# BOUNDARY

## ERIC FLINT &
## RYK E. SPOOR

BOUNDARY

Copyright © 2006 by Eric Flint & Ryk E. Spoor

A Baen Book

Baen Publishing Enterprises
P.O. Box 1403
Riverdale, NY 10471
www.baen.com

ISBN 10: 1-4165-5525-0
ISBN 13: 978-1-4165-5525-4

Cover art by Kurt Miller
Interior art by Randy Asplund

First Baen paperback printing, February 2008

Distributed by Simon & Schuster
1230 Avenue of the Americas
New York, NY 10020

Library of Congress Cataloging-in-Publication Data:
    2005035548

Printed in the United States of America

10 9 8 7 6 5 4 3 2 1

# DEDICATION:

*In memory of my parents Ryk Peter Spoor
and Dorothy Hansen Spoor*

*To Kathleen
And as always, to Jim Baen*

# ACKNOWLEDGEMENTS:

A hard SF novel of any scope requires the help of many people to make it convincing, and even with an earnest effort there are mistakes—or, sometimes, a decision to put story ahead of verisimilitude. If there are any mistakes seen in these pages, please place the blame squarely on the authors and not on our consultants, who did their best to keep us from looking silly.

## Thanks to:

Philip I. Moynihan of JPL NASA for his invaluable help on the operation and design of NERVA nuclear rockets.

John and Edwin Strickland for detailed input on the requirements of *Nike*, the journey of the Thoat, the Martian surface and subsurface, and other things aerospace related.

And:

Robert Zubrin, whose vision may one day make the journey into reality.

# PART 1: FOSSILS

*Problematica, n: a term used in paleontology to refer to fossils that appear to be either of unknown taxonomic origin, or whose occurrence in the location they are found contradicts current beliefs of the field.*

# Chapter 1

"Dear God, I'm going to die," muttered Joe Buckley, as the SUV bounced from one rutted pothole to another.

"Oh, come on, Joe, I don't drive *that* badly."

The silence caused Helen Sutter to glance over at Joe. His face was pale under its tan, contrasting all the more with his dark hair. His habitually cheerful expression was currently replaced by that of a man who has discovered he has a terminal illness and just two weeks to live. ". . . Do I?"

"Eyes on road! On the *road*!!! UNGH!"

The "ungh" was from the SUV's particularly hard, bottoming-out-the-shocks landing following yet another acrobatic leap across the roadbed, in an attempt to leave the rough dirt track and strike out across the rocky terrain nearby.

Helen gave a restrained curse and hauled on the steering wheel. The SUV responded, skidding slightly, but heading back into the center of the dirt track leading to the Secord ranch. Holding the line with one hand, Helen brushed her blond hair out of her eyes; as usual it was escaping the ponytail it was supposedly tied into. Despite the fact that it was early in the season and only eleven in the morning, Helen could feel a thin film of sweat on her forehead.

*Well, that's the life of a paleontologist,* she thought ruefully. *Pay all your grant money for the chance to break rocks, instead of getting sentenced to hard labor and doing it for free.*

"What's wrong with my driving?"

"Nothing, nothing." Joe paused. "If you're in the Baja 500."

"Oh, all right, I'll slow down. But who cut down your testosterone ration? As I recall, the first year we came out here, you almost got yourself killed trying to offroad along an arroyo. Nearly lost us our dig, too. Then the *second* year, you—"

"Hey, all right, already. It's just that I want to survive this summer. It's my last year."

Helen smiled a bit sadly. "I know. We're going to miss you, Joe."

"I'll miss it, too. But . . . push comes to shove, this is ultimately just a hobby for me. If I hadn't taken your course on a whim as an undergraduate, I never would have gotten interested in paleontology at all, it's so far removed from my own field of EE."

"Yeah, I understand. Now that you're closing in on your Ph.D., you don't have any choice but to clear everything else aside. I know, I've been there. We'll still miss you a lot—and take it from a pro that your skills as a paleontologist are a lot more than those of a 'hobbyist.' "

"Thanks."

The gate to the Secord ranch leaped into view as the SUV crested the hill and charged down the other side. Helen expertly maneuvered the vehicle through the gateway and pulled up to the sprawling ranch house in a cloud of dust.

Joe got out, pausing to let his legs steady, and possibly to give himself an excuse to watch Helen going first. As he was a several-year veteran, she ignored the matter. She was used to the fact that she got a lot of stares; in what was still a male-dominated profession, just about any woman got them. And in her case, a woman whose figure was still very good for someone close to forty years old. For a miracle, even, her face wasn't showing the wrinkles you'd expect from years of wind and sun in rugged country.

The door to the ranch house opened. "Welcome back, Dr. Sutter!"

Jackie Secord stepped aside and ushered them in with a wave of her hand. Combined with Jackie's striking appearance, the gesture had a dramatic flair to it that was absurdly out of keeping with its humble purpose.

But that was pretty typical of the young woman. She was Indian in her ancestry, on her mother's side. Her good-looking but intense face, black hair, black eyes and dusky complexion sometimes reminded Helen of a cartoon version of a Foreign Spy. Natasha, with a rural Montana accent.

To make the absurdity perfect, Jackie was a graduate student in engineering—and shared with Joe a fascination with space exploration. Her looks and liking for dramatic gestures aside, the young woman was about as down-home American as anyone could get.

Despite her intentions to become an astronaut, Jackie shared Joe's longstanding side interest in paleontology. That interest, as with Joe's, had been triggered years before by Helen herself—but not as a student. The first time Helen had showed up in the area, she'd introduced herself to the Secord family since they were one of the largest landowners around and she needed their permission to conduct digs on their property.

Their daughter Jackie—then eighteen years old and a high school senior—had promptly attached herself to Helen as a combination guide and gofer. Since then, Jackie had become one of Helen's main local contacts and a constant, helpful presence at the digs. She'd developed into a top-notch amateur paleontologist, in fact, and usually tried to spend at least part of her summers on one of Helen's digs.

"What's with the 'Dr. Sutter' business, Jackie? It's been 'Helen' for years, remember?"

Jackie grinned. "I figure I gotta practice up on my formalities. I'm not all that far behind Joe when it comes to getting my doctorate—and God help me if I start breezily referring to the head of *my* committee as 'Frank.' So what's up for this year?"

"Same as ever," Joe said, coming in after Helen. "Spend a couple months working ourselves to death to dig out a few fossils just like the ones everyone else has. Write some papers about them that no one but us and the reviewers will read. Then Helen and company write another grant proposal."

"And Joey's still the optimist, I see."

Joe winced. He detested being called "Joey," Helen knew.

But some years before, when they'd both been undergraduates, Jackie and Joe had been casually "sorta-dating" for one summer. Her pet nickname for him had probably seemed cute then. Now, of course, it was inescapable, though he wouldn't put up with anyone else using it.

Laughing, Helen nodded. "As always. Seriously, I thought we might try that area a bit north of the last dig. The indications we had seem to show that some of the random fossils come from that area in the runoff."

"You stop by Jeff's?" Helen wasn't sure, but Jackie's gaze seemed somewhat more intense than usual.

Jeff Little owned a souvenir shop in the nearest town, and specialized in buying and selling fossils from the local rock hounds and collectors. If a new group of fossils started showing up, he was generally the first to know.

"Yes, we did. He didn't seem to have much new, except one bone that might—*might*—have come from a dromeasaur or related species."

There was no mistaking the gleam in Jackie's eyes now. "Well, Jeff doesn't get *all* the good stuff. After the time I've spent working with you, I can spot the real winners out in the field if I run across them. Most of that stuff he gets is junk."

"Sure, you showed me your better pieces last year, too. Saves us having to bargain with Little for them."

"I've got something really nifty this year, I think. Came down in the year's runoff, and I think I've got a good idea where it came from. Be right back." Jackie trotted upstairs to fetch her prize.

Jackie's mother had come in from the kitchen by then. "Would you like some lemonade?" she asked, then gestured at the couches and armchairs scattered about the sprawling ranch-style living room. "And why don't you two sit down a spell before you go out there to start your digging?"

"Don't mind if I do," Joe said, sighing histrionically. "A chair that isn't bouncing up and down will be a comfort."

"Cut it out, Joe!"

Jackie came clattering down the stairs, holding something behind her. "Ready?"

"Let's see it."

A few minutes later, Helen looked up. "Joe, take a look at this."

Joe put down the lemonade Mrs. Secord had handed him, rose from the couch and joined Helen in staring at the object.

It resembled nothing so much as a large blackish shoehorn— Helen estimated it at around fifteen centimeters long and ranging from three to six centimeters wide, with a concave side and a little hook on the narrow end.

"Some kind of brachiopod relative?"

"Not one I'm familiar with. Look at these marks here."

Joe frowned, then took the object and studied it more closely. "Well, it's definitely a fossil, and . . . those sure look like muscle attachment scars. But what're they doing on both sides of this thing, if it's a shell? Should run down only one side, shouldn't they?"

"That'd be my expectation, too. But if this is a bone, why is it so thin and concave? I've never even heard of anything like that."

Joe was good at visualizing anatomy—much better than Helen, in fact, who always had to sit down and sketch it out a piece at a time. His face now screwed up in concentration. "If you had a. . . no, no, that wouldn't make sense. Oh, but maybe . . . no, not that either. I suppose if . . ."

He turned the fossil over, examining the backside carefully. "Darn. No sign of it being a piece of something else, either, which might have explained it." He turned it over and over a couple more times, shifting his point of view as though it might suddenly become an obvious and familiar fossil from some different angle, then handed it back to Helen.

"Okay, you win, Jackie. I'm beat. Do you know what it is?"

Jackie shook her head, looking excited and trying not to—after all, she wasn't a high school girl any longer, and hadn't been for a number of years. "No, not really. I knew it didn't look like anything I'd seen before, but I was sure you people would know right away. Are you guys putting me on? You really, truly don't know what it is?"

"Really, truly, Jackie," Helen said. "I've never seen anything like it, or heard of anything like it. You say you know where you found it?"

Jackie looked hurt. "Of course I do, Helen! Haven't I been keeping a journal since my second year doing this?"

"I'm sorry. I should have said: will you show us where you found it, and where you think it came from?"

"Of course. Let me get my hiking boots on, and we'll go out there now."

"There" turned out to be a few miles out, not all that far from the old dig site, but to the northwest up a small arroyo. "I found it lying over here, half under some sand. I think it washed down from somewhere up the arroyo."

Helen measured the area by eye, trying to visualize the rains, the wash coming down, the size of the fossil.

She thought Jackie was right. "Let's go up a ways, then, and see if we find anything."


Luck, luck, luck.

The word kept repeating itself over and over in Helen's mind, as she stood there looking at the wall of the arroyo in a state of half-shock.

"Jesus Christ," Joe repeated for the fifth time, finally straightening up from his examination. "Helen, that's a *Deinonychus*, or I'm just a first-year student."

"And if the rest is in the same condition, we've got ourselves a fully articulated skeleton."

Amateur or not, Jackie understood how very rare that was, and her excitement was only restrained by an attempt to be more professional and dignified than the professionals around her. Theropod skeletons, like the *Deinonychus*, were rare enough to be noteworthy, but fully articulated skeletons—skeletons that had remained pretty much connected as they had been in life—were vanishingly rare.

Helen glanced down the arroyo, frowning. "Odd, though."

"What's odd?"

She pulled out the unknown fossil. "If this came from here, there's no way it's a shell. Not of a water dweller, anyway."

Joe nodded. "These are land formations; late Cretaceous, maybe even Maastrichtian."

"No 'maybe' involved, Joe. Look at where your hand is."

Joe looked at the rock wall he'd been leaning against. "What—"

He suddenly started laughing. "You can't be serious, Helen! It's like pulling three jackpots in a row at Vegas!"

"What is it?" Jackie asked, seeing the narrow, dark band both Joe and Helen were staring at. Then she whipped around, eyes wide.

"You mean . . .?"

"Yes." Helen was hardly able to believe it herself. "It looks like our fossil is sitting right smack on the K-T boundary."

"Where the comet—um, sorry." Jackie caught herself before finishing the sentence. She tended to forget that the Alvarez Hypothesis was still a touchy subject for a lot of paleontologists, even if she herself thought it was a darn neat idea.

"Yes, where the comet." Helen said the words with a half-snort, half-chuckle.

Fortunately for Jackie, Helen was less hostile to the Alvarez Hypothesis than most members of her profession. She didn't doubt at all that an impact had happened at the K-T Boundary, which marked the end of the Mesozoic Era. She simply questioned whether it had the worldwide cataclysmic effects that the hypothesis proposed. There were other impact craters about as big as the one in Yucatan, after all. The Manicouagan, to name just one. But they'd had no discernable ecological effects at all; not even regional ones, so far as anyone could determine.

Nor had anyone ever really explained, to Helen's satisfaction, exactly *how* the impact had killed off so many species. Nor the peculiar mechanism by which it had killed off some, but not others. In what mystifying manner, for instance, had it killed off all ammonites—but spared their close relatives, the squids and the octopi? These were the sort of nitty-gritty questions that paleontologists focused on, and that physicists tended to ignore.

Still, she was willing to entertain it as a valid and testable hypothesis. In truth, she'd privately admit to herself, Helen's residual animosity toward the Alvarez Hypothesis was emotional rather than intellectual. Like most paleontologists, she was often rankled by the overbearing arrogance of many of the physicists who were so charmed by the hypothesis and took it as Revealed Truth. When they pontificated on the subject, physicists tended to dismiss the inconvenient facts paleontologists kept bringing up, much like an exasperated adult brushes aside the foolish questions of little children.

One of those facts, however, was that there was no evidence that any dinosaur had survived till the end of the Cretaceous. But now. . .

It looked as if they'd found the evidence.

"Yes, where the comet," she repeated.

She dusted her hands off on her jeans, and straightened up. "It's going to be a hike back and it'll be getting dark in a few hours. Even if it weren't, we can't do anything yet. This is on your folks' land, Jackie. We'll have to get their permission to dig here, and I've absolutely *got* to call the Museum of the Rockies. Probably a few other people."

She took a long, slow breath. "This is going to be a big dig, Jackie. Whatever your funny fossil is, it's led us to the mother lode."

That night, on the telephone from her motel room, she conveyed her excitement to the director of the Museum of the Rockies. It wasn't hard, actually. Ever since the days of Jack Horner, the museum had prided itself on its eminence in the world of paleontology, especially dinosaur paleontology. Director Bonds immediately grasped the significance of finding what appeared to be an articulated velociraptor skeleton on the very edge of the K-T boundary. He promised to give her the full support of the museum.

In fact, he even came out himself, three days later. By then, Helen, Joe, and Jackie had been joined by Carol Danvers and Bill Ishihara, the other members of Helen's team. Three days of careful digging had uncovered the entire lower half of the fossil. And, in the process, they had found the leg bone of another velociraptor underneath it, the body apparently extending off to the side of the first.

Helen heard the footsteps coming up behind her, but continued scraping away. The smell of chipped rock, a dusty hot scent that always reminded her of striking flints, lingered strongly in the bright heat of a Montana summer.

"Dr. Sutter?"

She finished freeing the small round stone that had been in her way, then stood up, dusting off her hands before extending one for a handshake. "Hello, Director Bonds."

Bonds was sweating and trying not to show how winded he was from the walk. He'd been quite a field scientist himself before he became director of the museum, and was probably a little embarrassed to discover how far out of shape he was from a few years of chair-warming.

At a gesture of invitation from Helen, he squatted at the edge of the work area, the others clearing out of the way. "Marvelous. Simply marvelous. A death scene, you think?"

Helen scratched her chin thoughtfully. "Too early to tell. There's something . . . Well, let me hold off before I jump to conclusions. But look at this. See? That's the K-T boundary, all right. There's no doubt about it."

"Jesus." The director was practically bouncing up and down in restrained professional excitement. "No one's ever found a dinosaur this close to the boundary!"

"Close?" demanded Helen. "It's not close. *It's right on it.*"

# Chapter 2

Two weeks later, Bonds was back again, bringing more help and equipment. By then, Helen and the people on her crew had managed to clear the first skeleton, half of the second, and had discovered yet a *third* on the other side of the first. To say the museum director was happy would have been an understatement on a par with saying the *Titanic* had experienced some difficulty on its maiden voyage.

Helen, Joe, and Jackie were also clearly happy, but someone who knew them better than the director might have noticed something a bit odd in their reactions. They welcomed the newcomers and showed them around, agreeing that it was clearly a death scene, but saying that they hadn't drawn any firm conclusions as to the sequence of events yet.

That was true enough, as far as it went, Helen thought, but . . .

They relaxed a bit once the director left. Helen needed to talk to the new paleontologists alone, without the director hearing things that might make his funding the venture politically difficult. It was extraordinarily hard to think that way, but with what they were finding, the circumstances were also extraordinary.

"Funny." One of the new guys, Michael Jennings, shook his head slightly. "The way the skeletons sit, I don't think they were fighting at all. Drowned, maybe? Flash flood?"

"Maybe," Jackie said.

"Found any wounds?" another asked. "Broken bones? Evidence of toothmarks? Clearly they didn't get eaten much, or whatever did it would've taken them apart."

"Yeah," said Joe. "There's some marks on the skeletons. Look here, around the pelvis." he pointed with a stick to the first skeleton.

The newcomers gathered around and shone flashlights on the exposed fossil, as the sun was starting to go down and long shadows were gathering in the arroyo. For several minutes there was silence.

"What the hell made that?" Jennings finally asked, frowning at the three neat half-centimeter holes that appeared to punch completely through the pelvic bone.

"Looks almost like a bullet hole." That was offered in a jocular tone by one of the other new arrivals, Ned Rhodes. But the quip trailed off a bit too abruptly.

"Too neat," Jackie responded immediately. "My dad's hunted all his life, and I've gone with him. A bullet would've mushroomed when it hit the bone, if not sooner. And even if someone had been using military-grade jacketed bullets, the holes are too small for the caliber guns you'd use to hunt big game."

"Funny thing, too." Helen extended her hand, showing several small, round, dark-brown pebbles. "These are all over the area."

Jennings took one and studied it, then put it up against one of the holes. It was clear that they were essentially identical in size.

"Bizarre. Cysts that cause bone loss, eat it away or something?"

Helen's eyebrow quirked upward. "Now there's an interesting idea, Mike. We'll have to section a couple of these, see what's inside."

"They all look the same size. Are they?"

"Within the limits of my field equipment, they're identical. Perfectly spherical and measuring, by field micrometer, 4.65 millimeters in diameter. We've measured ten of them at least, and all of them are just the same."

Dr. Sean Carter, the senior of the newcomers, had been silent until now. Finally he spoke. "Um, Helen, don't take this the wrong way, but are you sure . . . uh . . ."

"That there's been no contamination of the site? Yes, I'm sure. And I've kept detailed notes from the beginning. Even more detailed than usual, in fact."

The newcomers were silent. Helen Sutter had the reputation, among other things, for being one of the most meticulous field paleontologists in the country. Her notes were used as models in at least two textbooks and an unknown number of classes. If she said she was taking unusual care, the only thing that would have kept the site more pristine would have been not to dig it at all.

Carter was studying the bones and their positioning. Helen saw him judging angles, glancing along certain lines, then picking up one of the dark brown pebbles and studying it pensively for a long time, while the others continued their examination of the site.

It was clear to Helen, though, that none of them were looking at the precise features that Sean Carter was. That was no surprise. If Helen had the reputation for being a fanatically careful field worker, Sean Carter's reputation for obsessive attention to detail made her look like a dilettante.

Carter never missed a single clue in the study of a fossil. There had been one wag a number of years before who had jested that Carter could probably visualize the entirety of the Cretaceous *in toto* from a single bone. What he was seeing in this death scene bothered him more and more. She could see his brow wrinkling so it looked like he was in actual pain.

Finally, he turned back to Helen. "Could I speak to you for a moment?"

"Sure, Sean. Come on, let's take a little walk. I'll show you where the first fossil came from."

Carter said nothing until they were well away from the others. Helen knew Sean Carter. He was the kind of man who hated anomalies—they disordered his ordered view of life and his profession—but he also hated avoiding the truth. The current situation was clearly causing him a strain.

"I'm not sure what you have here, Helen. I can tell you have an idea of your own, and I'm not sure I even want to think about what it might be. But I'm worried, very worried."

"What has you worried, Sean?"

Carter snorted humorlessly. "Helen, you've been doing this excavation. Don't tell me you can't see it."

"Maybe I do, but I want to hear what you see, without me biasing your opinion."

"Fair enough." He gazed back at the site. "The three skeletons, near as I can tell, are in a rough semicircle. They do not appear to have been fighting each other. In fact, it looks to me as though at least one, possibly two, of them were trying to *leave* the area. And I don't see any clear indication of what killed them, unless it's those odd holes. But then, what made those holes? Those pebbles, are they cysts? I doubt it. Perhaps they were, as suggested, part of an infection— perhaps one that had some kind of psychological effects, as a number of parasites do, and could have caused erratic behavior . . . but . . ."

He studied the area again. "It's hard to tell because of the effect of tendon contraction on death, but it also looks as if they did not die immediately. More as though they spent a bit of time thrashing in pain."

"And your conclusions?"

He frowned even more. "I'm not sure I have any. But if there's more to be found here, I have a depressing feeling that it will be even stranger than we've already seen. Be careful. You must be *very* careful."

"Sean, come on. I'm being as meticulous as anyone can be."

"I'm not talking about your field methods, Helen, and you know it. 'Careful,' I said, not 'meticulous.' You need to be more *careful*, if you're dealing with something . . . unusual. And no matter what, this is just too damnably unusual."

Helen knew exactly what Carter meant. Paleontology had been plagued by fraud, misinterpretation, and personal feuds ever since its beginnings: the Piltdown man, the legendary rivalry of Marsh and Cope, the faked "feathered dinosaurs" from China in the 1990s profiteering on actual feathered dinosaur discoveries made around the same time, and a dozen other such episodes. That, added to the confused sensationalism that had accompanied the field in the public eye for more than a century, meant that paleontology was possibly the most conservative field of science on Earth. Downright reactionary, Helen sometimes thought.

The more outré a claim was, the more violently a segment of the field would fight it. Bakker had not even invented, but merely revived, the claim of possible warm-bloodedness in dinosaurs in the 1960s, and it had taken most of his career to make that a respectable claim in many peoples' eyes.

"Well, what do you expect me to do, Sean? Stop working on this dig?"

"No, no. Of course not. It's a marvelous dig. I'd give just about anything to be the one who found it. But you need to find a way to make it foolproof. The dig, I mean."

Despite the tenseness of the situation, Helen almost chuckled. "I'm taking even more records than usual, Sean. Photos practically every millimeter we uncover. Multiple people's testimony. A much more extensive use of satellite imagery than usual and a thorough aerial survey in multiple spectra. What else can I do? It's not like I can just take a look at it before . . ."

She trailed off. "You know, Sean, I might just be able to do something more, after all, now that I think about it. Come on."

Returning to the knot of paleontologists and assisting folk, she called out. "Hey, Joe! Didn't you tell me once that you knew some guy in college, a couple of years behind you. Some kind of genius at imaging?"

Joe immediately understood. "A.J. Baker. And he wants something challenging and fancy to show off with, too. He's just starting working with us on the Ares Project, you know."

"No, I didn't. One of you Nuts That Roared, is he?"

Joe grinned. "Yeah, and he loves that rep. Anyway, I'll bet he could get us a picture of the whole scene before we go any further."

"Pictures through *rock*?" Jackie asked incredulously.

"Better believe it," Joe said. "Really, he can do things with GPR, ultrasonics, and other things that even JPL and DARPA couldn't match. Let me give him a call and see if he'll do it."

Helen turned to Carter. "What do you think, Sean? Will that play?"

"It certainly can't hurt," he replied, scratching his cheek. "And it's easy to justify, if he'll do it for a reasonable fee. If you know the disposition of the fossils ahead of time, it's far easier—which means cheaper in the long run—to do a major dig. Director Bonds will be happy to arrange funding for something like that."

Helen nodded. "Call up your whiz kid, Joe. Tell him he's got the chance of a lifetime here. And he won't have to wait to travel to another planet for this one."

# Chapter 3

The black and silver helicopter wailed to a landing at the end of the arroyo. As the blades slowed to a visible speed, the rear cargo door opened and a tall man hopped out. He was dressed in black jeans, a shiny royal blue shirt, and had a backpack slung over his shoulder. The outfit combined with mirrored sunglasses and a full, shaggy, golden mop of hair made him seem very young.

He waved at Joe, barely evading the rotor blade as he jogged out to meet them. "Yo, Joe, what's doing? You'd better not have been shitting me on this—whoops, excuse me!"

He'd caught sight of Helen and Jackie. "You must be Dr. Sutter? Your pics don't do you justice. A.J. Baker, at your service."

He made an exaggerated bow so low that his backpack flopped down over his head and he banged his nose against a large pouch fastened to his belt. "Ow! So much for my suave European manners. I knew I should've settled for American ones. Oh, wait, that's right, I don't have any."

Helen couldn't restrain a smile. She knew that behavior from many a class she'd taught to bright young people, mostly male. Baker was clearly inherently shy, and the classic word "overcompensation" explained his noisy entrance.

"Helen Sutter. And this is Jackie Secord. She found the . . . anomaly."

"Glad to meet you both."

They shook hands, and then Helen asked: "Mr. Baker—or is it Dr.?"

At the last word, A.J. gave an odd twitch—or maybe she just imagined it. "Just A.J., Dr. Sutter. I'm at the dreaded A.B.D. phase, and probably won't ever finish the dissertation if I keep this busy."

The helicopter roared back to life behind them, making Helen jump. She wasn't accustomed to helicopters as a means of transportation to a paleontological dig. She glanced back to see that after depositing three moderate-sized cases on the ground, the copter was leaving. "How did you afford that thing, anyway? And you didn't bring your team?"

"I *am* my team, pretty much," A.J. said matter-of-factly. "Back at the labs I can get other people and use bigger equipment, but for fieldwork I just need what I brought. As for the chopper, it's a freebie. One of Ares' backers is stinking rich and offered to let me use it when I wheedled him. I'll have to arrange different transportation out, though. He only wheedled so far."

"No problem. We can give you a ride back."

Baker smiled. "I figured. And now, I'd better go back and grab those cases."

"We'll give you a hand. You're coming to help us, after all. Are you sure you aren't going to have to charge?"

"Well, there'll be a nominal fee, to make it all official. And expenses, of course. But if it's interesting, it's worth doing for publicity and professional respect. The Ares Project can always use more."

Helen nodded. The Ares Project was an attempt to send a manned mission to Mars following the approach Robert Zubrin had called "Mars Direct." It was mostly based in private enterprise and, like any major private attempt to do something scientific that seemed to have no prospects for immediate profit, it was perennially short of funds. But it was probably even shorter of the sort of "official respect" that it needed to drum up more support and financial backing.

"I think you will be more than satisfied with the challenge and the subject matter, A.J."

When they reached the cases, Helen picked up one of them. It was startlingly heavy, but Helen set her jaw and forced herself to carry it as though it wasn't any heavier than she'd expected. She wasn't sure why. Habit, she supposed, of never showing weakness in a profession that was still mostly male-dominated.

By the time they reached the dig area, her arm felt like it was about to pull out of its socket and she was cursing her perverse pride.

Then she caught A.J. grinning at her.

"You know, I usually get help carrying that one, ma'am."

"Then why didn't you offer any, you twit?" Joe demanded.

"She seemed to want to handle it. Who am I to tell her otherwise?"

With a groan of relief Helen put the case down. "Just what is in there?"

"Fuel-cell generator. Some of the gadgets I'm going to use need some pretty high-power juice, and I knew this dig wasn't exactly going to have electric outlets handy. Now, you just give me some peace and quiet to set up and test some stuff, and I'll be able to get started."

Helen indicated a tarp and field tent nearby. "We set one up for you near the site. You'll need us to show you what to do, right?"

"Certainly. I'm no paleontologist. I need to see what you need done, and you'll probably have to give me feedback on the data, so I can refine it to what you really need."

Helen caught a faint glint of color from behind the mirrored glasses as he entered the darker area of the tent. She realized that A.J. must be using a VRD or projective display on or from his glasses.

"I'll give you a holler when I'm ready."

They spent the next hour or so making sure the site was cleared of anything that might interfere with A.J. Baker's work—tools, canvas coverings, they even swept away dust. Finally Helen heard a call from the tent. She went over, with Jackie and Joe following.

"You're ready, A.J.?"

"Ready to work my magic, yes, indeed." A.J. turned. To Helen's astonishment, there appeared to be a literal halo of light hovering around the man's head. A gasp from Jackie confirmed it was not her imagination.

"Oh, for the love of—A.J., you showoff!" Joe snorted. "And there's no way it should be a halo, anyway. Why not horns?"

"How do you *do* that?" Jackie demanded.

A.J. patted the large pouch on his belt. "Fairy Dust. From Dust-Storm Tech. Finest intelligent dust sensor motes on the planet. These are integrated with micromotile units to let them fly, as long as I can either keep' em supplied with enough power to scavenge—or I'm willing to let them drain the hell·out of the onboard batteries for the sake of a few seconds of showing off. Yeah, that's a cheap stunt using their illuminators, but it's fun."

He opened the flap. The halo, which at closer range appeared to be made up of hundreds or even thousands of individual tiny sparks of light, poured itself into the pouch.

"These things aren't toys, though. It's the heart of my approach. Thousands of ultrasensitive sensors all over the survey area, networking themselves together automatically, then using all that data to pull out a *really* detailed picture of whatever lies below. The trick is knowing what sensors and modalities to use and how to combine them and process the data the right way. Now, let's take a look at this dig of yours."

As they headed to the dig area, Jackie glanced at the belt pouch curiously. "I've heard of them being used for things like inventory tracking and so on, but . . ."

"That's just the tip of the iceberg," A.J. said. "Even back in the first decade of this century, when Dust, Incorporated, Ember, and a few others first started making intelligent sensor motes, it was clear there were a *lot* of potential uses for distributed sensor and computing networks that were embodied as near-microscopic motes that each had their own power, communication, computation, sensor, and memory capacity. I honestly don't think I could list every use I've thought of for these things in the past few years."

"So these motes can look right through the rock?"

A.J. laughed. "Not exactly. Let me take a look at what we have and I'll explain a little more."

Helen showed him around the dig area, letting the imaging and sensor expert kneel down to examine the fossils and surrounding rock. She saw him reach into the pouch and then let fall a ghostly shimmer of the dust-mote sensors across the area. From the side, Helen could see that the light behind his glasses was directed into his eye; what she'd seen vaguely before was the reflection. A Virtual Retinal Display, then, rather than a mini heads-up display projection. The VRD flickered brightly from his eye for a moment or two.

"Hmm, interesting." The imaging specialist seemed to have the habit of talking to himself. "Yeah, we can work with that."

He turned back to Jackie. "The motes are really excellent at sensing things, and if I combine the signals from thousands of them across the area, that's great—but only if there's something to sense. And there's no way anything their size can produce the beefy signals I'm going to need. Penetration through rock depends on a lot of different things—the type of signal, the wavelength, the precise type of rock, presence of moisture, and the power available probably being the most dominant, although there's a bunch of other ancillary ones. For the most part, I can control three of those variables—type, wavelength, and power. The trick here is that we have something of a dilemma. We want lots of penetration, but we also want lots of detail. As a rule, penetration increases with increasing wavelength—but the level of detail that can be detected *decreases* with increasing wavelength. If I want a shorter wavelength to give me a readable return, then I need a lot of power."

Helen nodded along with Jackie, as A.J. continued to carefully sift his Fairy Dust onto the ground in the area of the fossils and the rock still left to be removed.

"So what do you use? GPR? Seismics?"

"The short answer is yes." A.J. grinned. "Ground Penetrating Radar is just fine, for some things. But for others, some acoustic signals are good. Seismic shock is related to acoustics, of course, but I can induce different signal characteristics with acoustics than with a simple seismic signal. I can also sometimes get results with powerful magnetic fields. They react with the metals in the ground and bones, and bones are often packed with metal compared to their surroundings. I also use radiation detection—as I'm sure you know, sometimes fossils accumulate significant radioactives."

Helen nodded.

"There have been times I've used radiation directly in imaging, but that's not really practical in this setting, so I'll have to settle for whatever I get on the passives. Straight centimeter-scale radio waves on as high power as I can manage is another thing I'm going to try. While that wouldn't normally penetrate very far, a lot of your fossils here aren't all that far below the surface. I also try to use digital pulses where possible."

"Does that make them penetrate farther?" Helen asked. It didn't seem likely to her.

A.J. shook his head, smiling in acknowledgement of

her doubtful tone. "Not directly, no. But what it *does* do is make it much, much easier for me to pick up the return signal from the noise, because I can listen for a specific pattern. I know what I'm looking for, in essence, and that really increases the chances of picking it up. Where the motes come in is in registering the returns from all different modes in thousands of closely related vectors, which the sensor net can coordinate and extract as precise survey points in spacetime. The motes construct their own ad hoc network and then derive their own relative positions with very high accuracy. Between time-of-flight, multiple triangulation, and a few other tricks like performing interference patterns, the network characterizes itself to within very small fractions of an inch. This means that the combined received signals are known to an extremely high degree of accuracy. That takes some processing time—that's what it's doing now, since I've stopped playing Tinkerbell.

"So once the network's fully characterized, I start setting off the signal pulses. I let the network know"—he tapped his glasses and the virtual control interface that only he could see—"exactly what signal I'm about to send, then trigger it. The net records all the responses it can, I hit it with another pulse; maybe change modes, it starts building up a rough picture. I examine it, see if I've got something coming up. Maybe I go back, do a few more GPR or radio shots, or try another acoustic signal, or shift frequencies. Eventually, I've got all the data I think will be useful. Then I can really go to town on this stuff; sensor fusion, bandpass filtering, synthetic aperture, Kalman and Weiner filters, all that kind of thing, plus some tricks of my own.

"With a handful of these motes and no special signal

generators, I can use the ambient sound to locate and determine the number, direction, and general composition of your tents—without any of my dust motes actually touching the tents. Heck, with equipment twenty years older, I could send any two of you off to have a conversation, and not only locate you, but pick out your entire conversation, whispered, on the other side of a hill three hundred meters off. These motes have access to my own neural net code, expert systems, fuzzy logic structures, all sorts of stuff in the control unit and local heavy-duty processors, like in the main control unit here."

He patted another simple metallic box on his belt. "Give me powerful signal sources, and I'll guarantee to map out anything you want, above or below ground. And in this case, I'll even guarantee that you'll have enough detail to count teeth in a skull."

"Can you keep a record of how you produce the results?" Helen asked.

"Not only can I," A.J. answered, pacing out the area again as though measuring it, "it's pretty much part and parcel of the process—nice alliteration there, huh? I keep the raw data and track the sequence of filtering and analysis, all the way in. I have to—sometimes you don't get the best results and you need to experiment by taking out one step, moving it to another point in the sequence, and so on. It can make a big, big difference in the final results whether you filter first and then run an enhancement process, or enhance first and then filter, for instance. Pillage, *then* burn, so to speak."

He stopped, nodded to himself, then turned back towards the tents. "Well, it's getting pretty dark out here, but rather than waste time, I'll just get started."

�֎    ✖    ✖

Jackie and Helen held the lights as A.J. unpacked a number of devices with thick, rugged power leads.

As he did so, Helen studied him, a bit surreptitiously. Somewhat to her surprise, she was starting to find the man interesting.

In many ways, A.J. Baker was obviously a classic geek. Who else got that enthusiastic about dry-as-dust technical matter? But the muscles visible in his arms when he hefted the first case—the one that had nearly pulled Helen's shoulder out of its socket—made it clear that A.J. was in far better physical condition than the average geek.

On a personal level, the muscles impressed Helen even less than the flamboyantly awkward geeky mannerisms. But she found the combination rather intriguing. It reminded her of . . .

Well, herself, actually.

Since Helen didn't have that damnable male ego to deal with— the one that crucified every high school geek in existence—her own mannerisms weren't as awkward as A.J.'s. At least, she hoped not. But she could get just as enthusiastic when discussing paleontological issues, which were often *literally* as dry as dust. And on the few occasions when she ventured into public gymnasiums for a workout, she usually got admiring looks from all the men present and envious ones from the women. Even from women half her age.

From men half her age, she *always* got admiring looks. Ogles, often enough, to call things by their right name.

The thought of young men rallied her. *Stop this, woman. He must be fifteen years younger than you are.*

Thus fortified, Helen went back to studying A.J. from

the perspective of an expert in one field watching another at his own. She did her best to ignore the treacherous little voice at the back of her mind, as it worked its way through simple mathematics.

*Don't be silly. He's not as young as he looks. Can't be, not even in his cutting-edge field. He's got to be at least twenty-five or twenty-six. Maybe twenty-seven. Subtracted from thirty-eight, that is* not *fifteen years younger. It's only eleven. Maybe even less.*

Shut up.

"Okay, here we got your GPR unit." A.J. held up a wide metallic antenna unit, followed by a cylindrical object that looked like a solid rod of metal but probably wasn't. "And this here's the impactor for seismic signals, some electromagnetic pulsers—keep metal and electronics that aren't shielded *well* away, folks—and my own shriekers. Highpower ultrasonic pulsers."

The "shriekers" were strange things, looking a bit like large versions of the paddles found on a defibrillator unit, but ending with quivering blobs that looked like nothing so much as firm blue jello. They were labeled *Kaled 1* and *Kaled 2*.

"What's that stuff?" Jackie asked, pointing to the blue blobs.

"Couplant gel. The attenuation of the signal through air is something fierce, so you try to use couplant to bring it more directly to the target. I wash the area off with a high-pressure water jet, then push the gel up against the rock. That increases the efficiency by many times. Even so, it'd be just plain useless without the Fairy Dust. You can immerse a sample in liquid and get good results, but in the field you just wouldn't get the penetration needed. With the sensor motes properly programmed and all over the place, and digitized pulses for signature return filtering, I can get results out of returns almost a hundred times weaker than I could with normal sensors."

"Anything else we can do to help?" Helen put in, seeing that he was now laying out his devices in a carefully planned order.

"Yeah," A.J. said. "Go away. Meaning no offense, just that once I start taking the readings the more people and objects in the area, the harder it's going to be for me to compensate for the signals. I have to sit dead still while the data's being gathered, and even so I'll probably be having an effect that I'll notice later."

"No problem, we understand." Helen and Jackie started off. "Let us know when you're done."

"Sure thing," A.J. replied absently, already staring at a display on his VRD unit. "Your problems are just about over."

# Chapter 4

"What the hell is *that*?"

A.J. was taken aback by the vehemence of Helen's question. "Hey, cool down. And why are you asking *me*? You're the paleontologist. I just image what's there."

Joe shook his head, then bent down to A.J. and spoke quietly. "Look, I don't know what you think you're doing, but cut out the joking and give us the real data."

A.J.'s eyes narrowed. "That *is* the real data. Top of the line. Imaged in three different spectra, multiple wavelengths, filtered, neural-net-processed, compared with known data for verisimilitude, and data-fused and analyzed out the wazoo. If I wasn't doing this for you and my own entertainment, you'd be paying about a hundred grand for this little job—over and above expenses. That is exactly, precisely, and inarguably what is down there."

"But that's just . . . impossible," Joe said defensively. He gestured at the projected image before them.

The computer-enhanced graphic showed the entire dig area in three-dimensional, mostly pastel false color. The rock still to be removed was present as an outline, an overlay of faintly gray glass. The fossils of the three raptors were clearly visible, the two newer ones now fully visible in their curved death poses. In addition, two *more* raptor skeletons were revealed, one on either side of the other three, making a rough three-quarter circle around the perimeter of the dig area. All five skeletons were fully articulated, possibly the finest specimens of *Deinonychus* ever uncovered— and all of them were sitting on a stippled red and purple layer that was the K-T boundary itself. White dots showed the position of hundreds of the strange pebbles, both around and past the raptor skeletons.

But it was what squatted ominously in the center of the image, in the middle of the rough circle delineated by the fossilized predators, that was the focus of such utter disbelief. It was large—close to four meters long, from end to end—and was as clearly defined as the other skeletons. The problem was . . .

"That's not even a skeleton," Helen said finally. "I'm not sure *what* to make of it."

"I thought it was like some kind of squid," A.J. said. "I know there was a lot of squiddage back then. Squids with shells, if I remember right. Ammonites, they were called?"

Joe frowned. "Well, we do have a sort of cephalopodic outline here." He sketched an elongated oval in the air. "Those could be tentacles, sort of. I only see three of them, though. And it looks almost like there are more at the rear."

"A lot shorter, though," Helen pointed out. "And much

of the rest looks like it *is* a skeleton. Well, sort of. Weird though it is, that part here, near the longer, um, tentacles, looks like a skull to me, and it's attached to these other parts. But it's not an ammonite or any kind of shell, that's for damn sure. And what's the segmentation effect we have here? What are those things you're rendering in blue, A.J.? Look like layered armor plates or something."

A.J. shrugged. "Like I said, don't ask *me* what they are. But I can extract one for you, no problem."

He glanced into his VRD, mumbled some barely audible words, tapped out orders on an imaginary keyboard, and suddenly one of the "plates" glowed and seemed to spiral up and expand, filling a secondary window at the top of the image.

There were immediate startled exclamations from the three others in the tent.

"My god, Jackie. That's your mystery fossil!" Joe almost shouted.

If Helen had had any lingering thoughts that A.J. was playing some kind of practical joke, this eliminated them. None of them had mentioned Jackie's unique find to him, and A.J. certainly had never had a chance to see it.

Yet there was no doubt about it. The "shell" Jackie had found was now revealed to be one of many sequential components in what appeared to be some kind of arm.

"And the . . . tentacle on the right," Joe said, pointing. "There. It's shorter than the others. I'll bet that it lost part of the arm, maybe in a fight with the raptors, and so that part got weathered out."

"But what *was* it?" Helen demanded, returning to the main question. "How do those plates come into the picture? They're not armor—the attachment points make that clear. They're internal structures of some kind. But I don't see any ordinary bones or anything, so . . ."

"Maybe they *are* bones," Jackie suggested quietly.

Helen stopped short and looked more closely at the image. Her classes in reconstruction stood out more clearly now in her mind than ever before. She visualized the connections, the necessary methods for locomotion, the attachment points as related to the way the—arm plates?—were clearly meant to fit. She could see Joe's face going through the same steps, and that Joe was finding the conclusion hard to believe.

"A.J., can I use your interface?" she asked. "Or can you hook the simulation up to something I can access?"

"Your portable have standard wireless? Sure, hold on." A moment later, he said, "Okay, tell it to access WEIRDSIM. The interface should be pretty straightforward."

Helen saw the interface come up in front of her. Not that different from the one she used at the lab, actually. A.J. clearly understood the totality of his field, including user requirements. For several minutes there was mostly silence as Helen patched in her own reconstruction data, modified it, cursed softly as she realized she needed something unique, queried the Net for a formula that would describe what she wanted, added that in.

"Here goes. Take a look at this."

The general display flickered, and a long, slender window opened across the site display. The plates moved forward and backward in a motion similar to that of a telescope or old-style antenna, the individual parts extending to make a longer unit, then pulling back to retract the tentaclelike arm into a shorter, fatter configuration. It flexed and moved in a manner that was both familiar and subtly, disquietingly wrong. A stick-figure simulation showed the shorter, wider "tentacles" moving in a peculiar rhythm that pushed the weird thing along with surprising speed.

It certainly wasn't impossible, mechanically or biologically speaking. But it was clearly not a method of locomotion used by any form of life that Helen had ever seen or read about.

Joe's head lifted and he stared incredulously at the imaged fossil again. He then turned to Helen. She lifted her head, stared into his eyes, and then nodded slowly.

"My god. Helen, this is *it*! This is the biggest find in three centuries—in history, dammit!"

"And you and Jackie might want to get very far away before I finish this dig, too," Helen said softly.

"What the—? Oh."

Joe and Jackie looked at each other. Their expressions showed that they understood what Helen was saying.

A.J., however, was obviously in the dark. "Um, what's the problem? One second you're practically ready to start writing your Nobel Prize speeches. The next minute you're acting as if Jack the Ripper just came in."

Joe pointed at the image. "If Helen publishes a full report on that, it'll probably wreck her career."

"Well, not quite that," Helen said, shaking her head. "I've got tenure, after all, so I'd keep collecting a paycheck. But it would most likely get me relegated to the status of a crackpot. At least in the eyes of most of my colleagues."

"So screw 'em," A.J. snorted. "They don't believe you, too bad for them. It's right there in front of 'em!"

"A.J., that may work for you—your imaging work deals

with real solid stuff that no one can argue with. But pale-ontologists are more in the position of detectives trying to figure out what happened with only a handful of clues."

Joe's tone of voice was that of a parent trying to explain the facts of life to a stubborn eight-year-old. Given that A.J. was, in point of fact, not more than a year or two younger than Joe, Helen found it somewhat amusing.

But she could see that A.J. was beginning to bridle at the tone, so she intervened.

"Look, A.J., it's just a fact that paleontologists tend to be very conservative, in a scientific sense. Nor, by the way, do I say that critically. Joe's right, you know. We *do* have to work from mostly disconnected facts, just like detectives—and the fossil record is about as far removed as you can get from what anyone in their right mind would call a 'perfect crime scene.' Our data is hundreds of mil-lions of year old, and fragmented to boot. There's so much gray area—so many different ways *anything* can be interpreted—that members of my profession generally look cross-eyed whenever somebody comes up with a sweeping proposition. Especially one that flies completely in the face of previous findings."

A.J. set his jaw. "So, what are you saying? You want to dump all this data and forget the dig?"

"Hell, no!" Helen said. She glanced at her two co-workers. "They're just worried. Mostly about me, and it's really sweet of you, Joe." Joe blushed.

"No, I just had to make sure they knew what might happen. You, A.J., I'm not worried about. Like Joe said, on your side no one will care what my interpretations of the data are, as long as the data you got is bona fide—and my excavation *will* prove that beyond any shadow of a doubt. But if I'm going to survive professionally, I'm going to have to be very, very careful about how I report this."

A.J. shrugged. Somehow he managed to make even that gesture a bit theatrical.

"Hey, as long as my pretty pictures don't go to waste, I'm happy. And if you end up in a controversy, it'll be free publicity for me. But it'd be a crying shame for them to be stupid enough to blackball you. I can tell a professional when I work with one."

He stretched. "Well, it's off to bed for me, and then back to the lab tomorrow. Thanks a lot for calling me in— this has been pretty challenging *and* interesting—and looks like it's going to be fun to watch the fireworks coming up." He grinned and headed off to the tent they'd set up for him.

"So," Joe said finally, after A.J.'s footsteps had faded away. "How are you going to approach it?"

"I don't have to decide yet, Joe." Helen was still staring at the image of the impossible. "I have some vague ideas, but I've got months to finish the dig and it'll be at least a year after that before I can get anything published. I think I'll just wait and see what comes up. Wait and see."

# PART II: QUARRELS

*Controversy, n: a prolonged public dispute,
debate, or contention; disputation
concerning a matter of opinion; contention,
strike, or argument.*

# Chapter 5

A.J. Baker skipped down the hall, drawing tolerant stares from other members of the Ares Project. He might have just turned twenty-eight years old, but after the year or so he'd been with Ares they had stopped expecting him to act much more than eighteen. He bounced through Glenn Friedet's office door, making the harried-looking project director jump.

"I swear, A.J.," Glenn sighed, "more than half of my gray hairs come from you."

"Well, let me see if I can make your day a happier one, Fearless Leader." A.J. slapped a sheet of paper down in front of Glenn.

That got Glenn's attention. "Paper? From *you*?"

A.J. grinned, smugly aware of his reputation as someone so far out on the bleeding edge that he considered paper and papyrus to be equally outmoded.

"You won't begrudge me the death of *that* tree, Glenn."

Glenn's gaze scanned the paper. "They went for it!"

"You better believe they did!" He bounced around the office. "Yeah! Yeah! Yeah! I get to build Tinkerbell, Ariel, and the rest of my Faeries! And get to make all the rest of your engineers modify the designs on *Pirate*!"

The latter made Glenn wince. Wince twice, actually, first at A.J.'s official use of the very unofficial nickname of the Automated Arean Reconnaissance Rover and Return module. Officially $A^2R^3$—which had led to its own spate of Star Wars jokes—the longhand acronym AARRR had been pronounced in such a way as to inevitably be followed by "matey," "walk the plank," and so on, thereby causing the obvious moniker of *Pirate* to refer to the test vehicle.

The second wince was at the equally inevitable complaints the redesign would engender from the engineers.

A.J. recognized both winces with satisfaction. "Hey, Glenn, I told them I would win this one. They should've planned for it."

"Actually, they probably did. But with two more months going by than we'd expected, we were getting pretty settled into the other design."

"So, do I call up NASA and tell them to keep their money?"

Glenn laughed. "Not a chance. We can use all we can get, and none of the critical construction stages have been passed yet— though this was close."

"I'll go get things started in RDD, then. You get someone processing the files—I've already digisigned everything to authorize my end and you'll find the secure contract files in your inbox."

A.J. jogged out, giving another whoop of triumph as

he exited the office area. His grin grew even wider as he headed toward Research, Development and Design.

It was finally sinking in. Despite his words, he hadn't been nearly so sure NASA would go for his proposal. It made sense, true, but sense often didn't have much to do with government contracts, especially when the government agency in question was competing with the proposing private organization.

The Ares Project.

It had been A.J.'s dream since he was a kid to be able to go into space, and especially to land on Mars. But despite some initial rumbles in that direction in the very early part of the twenty-first century, the government's efforts to land a manned mission on the Red Planet had progressed only haltingly, with the vast complexity, immense inertia, and often wrongheaded design strategies that had characterized government space missions for years.

With a new generation of engineers agitating for private space missions, the U.S. government had finally authorized a few incentives for private space work. A series of prizes had been established for achieving certain space-travel goals, with a general eye towards eventually reaching Mars.

The prizes involved were mere pittances, needless to say, from the point of view of most government agencies and megacorporations. But they were large enough to warrant an attempt by moderate-sized consortia of interested organizations. The idea itself had its genesis in Robert Zubrin's *The Case For Mars*, and the Ares Project had been formed to seize the opportunity. Many of the founders were, of course, the same people who had hounded the government into arranging the prizes. Collectively, the group had gained the nickname of the Nuts That Roared, for their Grand Fenwickian victory over the ponderous and generally unswervable inertia of official space programs.

The public had started to take notice when the Ares Project successfully orbited, deorbited, and retrieved a fully functional man-capable space module—and did it for a million dollars less than the prize money for that achievement. But it was the follow-on *Ares-2*, a smaller but fully automated sensing satellite, that galvanized public opinion. The completely privately constructed spacecraft reached the Red Planet, used aerobraking to achieve orbital velocity, and sent back multiple high-quality images. And did it at a smaller cost than any equivalent government probe to date.

Stung into high gear by these successes, the politicians had showered money onto the space program. NASA and its associated partner agencies suddenly found themselves with quadrupled budgets and a mandate to get a manned spacecraft to Mars—and the unspoken mandate to manage the task before the Ares Project beat them to it.

Politics and government approaches still influenced the work at NASA, of course, and part of that caused NASA to avoid using many of the approaches which Ares used. This suited members of the Project, like A.J., just fine. If NASA decided to copy their methods, it might well outdo the Project despite its current lead.

For A.J.'s purposes, one important way in which they *had* taken a lesson from the Project was to avoid what Zubrin had called the "Siren Call" of the moon: i.e., to see the establishment of a moon base as a necessary precursor to a Mars expedition. The important way in which they had *not* taken that lesson was politically connected. The moon-base faction had been persuaded to give up on a Luna base, and a compromise reached: that a base would be constructed on Phobos, one of the two moons of Mars.

This was not something the Ares Project was directly interested in, but it made a lot more sense than building a base on Earth's moon. Phobos had no gravity well to speak of, and aerobraking in Mars' atmosphere could help in achieving a matched orbit at a reasonable cost. That done, the closeness of the moonlet would allow excellent surveying of parts of Mars.

Better still, there had been some indications from prior probes, including the ill-fated Soviet *Phobos 2*, that there might be some fossil deposits of water on Phobos, which was over twenty kilometers wide. That wasn't really surprising, since both Phobos and its brother moon Deimos were suspected to be captured outer-system bodies, possibly the cores of former comets. So the Phobos project was justifiable on its own terms while still being reasonably well integrated into NASA's overall mission design. And—always a critical factor in the world inhabited by government agencies and the megacorporations with whom they maintained an incestuous relationship—the Phobos project kept the existing vested interests happy. A moon base, after all, was a moon base, regardless of what moon it was on.

It was here that A.J. had seen an opportunity. Obviously, no one—neither government regulatory agencies nor private insurance companies—was going to let the Ares Project blast human beings into space without firm proof that all aspects of the proposed system would work safely. *Pirate* was an unmanned device designed to demonstrate the most critical aspects of the system: to be able to travel to the Red Planet with no return fuel, just a small store of "seed" hydrogen; to be able to create fuel from Mars' atmosphere; and then return to Earth using Mars-manufactured propellant.

A rover unit was to be deployed during the atmospheric fuel manufacturing stage to do surveying of the area, which was one of the prime locations currently considered for final landing of a manned mission. It would also leave the first "hab"—habitable enclosure—on Mars, although it was a scaled-down version from the full-scale "tuna cans" in the forthcoming main prep flights. The "hab" would serve as a testbed for the long-term operation of some of the systems and as a radio beacon as well.

A.J. had proposed a modification of this mission profile which would serve NASA's interests and those of the Ares Project: instead of immediately landing, *Pirate* would aerobrake into an orbit close to that of Phobos, and would release a number of independent, remotely controllable sensor-probe units. The probes would survey Phobos carefully from all directions in a number of spectra, helping them to select the best places for NASA's base. *Pirate* would then deorbit and carry out its basic mission. Though now, probably, with no rover or a much smaller one, to make up for the extra mass of the sensor drones that A.J. called his "Faeries."

The price tag for A.J.'s proposed modification was substantial for Ares—around twelve million dollars—but was far, far less than NASA would have to spend on any similar mission. Assuming they could do it at all—which, as far as A.J. was concerned, they couldn't. They didn't have *him*, and that meant that they simply wouldn't be able to design sensor drones good enough.

Apparently, NASA agreed, because they had accepted his proposal and hadn't even quibbled on the price.

The doors slid aside as he approached. "Joe!" he bellowed, making everyone in the room jump. "I believe in Faerie tales!"

Dr. Joe Buckley frowned at him for a moment before catching on. "Well, dammit, why'd they have to wait so long? We've spent the past two months refining the rover designs and the interior supports. Not to mention—"

"Oh, don't gripe, Joe. You'll still get to build the rovers. They'll be used in the next launch—hell, they'll be used in every mission we land, I'll bet. But this first mission will help pay for your rovers, and it's not like all of you won't get something to do in the redesign. I'm going to need half the machine and prototyping group to whip up prototypes of the Faeries. You'll want to try to design a chibi-rover to do at least some of the other stuff we wanted to test on the ground. The main capsule guys are going to need to design the drop-off module so we can match them up with Phobos' orbital speed exactly. I sure don't want to have to make the Faeries try to play orbital catchup; it'd play merry hell with the mass ratio and energy budget. And we'll all be playing games to figure out the best design for the drive systems on the things."

Joe grinned. "Sure. But you know how we engineers hate being kicked out of a nice comfortable rut. Now you're going to make us all *work*."

"True. Still, don't I get *any* thanks for bringing us in about twelve million bucks?"

A.J. found himself blushing as the entire engineering group on duty answered by giving him a standing ovation, something he hadn't actually expected. If there were going to be serious gripes about the changes, apparently they weren't going to be addressed at him.

"Umm . . ." The claps trailed off, leaving him in an awkward silence. "Thanks. Thanks a lot, guys."

"Aw, c'mon, you're embarrassing him!" Joe said, grinning. "Next he'll start getting teary-eyed and thanking the Academy and all that kind of thing. Enough of all this, let's get to work—we've got a hell of a lot of redesign work to do, and if we want to make this launch target, we've got just six months to do it all!"

# Chapter 6

"For the last time, Joe—*no.*" As if to emphasize the point, she sat down at the desk in her office with a solid-sounding plump that properly belonged to a woman much heavier than she was.

"It's not going to hurt *my* career, Helen!" Joe Buckley looked just as stubborn as Helen did. "I've gotten my doctorate now, and as far as the rest goes . . ." He snorted derisively. "I doubt if more than two percent of the people in my field know the difference between a triceratops and a tricycle—and less than half of the ones who do could care, anyway."

"That's not the point, and you know it," Helen said bluntly. "You want to do the spaceman thing just like your friend A.J., except you're willing to follow the standard route with NASA if the Ares Project doesn't pan out. Well, Joe, you and I both know that there's nothing more political than a national space program. Get associated with the wrong weirdos and you'll never get picked. It doesn't matter what your colleagues think—*they're* not the ones who call the political shots at NASA. And I might well be the absolutely wrong weirdo."

"Come on. The way you've written the paper, no one can gripe at you. It's not like you even say anything controversial."

Helen laughed humorlessly. "Joe, you worked with me for *how* long? And you still think they can't gripe any time they want to? Of course, they can. And they will, because they'll notice exactly what I'm *not* saying—when, normally, I'd be expected to say quite a bit. At the museum next week they probably won't tear me to shreds, but after the paper comes out publicly and the axes start getting ground . . ."

She shook her head. "By the time of the North American Paleontology Conference next year someone will absolutely crucify me. Might even be Nicholas Glendale."

Joe grimaced. Glendale was far and away the best known paleontologist in the country. And, somewhat unusually, his popular acclaim was matched by professional respect from his colleagues. Tall, handsome, with salt-and-pepper hair and a toothy grin, Nicholas Glendale was a regular figure for interviews, movie consulting jobs, and had written several best-selling books on paleontology.

He'd also been a solid fieldworker, early in his career, though he hadn't done any fieldwork in many years. For at least a decade, now, he'd been generally considered one of paleontology's top theorists. He had, in fact, been one of Helen's instructors for her graduate work—and probably the best.

If Glendale did decide to weigh in against Helen's work, she could really be in for trouble.

Helen saw the wince and smiled wryly. "You finally get it. And no, my chivalrous friend, there's nothing you can do about it. If you were thirty years older and at the top of the profession, maybe. But then you'd most likely be on the other side, anyway. If things work out well, don't worry. You'll all get the credit you deserve. I'll shout it from the top of the library building, if I have to."

"I'm not worried about that!"

"Maybe not, but *I* am. That's the part that rankles most about not putting your name—and Jackie's, Bill's and Carol's—on this paper. I feel like I'm cheating you, even while I'm trying to keep you out of the mudslinging. The only reason A.J. is listed is because his field won't care about ours, and it's really our only payment to him for the work he did."

"Well, then, don't worry, okay? None of us think anything like that."

He glanced at the sheaf of papers that summarized the many months of work Helen had done at the dig. Joe himself, along with Jackie, had only participated that first summer before their engineering careers made any further such time-consuming sidelines impossible.

He grinned as he once more read the name in the title. "And Jackie, at least, is getting her credit right there."

". . . of *Bemmius secordii*."

Helen finished and looked up. She tried to maintain a detached and professional expression, but it wasn't easy. Half of her wanted to burst out laughing at the expressions around the table, and the other half wanted to dive into a foxhole.

The room was silent. For a long time.

Finally, one of the visitors cleared his throat and said: "The study of the raptors is brilliant. But I noticed that you don't speculate on the holes in the skeletons. Or on the—ah, pebbles—that you found scattered about the site."

"That's true," replied Helen. "I simply reported the facts. People can draw whatever conclusions they choose. I don't feel I'm in a position to do so. Michael Jennings feels he has an excellent explanation for them, however, and he will be describing his theory in a separate paper."

Silence.

Another visitor spoke.

"Your treatment of the new species is also very restrained. The description is excellent, and I personally found your analysis of the presumed shape and locomotion quite convincing. But again, you draw no general conclusions. You don't even attempt to locate the animal within any established phylum."

"You're right. Where would you put it?"

Silence.

After another long pause, Director Bonds spoke.

"One small point, Helen. I'm a little puzzled by the name you've chosen for this new species. The species name is for the Secords, of course. But why the generic name?"

Helen managed to keep from smiling. "Oh, I don't know. I needed a name, and that one just came to me."

Fortunately, none of the people in that room were regular readers of science fiction. So she got away with it.

*That was the easy one,* she thought to herself an hour later, relaxing in the chair of the borrowed office. The museum had supported the dig, was getting the skeletons, and had every reason to accept whatever they got. But the peer-review process was bound to get interesting. By the time the paper came out publicly, months from now, the whole field would be alerted to the gist of its content. That would generate an instant academic brawl, which would reach a climax at the major conference next year.

The phone rang. Startled, she stared at the warbling instrument for a moment before finally picking it up. "Dr. Kamen's office, Dr. Sutter speaking."

"What's up, Doc? How'd the grilling go?"

Even over the phone, Helen recognized the exuberant voice. She was startled to hear it, though. She wouldn't have thought that, after more than a year, A.J. Baker would have still been following her work. She knew from Joe Buckley that his friend Baker was up to his eyeballs in his own project at Ares.

That's . . . kind of intriguing, actually.

She shook off the thought. "Not too badly, A.J. They knew I was dancing around certain subjects, sure. But they didn't want to go there either, so that works out pretty well for me."

"I still say I'd just go for it. Hit 'em with the truth and to hell with the rest."

"Oh, how I wish. Apparently, when it comes to professional status, your field works differently than mine."

"Well, yes, that's true. In my trade, there are those who are good, those who are excellent, and those who are divine. I have sufficient worshippers to qualify for the third category."

"And you're the most modest person you know, too."

He laughed. "Damn straight! So no one caught on?"

"Well . . . The director did ask about the name. But

either he didn't quite get it, or he was really working hard on ignoring it."

"Maybe everyone else will do the same."

"Ha. I laugh. And I laugh again. Everybody at the museum is friendly. Some of the people in this field are long-standing professional rivals of mine. Outright *enemies*, in the case of at least one or two. And they'll all have lots of time to read over my paper, once it comes out. For that matter, plenty of them will be reading it already.

You can bet copies will get circulated ahead of publication, no matter what the rules are. Oh, they'll be ready for me and Bemmie, A.J., don't you worry about that. Come along to the conference next fall. You can see me get burned in effigy. It'll be a big bonfire, too, with them having almost eighteen months to pile up the firewood."

"I'd love to, but it'll probably be impossible." A.J.'s voice sounded sincerely wistful. "Especially since I'd gladly roast anyone trying to light flames under you, and—if I do say so myself—I'm damn good at roasting people. 'To Serve Man' is my favorite bedtime reading."

Helen laughed herself at that. A.J.'s cheerful delivery made the whole conversation lighter. "So come on, then! The conference next year will be held in Phoenix, which isn't even that far away for you."

"No, it isn't—even allowing for the fact that New Mexico and Arizona are both big states. Hell of a scenic drive, too. But the problem isn't the travel time, it's the time I'd have to spend at the conference. Alas, though it devastates me, dear lady, I fear I cannot, for duty doth call."

A.J. had put on a very exaggerated Ye Olde English

accent for the last sentence, but promptly lapsed back into his usual Wiseass American. "We're kicking into high gear over at Ares, and I've been given the green light to go all-out in designing my sensor gear. You're talking to the man who's going to be first on Mars. Well, at least by proxy, but I get to design and run the proxies. And, who knows, maybe I'll actually get sent myself. Still, by next summer I'll be working round the clock and I doubt very much I'd be able to go attend a paleontology conference. Send me lots of pics and a transcript, though."

"You want pictures?"

"Of course. Mostly of you, though, not the stuffy old professors."

A.J. was too hearty with the flirty approach. But he segued back into the dry humor that Helen thought fit him much more comfortably. "Though if you can get some pics of people about to explode with outrage when you read your paper, I'd enjoy that also. By the way, thanks loads for the 3-D model you made of Bemmie. I have him as my wallpaper at work."

She heard a voice in the background. "Whoops! Gotta go, Dr. Sutter. Hey, hope you enjoy the e-mail I just sent! Bye!"

"Goodbye, A.J." she said, but he'd already cut off. Her portable pinged, signaling that A.J.'s message had arrived. She saw it contained an animation file, which she opened.

A flying saucer floated down the screen, disgorging a rather disquietingly cute *Bemmius*: squat, overly short, with exaggerated eyes and a completely anatomically wrong smiling mouth under the three forelimbs.

Bemmie scuttled in its odd way across a simple

landscape, coming upon a bunch of similarly overcute raptors. Bemmie held up a sign: TAKE ME TO YOUR LEADER. The raptors leaped at him, there was a struggle, and over the now unconscious body of Bemmie one of the raptors held up another sign: LEADER? I THOUGHT HE SAID LARDER!

She laughed again, even though the joke was pretty lame. He'd clearly put some work into that one. Bemmie might have been given a sort of face against his anatomical realities, but it had taken some thought to create a cartoon version of his actual locomotion style.

She dictated a quick, appreciative thank you, and then stood up. It was time to start working again. For the next year and a half, she wouldn't have much chance for relaxation.

# Chapter 7

Jackie Secord gripped the frame of the observation port tightly, staring at the strange assemblage of spherical tanks, tubing, and massive bracing structures within the almost unbelievably huge enclosure before her. Behind, a calm voice continued the countdown. "Five . . . four . . . three . . . two . . . one. . . *Firing.*"

From the center of the assemblage a monstrous tongue of flame reared up. Even through the soundproofing and vibration-absorbing material of the test facility, there came a deep-throated, thundering roar that shook the room. The sound went on and on, an avalanche of white noise that overwhelmed even her shout of triumph. It also wiped out the continuing counts and updates of the engineers, who had to resort to electronic communication rather than attempt to make themselves heard over the force of that unbelievable sound.

Finally, when it seemed to Jackie that even her bones

were vibrating from the unending song of power, it cut off. *Then* she could hear the yells, the whistles, and leaped into the air herself with a cowboy whoop.

"It worked, it *worked!*" she shouted, ears still ringing with that impossible noise.

"And why should it not?" the deep, sonorous voice of Dr. Satya Gupta inquired calmly. "The concept was proven decades ago. It was merely a new design that needed to be tested."

"Dr. Gupta, you can't stand there and tell me you didn't feel anything—any nervousness, any anticipation—while we were counting down to the first firing!"

The dark eyes twinkled. "Well . . . anticipation, certainly. The success of such a project, this is the reward of an engineer."

Jackie loved that considered, deliberate delivery, with the exotic combination of Indian and English accents flavoring Dr. Gupta's precise and well-crafted speech.

There was nothing unusual about Gupta's appearance—dark skin, black hair, symmetrical and well-molded face with a hooked nose over a brilliant smile, and he always dressed as though attending a formal dinner. Nothing unique at all, unless you counted the sharpness of those black eyes. It was Satya Gupta's *voice* that caught one's attention.

Everyone remarked on it, sooner or later. When A.J. Baker had met Gupta, he'd said: "So *that's* what Saruman is supposed to sound like."

Being A.J., he'd said it right in front of Gupta, too. Fortunately, the Indian engineer had a good sense of humor and hadn't been offended.

"So you never worried about something going wrong?"

Gupta gave an elaborate shrug. "It is always possible for there to be a failure, of course. Why else do we engineers always try to allow for all possibilities—and then add more reinforcements, just in case? On the other hand, a machine that is designed correctly should work. It *will* work. On this premise, Ms. Secord, our entire civilization depends."

Jackie almost laughed. Coming from anyone else, Gupta's little speeches and saws would just sound pompous; coming from him, they were simply right.

"Still—a nuclear rocket, Dr. Gupta! We just fired the first nuclear rocket since NERVA shut down!"

"Speaking for myself," Dr. Philip Moynihan said from his chair near the observation port, "I knew perfectly well it would work, and I still feel the same way Jackie does." The very elderly researcher was the only living man in the room who had participated in the original NERVA tests in the 1960s. "It's wonderful to see the new rocket fired for the first time."

Steven Schiffer, as was his way, added a cautionary note. "If the scrubbers don't make the outside air as clean as it was before the firing, it may be the *last* firing, too. The licensing hassles to permit this were something hellish. If one of the counters outside the range so much as hiccups, they'll probably come in and seal the whole complex." Gloomily: "With us in it, under a million tons of cement."

"And if they do that," Dr. Rankine said from his position at one of the analysis stations, "We'll just fire Zeus up again and blow a hole in the cement. Peak thrust of four and a half million newtons—call it just over a million pounds."

"Sweet! That'll give us something to fly from here to Mars on!"

"I still prefer 'Old Bang-Bang,' " grumbled Dr. Hiroshi Kanzaki.

Jackie rolled her eyes. The Japanese engineer's attachment to the old Orion design had always struck her as just barely short of obsessive.

"Oh, sure," she jibed. "*That* would be a lot easier to get authorized. 'Hi, we're going to take this huge honkin' plate of steel, put our ship on top, and then light off a chain of nuclear bombs under our asses to get us moving. In your back yard.' "

Kanzaki was never one to take a jibe without a rejoinder. "Well, you can't argue that us going for the nuclear rocket hasn't taken the heat off your boyfriend."

"A.J. is *not* my boyfriend!" Jackie replied automatically, for what was probably the three thousandth time.

The rest of what Kanzaki had said was true enough. The Ares Project also needed nuclear reactors to pull off some of the projected stunts, like generating new fuel on Mars for the return trip. If the government hadn't already been planning to make extensive use of nuclear technology in space for its own projects, A.J. and his fellow Nuts would have had hell's own time trying to convince anyone to let them fire off something loaded with fissionable materials into the sky.

"No doubt. I'm sure they're all grateful for that minor favor. Still, it means we get the real drive system while they're playing with bottle rockets."

That was greeted with another euphoric roar of agreement. Ever since they began, the space programs of the world had been stuck using chemical fuels to catapult loads into space. While that was perfectly acceptable for simple small orbital work, the fact remained that to explore the rest of the solar system demanded some other method of propelling a spaceship.

Many alternatives had been proposed, but they all had one of two disadvantages. Either, like solar sails or electric drive systems— sometimes called "ion" drives—they provided miniscule amounts of thrust. Or, they required a power source of such magnitude that only something like a nuclear reactor could provide the *oomph* needed.

In the case of Orion—"Old Bang-Bang," in their parlance— the design cut out the middleman entirely and detonated nuclear explosives like firecrackers under a tin can to kick a truly impressive payload upwards. However, with the paranoia against all things nuclear—even controlled reactions like NERVA—no such design had ever really been given a chance to get off the ground, so to speak.

But with the impetus to get to Mars suddenly in overdrive, it was clear that some superior drive system would be needed for the projected spaceship that NASA intended to send to Phobos and, thence, to Mars. With that demand, the NERVA program—Nuclear Energy for Rocket Vehicle Applications—had been reborn. Even in its prototype stages two-thirds of a century before, NERVA had demonstrated the immense thrust of two hundred and fifty thousand pounds. The specific impulse, which meant the amount of time that one pound of propellant could be used to produce a thrust of one pound of force, had been over eight hundred seconds—far greater than that which could be obtained from chemical sources.

While other theoretical systems, such as VASIMR,

offered superior overall performance, they remained theoretical. All of them required major technological breakthroughs, such as controlled commercial fusion—still eternally twenty years away—or specialized materials design. NERVA was in fact the simplest overall concept available. It used nuclear power to heat reaction mass to tremendous temperatures and pressures, and then let it squirt out. Simple, but with proper design reasonably efficient and vastly powerful.

"What was our specific impulse?" she asked.

"Eight hundred ninety-two seconds," Rankine answered smugly. "Pushing the calculated limits already. I'll bet with tuning we can crack the nine hundred second barrier!"

Jackie's phone pinged. "Yes?"

A.J.'s image appeared in front of her, courtesy of her VRD. "Congratulations, Jackie! Looks like you hit a million pounds of thrust there!"

"How the hell do you know that? You didn't play Tinkerbell with *me*, did you?"

A.J. gave an exaggerated look of wounded pride. "How could you even consider such a thing, Jackie?"

"Because it's just the kind of thing you'd do!"

He waved a finger in the manner of a prissy teacher. "Certainly not. Planting unapproved sensors inside that complex would be illegal, and the last thing I want is to get hauled up before the law."

He paused a moment, obviously fighting a grin. "Now, monitoring it from *outside* and performing my own unique analyses on the data, that's a different matter."

A.J. made a theatrical frowning glance to the side, as though consulting some very complex and important display out of her range of vision. "And it looks like you can tell your friends not to worry about having your tests cancelled. According to my data, the air you're venting is actually coming out below ambient rad levels."

"Showoff."

"Well, true. Let me make it up to you—meet Joe and me in Alamogordo and we'll buy you dinner. We both have something to celebrate!"

"You too?"

"Yep. Ted's Steak and Lobster, how's that? Meet you there at eight? Great. See you!"

"Hey, wait! What—" But A.J. had cut off. "Oooh, he is so . . ."

"Your boyfriend annoying you again?"

"He is *not* my boyfriend!"

# Chapter 8

"I'm not?" A.J. pulled an exaggerated sad face.

"No, you're not," stated Jackie firmly, as she slid into the booth seat opposite A.J. and Joe. "And stop pouting. You look cuter when you smile."

The sensor specialist brightened. "I'm cute!"

Joe shook his head. "She said you're cut-*er*. All that means is that you're less annoying when you smile than when you sulk. She's the precisionist type, don't forget."

"So," Jackie said, ignoring their byplay. "Obviously everyone knows what I'm celebrating. What about you guys?"

After A.J. filled her in on the latest news, Jackie jumped up and hugged him, nearly spilling water all over Joe. "Congratulations! That's wonderful news!"

"Dammit, Jackie, watch out." Joe blotted up the spill with a handful of napkins. "Or you'll get in trouble for consorting with the enemy."

She resumed her seat. "Yeah, right. Like they don't already believe I'm consorting. Do you know how often I have to repeat the fact that A.J. and I are not dating?" Jackie studied the menu and her eyes widened. "Holy sheep, as my dad used to say. Celebrations shouldn't leave people broke!"

"Don't worry, I'm paying." A.J. spoke before Joe could even respond.

"Oh, A.J., you don't have to—"

"It's no biggie, guys. Seriously."

Joe raised an eyebrow. "Paying for Jackie, I can understand, but I doubt I'm that good to look at."

"No, you're ugly. I'm paying for you out of pity."

"You are funny, A.J. That is why I'll kill you last."

There was a break in the banter as the trio considered the many options on the menu. The ordering process was delayed as Joe interrogated the waiter sternly on the precise methods of cooking employed, the spices, and a number of other issues. Jackie saw A.J. roll his eyes.

Joe was a gourmet; and, quite possibly, the most ungodly picky eater either of them knew. Apparently, however, the waiter's answers satisfied him, because he finally leaned back and selected stuffed portobello mushrooms with lobster and king crab for an appetizer, with grilled swordfish marinated in red wine sauce for his main course.

A.J. had taken all of three seconds to make his choice of calamari followed by a broiled lobster. Jackie wasn't quite that fast, but she'd still managed to order her grilled vegetables with dipping sauce and surf-and-turf combo in far less time than Joe took.

"I can see why you said you don't go out to eat with Joe very often."

Joe gave a tolerant smile. "Oh, you complain now, Jackie, but that's because you aren't in Ares."

She looked quizzically at A.J. "Just what does Joe's mania for cuisine have to do with the Project?"

"Well, everyone in the Project has to wear more than one hat. It so happens that Joe is in charge of the consumable supplies aboard the ships."

"Ah. Light dawns."

"Which," A.J. added, "is one of the reasons I pay for his meals. He's going to be picking mine when we go."

"So you're actually *going*?" Jackie couldn't keep her voice from rising on the last part, nor exclude the envy.

"About ninety-five percent chance. I'm in training already."

"Not that he really needs much," Joe said. "A.J.'s always been in good shape. I'm the one who has to really work."

"Don't tell me you're going, too!"

"Not all that likely. But possible. I'm a candidate, but nowhere near the front of the pack like A.J." Joe shook his head. "Basically, for me to go up, some of the others have to either get disqualified or quit. Or else something new has to turn up that gives me some special qualifications that other people don't have."

He eyed Jackie sympathetically. "What about you? The *Nike* is going to be *big*. We've heard it'll have a crew as large as ten people. Maybe even more."

Jackie knew she didn't look very optimistic. She didn't feel optimistic, either.

"Maybe. There's hellish competition. I'm going to be starting training next week, but I don't think they'll want more than one drive systems engineer aboard, and Dr. Gupta isn't about to step down. If the crew size was maybe half again larger—leaving enough room for an assistant drive engineer—then I'd have a real chance."

"You're a good electrical and micro-electro mechanical systems engineer, too."

"Thanks, but they've got qualified specialists for that. Again, the problem is the crew size. I'm everybody's favorite second banana, but with a crew of only ten there's just no room for any second bananas. If the *Nike* were twice the size—" She shrugged. "But it isn't. So all I can do is hope."

"Well," said A.J. brightly, "if both of you stay back, you can at least keep busy cheering me on."

It was Joe's turn to roll his eyes. "A.J., sometimes you are really a . . . "

"Self-centered jerk?"

"I wasn't going to say it," Joe muttered, still staring at the ceiling.

"I *was*," Jackie hissed.

Joe brought his eyes back down and changed the subject. "So, Jackie, today's test—any hitches at all?

"Not a one, so far. We may—wonder of wonders— actually finish a project ahead of time."

"Isn't that, like, completely against government regulations?"

"Normally, sure. But as we are currently under what amounts to an order to kick your sorry civilian asses, we've actually got permission to do things at real speed."

"The ass-kicking is going to happen in the other direction," A.J. jeered.

Jackie just smiled. "Possibly. But we've got a big fat government butt to absorb the punishment, where all you've got is skin and bones. Besides, if we can actually get close enough to launch this mission, I don't think it will matter. Especially if we can get everything done we've got projected."

"Well, I'll do my best to make it easy," A.J. said. "I'm really looking forward to doing this one. I'll actually get to play in both sandboxes at once. I stay on Ares' payroll and get to design all their cool stuff, but when the Faeries actually get down to business, since that data's going to belong to NASA, I'll be working in Mission Control with the big boys. Does it get any better than this?"

Joe laughed. "Probably not. I suppose I'm a little jealous, but hell, if it's adding that much to the department budget I can't really complain." He looked back at Jackie. "So how's the *Nike* design going?"

"Mostly hush-hush, but I can tell you she's going to be really big. More than one main engine to shove this lady along."

"I'll admit NASA did one thing right," said A.J. "At least they gave her the right name for the job."

He raised his glass over the arriving appetizers. "It may be disloyal, but here's to the winged Goddess of Victory, Nike!"

The others clinked their glasses with his, Jackie managing to control her irritation. Jackie had plenty of criticisms of NASA herself, but as time went on, she found A.J.'s incessant jibes were getting more and more annoying. As she'd often found with hardcore libertarians like A.J., if not with someone like Joe, the man could be insufferably smug—and amazingly blind to the contradictions in his own attitudes.

In this instance, she'd admit, Jackie happened to agree with A.J. She wasn't sure who, in the vast bureaucracy of

NASA, had first come up with the name, but it was appropriate in so many ways. The Greek/Roman pantheon had, of course, been the source of the planetary names, and Mars—Ares to the Greeks—was the God of War. However, the Greek pantheon had another deity of war: Athena, goddess of wisdom and warfare. Athena was symbolic of the necessity of war waged with rationality and control, while Mars/Ares was the symbol of its destructive savagery. NASA's first goal, however, was Phobos, one of the two moons of Mars, named after Ares' companions Phobos and Deimos: Fear and Terror. But Athena had her own companion, Nike. Thus the ship was named, and the motto of the Phobos Expedition was born.

She raised her glass and repeated it. " 'Conquer Fear.' "

They drank again. When she lowered her glass, Jackie found that she was still irritated enough to do a little needling of her own.

"A.J., explain to me again exactly how you guys are proposing to finance your junket—besides begging money from NASA? I've never been able to figure out how the abracadabra works."

"Oh, you mean instead of mugging the taxpayers and blowing their dough on expensive boondoggles?" A.J. grinned. "Well, you know about the prizes."

"Right. That's some money, and I suppose if you guys manage to have everything work right, that'd finance a good chunk of things."

"So far it's done real well for us. But it only pays for you being first, don't forget. If you have a reason to do things more than once— and we have a number of reasons we have to do multiple launches and landings—you'll start burning through whatever small profit you might make on the prize money after development. So as you imply, we need other sources.

"So first we got people who believed in it enough to be willing to donate money to the cause, work for cheap, and so on, to keep costs down. Then we started looking for angels—investors who wanted to be in on private space ventures."

A.J. leaned back, stretched, and then attacked his calamari for a moment. "Of course, the problem there is that even though a few ventures like Rutan's managed to make space before, they never got a chance to do much with it except some touristy stuff, so there weren't too many angels left. That meant we had to actually promise something."

"You started selling Mars, right? But you don't own the planet, so how can you sell it? That's what I don't get."

Joe held up an admonishing finger. "My dear girl," he said in a pompous tone, "we aren't *selling* Mars. We are selling the option to own property on Mars on the specu-lation that we can arrive there first and, therefore, claim that property by virtue of our arrival."

"Isn't that the same thing? And isn't it against interna-tional law to begin with?"

"Not exactly," A.J. said defensively. "If you look at it cold-bloodedly, what we're really doing is essentially a legal form of gambling. There's a reason they call the finan-cial section the 'Harriman Division' at Ares. This is land speculation based on the potential opening of a new fron-tier—something Heinlein mentioned in his story 'The Man Who Sold the Moon.' "

"In other words, it's a hustle." Jackie made no attempt to keep the sarcasm out of her voice.

"The fact is," she said forcefully, dropping her innocent pose, "that your scheme *is* against international law—going back at least to the Antarctic Treaty of 1959. The principles of which, I remind you, were reaffirmed in the treaty regarding use of the moon in 1967. Not to mention about a jillion UN resolutions that the United States is signatory to. What you're gambling on—more precisely, trying to get *other* people to gamble on—is that if you can land on Mars first, you can get at least some of those treaty provisions lifted."

A.J. and Joe were both looking defensive now—and the term "defensive," in the case of A.J. Baker, was a very difficult one to separate from "belligerent."

Joe, however, responded first. "Yes, Jackie, we're gambling—or asking others to, if you prefer. But what we're gambling on is not *whether* it will be done, but how quickly it will be done."

"What makes you think it will ever happen at all?"

"Because, to put it bluntly, Mars will eventually be habitable. The engineering to make it livable is already known to be possible, and relatively quickly—unlike the ten-thousand-year job it would be to terraform Venus. Antarctica really isn't, and there's a biosphere already on Earth that you can't risk disrupting in order to make it habitable. The Moon is a useless rock. Basically, those treaties hold because no one wants the areas involved badly enough to kick about it, and because there's no real motivation for lots of people to go there."

He took a bite, savored the flavor. "Mmmm . . . Now, if you want people to live somewhere else, you have to offer them something. And if what you want is for the place to be self-sustaining, you're talking about getting everything from farmers to miners to management people there. History has shown that, especially in frontier locations—and Mars will most definitely be a frontier—one of the big driving forces is the ability to get your *own* place relatively cheap, or potentially even 'free.' I put little verbal quotes around that because, of course, you'll be working your tail off to live on your land. You'll not be getting the best immigrants if what you do is force a lease or rental agreement on everyone. They will want to *own* the land, and I think the governments of the world will recognize that a separate *habitable* planet is an entirely different kettle of fish from some deserted, airless rockball like the Moon."

Jackie nodded. "Okay, it's not quite a con. You're right, it's a gamble. You're betting that the potential of a frontier will cause political pressure, on the one hand; and the thought of the potential profits from owning and exploiting an entire planet, on the other hand, will cause pressure from major industrial and financial interests. And all of it happening fast enough to make a difference in the laws to your benefit."

"Profit motive and a need for freedom are strong incentives. I think it's worth betting on, and so, apparently, do our investors."

"Fine. And let me tell you what *else* is true, Mr. Sudden-Expert-in-History. Your parallel between the American frontier of the nineteenth century and the Martian frontier of the twenty-first conveniently overlooks the fact that a *lot* has changed in two centuries. It's not going to be Ye Plucky Pioneer racing his Conestoga in a land rush, it's going to be Ye Megacorporation gouging the hell out of everybody to *allow* them to go to Mars—on Megacorp's terms.

Or do you think every would-be pioneer can build his own version of the *Nike*? If you ask me, your scheme—even if it works—isn't anything more than a fancy recipe for bringing back indentured servitude. In the name of 'freedom,' no less. And that's true even for American or European or East Asian would-be emigrants, much less—"

She broke off suddenly and took a deep breath. Then, decided she wasn't really in the mood for a full-bore argument. "Ah, never mind," she said, digging into her own food.

Fortunately, A.J. and Joe were just as willing to let it drop.

It was an old argument anyway, and one which in all its permutations the three of them had been bickering over for years.

A.J. and Joe were both libertarians in their political leanings—A.J., flamboyantly so; Joe, moderately so—and Jackie wasn't at all. As far as she was concerned, the splendid-sounding word "libertarianism," when you scratched the surface, all too often just meant "Me-me-me-me-me."

On the subject of who really owned Mars—or ought to—Jackie tended to agree with her boss, Dr. Gupta.

"I see, "he'd said to her mildly once, after she explained the Ares Project's scheme." Finance Mars exploration by selling Martian land to wealthy speculators. Well, that will certainly be to the benefit of a billion of my former countrymen. Most of whom can't afford to own an automobile. Or a bicycle, often enough."

It was easy to deride government agencies for being bureaucratic. Jackie had done so herself, many times—and had to deal with NASA's often amazingly stupid decisions and procedures far more directly than A.J. ever did. But, in the end, she didn't really think that handing the world—the whole damn solar system!—over to people with the single-minded and ultimately self-centered focus of A.J. Baker would be any improvement. At all.

The problem wasn't even with people like A.J. anyway, much less Joe. The problem was that the kind of people they'd get to provide them with the sort of financial backing they needed usually did *not* look at the world the way they did. A.J. might be self-centered in terms of his interests and his personal focus, but he wasn't a damn bean counter. Money, as such, ranked so far down on his list of priorities that it barely made the list at all—and then, only as an afterthought. Allowing for his more practical nature, the same was true of Joe.

Jackie doubted that the Ares Project's fund-raising scheme would really work, in any event. She knew Ares had picked up enough financial backing over and above the prize money to keep their operations running—albeit always on a shoestring budget. But she thought their assessment that a successful landing on Mars would start unraveling almost three-quarters of a century's worth of international treaties forbidding the private exploitation of Antarctica and extraterrestrial bodies was . . .

The proverbial pie in the sky. If anything, she thought it was more likely that the treaties would be strengthened. Nor could she really envision any government—certainly not ones as strong as the United States or China or the European confederation—allowing any private enterprise to build spacecraft which, push comes to shove, could serve as platforms for weapons of mass destruction.

But, she reminded herself again, there was no reason to turn the subject into a loud argument over this particular meal. And who knew? When the dust all settled, they might wind up with an immensely complicated mixture of public and private methods. It had happened before, plenty of times. The kind of compromise that satisfied nobody, but didn't create enough resentment for anybody to really want to pick a fight over.

A.J. still seemed to be a bit sullen. But Joe apparently shared Jackie's sentiment.

"Enough of that," he said, pushing away his plate but obviously referring back to the earlier dispute. "Come one, Jackie, let's get to the good stuff. Tell us what it was like to test a NERVA rocket!"

# Chapter 9

Helen gritted her teeth, willing herself to keep still in her chair. It helped that she had clamped both hands on the armrests to make *sure* she didn't move. If she let go of the armrests, she'd probably leap straight over the three rows of seats ahead of her and strangle Dr. Alexander Pinchuk with her bare hands.

Helen had first encountered Dr. Pinchuk in her second semester as a graduate student. He'd been a visiting professor. Within a month, she had come to detest the man. Nothing in the years that came after, as she encountered Dr. Pinchuk time and time again— either personally at conferences or indirectly in professional journals—had changed her opinion except to deepen it.

Wine improved with age. Dr. Pinchuk did not. The sarcastic nickname he'd been given by graduate students—*Alexander the Great*—had derived from the man's egotism. A decade and a half later, coming toward the end of a career that had never been very distinguished, Pinchuk was as sour as vinegar.

Dr. Myrtle Fischer, an old classmate from those graduate student days, had hinted to Helen that she might want to attend Pinchuk's talk at the conference. Not that Helen had really needed the hint, given the title of the talk.

Frauds, Fakes, and Mistakes: An Overview of Questionable and Falsified Paleontological Evidence and Methods.

Leaving aside Helen's personal dislike for Pinchuk— she'd spent some considerable time avoiding him over the past many years; said avoidances including one outright rejection of a pass—she'd also taken him to task in several articles and at least one conference for sloppy fieldwork, something that he'd been perennially guilty of.

Pinchuk, among other things, had a nasty streak. He not only kept grudges, he fed them and bred them.

At first, the presentation seemed a good review of the history of the field, with a focus on misperceptions and outright fakery. But soon a theme emerged, wherein Pinchuk kept returning to the present and asking the question of whether such a fraud could be perpetrated in modern times. Each time, presenting a little example of how such a thing might be done. And each little example was, in fact, clearly drawn *from her own dig*. Without saying anything directly, the slimy bastard was implying that she'd faked Bemmie!

The fact that the accusation bordered on the ludicrous wouldn't necessarily keep anyone from believing it. Dr. Pinchuk had done his research well. Helen was a bit astonished, in fact, when she finally realized how much effort he'd put into it.

The approaches he described would, in fact, make it possible to create a fake even as complex as *Bemmius*, given the advances of current technology. People would ignore, or be unaware of, the other facts—for instance, that to *make* such a fake dig and set it up as described would take far more money and time than she'd received in grants over the past ten years. And that he was implying that the Secords were also in on the scam, as were all of Helen's associates and assistants.

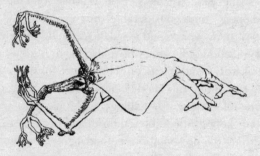

*Original drawing by Kathleen Moffre-Spoor.*

That made her even madder than the accusations against herself. She'd been prepared for something to be brought out against her, though the brazen effrontery of this approach went far beyond anything she imagined, but not for accusations against her friends.

And now she was aware of the surreptitious glances being sent in her direction. She wasn't the only one who was catching Pinchuk's references. She wondered if it would do more harm than good to try to confront him.

But . . . no, he was surely ready for that. If he'd spent this much time preparing what was obviously *both* an actually worthwhile paper *and* a carefully crafted strike at her, he wouldn't have neglected to cover the likelihood of her presence.

She could just ignore it, but that might give it more credibility. Helen ground her teeth together as Pinchuk unctuously began a discussion of another possible technique that "the paleontological field must keep vigilant watch for."

Just as she felt she couldn't possibly keep seated any longer, someone else spoke.

"Pardon me, Dr. Pinchuk."

That deep, warm voice, clearly audible around the auditorium without benefit of microphone and speakers, yanked Helen's head around almost as though by a string. It was the voice she'd been dreading all weekend, since the big annual paleontological conference began.

Dr. Nicholas Glendale rose from a seat in the back as Pinchuk recognized him.

"Overall, Doctor, an excellent piece of work," Glendale began. Helen's heart sank. Attacks from Pinchuk she could handle. Overall, she outpointed him professionally—by a big margin, in fact—and everyone knew it. But Glendale was, quite honestly, out of her league. As a paleontologist, Helen today was probably just as good—better, in fact, in the field. But in terms of reputation and professional politics, there was no comparison.

"But while it's certainly instructive to think on past events," Glendale continued, "I think you are missing an opportunity with your review of potential techniques for modern fakery."

She could make out the barely restrained grin on Dr. Pinchuk's face very easily. "Indeed, Doctor? How so? I would be glad to elaborate on any of the points I have made so far."

Glendale returned Pinchuk's smile with his charming white-toothed grin. "I'm not speaking so much of the points themselves. While, as you say, they could be elaborated upon, your descriptions were more than sufficient to get across the important elements. What I mean is that you weaken your argument by presenting it piecemeal. The audience can be left with the impression that one piece or another of some dig could be faked, but without the understanding that an entire dig could be successfully falsified."

He raised an elegant eyebrow, questioningly. "Unless I am misinterpreting you?"

"Not at all, Doctor, not at all! You're quite correct. Even a dig of quite considerable size could be effectively faked with the right techniques, even today, and proving it after the fact . . . Well, perhaps in twenty years. But we know what can happen in twenty years—and how hard it would be to eradicate false impressions that remain for that long."

"I think," Glendale said, nodding in agreement, "that it would be instructive if we could go over, step by step, the faking of such a dig from start to finish. Unless I am imposing too much, Dr. Pinchuk?"

By now, Helen thought, Pinchuk's professional smile was clearly straining to break through to some version of **Evil Overlord laughter**.

"I wouldn't mind at all, Dr. Glendale, as long as the audience doesn't. After all, I still have a few parts of my retrospective left."

To judge by the anticipatory murmur that followed, Helen was probably the only one in the room who would rather just see the subject dropped. Pinchuk's eyes carefully avoided hers, giving the impression that he was utterly unaware that she was actually in the room—except that his smile widened momentarily when his gaze passed nearby.

"Well, then, Doctor, let's see what we can do." Glendale joined Pinchuk on the lecture stage, without asking for an invitation. "We need a large, sensational fossil we want to fake. To make it really challenging, it should be something that's completely impossible in the fossil record. Something truly—"

"Alien?" Dr. Pinchuk finished, innocently.

"Alien?" Glendale mused on that theatrically for a moment. "Certainly an excellent candidate, but I think we should stick with something for which there's anecdotal evidence, so to speak. How about another creature of myth? A unicorn? No, something like that actually could have existed. Ah, I know. A dragon! Your classic dragon, four limbs plus two wings, tail, and so on. Fire-breathing metabolism, the works. And to be proper about it, let's put him in the Age of Dinosaurs—always a favorite for sensationalism."

"Perhaps right on the K-T boundary?" That suggestion came from a member of the audience. Helen couldn't quite see who it was.

Glendale looked rather torn, but Dr. Pinchuk nodded. "Oh, come on, Dr. Glendale. It allows the demonstration of all the techniques in one example."

He sighed. "Oh, very well, but the combination is ludicrous."

The talk, now an exploration in theoretical paleontology gone bad, continued. Glendale and Pinchuk alternated conversation as elements of the phony dig were explicated. For authenticity, Pinchuk demonstrated the use of actual fossils and how they could be effectively "salted" to the dig. Glendale raised objections of mineral consistency and solidity, pointing out that in order to fool observers and the cameras one would have to effectively fake rock. Dr. Pinchuk countered with numerous exhibits of replicated stone from recent laboratory studies— including one sample which looked suspiciously like the stone from which Bemmie had been dug. If that part was possible, Glendale conceded, it would take care of many of the objections.

"Now, the skeleton itself would be a problem," he pointed out. "Perhaps you could use similar techniques to replicate the fossilized bone. But how would you make a convincing design for the creature?"

Pinchuk was tall, very skinny, and had outsized elbows. The way he seemed to stoop over that question, even while sitting, reminded Helen of nothing so much as a vulture. A vulture with disheveled graying red hair, just to make things worse.

"Ah! Excellent question! Let me refer you to my earlier images, Figures 19 through 23. As you can see, combining a modern 3-D modeling package with data on fossil formation, then putting the model through the desired process, leaves a model of a fossil in all the detail you desire. In fact, you'd probably want to damage the model some to make it look believable—here, let's rip off part of our dragon's wing and leave it over here. Then we can arrange to find the dig through this piece."

A little titter ran through the audience, at this latest of Pinchuk's none-too-subtle jabs at Helen's work.

"Excellent thinking, Doctor," Glendale said approvingly.

Glendale continued to analyze the phony dig, and Dr. Pinchuk eagerly supplied explanations for every objection. Finally, the entire structure was complete.

"If I may say so, Dr. Glendale," Pinchuk triumphantly concluded, "I believe between us we have built an ironclad case. Such things are possible today."

"Ironclad indeed, Doctor." Nicholas Glendale was smiling broadly. His gaze swept the audience. When it reached Helen, staring in paralyzed fury, she thought she saw one eyelid dip—ever so slightly—in a wink.

What . . .?

"I have, in fact, been verifying your facts as we went along." Glendale patted the glittering ornament which was his personal data center. "They check out very well, although you are considerably more optimistic with a few elements than I feel comfortable with. Still, you've made an excellent case. A large dig such as this could indeed be faked, even well enough to fool modern technological investigation. Of course, doing so would cost—at rock-bottom minimum—about . . ."

He looked down to check his figures. "Forty-six million dollars. Or, to put it another way, approximately six hundred times the annual salary of a fully established paleontologist."

Dr. Pinchuk's grin seemed to freeze on his face, and a hush fell over the audience.

"Forty-six million . . . Well, it's true that—"

"No matter," Glendale said breezily. "While it's clearly

ludicrous to contend that *any* large and important dig could be faked in the real world"—his emphasis was sharply defined and unmistakable to everyone in the room—"your points still stand well on their own. Smaller fossils and digs are well within the capabilities of well-off notoriety seekers—millionaires, really, they'd have to be, to throw *that* much money around—and certainly should be watched for."

The good humor seemed to fade a bit from his expression. "I just wished to caution the observers to draw no conclusions about large excavations from our admittedly overly ambitious example. Such a falsification, though within the realm of the theoretically possible, would be so expensive as to make it, in the real world, something out of science fiction. Fantasy, I should say."

He gestured to the image of the falsified dragon fossil. "As fantastic as our draconic friend here. It would not only require money, but multiple coconspirators in laboratories and at the dig itself. The latter is what truly dooms any such attempt at fakery, of course. Money itself doesn't talk, but in conspiracies we must all remember what Benjamin Franklin said."

He paused, smiling at the audience, and finished. " 'Three can keep a secret—if two of them are dead.' So be suspicious when someone hands you a fossil of Tinkerbell, but don't worry about something much larger. It may be weird, and the discoverer may be misinterpreting the data. But it's real. Don't think for a moment it isn't."

He shook Dr. Pinchuk's hand with great enthusiasm. Since Pinchuk's whole arm seemed to have gone completely limp, it looked as if Glendale was shaking hands with a very large rag doll.

"Thank you very much for an entertaining diversion, Dr. Pinchuk! Well, I'd best leave you to finish up." He bowed to the audience. "And thank you all for your patience."

There was thunderous applause as Dr. Nicholas Glendale left the stage. Helen would have added to the applause, but on forcing her hands to release their grip she'd found they hurt too much. A huge weight was lifting from her shoulders. She couldn't help but laugh as she saw Pinchuk, still shell-shocked, try to resume his speech.

But his audience was already up and leaving. They knew what had been happening, under the surface. And now that Glendale had utterly demolished him, there was nothing left to see. She waved cheerily to Pinchuk, then headed for the exit herself.

# Chapter 10

"Reactor cooking?"

"Ruth's doing just marvelously, Joe." Reynolds Jones looked up from the readouts of the large atmosphere chamber. "Producing fuel and oxygen both at near-optimum efficiency in our little simulated Martian atmosphere."

Jones was a tall, slender, black-haired man with a faint speech impediment that, combined with his prissy schoolmaster's vocabulary and gesticulating conversation style, made virtually everyone sure that he was gay. Or, as Joe's father used to put it, "walked the other side of the tracks."

Joe had his doubts. First, because he was generally reluctant to typecast people. Secondly, because he didn't think anyone could be *that* much of a stereotype.

It didn't matter, anyway. Whatever Ren's sexual orientation might be—and no one at Ares really knew—one thing that was sure and certain was that he was a master mechanical engineer. Better still, he had enough knowledge of chemistry to make him an ideal team member for designing and building all of the chemical reactors that would transform native Martian materials into everything human beings needed to live there.

That made him, arguably, the single most irreplaceable member of the team. The strategy of the Ares Project pivoted on a premise advanced by Robert Zubrin long before: that an expedition to Mars only needed enough fuel and supplies to get there. Surviving on Mars, and returning to Earth, could be done using the materials found on the planet itself. If that premise proved to be unworkable, everything else became a moot point—and it was Reynolds Jones, more than anyone, who would be the person to make it work. Or find out that it wouldn't.

"You can actually see the levels going up as we watch," Reynolds added.

"Ruth," the reactor in question, was deceptively simple. A test version of a close relative had, in fact, been created by Zubrin himself to prove the basic concept. A ruthenium-iron-chrome catalyst in a long pipe combined hydrogen with Martian carbon dioxide, producing methane gas for fuel, along with water and carbon monoxide as useful byproducts.

The reaction used was a variation of the Sabatier process. Once started, the process produced enough heat to maintain itself. The water was electrolyzed using an advanced solid polymer electrolyte (SPE) unit similar to those developed years before for use in nuclear submarines to produce oxygen and return hydrogen to the catalytic process in the reactor. Meanwhile, the carbon monoxide was led off to other processes or stored for later use. The various components— attachments for power; tubing for leading the gaseous and liquid products to their destinations of liquefaction, compression, storage, or transfer; the compact shape of the custom SPE unit; and the connections for control circuitry and valves—were carefully distributed to leave the unit clear of obstructions. That was critical, because it operated at significantly high temperatures.

The basic tube-shape was still visible, however. Several other devices, of different construction, were set at separate locations around the atmospheric chamber.

Jones turned towards Anne Calabrio. "Annie, watch that carbon dioxide flow. We have to keep the pressure just right, and I think the program's not handling the valves properly. Something's wrong, anyway. The ratio's fluctuating more than it ought to."

"I'm on it, Ren. But with three experiments running at once, it's hard to maintain it all. I know we need to do this, checking for cross-interactions and all, but still, it's getting into pretty chaotic territory here."

Anne frowned. "Lee, can you throttle Ferris back some?"

"Throttle it back?" Grimes complained. "C'mon, Annie, I'm just gettin' started here!"

Anne's blue-eyed glare pinned Lee to the wall. The former Marine Corps lieutenant winced and raised his hands.

"Okay, okay. Gimme a sec. I was just starting to see some results here—and demonstrating iron production is going to be a pretty major experiment for us when we land, right?"

"Sorry, Lee," Reynolds said soothingly, "but remember, they're all tied together. We have to coordinate. When you start drawing the gas out of the system, the others have to adjust their timing so that each of us manages to support the other. It won't do us any good at all if you pull down the carbon monoxide when it's supposed to be used for a cleaning cycle. Or, worse yet, take too much hydrogen out of the main cycle."

Grumbling, the metallurgy specialist started shutting down the reactor that created iron by two separate paths. One combined hematite—an ore of iron that gave Mars its distinctive rust-red color—with carbon monoxide to produce iron and carbon dioxide. The other used hydrogen in a cycle that produced iron and water, with the water going to electrolysis to get more oxygen and return the hydrogen to work.

Lee Grimes was justifiably proud of the design. It allowed them to test and demonstrate both methods for producing usable iron, in a very small space.

"Part of the problem," Lee said, his tone conciliatory, "is that we're not really on Mars now. The damn chamber isn't big enough for us to drive things at full speed, at least not without a lot more ramp-up testing."

"Well, that's what we're all here for." Ren turned to Buckley. "Joe, what do you think?"

"I'd like to see if you can get Lee's experiment running again," Joe admitted. "Sure, our fuel-oxy reactor's big enough for primetime and combines reactions efficiently, but it's nothing spectacular. Making iron from Martian materials, now . . . *That's* going to be a demo that will make more investors really start thinking. And I'd like to see a demo of the ethylene reactor and the brickmaker, too."

"Ethylene coming up!" Anne said cheerfully. "Lee, once I get Ethyl running, you can restart Ferris. Use the hydrogen reaction, so I can grab the carbon monoxide from Ruth. Once I get that all balanced, we can try Porky."

" 'Porky'?" Joe repeated, puzzled.

Lee gave an explosive snort of laughter. "You haven't heard that one yet, have you? The heat cycle on the brickmaker was hogging all the energy, since we haven't got a nuke reactor right now. To use the waste heat to cook the bricks, we need to pull it off the mains and use electric heaters. When I said that to Annie, she said to me: 'Well, yeah, it's the Third Little Piggie.' "

"Lee didn't get it immediately," Reynolds chuckled. "Until I pointed out it was making our house out of bricks."

"You *do* realize we'll need more respectable names for our advanced technology than Ruth, Ferris, Porky, and Ethyl?"

"Joe, stop worrying about the damn investors." Anne coded in several instructions to the system, causing Ruth to increase production and Ethyl to start in. "We've got perfectly good, dull, respectable names full of stupid acronyms for them."

Meryl Stephenson and Bryce Heyers from the next lab poked their heads in. "Hey, guys, can we use some of the— Oh, hi, Joe. Big demo for the boss, eh?"

Joe smiled. "Something like that. Look, I'll be by your lab in an hour or so. We need to—"

A buzzing noise sounded from one of the panels. Reynolds' head snapped around. "That's—"

Joe was just turning towards the panel when the world split open.

⌗     ⌗     ⌗

Even through his headphones, A.J. heard the sharp boom of the explosion, and felt the floor jolt under his feet. The phones shut off as A.J. leapt from his chair and dashed for the door.

"What happened?"

"I don't know," said Melanie Sherry, standing indecisively. "But it sounded like it came from Engineering."

Other people in the hallway blurred past as A.J. sprinted towards the doors. He burst out into the open.

As he ran towards the testing area, he could see that it was bad. Black billows of smoke, lit from beneath by orange flames, curled upwards from the shattered Engineering wing, near the Atmospherics Testing area. He felt his stomach tighten. Joe had been planning to test some of the catalytic generation processes today.

He skidded to a halt in a scattered jumble of stone and brick. A few others were hesitating, like him, before plunging into the yawning, smoke-belching ruin.

"Joe!" he shouted. "Reynolds! Annie! Lee!" He could hear the distant wailing of fire and emergency medical vehicles approaching.

Setting his jaw, A.J. started in. But then, startled, backed off almost immediately.

Something loomed up in the smoke, emerging slowly, backlit by the flames, seeming almost to materialize like a monster in a bad action movie. It was too wide and squat to be human. A broad, blocky silhouette that wavered like a black ghost . . .

A.J. gave a shout and charged forward. "Joe!"

Joe Buckley gave a faint grin through the soot on his face, as did Reynolds Jones from beneath the reflective heat blanket the two had around their shoulders.

"I don't believe it. We made it out alive."

"Christ, what the hell happened? Never mind!" A.J. interrupted himself and reached for the blanket. "Give me that. The EMTs will be here soon."

Wrapping the blanket around himself, he plunged into the building, ignoring the shouts of people behind him.

Acrid chemical vapors spiked into his lungs as he reached into his pouch and grabbed a small, somewhat malleable ball. With all his strength he pitched it into the darkness ahead of him.

His VRD lit up almost instantly, matching the data now coming in from the sensor motes being scattered through the shattered interior by the ricocheting "scatterball" against the filed building plan. The data was patchy but good enough to work with.

The air was bad, very bad, but it wasn't going to kill him right away. Atmospheric chamber gone kablooey. Bodies . . .

There! And alive!

A.J.'s eyes stung terribly, but he blinked and fought the tears away. Then, suppressed a cough with desperate effort. If he started coughing now, he might not stop until he'd finished himself off.

A.J. tapped out commands on the virtual control panel in front of him as he stepped over a sensor-outlined block of rubble to get nearer to the body. The ad hoc network was coming up and trying to link in with the emergency vehicles' frequencies. *There! Got it!*

As he squatted next to Anne Calabrio's unconscious body, A.J. broke into the EMT frequency. "I've got a live one in here. We may have a few others. I think . . ."

He almost started coughing, then rasped out: "I think

I can get out with her, but tie in with . . . local net. . . maps. . . "

He stopped talking and got Anne's limp form over his shoulders. The body was damnably heavy, even though Annie wasn't at all fat.

A.J. just didn't seem to have much strength. Unusual, for him.

It was puzzling. And the VRD wasn't focusing right at all. What the hell was wrong with it? It was supposed to project straight to the retina, focus shouldn't be . . . a problem . . .

A.J. stumbled and almost fell. *Oh, shit. I'm the one having trouble interpreting.*

He could make out some symbols showing that the conditions were already far worse than they'd been when he entered. His head was spinning. Which way was out?

He couldn't tell. Black smoke was everywhere. Light, he needed . . .needed to find . . .

He was on the ground, blood in his mouth, hurting. He realized he'd fallen. Someone . . . Anne . . . was on top of him.

*Got to get up. Get* up, *dammit!*

Light drew him. Orange flickering light. No, he realized, that was bad. *Fire bad! Fire bad!* The words came into his head from some long-distant movie.

With a supreme effort, A.J. forced himself upright. The VRD had failed. Maybe the fall, maybe soot on the optics, who knew? It didn't matter. A.J. doubted he could have understood it at this point, anyway.

He dragged his feet forward, one step at a time. Just one step more. Now just another step.

*It's a building, not a catacomb! You only have a few . . .*

The wall smacked him in the face.

He knew that wall texture, though. He was near the back of the Atmospherics area. He'd gotten turned around and headed in just the wrong direction. A hacking cough hijacked his breathing, forcing him to stop and almost drop Anne. Disembodied knives stabbed deep into his lungs. Somehow he got the pain under control, and managed to turn around.

But there looked to be flames everywhere! He'd have to run through . . .

Running seemed out of the question.

A dull explosion punctuated his oxygen-deprived panic. *Move! Have to try!*

A.J. managed a sluggish trot. It was already stiflingly hot, but every step towards the flames seemed to double the heat. The pain in his lungs . . .

*I can't die yet, dammit. The Faeries haven't flown.*

Then he was falling.


A.J. stirred slightly. Joe came alert, looking down at his friend's reddened skin, scorched hair, and streaks of black soot that even scrubbing hadn't yet managed to eradicate. The blue eyes opened slowly.

"J-Joe?" The normally exuberant voice was barely a whisper, almost a hiss.

"Take it easy, man. You were really touch-and-go there for a while. You crazy sonofabitch." He extended a small cup to A.J. "Try to sip a little water."

A.J. sipped, grimacing at the pain in his throat, but sipped more anyway, trying to rehydrate the nearly cooked tissues. "Anne?" he finally managed, his voice now more of a croak.

"Alive. And so are Lee, Susan, and Lindy. Meryl and Bryce, too. Anne's doing fine. She'll have a scar on her head from where a chunk of metal hit her, but the concussion was minor and because she was unconscious and not doing heavy work, her lungs are in decent shape. She didn't inhale much. Lee, well . . . he lost his left leg."

A.J. winced. "Oh, hell."

"Come on, A.J.," Joe almost scolded. "He's lucky to be alive. Wouldn't be—neither would most of the others—if it hadn't been for you."

"*Me?* Ha. I went charging"—he coughed slightly and his eyes watered at the pain—"charging in there like an idiot and got myself trapped. Anne, too. And never did anything at all for Lee."

"You certainly did, you moron," Joe retorted, with a touch of affectionate exasperation. "You also tied all your sensors into the local net, and with that the firefighters and EMTs who just happened to also have masks were able to navigate through the mess and find everyone in jig time. Apparently they caught you just as you were about to fall into the fire. So you did land yourself in the hospital, but you almost certainly kept the rest of us out of the morgue."

A.J. looked somewhat gratified, if still embarrassed over having turned himself into a victim. "Still. With a leg gone, Lee's hopes to be on the mission are over." That was true, but Joe wanted to change the subject. Obviously,

A.J. hadn't yet figured out the implications of Joe's earlier statement that Anne's lungs were okay.

A.J.'s . . . weren't.

His good looks had miraculously come through untouched, except for a small scar on one cheek that would just draw more attention. But A.J., unlike Anne, *had* been breathing heavily in that holocaust.

The air in there hadn't simply been "bad" toward the end. It had been toxic. There'd been almost no oxygen left in the interior of the building. Instead, it had been filled with poisonous vapors from burning plastics, chemicals used in the engineering experiments, carbon monoxide and nitrogen oxides from the intense heat, particulates—a sheer witches' brew that would have felled most men with a single breath. Joe knew the doctors were astonished that A.J. had survived at all, much less managed to move around as much as he did. Under the flamboyant exterior, the man was about as tough as any human being could get.

A.J. finished the cup of water as a nurse came in, checked his IVs, and went to get the doctor.

"What happened?" he asked, after she left.

"Not quite sure yet," Joe admitted. "It'll be a while. I *think* that we had a leak somewhere that caused oxygen to get into the mix, and once it started running away on us . . . anyway, we'll know in a couple days."

"Play merry hell with our schedule," A.J. said gloomily. Then, obviously trying to cheer up: "Hey, how'd you and Ren get out, anyway? I thought you were a goner!"

"Damn near was. I don't remember it all clearly, and neither does Ren. Near as I can figure, when the tank went up, the shockwave threw both of us towards the wall that blew out. A fire blanket was in the mess next to me, so I threw it over myself and Reynolds, and managed to get him to wake up so we could get out."

"You seem to make a habit out of this kind of thing."

Joe grinned weakly. He had a reputation for nearly

getting killed—a climbing accident in which a belaying rope gave way, an explosion in a model rocket when he was a kid, going off a cliff in a car with no brakes, and a few other less spectacular but no less dangerous events.

"It doesn't get any less scary, let me tell you. If anything, it's worse—I'm sure that somehow, somewhere, fate is saving me up for a *really* spectacular finish."

"Well, I guess this one wasn't quite good enough." A.J. leaned back as Dr. Mendoza came in. By the time Mendoza finished his examination, A.J. had actually fallen asleep.

"He must be exhausted."

"He's got a ways to go yet, Mr. Buckley," Mendoza said briskly. "We'll be keeping him here for at least a few days for observation. With all the fumes he inhaled, and the high temperatures, he has significant damage to his lungs. Hope for the best, of course, but Mr. Baker is very lucky to be alive. I will be surprised if he comes out of this with more than eighty percent of his former lung capacity."

Joe grimaced. Eighty percent . . .

That would be enough to knock A.J. off the Mars mission. You didn't send people with respiratory problems into space.

"Please do what you can, Doctor. He's on the short list for the mission."

Mendoza nodded. "I know, and I will. But I can't do miracles. He'll have to do that himself."

Joe couldn't help another smile. "Well, as he'd say himself, that's his main job. Making miracles."

# Chapter 11

Helen had intended to wait for Glendale outside another lecture late that afternoon, in order to thank him. But the call from Jackie Secord telling her about the accident at Ares not only distracted her for too long, but left her feeling much too depressed. Instead, she returned to her hotel room and spent most of the evening on or by the phone, waiting for further news.

She was finally able to talk to Joe himself. That was a source of much relief, regarding him, of course. But the rest of the situation was very unsettling. In an odd sort of way that Helen still couldn't define—she'd only spent a few hours in the man's actual presence, after all—A.J. Baker had come to be an important person in her life. The idea of him dying was . . . horrible.

Early in the morning, though, Joe called again.

"He'll survive, Helen. The doctors say there isn't any doubt about that at all, any longer."

"Oh, thank God."

There was a little pause. "But he won't be one hundred percent again. Never. The damage to his lungs was just too extensive."

"How bad is it?"

She could almost hear the shrug on the other end. "Depends how you look at it. From the standpoint of most people, not bad at all. After a few months, you really won't be able to tell the difference, under normal circumstances—at least, that's what the doctors say. He won't be running any marathons, of course."

Helen chuckled. "Did he ever?"

"As a matter of fact, he did. Twice, once in the big Boston one. He even had a pretty respectable finish. The truth is, Helen, A.J. is one of the few geeks I've ever known who could have been one hell of an athlete, if he'd wanted to. Which he didn't, but he's always been in top physical condition. Even studies martial arts, if you can believe it. That's partly why he was placed so highly in the running for the expedition. Now . . ."

Suddenly, Helen understood. "Oh."

"Yeah. 'Oh.' Traveling to Mars just doesn't fall under the label 'normal circumstances.' And you know how much it means to him."

"Yes, I do." She took a long, slow breath. "Well, let's hope for the best. And let's also not forget—and make sure you remind him, Joe, when he needs it—that as long as you're alive you can still hope."

She finally caught up with Glendale in one of the hallways later that morning.

"Dr. Glendale—Nicholas—thank you."

The famous smile was muted but sincere. He didn't try to pretend he didn't understand, either.

"Helen, there's nothing I despise more than a hatchet job. And that was one of the most cleverly repellent things I've seen in years. It was, I assure you, a genuine pleasure."

"So you believe . . ."

"I believe that you have found the most interesting case of *Problematica* on record," Glendale said firmly. "Nothing more than that, Helen. I know you have some rather . . . extreme conclusions. But. . . "

"But? Nicholas—"

She more or less dragged him into a side room, away from the circulating masses. "*Look* at it. There isn't a phylum that even comes close. The means of locomotion is utterly alien to this world."

Glendale winced. She could see he had been hoping to avoid this conversation entirely.

"Helen . . . my dear . . ."

He stopped, looked at her, sighed, and then shifted into his professional persona that she knew so well. "Dr. Sutter, I suppose it would be easiest to speak directly about this. Can we do that? I know everyone else, including yourself, is avoiding direct statements. Can we be straight with each other here?"

Helen nodded.

"Very well. Dr. Sutter, your theory, and presumably that of your co-workers, is this: that the anomalous fossil you have named *Bemmius secordii* is, in point of fact, the remains of an alien creature. A star-traveling visitor to our world, who had the misfortune to encounter some of our nastier native predators sixty-five million years ago, and paid the price. Although he managed to finish off the predators as well, through the use of a weapon which used the ceramic-type pellets you found on the site as projectiles. Am I basically correct?"

Helen found herself hesitating momentarily. She didn't think any of them had ever—even to each other—put it so directly. It had been more an assumption than anything else. But what other explanation was there?

"Yes, that is correct."

"An attractive theory, certainly. We all want to have something sensational in our careers, and I remember you well as an undergraduate. You were something in the way of my star pupil. Science fiction was one of your favorite reading areas, too, as I recall. So, naturally, such an explanation would occur to you when confronted with something that bizarre."

"It would occur to a *lot* of paleontologists. I would have bet it would occur to you, too."

Glendale laughed. "Oh, it most certainly would occur to me. *Did* occur to me, I should say, the moment I finished reading your initial report. I'm an occasional reader of science fiction myself, as it happens. Unfortunately— or fortunately—I am also far too aware of the logical flaws involved to retain such a theory for very long."

Helen felt her jaw setting as it always used to when she started arguing with Glendale. She reminded herself sharply of how often that had presaged her getting roundly trounced in an argument, rather as Pinchuk just had.

"What other theory is there?"

"There are many possibilities, Dr. Sutter. Instead of immediately offering one, I want you to consider what you are asking us to accept.

You are, as a paleontologist, intimately aware of the probabilities involved in fossil formation. You may not, perhaps, have considered the probabilities of other events quite so closely, reasoning—with some justification—that there wouldn't be sufficient information to judge them by, anyway. Still, let me summarize."

He held up one hand and began counting off the fingers with his other. "You want us to believe the following unlikely chain of coincidences:

"First, an alien from another world arrives here. Perhaps you have never considered how very improbable that is, what with all the science fiction books and videos ignoring that very point. But from everything we currently know, such travel between the stars is hideously unlikely, even for us. And, so far, we have absolutely no evidence that there *is* any other life in the universe. We may assume it, but thus far there is not the smallest shred of acceptable evidence that it exists at all.

"Second, this creature lands on our world and manages to get himself killed. Perhaps not so farfetched.

"Third, that he was traveling completely alone. That seems a ludicrous assumption unless we allow for truly space-operaticlevel technology—and in that case, what was he doing protecting himself with what amounts to a fancy shotgun? Or, if he wasn't alone, that his fellow beings didn't bother to retrieve his body. Human cultures do not just leave bodies to be savaged by random creatures, and I find it hard to believe that alien ones would either. Or, of course, something else killed off his fellows coincidentally before they could interfere or retrieve the body.

"Fourth, that he managed to injure most if not all of his attackers— but not swiftly enough to keep from being killed himself, though the injuries he dealt made them expire just a short distance from him. Close enough that they could all be found together in a single death scene, sixty-five million years later.

"Fifth, that of all the untold trillions of death scenes across the entire world over the past hundreds of millions of years, it was *this*—already utterly improbable—death scene that just happened to be one of the very few preserved as a fossil."

Having run out of fingers, he lowered his hands. "And, finally, to add insult to statistical injury, you want us to believe that all this just *happened* to occur at the very moment the asteroid or comet struck the Yucatan. So that all of these perfectly preserved corpses ended up literally sitting on the K-T boundary."

He gave Helen a level stare. Not an unfriendly one, no. But it was just as disconcerting today as she remembered that stare being when she was a young graduate student.

"Helen," he said softly, "I just demolished Pinchuk by showing the mathematical absurdities that his scheme would entail. I can assure you—this is my own field of expertise, as you know—that if I subjected your theory to the same sort of mathematical scrutiny, the results would be several orders of magnitude worse. I did a rough estimate, as it happens, the moment I finished your paper. I stopped once I realized that your theory is statistically more improbable—*far* more improbable, as a matter of fact—than the existence of dragons and unicorns."

Helen couldn't argue with the statistical improbabilities involved. She was not an expert on the math involved, the way Glendale was, but she knew enough to know that he was right. She'd been bothered all along by the cumulative series of unlikely coincidences, and had no good explanation for them herself.

Still . . .

Helen was a *fieldworker*, not a theoretician like Glendale.

"But facts trump probability, don't they, Nicholas?"

"Certainly, Helen. Facts always trump theories. And if you had found that our mysterious friend had a fossilized repeating shotgun on his person, I would have conceded immediately—and then wracked my brains trying to figure out how to explain the improbabilities involved. In this case, however, I think what you are seeing is something still very improbable, but at least a couple of orders of magnitude more likely than fossilized aliens. That is, a creature of a previously unknown phylum which, through quite amazing probability events, has not had any of its precursor forms discovered previously.

"Or," he added, "which I personally think is what we'll find, that such fossils *have* been found but weren't recognized for what they were. Helen, I suspect that if you could take a few years and search through the miscellaneous fossils in the New York Museum of Natural History and similar places, you'd find some misfiled shells that are, in fact, parts of precursors to your *Bemmius*. Such things happen often enough, as you well know. Look how long it took before we finally realized what the conodonts were. This is just an extreme version of it."

He looked aside, for a moment, pensively. "It may even be less unusual than it seems, for that matter. The oddity isn't really the design of the phylum, after all, if you consider the incredible range of evolutionary possibilities we can see in the Burgess Shale. Is Bemmie really so out-landish, matched up against *Wiwaxia* and *Opabinia* and *Anomalocaris*—not to mention *Hallucigenia*? For that matter, it occurred to one of my current graduate students, when we discussed the subject, that your initial impression may actually not be far from the truth. Imagine an offshoot of the cephalopod family which took to land; had some of its tentacles migrate and become shorter for movement, and others evolve for manipulation or catching prey on land. It develops the platelike supports for land propulsion and the skull is the internalization of the shell. Farfetched, perhaps, although . . ."

He shrugged. "You know as well as I do that the real mystery is not the creature itself; it's explaining why we haven't seen any previous indications of such a phylum in the fossil record. But if the lifestyle of such animals kept them away from conditions which lend to fossilization, it's by no means impossible. And what's certain, mathematically speaking, is that the discovery of even a large, highly evolved representative of an unknown phylum is still a far, far more likely event than the fossilization of a singular alien from some distant planet."

She suddenly felt exhausted, emotionally as well as physically. Her extended session of fury in Pinchuk's lecture, the abrupt relief, the lack of sleep from worrying about A.J.'s condition—and, now, the realization that even her defender didn't believe what she'd found, had drained her.

"I don't know about that." She summoned enough energy for a last sally. "I do know this—and so do you. Using that same method of statistical analysis, you can demonstrate that the likelihood of a universe emerging which could eventually produce intelligent human life on Earth is every bit as farfetched."

Alas, Glendale just grinned. "Yes, you're right. I hate to think how many innocent trees have been slaughtered to provide the paper for the endless debate over the anthropic principle. But there's still a fundamental difference, Helen. Facts *do* trump theory, and here we have a *fact*. We *know* there is life here on Earth, and we *know* it's produced other phyla of life, including intelligent life. We have no such evidence for life on any other planet. Much less intelligent life. Much less life so technologically advanced that it can visit our own world."

He spread his hands a bit. "My own hypothesis is admittedly unlikely. But it is less unlikely than your own—and has the great logical advantage of being based on facts that we *know* to be true."

He looked at her sympathetically. "You're wiped out, Helen, and no wonder. You've been worrying about just this sort of reaction for weeks, and it's not doing you any good. If you'll just accept that what you have is a wonderful *terrestrial* find, and write up some papers that way, you'll find it's a lot easier to sleep at night—and idiots like Pinchuk won't be able to bother you."

He checked his watch. "I have a panel in five minutes. Helen, take care. You have a magnificent find; just stop thinking of an explanation that really doesn't hold water, even if it does look, well, a lot cooler than any other explanation out there."

After Glendale left, Helen sank into one of the empty chairs nearby. "I wish I could do that, Nicholas. But—unlikely or not, impossible or not—I'm sure that *Bemmius secordii* died a long, long way from home."

# PART III: FAERIES

*Paradigm shift, n: a sudden, transformative change in world view, generally the result of new information or events which render the prior world view ineffective in describing the world in which the person or civilization now finds itself.*

# Chapter 12

"No, it's okay. You *deserve* to go, Joe."

"I didn't ask for them to do this."

"Are you deaf, Joe? I said it's okay."

To someone who hadn't known him for years, A.J. sounded like he was one hundred percent recovered. Joe, though, could hear both the overemphasized casual tone and the very slight roughness, the latter indicating the cause of their current discussion.

A.J. put his VRD glasses back on, pointedly trying to act as though it was a normal day at work. "I knew something like this would happen once the doc had his little talk with me."

Joe put a hand on his shoulder. "Cut the crap, A.J."

The blond imaging whiz sat still for a moment, trying to maintain a casual pose. But it collapsed and A.J. tore the glasses from his face, flinging them down violently.

"God *damn* it. *Damn* it!" His voice broke, bringing a

sympathetic sting to Joe's eyes as he saw actual tears break through A.J.'s reserve and spill down his face before he savagely scrubbed them away with his sleeve.

"I shouldn't be crying about this. I shouldn't even be *angry* about this. I did it to myself, didn't I?"

He tried to stop the rant, choked off a sob, and dissolved into a racking cough. Joe waited until his friend had recovered breath and some self-control.

"Yeah, you did do it to yourself. Saving my own engineering staff. The whole project, really. Look, A.J., the Faeries are on their way to Mars right now. You watched the launch yesterday. You'll be exploring Phobos soon, on schedule, and if you hadn't pushed yourself past the limit, we'd have missed that deadline. I can't override the docs, A.J., but no one can take away what you've achieved, or what you're *going* to achieve."

A.J. glowered down at the table, obviously trying to keep from crying, shouting, or both again.

"And you weren't the only one who paid that price. There were two, three other people ahead of me, and the accident took them out one way or another. That's why I'm at the top of the list now."

The blue eyes closed again. A.J. took a deep, carefully controlled breath that still held a faint wheezing note, a sign of the damage to his lungs. When his eyes opened again, the fury was fading from them.

"I know. It's just . . . going to take me a little time to accept it, okay? I was so close to that part of the dream. I knew they hadn't actually decided the crew, but I sort of assumed I'd be on it."

"And so did everyone else."

"I'm not entirely off the list," A.J. said after a pause.

"The doc said I was down to eighty-two percent of my normal—former—capacity, and there were things that could trigger other problems, but that it wasn't absolutely out of the question, depending. The rest of me is healthy."

"Well, that's good. Maybe then on the next trip . . .?"

A.J. nodded, a bit too lightly. "Maybe so. But I should get to work. Have a lot of things to do before I move out to JPL and handle the Faeries for NASA."

He picked the glasses back up and put them on. A moment later, he took them off, stared at them, and then suddenly burst out laughing, a laugh which also turned into a short coughing fit.

"Just perfect. I've killed my VRD."

He stood up. Then, so suddenly it startled Joe, turned and hugged his friend. "Thanks."

Joe recovered and returned the embrace. A.J. wasn't affectionate with too many people, but with those few he tended toward unabashed displays of joy and sorrow. Joe appreciated the fact that

A.J. considered him one of those few. "Thanks for what?"

"For making me explode, letting it all out. It'd be a poison if I kept it in. I know myself that way."

A.J. wasn't really all right yet, Joe knew, but at least he'd acknowledged the anger and started to face it. They needed that anger worked out as fast as possible, because the Project still needed A.J. badly, and Joe very much did *not* want to lose one of his best friends over something like this.

"I guess I'd better go pick myself out another VRD. Congratulations on making the crew, Joe."

"Thanks, A.J."

The imaging specialist walked out, just a bit more slowly than he might have a few months before, shoulders slumped the least little bit. Joe heard himself sigh. *What a goddamned shame.*

Helen rubbed her eyes and pushed back from the desk. Opening her eyes, she found that the tests had, alas, not magically finished grading themselves as she had hoped.

"What I wouldn't give for a distraction," she muttered. Being a professor had its advantages, but this wasn't one of them. Especially with the quality of students these days.

She suddenly chuckled, remembering that her father—a professor of long standing himself—had made the same complaint, and mentioned that *his* favorite professors had done the same. If all of them had been right, by now she should be teaching a class of mostly australopithecines.

Opening up the next test file, she winced. Perhaps she *was*. Was it really so very difficult for a student to master basic language skills before entering college? Yet Jerry was always attentive in class, and he didn't do badly on the lab practicals. He just could not seem to put into written words anything he knew. Maybe he needed a verbal examination.

Her phone dinged, then gave voice to a four-note chime that she hadn't heard in months. "A.J.!"

"What's up, Doc?"

"To my neck in tests, is what's up," she answered. The tanned face displayed before her had the subliminally odd cast that came from generating the face image based on the actual face, but using sensors set at a much different location than the apparent camera viewpoint. Still, there was something about the expression that seemed additionally wrong.

"What about you, A.J.?"

"Oh, I just . . . thought I'd give you a call. It's been a while."

"Uh-huh. I'm actually a little pissed at you. I also got a call from Jackie Secord. About five hours ago."

"Oh."

"What the hell is wrong with you, A.J.? She calls to give you some good news and you practically freeze her from long distance. Then won't answer her calls? I know the two of you argue about a lot of stuff, but that's just plain rude."

A.J. was silent, but his expression was failing to maintain the usual open and carefree look. The imaging expert looked . . . miserable.

Helen couldn't recall ever seeing him even look momentarily glum. She was silent, waiting. He obviously had some kind of trouble, but she wasn't going to let him completely off the hook.

"Yeah. I had better send her an apology. She . . . it was just a really, really bad time to call."

"A bad time to call? Come on, A.J."

"You know what she called about?"

"Well, of course. She's made the cut to be on *Nike*'s crew. It's not guaranteed yet, but things are looking much better than she ever—"

"I've been grounded."

It took a moment for Helen to grasp what A.J. meant. "Grounded? I didn't . . . Oh, God. You found out today?"

The answer was almost a whisper. "Yeah. Joe managed to talk me out of a major tantrum, so I went out to get myself new shades, and while I'm doing that Jackie calls me out of the blue."

"Oh, A.J." She didn't honestly know what to say. What *could* she say?

"I figured you might understand better than anyone."

"Huh? I'm not one of you space cases."

"No," A.J. conceded. "But you've had your career take a down turn because you did something you knew was dangerous to it, even though you really didn't have a choice."

"I thought . . . Joe called me last week. He told me your recovery was going very well, according to the doctors."

"Yeah, I guess. The way the doctors look at it, which isn't the way I do. I'm not blaming them, you understand. They did what they could. Twenty years ago I'd have lost a lot more function, and fifty years ago they'd have written me off, even if I'd lived to get out of the fire. I'm a little better than eighty percent; but in space, they're looking for a hundred and ten percent, you know?"

"Even so, I can't believe they've taken you off the list entirely!"

"Well . . . no. But I'm down around where Joe was. Oh, and just by the way, Joe's now on the list for Ares."

No *wonder* he hadn't been able to handle Jackie's call! His two best friends got the nod just as he got the boot, and then. . .

"I'll have to congratulate him. But. . . that must hurt."

"A lot." The roughness in his voice became apparent as he tried to control it. "More than I told Joe, though I know he knows me enough to know . . . does that make sense? And I feel like such a complete and utter *dickhead*,

Doc. I shouldn't be mad at Joe, it's not his fault, and it's not Jackie's. There's no one to blame except a faulty valve that happened to blow a few months back. But I'm still mad at him. I'm so fu—frigging mad that I could punch him out, and all the damn doctors, and I'd take a swing at Jackie if she wasn't a girl. Because, dammit, it's my dream. *Mine*."

"I know," she said softly.

"And here I am, crying to you. I sorta cried in front of Joe before, but I can't really do that. And my folks, well . . ."

He didn't finish, but she already knew that A.J.'s parents had been killed in an auto accident several years earlier. "So I guess you get the really short end of the stick. First Jackie gets to tell you what a jerk I am, and then I get to tell you in person."

"Why me?"

A.J. wiped his eyes—his image had blurred for a moment and then suddenly refocused, this time clearly coming from a camera that was actually transmitting his real picture—and sagged back into a couch visible behind him.

"Why? I guess. . . Because you're outside of it all, Doc. I know you, and you know all of us, but you're not in the space race any more than I was in the game with you bonediggers. You're not competing with us."

"I see. Well, I'm honored, I guess."

A.J. managed a weak chuckle. "I also knew I would get straight talk from you. But you wouldn't make fun of me, either, because you know what this means."

"People don't make fun of you, A.J."

"How very little you know. Maybe not now, but if you

have it happen enough when you're younger . . . "

"True, true," she admitted. "I managed to avoid most of that, but I can't deny I've seen enough of it."

She studied A.J. for a while in silence. "So what are you going to do?"

"Well, my job. What else? I'm still going to be running the Faeries for NASA, and I've got buttloads of other sensor work to do. But if I'm not going, I suppose I'll have more free time. . . "

"Maybe you can finally finish up that dissertation and be Dr. Baker."

There it was again, that tiny little twitch. "Nah, I don't think so. I don't really need it, with my rep. I've got other things to do."

"Okay, A.J., give. What's with you and the title 'Doctor'?"

To her surprise, A.J. blushed. "That's my deepest and darkest secret. Joe knows it, but he was sworn to solemn secrecy."

"So . . . ?"

The imaging genius rolled his eyes. "Okay, okay. Have you ever heard of an old TV show called *Doctor Who*?"

Helen nodded. "Sure. I was a sci-fi fan when I was younger, myself. I've even seen a few episodes when they reran them for a while."

"Well, both of *my* parents were Whovians. *Fanatic* Whovians, though at least—thank the gods—Who fans tend to be more civilized. But still . . . my dad's first name was Thomas."

"Tom Baker." She was still puzzled.

"He was probably the most popular and well-known Doctor in the series."

*Now* she remembered. "Oh, yes. He was the tall one with the scarf."

"Yes. Well, like I said, they were real fans. So the word Doctor has some very strong associations for me. Especially with my name."

"A.J.?"

"A.J. is short for my real name. Adric Jamie, for their two favorite male companions. I suppose I should be grateful that I wasn't born a girl, or I would have been Romanadvoratralundar Leela."

"Jesus. You're kidding."

"I'm not. I loved my folks, but I swear, there were times I thought that killing them would have been justifiable homicide."

"Do you have a . . ."

"Sister? Yes, actually. And yes, she does have that name. Well, Leela Romana—mom had gotten to choose first when I was born, so dad chose the first name when Lee was born."

"Your parents were definitely in actionable territory there."

A.J. laughed, the first relaxed sound she'd heard from him. "It could've been worse, I guess. I'm named after a supergenius who adapts to any situation and an honest, courageous, and really tough Highlander warrior. And other than their little obsession they were really great folks." He looked sad, but no longer on the edge of tears. "Thanks, Doc."

"You're welcome. At least now I know why you go by your initials. And to be honest, I was hoping for a distraction."

"Let me guess. Test time."

"Right in one."

"Well, much as I know you won't thank me, I'd better send you back to the test papers. And then go bite the bullet and see if Jackie will accept a groveling apology."

"If you can get past the first few moments and she finds out why you went off on her, I suspect it won't be a problem. But you'd still better do some groveling. It will do you good, anyway."

"Okay, on *that* note, good night, Doc."

"Good night, A.J. And, hey—keep in touch."

"I will. Bye." His image vanished.

Helen shook her head. What a mess. Glancing at the screen, she sighed again and began the long task of grading.

# Chapter 13

"Coming up on confirmation. Reacquisition of signal due in five, four, three, two, one . . ."

A.J. held his breath. *Please don't screw up now,* Pirate.

". . . waiting . . . waiting . . ."

"Are the Martian antispacecraft defenses up again?"

"Wait—we have a signal. *Pirate* reports all functions green."

"Trajectory?"

"Looks to be slightly hot. May need a short burn for final match. Running the figures now . . . within safety margin. We are go for ISM release at Phobos rendezvous."

The room, momentarily silent, echoed suddenly to the explosive *whoosh* as A.J. finally took another breath. Good-natured chuckles followed.

"A little nervous, A.J.?" Diane Sodher asked with a grin.

"Oh, maybe just a little. I mean, it's not like there's anything important riding on this mission."

"You mean like your rep and half of Ares' money?"

A.J. grimaced.

"Well, you let me know when you're ready to relax." The spectacularly redheaded info specialist winked at him and turned back to her station. A.J. managed to keep from looking either nervous or smug. Diane had been flirting with him for weeks, ever since he started coming to Mission Control regularly, but he'd been too worried about making sure everything worked right to risk fraternizing with the enemy, so to speak. But after tonight, maybe . . .

"Burn to match orbits set for 1435:04. Deployment of ISM units will follow at approximately 1600 to allow for verification of burn success and deployment readiness."

Time for him to take a break. Once the deployment happened he was going to actually have something to do for a change. He couldn't control the Faeries—the Independent Sensor Modules or ISMs in official parlance—in detail at a distance, of course. The speed-oflight lag meant that even at closest approach to Mars, he'd still have a round-trip delay measurable in minutes; at maximum distance it was close on half an hour. But he could give them a lot of general guidance, especially if he thought ahead carefully.

He'd been doing a lot of mission profile planning for the past several weeks, including disaster contingency plans. Hopefully *that* part of his work would turn out to be wasted. A.J. intended to work out all the systems to their fullest extent, and that meant he would actually have to take a few risks—something he couldn't do if he lost any of the Faeries on deployment. He'd need them all intact before he could take chances.

A drive and a late lunch sounded like a good idea. If he were back at Ares he could've grabbed Joe to go with him, but things weren't quite that casual here at NASA. Most people were busy right now, anyway. He headed to the parking lot and was soon driving down the commercial strip in the nearby town, looking for something appropriate.

*Not fast food, thanks very much*, A.J. said to himself as the neon and brighter lights of said establishments tried to beckon to him. *I need real food to keep me going tonight. Well, real food and then a sack of doughnuts and coffee. Ah, there we go, a steakhouse!*

Getting a table in midafternoon was easy; the place was almost empty. He checked the menu, ordered, and then sat there in the quiet, waiting.

A.J. hated eating alone. After chewing on the problem for a moment, he pulled out his phone and dialed a still-familiar number.

The tanned face that materialized in his VRD vision was streaked with sweat and dirt, and the golden hair pulled back but escaping in tangled disarray.

Damn, but she looks good.

"What's up, Doc?"

"A.J.!" Helen Sutter's smile was brilliant against her honey-dark tan. Then she frowned in mock annoyance. "And *will* you stop greeting me like Bugs Bunny?"

"Better, ah say, girl, better than Foghorn Leghorn!" A.J. retorted in his best drawling bellow.

That got a laugh. "True enough. Well, as you can see, I'm in the middle of a dig right now. What's up with you, almost-Doc?"

"I'm in a restaurant completely alone, and wanted to

see if I could at least have virtual company. I thought you might be able to indulge me. Time for a call?"

"Oh, I suppose I could take a little break. But if you're in an even vaguely respectable place, I sure hope you're not using a projector. I'll bring down the tone of the place. Badly."

"Purely for my eyes only. But even just like you are, you'd bring the tone of any place way up."

"That's why I put up with your antics—you know how to flatter a woman."

"Flattery? Never. I just tell the pure and honest truth. The secret is knowing that women like you never believe that they really *are* gorgeous."

Helen studied him for a moment, her head cocked a little. The expression on her face was a bit disconcerting to A.J. A sort of distant amusement combined with . . . something else, that he wasn't sure about.

He was reminded, not for the first time, that badinage with a very intelligent woman twelve years older than he was could be a chancy proposition.

Abruptly, Helen changed the subject. "So what's up with your work now?"

"The Faeries get to fly in a few hours. *Pirate* just succeeded in the aerobraking maneuver to get her into a closely matching orbit to Phobos."

"That's great, A.J.! I'll bet you're excited."

"Yeah. Yeah, actually, I am."

Helen's head was still cocked, subtly inviting an elaboration.

He was rather surprised to find he meant it. After being taken off the flight crew, he'd spent weeks working simply because he hadn't had much else to do and he didn't know how to just slack off. He was out of practice, having been working like a demon since he was fifteen. "You know, I really am!"

Helen's smile flashed again, this one warmer and with a touch of sympathy. "I'm glad. I could tell you weren't doing well at all for a while there, even though we only talk occasionally. Your e-mails just didn't have the usual A.J. edge."

"You mean bad puns and stupid humor."

"That too," she said, chuckling. "But really, you have a voice all your own. And as annoying as you can sometimes be, it's a signature that comes across even in a typed note. When I don't see something that says 'look, I've got something really cool to tell you' in the note, and instead get something that just reads like a thank-you note, I know something's wrong."

"Well, have no fear, Milady Bonedigger. A.J. the Great, Imperator of Imaging, Sovereign of Sensors, Dictator of Detection, has returned!"

Plates rattled. "And my lunch has arrived. I would share some of it, but somehow I don't think it'll work out."

She looked wistfully at the table. "You are a cruel man, to call a woman who's working here in a hot desert and then taunt her with real food and drink when all she has"— she held up a small wrapped object—"is a granola bar and a canteen of warm water."

"True, true. But it's an artistic kind of cruelty. I'll make it up to you, whenever you're back from digging. You name the place, I'll pay the check. Joe and Jackie could even join us, if you time it right."

"I'd love to see them again. I know they've been busy in their training, though."

"Don't worry about it. They can get enough time off to drop in and see an old friend, I guarantee you." A.J. started in on the salad. "If this really bothers you, I can cut off. I mostly needed company while I was waiting with nothing much to do."

"It doesn't really bother me. But I probably should get back to work."

"No problem. Thanks for taking the time. Now, and before."

"Anytime. Later, A.J. Let me know how everything goes!"

"I will."

The image of the paleontologist vanished, and A.J. dug in. Now that he realized how excited he was, he was impatient to get back. There were things to do, and he was the one to do them!

# Chapter 14

Release of ISM units completed successfully. All units showing on the green."

"*That's* the way to do it," A.J. said triumphantly. "Okay, time to get to real work."

A.J. checked the release pattern and observed that the Faeries were in proper station-keeping mode with respect to each other. *Pirate* was already moving away to a safe distance preparatory to making its final deorbit burn.

That was fine with A.J.. He knew what he was going to do with the Faeries, but he wanted to tweak all the instructions to reflect exactly the situation around Mars. The release had occurred just one hundred and sixty thousand meters from Phobos—a bit less than a hundred miles.

The Faeries were equipped with electric or, as A.J. preferred to call them, "ion" drive systems. They were low in actual thrust—the optimized designs on the Faeries would, at full power, shove the sensor platforms forward with an acceleration of all of one-fiftieth of a gravity. But the ion drives made up for it with specific impulse ratings that were beyond even the wildest fantasies of nuclear rocket enthusiasts, measured not in hundreds but in thousands of seconds. That made it possible for objects like the Faeries, which were small enough that A.J. could have picked them up and carried them, to hold sufficient reaction mass to travel significant distances and stop at their destinations. It was critical to give them that ability, since the availability of high-thrust drives such as compressed gas, rockets, or similar approaches was tremendously limited on small probes.

As everything was on the green, A.J. was going to have one of the Faeries—Ariel—run ahead of the pack, trying to reach Phobos at maximum speed, while the others would take much more leisurely approaches. This would be a test of the Faeries' navigation skills, the precision of his programming and the engineering departments' design work, and of the efficiency and precision of the drive system. At that distance . . .

*Close enough for minimal orbital mechanics to take part, $1/2at^2$, we get . . . um . . . a little over twenty-one minutes, full acceleration for 10.66 minutes and a smidge, flip and decel for same amount of time.*

The other Faeries—Titania, Tinkerbell, Sugarplum, and Rane—would follow at a more sedate pace, getting to their stations around Phobos in a few hours. He worked the precise numbers and course data carefully, then transmitted the orders to the Faerie Fleet.

"Well, in a while we'll start seeing some action," he said, leaning back and glancing around. "Say, about an hour. Though if you'll watch Titania and Rane's transmissions, you'll get to see the *Pirate* do its burn and start true deorbit. They'll try to hold the image as long as possible, another test we programmed in them before we started. That will demonstrate how well they can track. Tink's doing some GPR on Phobos before approach, while Sugarplum will be seeing if I can get good returns from Mars with the same equipment. Probably not, but it's worth a try."

"Where's *Pirate* landing?"

"We're combining science and sightseeing. Landing track will take *Pirate* right down the Valles Marineris, and our target landing site is somewhere near the Melas Chasma. There's a lot of interesting possibilities to be found at the bottom of the Valles, and Melas Chasma has some of the best potential for all sorts of stuff, including mineral finds of various sorts. You'd have to ask some of the others back at Ares for more details. I'm not as up on that as on other things."

"How long do you think you'll be working here tonight?" Diane asked, curious.

A.J. laughed. "Possibly all night. Or until the caffeine runs out. I may not be able to control them like a video game, but watching what they're doing and making decisions as I start getting a real picture of what Phobos is like is a job that can't be entirely left to machines. I don't think I'm going to want to just hand it over to automatics for quite a while yet. Until I know what I'm dealing with, I won't—and the Faeries won't—know what the best approaches are, especially for locating the best places to land the base materials."

That was, of course, the main purpose of the whole

exercise: to survey Phobos with an accuracy and detail never before attempted, including interior imaging if possible, so that the best location for the Phobos Base could be determined.

"Once the data really starts flowing, no one bother me. I'm putting my earphones on now." He suited action to words, and the exuberant sounds of Tenkuken's *Battle for Heaven* blotted out any possibility of being interrupted short of someone physically poking him.

The latter would also be difficult as he had now brought up a temporary cubicle. That minimized disturbance in both directions, since it not only prevented people from casually walking up to him to ask questions, but also screened him from view and at least partially from hearing. A.J. had a habit of talking to himself or playing VR games while waiting for the next round of Real Work. It was only a matter of courtesy to try to minimize the amount of such antics his co-workers were exposed to.

Initial GPR data was starting to come in from Tinkerbell and Sugarplum. That was what he was currently interested in, but he left the feed from Titania and Rane up so that anyone interested could track *Pirate*'s progress.

Excellent, the returns were coming in loud and clear from Phobos. It wouldn't be too long before he could start building up an idea of what he had there. Surprisingly, he was actually getting some usable returns coming back from Mars. Well, with the lowest orbit of a natural satellite known—less than six thousand kilometers—he wasn't trying to scan from nearly as far out as he would otherwise. He stored that data for later analysis; it wasn't part of the main project.

A shadowy image began to build up on his VRD. Phobos' density was known to be very low—not even high enough to be mostly carbonaceous rock. The moonlet's composition was a mixture of rock and ice, or it had large hollows inside. Either was a fairly likely possibility. The theory was that both Phobos and Deimos were captured outer-system bodies, possibly "burned out" comets or something similar.

Privately, A.J. had bet himself that it was a combination—there would be some hollows, and some ice as well. The latter was close to being a sucker bet, as some probes, notably the ill-fated Soviet Phobos probes of the late twentieth century, had actually detected some water outgassing from the little moon.

The GPR probes were slowly gathering enough data to start generating a 3-D model of Phobos. The moonlet was roughly oval in shape, with the giant ten-kilometer crater Stickney showing how close the little moon had come to being shattered eons ago. The model was slowly solidifying. Now it was a cloud of gray with just tanta-lizing hints of structure, but as time went on, he was sure he'd get more out of it.

Looking at the rest of the feeds, it was clear that he wouldn't have much to do—even just on the thinking end—for another half-hour at least, maybe more. So he keyed the system up to do alerts only when various tasks were complete, and logged on to the Elemental Flame VRRPG (Virtual Reality Role Playing Game) server net.

After about an hour with no particular alerts from the system,

A.J. switched over for a glance. What he saw caused his character Severn Four-Winds to exclaim "What the hell is *that*?" This necessitated some out-of-character explanation and a quick log-off.

"What *is* that?" he asked himself again.

The 3-D model of the miniature moon had become much more solidly detailed, since its ghostly first appearance of an hour or so ago. But the details that could be made out were . . .

Peculiar, to say the least. Some areas of the interior were blank, as though the GPR waves couldn't penetrate. That was pretty odd given what was normally required to screen out radar waves. There were rounded and blocky outlines, long curving lines seeming to radiate out from various points, and things that appeared to be hollows of a wide, flat nature.

A.J. started talking to himself. "Hmm. Well, this is over near Stickney. Result of collision? Maybe. It does radiate outward. I wonder if the other radiative areas coincide with impact events. It's the blank areas that are really funny."

A.J. wasn't really that knowledgeable with regard to astrogeological dynamics, but to his untutored eye it looked like half-melted conglomerate with crystal inclusions.

"Which, come to think of it, might not be far from the truth," he muttered. "If the things were outer-system, they must've been something like comets, so parts would certainly be melting at perihelion. And they'd be moving so fast that normally they couldn't be captured by something as small as Mars. So maybe they hit something—something that caused serious melting. Hmm . . . maybe . . . what if Deimos hit Phobos, or something like that? I'll have to get one of the orbital mechanics guys to model it. How fast would these things be moving if they came in from outsystem, and what would it take to get them captured by Mars?"

He checked the disposition of the Faeries. Ariel was very close to the surface of Phobos, no more than a mile off. The other probes had stopped about six or seven miles away and were bracketing the nearly fourteen-mile-long moon in a designed attempt to ensure that no point on Phobos' surface would go unmapped.

"Okay, let's get fancier."

A.J. considered the arsenal of sensors at his disposal. The Faeries were, in some ways, the most advanced instrumentation packages ever constructed, and they had an awful lot to offer. The primary modality on Earth was sight, so naturally the Faeries were well equipped with cameras. Visible light, ultraviolet and infrared—with their optics sealed between synthetic diamond windows for protection.

Unfortunately, the real detail he needed—down to a foot or less—he couldn't get at this distance. With a field of vision of only sixty degrees, he wasn't going to get much better than five feet or so, even with interpolation and super-resolution tricks. Narrower FOVs would have been better, but the tradeoffs involved had torpedoed that. He'd even had the engineers try a synthetic FOV approach, but that ran into problems with light-gathering capability which would take too long to solve.

"If only I could use something with decent resolution," he muttered, not for the first time.

The problem was an old one, dating back to the onset of space exploration. There was almost always a big lag between what technology could do on the surface and what you could get to work up there, with the radiation, vacuum, and other things to cope with. The gap had only gotten bigger in the last decade or so, because with most of the advances hinging on how much smaller and more efficient they could make the gadgets, they'd been getting progressively more sensitive to minor problems.

Tons of minor problems were pretty much what space handed you all the time. Cosmic rays, outgassing from vacuum, the list went on and on. And there was no corner store on the way to pick up a replacement. That meant that you couldn't afford to use something that wasn't fully space qualified on an interplanetary voyage. For a jump to orbit and back down, maybe, but not across a hundred million miles.

So, for the Faeries, A.J. was stuck with something not much better than he could've gotten on the street twenty years ago. Barely twenty-five megapixels in the visible, and worse in the IR and UV spectra.

But there was no point regretting the inevitable. A.J. had IR— near, mid, and far—along with visible and three UV bands. He had GPR, which would certainly be needed. Other frequencies of radio might prove useful, especially if he used the X-ray approach—have one transmitting and the other receiving. Measurement of heat signatures and any chemical emissions would be vital. If there were major caverns or differing composition beneath the surface— which did, as suspected, seem to be covered with about a meter of regolith—the heat absorption and radiation should show some differing patterns.

The other real bottleneck was data transmission. Even with all the advances made in other technology, the speed of data transmission from miniature sensor craft like the Faeries was only slightly better than that from old dial-up modems. That meant that most processing had to be done on the Faeries. Even one full-size image would take a significant time to send. And this was even though they were relaying through a separate satellite, put there by NASA a few years back, which had as its sole purpose being a communications facilitator.

The Faeries were advanced. Still, as they had to be space qualified, small, and mobile, their CPUs didn't have anything even vaguely like the power of current processors. With the transmission limitations, they couldn't send back too much data to be analyzed. That had to be reserved for truly unique work.

Both Tinkerbell and Rane's chemical sensing arrays were showing some water spikes. It was time to try mapping that out and see if he could get some idea as to where the outgassing was coming from.

It took another hour or so to figure out the optimal search pattern to cover with all sensors, and to ascertain the parameters of the low-power ion burns that each Faerie would have to perform in order to fly that pattern. Finally he was satisfied with the layout of search and sent out the directives. That, of course, triggered a slow-motion acknowledge-repeat-confirm cycle to ensure that all the directions had gotten through and were properly understood. Another hour later, he sent the final "go" confirmation.

He was tempted to go back to Elemental Flame, but there was business-related e-mail to answer and other work to do. And this part of the work would take a while.

A few hours later, the alert pinged in his ear, letting him know that he was receiving data from the completion of his survey pattern. He stretched and dropped the cubicle.

It was later than he'd thought. There was hardly anyone left around, except Bernie Hsiung over at the *Nike* construction section, overseeing some of the remote construction work in orbit. NASA had been assembling the material for *Nike* slowly but surely over the past year, and the work would continue for some time. Like him, Bernie often spent much of his time just keeping an eye on otherwise automatic processes, but it was still necessary to have someone around who had the capability to respond in an emergency.

"Let's see what we got. Hmm . . . the internals are still weird, I'm going to have to let the experts argue over this stuff. Water emissions as plotted over time . . . heating patterns correlations . . . There's water in there, no doubt, and possibly quite a bit of it. That'll make it a lot more attractive as a base. Transporting water is such a pain. Emissions and internal mapping plus heat signatures . . . Ah-ha! Two possible emission sources. Ariel, my sprite, come to me! Time for you to earn your living."

As Ariel was already closer to Phobos, A.J. would use her as his "point man." Ariel would examine the surface up close near the areas where water vapor was apparently escaping. If he got lucky, there would be a crack or cave in the area.

After another hour and a half, with Ariel now conducting its survey of the Phobian surface, A.J. headed off for a bathroom break. He stopped off for a candy bar and soda and then headed back. By then, Ariel's transmitters were showing the gray, soft-edged surface covered with fluffy regolith—powdered stone the consistency of flour—up close as it drifted along with a carefully defined path of examination.

The first emission site was a bust. There were some cracks, which clearly were the source of some of the outgassing. But they wouldn't have admitted a mouse, let alone a sensor drone the size of a large breadbox. Ariel continued along her way, approaching the locale of the second outgassing.

As it cleared a small crater ridge, A.J. couldn't quite restrain a triumphal "Yes!"

Even to eyes still accustoming themselves to the sharp-edged perceptions needed in the airless setting, there was a clearly darker streak that couldn't be anything other than a crack in the surface of Phobos. It seemed to be a crack yawning wide about two meters above the surface in one of the many little cliff ridges that meandered across the moon's surface.

"*That's* why it's not buried in regolith," A.J. muttered to himself. "Horizontal entryway instead of vertical. Hope that doesn't mean it's to some shallow deposit in the cliff."

As Ariel approached the crack, the automated sensor platform slowed according to prior instructions and directed illuminators into the chasm. It was wider than Ariel by a good half meter in any dimension. Ariel hovered, waiting for instructions. It wasn't permitted to proceed into the interior unless A.J. directly ordered it to.

There was considerable risk here, of course. The width of the crack was sufficient, but there was no way of knowing how far that ran, and even so the margin of safety was very thin. Piloting would be purely in the hands of the automatics, as there was no way A.J. could react in time to change anything that happened. And an accident could easily destroy Ariel.

On the other hand, looking at Ariel's sensor data, there was clearly water outgassing from below. Ice had to be present, possibly in significant quantities. And all of his other Faeries were running perfectly. Speaking cold-bloodedly, he could afford to lose one of them.

The call was entirely A.J.'s to make, since this was his project and no one else could make the judgments necessary. That fact didn't make it all that much easier. In some ways it made it harder, because if something went wrong he could hardly shove the blame away to someone else. But the way A.J. looked at it, finding out as much as possible about Phobos was his mission. He didn't see any reasonable alternative.

He went through the back and forth of order and confirmation once more. This time, once the acknowledgement came through, he stayed glued to his screen. It was true that he couldn't really do anything for Ariel if something went wrong, or at least not immediately, but he still wanted to know right away if something damaged her.

Slowly, turning on both ion and low-powered chem thrusters, Ariel drifted into the darkness, illuminating it with LED strobes timed with her frame captures to minimize power drain. Tinkerbell positioned itself above the chasm as a telemetry relay, since the farther into rock the drone descended the less signal would penetrate.

Twenty-two meters in, the dark lateral chasm intersected with another going almost straight downward. A.J., enhancing the view ahead slightly, could see that the lateral one narrowed and eventually ended a few dozen meters farther in.

"Excellent. Down we go!"

Ariel could also see the same thing, and despite being orders of magnitude less intelligent than her master, quickly reached the same conclusion. The little probe paused, rotated, and descended into the abyss.

Fifty meters down.

With a slow and steady precision, Ariel passed by gray-black rock with occasional tinges of other colors like reddish-brown. The crack descended at a slant, and its irregular walls showed that some sort of violence had caused its opening. That wasn't much of a surprise, of course.

One hundred meters down.

Ariel slowed and rotated, seeing a large rock blocking part of the crack dead ahead. It was clear to either side, however, so the automated sensing drone continued its descent, having chosen the left-hand side of the rock to pass by.

Two hundred thirteen meters down.

Dark shadows showed on either side of the crack, indicating another cavity or cavern. As Ariel drew level with this new intersection, it was clear that whatever cataclysm had caused this crevice to open had also caused it to cut straight across another long, slender cavern. Ariel hovered at the three-way intersection, consulting its own data to decide its course—further down, or into one of the two tunnellike cavern segments. A.J. did the same, in case he had to transmit to Ariel to abort and take a different route.

But Ariel made the same decision he would have. The flow of water vapor outgassing was stronger from one branch of the bisected cavern.

Here, Ariel had a bit more room to maneuver. The tunnellike cavern, oval in cross-section, was ten feet wide and eight feet high. Strange rippled formations were visible along the walls at regular intervals. A.J. was reminded of the scalloping he had seen in several caves, but clearly these odd shapes could not have resulted from running water over millennia. He wondered if cometary outgassing could have a similar effect.

Two hundred meters farther along, the tunnel reached a branching. One side turned deeper into Phobos, while the other stayed roughly level beneath the surface.

Tinkerbell was starting to show a clear drop in signal strength from its sister drone, but both A.J. and Ariel calculated that at least another three hundred meters would be possible before it would be time to decide on whether Ariel would have to go totally solo or not. Once more Ariel selected the path with the strongest H2O concentration—this time continuing along the original passageway.

Two hundred meters more, and the signal was starting to show some signs of interference. Suddenly the walls fell away on three sides, leaving only one—the side towards the surface—relatively level with respect to the prior tunnel. On Earth, this would be the equivalent of entering a large room in a cavern, with the relatively level side being the "floor." Ariel began a surveying drift around the dim, airless space, which seemed to be huge, something like a football field across. Its light began picking up other cavern exits along the "floor" area.

A.J. realized how stiff his neck was. He'd been leaning forward, watching tensely, despite the fact that on a VRD leaning forward was just useless. Amazing what instinctive reactions will do. For what must have been . . .

Two hours? It was heading for six in the morning! He got up, stretched hugely, and slugged down the rest of his now-warm soda.

Something nagged at the corner of his vision, which had been concentrated on the mundane for the past couple of minutes. He refocused on his VRD screen and sat down. It had seemed that there'd been a flicker of slightly different color . . .

Ariel had noticed it too, apparently. The probe had many subroutines for analyzing images, noticing anomalies, and returning to them. It was slowing and turning around now. Using gyros, it spun in place. Something flicked across the field of view, then stopped and was centered. Slowly it began to grow, with slight flickers of interference across it, as Ariel approached.

A.J. was barely aware of himself standing slowly, his mouth half-open, hand stretching towards the virtual screen, his hindbrain trying to reach out and touch the image glowing before him.

Inset into the wall, perhaps a meter from the nominal "floor," was a massive...

Something. It shone with a brownish-gold luster, undeniably metallic. It was symmetrical, a generally triangular shape with rounded sides and smaller, round-sided triangles at each corner. Across its surface, in curved sequences like waves, mysterious black and silver symbols marched in organized ranks.

Ariel had stopped with the object just filling its field of view. This target lay entirely out of its search parameters, and it was now waiting to be told what to do.

"Well," said A.J. to the empty air around him. *"That's* something you don't see every day."

# Chapter 15

"And *Seig Heil* to you too!" A.J. snapped.

"Cut it out," Colonel Ken Hathaway said tiredly. "First, I'm not the one slamming the lid down. Second, it's a perfectly reasonable response from the government's point of view." Hathaway's subtle southern drawl was heavier than usual, turning his "I'm" into "Ah'm"—a sure sign of annoyance, which A.J. failed to note in his own anger.

"You can't keep me from calling out! This was my project. You can keep the data, but you can't just shut me in!"

"We can, and we will, A.J. I know it's grating on your free spirit, but you'd better deal with it. Or do we have to take away all your toys just to make sure?"

A.J. got himself under control with difficulty. Ken Hathaway was one of the main driving forces behind *Nike*, and A.J. had worked with him for months now. He knew that the Air Force colonel wasn't really the problem. The truth was, A.J. liked the man.

The whole situation still rankled, however. "No. Okay. Sorry. But send it up the line to whoever came up with this idea—we should be broadcasting this worldwide, not sealing it up tighter than a bank vault!"

"No, I *won't* pass it up the line, and yes, we should, at least for the sake of your funders and mine. Like it or not, there's still politics to consider, and that includes things like national security. What if this turns out to be an alien military installation intact enough for us to learn something from it? Can you tell me there's a single country on earth that wouldn't want that for itself at first?"

Reluctantly, A.J. shook his head. "No, I guess not."

"I guess not either. And speaking as a soldier, I damn well do agree with the idea that if anyone's going to get the first shot at it, it's going to be *my* country."

"I'm not into patriotism. Buncha tribal instincts."

The colonel rolled his eyes, the extra white making them contrast even more with his very dark skin. "A.J., that's just the kind of attitude you *don't* want to express around the wrong people. Me, I don't care what you think, as long as you're not actively working against our nation. But some of the more rigid types have no sense of humor on that subject. Trust me, they don't."

He flicked the display to another page. "Now, they don't want to shut us down. In fact, it's top priority to find out whatever we can. So, if you'll promise me—not some faceless guys out there, but *me*— that you won't try to sleaze around the security, you can have your connection back and return to work. Your Faeries are the only things on-site, and we obviously won't be getting anything else there for quite some time to come. So you are set to remain the top-billed star of this particular show, and I'd like you to keep that billing."

A.J. gave Hathaway a sour look. Despite only knowing A.J. for a few months, the blocky, solidly built astronaut apparently had read him very well. A promise to some disembodied abstraction like the government that was trying to stifle the discovery would mean relatively little to A.J., but a direct promise to someone who knew and trusted him, that was something A.J. would never break if he could possibly avoid it.

"You sneaky . . . Fine. Fine, I promise, I won't smuggle messages out, and I'll keep your silence as long as you say. No one else can run the Faeries like me, and there's no way I'm going to let someone else try. Dammit."

Hathaway smiled. "Good enough. Look, A.J., I'm sorry. But remember—we all want *Nike* and Ares to have their shots. If you pull some stupid crusading stunt, all of us could get screwed."

A.J. nodded unwillingly. "Yeah. Okay, you can trust me. I won't mess things up for your people or mine. Just let me back at the Faeries, okay?"

"In a shot."

Hathaway picked up the phone and called the MPs. "Mr. Baker is cleared to return to work immediately. Aside from the standard comm shutdown, he's got priority on everyone else. Anything he needs, make sure he gets."

After he hung up, A.J. demanded: "What about people who are expecting me to call? I mean, none of my friends would possibly believe I'm not going to call them and fill them in."

"I have no doubt that you'll be given a chance to call

them soon— with some really clear guidelines on what to say, and a script if necessary."

"Ugh. You think?"

"I'd bet on it. Until they decide to release this, they'll be making sure no one can give it away. If you need to work with people, they'll find a way to bring them here and under the umbrella of secrecy."

"Aaaaugh. Well, hell with it, I'll go deal with my machines. They make sense and keep no secrets from me. You guys realize how lucky you are? I only told your people first because it was on your nickel. If you hadn't pulled the lid down right away, I'd have told half a dozen people by now. And if the data wasn't proprietary at this point, the transmissions wouldn't have been encoded."

A.J. paused. "By the way, I wasn't using the very top-level encryption on this stuff. It's possible someone will decode it eventually. I'd warn whoever's in charge of this circus that eventually—and that's a sooner rather than later 'eventually'—there *will* be a leak. From someone who received and decoded the transmissions, if not from some-one inside."

Hathaway nodded. "I'm sure they know that already. It's a constant concern in security—you can't keep any secret forever, so the question is whether you can keep it long enough to matter."

"Okay. Anyway, I'm going to go to sleep first. I haven't had any rest since I started this whole thing . . . damn, forty-three hours ago."

"Yeah, you'd better go get some shut-eye. You'll have a long day ahead of you whenever you get up."

A.J. nodded and walked out, his gait already showing some of the flatness of the truly exhausted.

❈    ❈    ❈

Jackie Secord tapped her foot as the system hesitated in opening the door. The guards nearby were unfamiliar.

*Guards? Why two of them? Never had any need for them anyway, the system's automatic.*

One of them was studying a screen in front of him. His partner was watching Jackie. The gaze didn't look hostile, but it wasn't friendly either; a neutral look that unnerved her more than a glare. Only when the guard at the screen nodded did the door to the operations area slide aside.

Jackie thought of commenting on the situation, but decided it wasn't worth it. Someone upstairs had probably gotten a bug up their ass about security, so now they needed some new tin soldiers and procedures. At least no one was asking for a strip search.

Reaching the main mission control area, Jackie glanced around. The golden mop of hair she was looking for was immediately visible, just slightly to the right of center.

"A.J.!"

A.J.'s face lit up as though someone had shone a searchlight on it. "Jackie? *Jackie!*" The slender, wiry arms hugged her close and then swung her around before setting her down. It was always a little startling to realize just how strong A.J. was.

"Whew! Nice to know I'm wanted around here, but you're getting a little overexcited, aren't you? I mean, it's not like I don't work for NASA. You could expect I'd drop by operations, once in a while."

A.J. grinned, but there was an edge to that grin. It looked almost like a sneer in some ways. "So you don't know yet? Damn, they're good."

"Don't know what? Who's good?"

Jackie looked around. It was odd, now that she thought about it. Things seemed a little restrained here—aside from A.J., for whom the word "restraint" would only apply when used in conjunction with the word "heavy."

Even the displays weren't showing the usual multiplicity of views. Most of them seemed to show some kind of movie set in an underground cavern.

"Where *is* everyone, anyway?"

"Briefing, I think. There's been a lot of . . . stuff going on here lately."

"You're being evasive, A.J., and that's about as unlike you as I can imagine. And what the hell is wrong with the publicity machine, anyway? I'd have thought by now pics from the Faeries would be on every space site in the country. But instead, aside from a few external shots that don't tell anyone anything, there hasn't been a peep out of you guys for two days."

She suddenly looked concerned. "A.J., the Faeries didn't, like, crash or something? They didn't die on you?" She knew that a disaster at *that* level would have left a hush for a while, and certainly put a sour look on A.J.'s face for weeks. But . . .

"Go ahead and tell her, A.J."

Jackie turned and saw that Colonel Hathaway was standing in the doorway that led to the central offices. "She's going to be up to her neck in it anyway," he added.

Jackie thought A.J. seemed to relax slightly. *So there was something he wasn't allowed to talk about? That explains his tension. Telling A.J. he can't talk is like telling Santa Claus he can't go "Ho, Ho, Ho."*

"Well . . . I guess it all starts right there." A.J. pointed to the screens with the slowly moving cave scenery.

"What does that have to do . . . with . . ."

She trailed off as she realized the symbols in the corner of the image denoted material being received from Phobos. From ISM-4, what A.J. called "Faerie Princess Rane."

Rane was traveling down a tunnel *inside* Phobos. Ariel was apparently sitting somewhere else inside the fast-orbiting Arean moon, serving as a relay for Rane.

"The cavern looks awfully smooth on that side," she began uncertainly, "but I . . ."

Her mouth fell open. "Oh . . . my . . . God."

Looming up on one side of Rane's field of view was a door. There was no other possible word for it. It was half-open, showing clearly the track or groove into which it was meant to fit. Shreds of some unknown material—probably a door seal—were still clinging to one edge.

*"Ohmigod."* She heard herself running the words together. "Ohmigod, ohmigod, A.J., that's a *door*, a door on *Phobos* for crissake, what's a door doing there?"

She whirled, about to put some pointed questions to the blond engineer, then stopped.

"No, you'd never do this kind of joke. That's *real?* Someone—or something—was on Phobos before us?"

Her mind was racing ahead of her words. That explained the guards at the door, A.J.'s comments, and why she hadn't heard updates on the Faeries' progress. Someone had clamped the lid down *hard* on the project.

"No joke, my fave NASA engineer. I'd say more some-*thing* than some*one* if I were guessing. We haven't found any remains yet, or if we have I haven't recognized them as bodies, and I think I would. Then, there's several doors we need to open. This one's partly open, but I'm not sure I can squeeze one of the Faeries through."

"So, if you haven't found any bodies, why do you say 'thing'? No, wait, let me guess—the designs."

"Right in one. The corridors aren't shaped the way we'd do them. At least, not where they were clearly cut instead of just adapted from cracks and caves already present inside Phobos when whoever or whatever they were took it over."

He pointed to the screen. "That door—look at it. It's more a semicircle, or a half ellipse. Either they were really short but liked very wide doorways for some reason, or they were shaped low, kinda wide, and fairly big. We've come across plaques and things set in the walls in places we might put signs—you know, 'Engineering that way, Life Sciences to the right'—and they're all set much lower down than we'd put them. Almost a meter lower down."

"So you have closed doors? Do you think . . . maybe . . .?"

A.J. shook his head. "Not unless they have some super-miracle materials and no need for power. There isn't any significant source of energy left on this rockball. If there was, the Faeries would have picked it up. And without some kind of energy, nothing's going to be alive here for long. But there might be some other stuff in the closed rooms."

Hathaway joined in. "We've had some of our other engineers going over part of the data A.J.'s been feeding us. It looks to us like something violent happened to the base—maybe a collision with something else, maybe some kind of internal cataclysm. But whatever it might have been, there's been a lot of damage to various areas.

Explosive decompression, shockwaves, the whole nine yards. If this was on Earth, there would probably have been cave-ins. As it is, there are places we can't get to easily."

"So," Jackie said, "maybe the doors that are closed got jammed during the disaster?"

A.J. nodded. "That's kinda what we're hoping. Yeah, it'd be pretty grisly for our alien friends who got stuck, since they'd have run out of whatever it is they breathed once the main base power went down. But it would also mean we'd have a good chance of finding something intact in there—bodies, maybe even equipment."

"Intact?" Jackie asked,

"Well . . . intact enough so we have a chance of figuring it out." Hathaway replied. "I doubt anything will work. But first we have to get inside."

A.J.'s grin was smug. "At least we actually *do* have a chance of getting inside."

Hathaway rolled his eyes. "Okay, okay, okay, yes, A.J., you were right and we were wrong. There *was* a point to putting manipulators on the Faeries. It was *still* a waste of resources. There was no way you could possibly have known what you were going to find."

"How can you call it a waste when we're using them? Besides, it was my grant money to spend. I was sure I'd have an occasion to use them for *something*. I'll admit, I didn't expect it to be something this big."

"You think the Faeries have the ability to move doors like those?" Jackie asked doubtfully.

"Not sure, really," A.J. admitted. "Maybe not. The systems were set up to be maximally configurable, and I'm going to be selecting the highest mechanical advantage.

And using three of them at once, if I need lots of force."

"What if something goes wrong? You don't want to lose three Faeries."

"I don't want to lose *one* Faerie. But it's not likely I'll lose any of them. Even if it goes badly, the worst I'd expect to happen is that they'll blow the manipulators or break them. They're not going to explode or anything silly like that." He pursed his lips. "A shame, in a way. If I could *make* them blow up, then I'd have a way to open at least one of the doors even if the manipulators don't do the trick. I'd originally planned for them to have Fairy Dust dispensers, but the sensor mote design ran into problems and had to be scrapped. They'll be up and running for the real mission, no doubt, but for this venture it just wasn't in the cards."

"No way to get whatever mechanism opened them in the first place to work?"

A.J. shook his head. "I don't think anything in this base is going to be workable any more. If the colonel's scenario is correct, something went wrong to keep these doors from opening in the first place. So even if the power was on, they'd be jammed shut anyway."

"Then what are the odds of them being openable now? Wouldn't the survivors have tried?"

"First, we don't know there *were* any survivors. Second, on the ones I'm interested in, I don't see any signs of heavy prying or other forcible entry attempts. And third, after all this time the seals and other things may have become fragile, turned to dust, or otherwise changed in their basic nature enough that force which couldn't move them before can do so now."

"What about vacuum welding?"

He shrugged. "There's a lot of different materials involved here. I don't think that will be a factor. Speaking of welding, I'm still playing around to see if there's some way I can get some kind of welding or cutting electron beam out of one of my babies, but I'm not hopeful. There are limits to the configurations I can get."

"When do you think you're going to try to get one of these closed doors to open?"

"Not for a while yet. We want to explore as much of the base as possible with all Faeries running before we risk damage to any of them. Oh, yeah," A.J. brightened again and waved his hand to activate some commands, "here's the real important jackpot aside from the discovery of the century."

The screen in front of them flickered, then showed another Faerie-eye point of view, drifting down a different corridor. Before it a large doorway loomed, mostly shut but with about two and a half feet of space on the one side where the apparently rotating valvelike door had stopped. The Faerie slowly drifted down to that level and spent a few moments making sure it could fit through the opening. Satisfied, it began to move forward again.

This room was huge. The "floor" slanted slightly in what would be the "downward" direction, but soon the smoothness vanished, replaced by a chaotic mass of dark brown and black, with occasional white streaks. The floor was rippled and scalloped and extended back into dimness, with deep hollows and narrow columns connecting it to the ceiling. The scalloping was almost scalelike, in some places. Much of it was dull and absorbed light almost like a sponge, making the range of vision even shorter than normal.

In a few spots there was a bright glint, a shine from something smooth. That seemed more common toward the rear, which was confirmed as the Faerie cautiously continued farther into the huge room.

"What *is* that?" Jackie asked finally, as she watched the images wend their way through an increasingly narrow and hallucinogenic set of passages of the dark material.

"Mud," A.J. answered with satisfaction. "Looks like it's more water towards the back, more dirt towards the front, which makes sense. It's been subliming away for a long time through that door and these passages. But even after all that time, there's still a hell of a lot of water there. Our unknown visitors were possibly aquatic, or amphibious, because this seems awfully excessive for a reservoir but very sensible for something like a staff mudbath/ swimming pool/whatever combined with a main water supply. From the surveys I've done, I think there's enough water left in this room to fill a cube a hundred meters on a side."

"A hundred . . . That's a million metric tons of water!"

"And all in one easily accessible chunk. Run it through a filter and I think you'd be able to drink it. Unless our extinct friends left some *very* long-lived bacteria behind. But I doubt if any diseases they had are something we could catch, anyway."

"So Phobos Base is definitely a go."

Colonel Hathaway smiled. "You could say that, Jackie." His wristphone buzzed. "I have a meeting to go to. There may be one both of you want to attend later, in a few days."

"No offense, Ken," A.J. said. "But I doubt I want to go to *any* meetings."

Hathaway's smile widened. "You'll want to go to this one, I think. See you people later, I have some business to attend to." As he turned to go, he paused. "Oh, and Jackie—this is under complete nondisclosure. You can't even tell anyone back at the labs, at least not yet."

She shook her head. "Ken, that's asinine. There's no way you can keep a lid on this very long. A few more days, maybe. But not much longer. Don't they realize that?"

"I think they do, Jackie. They're trying to decide how they want to approach it, and the time pressure is not helping. I'm trying not to add any pressure on our side. People, we can afford to wait. As you say, they can't keep this secret very long. When they do make that decision, I want them to think of us as the people who *didn't* give them a hard time over it. *Capice?*"

Jackie couldn't quite stifle a giggle at Hathaway's excellent "Mafia Don" accent, though his appearance didn't lend itself to the impression. "Okay, I get it. If we're the good boys and girls, they'll want to keep us all on the inside of whatever gets done."

"Exactly. So help me by not giving me any flack, and keeping A.J. from indulging his revolutionary impulses. Gotta go—important people waiting in my office."

As the door closed behind Hathaway, Jackie turned a mock-stern gaze on A.J. "No trouble from you!"

"I gave him my word," he said, a little sulkily, plopping into a nearby chair. "He doesn't need anyone to watch me."

"Oh, lighten up, A.J. You're getting to do your work, and you don't have to do much in the politics. Or would you rather have Ken's job? He's supposed to be in training for the *Nike* mission, but he's ended up being a part-time politician just to keep everything moving smoothly so that he *can* be on *Nike* when we launch."

She debated with herself, then sat down next to A.J. "You had your dream, you know. Remember how much it hurt to lose it?"

She could see he didn't quite understand where she was going with this, but he nodded, lips tight. The memory was obviously still painful, many months later. "Well, Ken has a dream too, a silly one that he's told to a few of us, the ones he was sure wouldn't laugh. You know what that dream is?"

"Well, no. He doesn't know *me* well enough to talk about anything like that."

"Ken's always dreamed of being the captain of a spaceship. And he just might make it. He's the highest-ranking military crew candidate right now, and he's got the training for it, and *Nike* is just about big enough to actually need a real boss. So if he seems a little uptight about anyone throwing a wrench into the works, remember he's on the edge of his dream too."

After staring at her a moment, A.J. smiled slowly. "Captain Kenneth Hathaway, commanding, NASA Exploration Vessel *Nike* . . ."

"Don't you *dare* make fun of him. Or tell him I told you. Or I'll—"

"Whoa, hold your horses. I was about to say 'that *does* sound cool.' " A.J.'s expression was grave. "Don't worry, I can respect a silly dream like that one."

# Chapter 16

The moment Madeline Fathom entered the office of the director, she knew the situation was unusual. Highly unusual.

Even given that the intelligence agency she worked for generally handled the most delicate issues of national security, it was still unheard of for the National Security Adviser to sit in on a meeting between the director and one of his field agents.

She was especially surprised to see *this* Security Adviser present. George P. D. Jensen. The common wisecrack was that his middle initials stood for "plausible deniability."

For the past two decades, due to a curlicue in the confusing welter of laws which had replaced the Patriot Act after its repeal, Madeline's agency had wound up becoming the preferred agency of choice for American presidents when they wanted to maintain as low a profile as possible in a security matter that was likely to become publicly contentious. The official name of the agency—Homeland Investigation Authority—was meaningless. Its critics commonly referred to the agency as "the President's Legal Plumbers." And the agents of the HIA itself joked that their motto was *The Buck Vanishes Here.*

"Please, Madeline, have a seat." With his usual old-fashioned southern courtesy, Director Hughes had risen to make the invitation. "I believe you've met Mr. Jensen before."

"Yes, sir, I have." She and Jensen exchanged nods after she sat down in one of the chairs in the lounge area of the director's large office. Madeline's nod was courteous; Jensen's was so curt it bordered on rudeness.

Jensen had not risen, needless to say. Even by the standards of Washington, D.C., the National Security Adviser was punctilious when it came to maintaining the pecking order. Superiors did not rise from their seats to greet subordinates, period; not even when the subordinate in person was a very attractive woman in her early to mid-thirties.

Not that Madeline cared. Bureaucrats came; bureaucrats went. She had her own motives for the work she did, and the approval or disapproval of people like Jensen ranked nowhere on the list. She was reasonably polite to them, as a rule, simply as a practical convenience.

There was silence, for a moment. As Madeline waited, she considered the seating arrangement. Director Hughes was sitting in a large armchair directly across the coffee table from her. Jensen was sitting to her left, on the couch. That was unusual, also. Normally, when she and the director met, they did so sitting across from each other at his large desk in the corner.

Of course, that would have required Jensen to sit on a chair no larger or more comfortable than her own. Can't have that.

The director suddenly beamed at her. He was a short, plump man with iron-gray hair and good-natured features. The iron-gray hair was real; the good nature was off and on; and the beaming smile brought her to full alert.

*This one's going to be a bitch.*

The National Security Adviser spoke. "There's a . . . situation, Agent Fathom."

Politeness had its limits. "There's always a . . . situation. Honestly, why do people talk that way?"

Jensen's face tightened. The director laughed. "You'll have to excuse Madeline, George. As I told you, she came into our world from the wrong direction. Understands our language, but doesn't speak it at all."

So they'd already been discussing her, including her personal history. Madeline wasn't surprised, but the knowledge didn't make her any happier. *Be a bitch* got ratcheted up to *be a pure bitch*.

The director shifted his good cheer back onto her. "I assure you, Madeline, this one really *is* a . . . situation. Unique, I assure you.

Utterly unique. We need someone to be there to watch over our interests—our *country's* interests—when many of those there, even on our side, won't have nearly so, shall we say, clear a vision of what must be for the future."

Madeline was a bit relieved. While the director was often given to dramatic little speeches, he rarely indulged in hyperbole. The assignments she liked were those in which she was really dealing with important issues of national security. Unlike most of her assignments, she thought sourly. Which, stripped bare, usually involved nothing more substantive than the petty internecine warfare practiced by Washington's spaghetti bowl of competing bureaucracies and security and intelligence agencies.

She put up with the second for the sake of the first. The government might be everyone else's scapegoat, but Madeline Fathom owed it her life.

"Show me, sir."

"You have your VRD on? Excellent. Watch. And then we shall talk."

After she'd watched everything, she had to take off the VRD glasses to stare. "Are you serious, Director?"

"Never more so, my dear."

She shook her head in disbelief. "This thing cannot be kept secret long."

The National Security Adviser's expression had never quite lost the tightness that her earlier wisecrack had put on it. Now, it came back in full force.

"Let's not be defeatist about this, shall we?" he snapped.

Madeline gave Jensen a glance so quick it was almost rude. As if flicking away a fly with her eyes.

The director intervened. "George, save that silliness for public speeches, would you?"

Hughes was still smiling, but he was also letting the steel show. He'd been the director of the HIA through three and a half administrations—and both he and Jensen knew that he would still be the director when the current administration was gone. For over two decades, Hughes had done such a good job of balancing the demands of security with the need to tread lightly on the liberties of the public that even the HIA's critics were fairly civil in their attacks. The political classes in the nation's capital considered him well-nigh indispensable—a status that was definitely not enjoyed by national security advisers who'd held their position for less than two years.

"I told you already—Madeline is one of my three best agents, overall, and without a doubt the best one for *this* assignment. She's got a better technical education than Berkowitz or Knight, and, unlike them, she's single and has no family ties."

In the brief, silent contest of wills that followed, Jensen looked away first. "Still," he grumbled.

Hughes wasn't about to let him off the hook. "Still . . . *what?* I do hope that the President has no illusions that we can keep this situation a secret for more than another day or so—and that he understands the consequences if it appears to the public, when it does finally surface, as if we were trying to hide something."

His face now pinched, Jensen stared at the opposite wall and said nothing. Madeline knew the man was not actually stupid, so she was quite sure he understood the realities of political life. But "not stupid" and "faces facts readily" weren't the same thing. The Security Adviser was obviously still in the throes of the standard bureaucratic reaction to all unpleasant news—isn't there *some* rug we can sweep it under?

"You remember the endless ruckus over UFOs and Roswell Area 51?" Hughes' shoulders heaved in a sound-less laugh. "Well, I can guarantee you that'll seem like the hushed tones of the audience in a fancy symphony hall compared to the hullaballoo you'll be facing— if there's even a *hint* that the administration tried to suppress

the news beyond the initial few measures that any reasonable person will accept as minimal security precautions.
And I won't even get into the international repercussions,
since that's not really my province." Relentlessly: "But it
is yours, isn't it?"

Jensen finally took his eyes from the wall. "Yes, I understand all that! It remains the case that we have no idea
what we may discover in that alien installation. There
could well be items of tremendous military significance."

"Of course," Hughes agreed, inclining his head.
Smoothly, the gesture slid from being a polite nod of
accord to a pointer at Madeline. "And that's precisely what
Ms. Fathom will be there for. Making sure the wheat
doesn't get mixed up with the chaff, so to speak."

Jensen gave her a glance that was every bit as quick as
the one she'd given him, and more openly hostile.

"She seems awfully young for the post. Meaning no
offense, Ms. Fathom," he added, obviously not caring in
the least if she was offended or not.

"Alexander the Great conquered the world by the age
of thirty-three," Director Hughes said cheerfully. "So I
imagine, at the same age, she can handle this little problem. And there's really no other suitable choice, George.
At your insistence, I showed you the dossiers of the other
senior agents."

"And I told you I'd be considerably more comfortable
if we went with either Knight or Berkowitz."

Hughes gave the man a look that was not so much hostile as simply weary. "George, cut it out. This is not a James
Bond novel and I am not M. If you want comic book
agents, go somewhere else. Try one of the cowboy out-
fits. Good luck finding an agent who can understand the

technical material involved well enough to know an alien weapon system from a bag of popcorn—and better luck still, finding one who won't get you involved in Martian drug dealing to finance the operation. Or have you forgotten *that* not-so-little scandal?"

The Security Adviser winced. As well he might. The President, then the serving Vice-President, had almost failed of election due to that mess—and Jensen's predecessor had lost his job.

Having made his point, Hughes eased up the chill and went back to his usual affability. "Look, George, here's the simple truth, bitter as it may be. My people are *civil servants.* Strip away their training, skills, and the fact that sometimes their job puts them in dangerous situations, they're not much different from your neighborhood postman. You want Jeffrey Berkowitz? Fine. Reinstitute the draft and conscript him. Failing that—no? you don't want to open that can of worms, either? didn't think so—then I wish you equally good luck getting him to accept this assignment. We're talking about a man who has three children still living in his home. You want Morris Knight? No sweat. Just find an instant cure for his wife's kidney condition and somebody to take care of *his* two kids. Do you really think you—or me, if I was stupid enough to try—could talk either one of them into leaving their families for a period of several years, at least two of which they won't even be on the planet Earth? And if they refuse, then what are you going to do? Neither of them are under military discipline and we're not at war, anyway. They'll just quit. With their skills and background, I can guarantee you they'll have jobs within a week that pay them twice as much as they're making now."

Jensen's jaws tightened. After a moment, he turned to face Madeline.

"And what about you, Ms. Fathom? Are *you* willing?"

While the director and the NSA had been having their little contretemps, Madeline had been pondering the same question. Not so much to find the answer—that was pretty much a given—but simply to find out how she felt about it.

She was . . .

Excited as all hell. *Mars!*

"Yes, sir," she replied stoically. "I'm willing."


The next ten minutes or so were taken up by a long lecture from the National Security Adviser explaining to Madeline the imperative necessities of national security, the supreme importance of her assignment to the fate of the nation, and the sublime nature of that nation itself.

Madeline put up with it, easily enough. Early in her career, she'd spent considerable time at public ceremonies and she knew the little tricks for getting through a long blast of hot air with no damage, when she had no security duties to keep her mind occupied. The one she favored most, which she used on this occasion also, was reciting the ingredients to her favorite recipes for bouillabaisse. She was partial to bouillabaisse, so she had eight of them. Enough to get her through most episodes of pointless windbaggery.

Throughout, of course, she maintained The Expression flawlessly. The one that she'd learned as part of her training and later experience in the field, and, like all agents she knew, considered every bit as essential when dealing with politicians and bureaucrats as body armor

was in dealing with desperate armed criminals. The
Expression combined *Personal Probity of Character* and
*Concern for the Public Welfare* in equal proportions, with
a generous admixture of *Calm Certainty That We Can
Do The Job* and just that little needed soupço n of *Eager-
ness To Tackle The Assignment.*

When Jensen was finally done, his earlier hostility
toward Madeline seemed to be on vacation for a while. A
short holiday, at least. She was not surprised. From long
experience, she knew that the period immediately after
giving a pompous and officious speech was as relaxing
and satisfying for bureaucrats of Jensen's type as the after-
math of orgasms was for most people.

He rose, nodded to her, and left the room. He did not,
of course, offer to shake hands.

"What a prick," she said dispassionately, after he was
gone. She made no attempt to keep the director from
hearing. She knew full well that his own opinion of Jensen
was no higher than hers, even though he'd never said
anything explicitly. The entire current administration, for
that matter, was held in no high regard by Hughes.

The director just smiled at her. "Ah, Madeline. Think
what a disaster your career would have been if you'd gone
into the Foreign Service and tried to become a diplomat."

"Could have been worse. I could have followed my first
inclination and joined the Secret Service. Then spent my
whole working life listening to speeches like that. And
maybe—fate worse than death— had to take a bullet to
let the windbag keep prattling."

He laughed softly. "Aren't you glad, now, that I saved
you in time?"

"Pretty much. I've still got a bit of a grudge over

Antarctica. I don't mind horrible conditions, and I can accept wasting half a year of my life. Putting the two together was a bit much."

"Well, look on the bright side. This new assignment will take a lot longer chunk of your life, and the conditions could definitely get worse than even Antarctica. But whatever else it'll be, it won't be a waste of your time."

"No, it certainly doesn't sound like it. How much authority will I have?"

"As much as you need."

She cocked her head skeptically.

"No, Madeline, I mean it. The reason the National Security Advisor insisted on sitting in on this meeting was because your assignment will be specifically authorized by the President. We're not going to have to work through the usual cut-outs on this one."

She pursed her lips in a soundless whistle. "I'll be damned. I would have thought hell would freeze over first."

"Don't overdo it. Whatever else, they are not stupid. They can't afford to play games with this one, and they know it. Even if the knowledge is making them choke a little."

The director picked up a large envelope on his desk. "This is your confirmation as head of security for the entire project. It's already got the President's signature on it. Jensen was here in case he decided to yank it at the last minute. Which—ha! by the skin of your teeth, you disrespectful hoyden—he didn't. I'll see to it that General Deiderichs gets a copy."

Madeline nodded. "All right. I assume you want me to start immediately."

"Magnanimously, I shall pretend I didn't hear that. Your flight to Albuquerque is already booked. Five hours from now, so don't dawdle."

# Chapter 17

Joe leaned back in his chair and gave vent to a long-drawn sigh of relief. "Not a single malfunction!"

"You expected some? In our peerless experiments? Why, Fearless Leader, how could you ever have gotten the impression that *anything* could go wrong?" Lee Grimes' voice drawled from the other side of the Ares control center. His prosthetic leg was propped up on the console in front of him, encased in one of the Western boots Lee preferred. "It's not as though anything's *ever* gone wrong here."

Joe laughed. It made him feel twice as good that Lee was not only still here, but able to joke about the accident that had cost him his chance to go to Mars as well as his leg. "Of course not. Still, that far away, it'd be a little hard to tweak the valves if something froze up."

"Told you to send me along. If I left my leg behind, I'd just about have made the weight limit."

"Yes, but there *was* the issue of air, food, water, that kind of thing. *Pirate* didn't carry any of those, remember?"

"Hmm. Okay, you could have just sent my leg."

"It's your *head* that I'd need to send."

"Ouch! No, I think I'll keep it where it is. Still, it's nice to watch everything running. Just look at that! Ferris will have a couple ingots made before we have to shut down."

"And there'll be water in the tanks and fuel to burn before long," Anne put in. "We're on target for *Pirate*'s return launch. Chibi-rover is happily surveying the landscape in Melas Chasma, too. One hundred percent success."

"Well, we don't know that for sure yet," Joe cautioned. "First, it ain't really over until the return launch and recovery. Second, A.J.'s Faeries have to pull off their miracle."

He frowned. "Speaking of which, I'm getting a little worried about that, actually. We haven't heard anything from him in four, five days."

"Oh, stop fretting, Joe." Reynolds was looking over his shoulder at some of the readouts, even though he could have pulled them up just as well on his own personal data center. "You know how A.J. gets. He runs until he drops, wakes up, and then starts running again. I'll bet that if we just take a look out on the Net there's a ton of stuff on the Faeries now."

"Probably." To satisfy his curiosity, Joe opened a connection and sent out a general search. A few minutes later, Lee caught the deepening frown on Joe's face.

"Something wrong, Fearless Leader?"

"I'm not sure," he said slowly. "Anne, Lee, why don't

you try pulling up something on A.J.'s progress with NASA."

A few minutes passed.

"That's . . . interesting," Anne said finally, with the tone of someone having discovered a nest of wasps just above them at a picnic.

"A.J. couldn't have dropped the whole ball *that* badly, could he?" Lee muttered. "I mean, he's an insufferable prick sometimes, but he's earned it, if you know what I mean."

"We helped him on those designs, guys. One, or even two, of the Faeries might have gone bad, but there's no way all of them did. We know the release went just fine, our own telemetry showed them separating and going their merry way."

Joe was frowning at the displayed information, or rather *lack* of information, as though it might suddenly change if he just glared at it enough. "But there's not a single pic here from later than, oh, I guess about six or seven hours after the Faeries were cut loose. And none of them are showing anything particularly close up."

" 'Something is rotten in the state of Denmark,' " Reynolds quoted.

"Marcellus to Hamlet, Act I, Scene 4." That came from Lee, as he continued a search for more Phobos data.

Ren looked startled. "I didn't take you for a scholar of Shakespeare, Lee."

"I'm not, really. But I did do some acting, years ago, and Marcellus was one of the roles I played." He shook his head. "Definitely rotten in the state of NASA, anyway. They've been giving out exactly diddly-squat since a few hours after the Faeries flew. No announcements, some vague talk about analyzing data, a few pics dribbled out that could have been taken a little earlier or later than the last official ones. But there's nothing giving us a real grip on what's happening."

"That makes no sense," Joe protested. "Even if somehow it all went wrong, there's no reason for them to clam up like this. They'd just try to slant it to make it look like we screwed it up."

He told his phone to dial A.J.

The phone screen lit with A.J.'s grinning face. "Hey, Joe, how's it going?"

"Fine, A.J., but we—"

"Ha, fooled ya! I'm not here or I'm too busy with my many fans to talk to you right now, but if you'll leave a message I'll—"

There was an audible *click* as a somewhat nettled Joe cut the connection. "I *hate* it when he sets his 'away' mode to that annoying little message. Fine, I'll ping him direct."

A few moments later he sat back, scratching his head. "He's not on-line."

Anne, Lee, and Reynolds all stared at him. "That's crazy talk, man. A.J. is off-line about as often as the Pope is Protestant. Okay, he's sometimes blocked or not answering, especially when he's sleeping, but off-line?"

"I'm not finding him."

Anne ran her own check along with Lee. "Looks like you're right. In fact . . . looks like he hasn't been on-line at all since about four in the morning the day after the Faeries flew."

Joe stood up. "That does it. This is all too weird. I'm going over to NASA to find out what's happening. What the hell, it's less than a two-hour drive."

"Well, okay, Fearless Leader," Lee said, after a moment. "But keep in touch. Or this might start to sound like those summer horror movies, you know?"

"Don't worry." Joe headed for the door. "I won't go into the basement, that's all."

"This way, sir," the guard said to Joe, opening the door to a stairway leading down.

Joe was a bit puzzled already. When he'd seen extra security at the entrance, he'd feared the worst. But instead they'd simply checked his ID and waved him through. And when he'd started to ask where to find A.J., they hadn't even waited for him to finish but had just said: "We'll escort you there, sir."

Come to think of it, he hadn't even gotten to A.J.'s name. Near as he could remember, he'd said: "Can you tell me how to find—"

He followed the guard down the stairway, through a well-lit hall, and finally through a set of double doors which opened into a large conference room.

"Joe! Glad you could make it!" A.J. said cheerfully. He was sitting on the other side of a long conference table in the middle of the room.

"Um, so am I. What is it that I've just made?"

His friend didn't answer immediately. Instead, he turned to the black man in a colonel's uniform sitting at one end of the table. "Pay up."

The colonel—he looked familiar to Joe, but Joe couldn't quite place him—gave a resigned smile, pulled out his wallet, and tossed a twenty to A.J. "It's a bet I'm glad to lose."

"I told you he'd be here," A.J. said. "I told them you'd

be here," he repeated unnecessarily to Joe. "I knew you'd get here pretty quick, too."

"How the hell did you know I'd be coming? I didn't even know myself until a little while ago!"

"Because," A.J. said in his lecture-room tone, "you attempted to call me, but hung up without leaving a message. Several talk requests tried to ping me. Two people from Ares tried to access my NASA contact info within the same time period. I knew you guys had finally woken up to the fact that something funny was going on. And knowing you, I was pretty sure you wouldn't sit around waiting to see what happened."

"Very well, Mr. Baker, you have had your—admittedly deserved—moment of triumph," said a new voice from behind Joe. "Would you please sit back down? And Dr. Buckley, please take a seat as well."

Joe turned and saw that the speaker was a tall man with brown hair, just starting to gray slightly, also wearing a uniform. He came through the same door Joe had entered from, and moved toward the opposite end of the long conference table from the colonel. Behind him came a number of other people, who filed quickly into the room and took their own seats. One of them was Jackie Secord.

"All right, sir," he said, squinting slightly at the man's uniform. He was suddenly glad he'd said "sir," as he recognized the general's stars: Three of them, no less. "Will someone tell me what's going on?"

"Don't worry, Dr. Buckley. You are not the only one in this room who needs a briefing, although you are, admittedly, the only one who has no information at all. Everything will be made clear in a few minutes. I believe some introductions are in order. I am Lieutenant General Martin Deiderichs. I have been put in command of this operation, at least for the time being."

He indicated a petite blonde woman to his left. "Madeline Fathom, security liaison. You are already acquainted with Mr. Baker and Ms. Secord."

The Fathom woman smiled brilliantly, an expression Joe couldn't help but echo.

*She's one cute package. And I think she knows it. And if she's doing security liaison, she's not just ornamental, that's for sure.*

"Ms. Diane Sodher, Information Analysis." The red-head in the lab coat waved.

*Was that the one A.J. mentioned? If so, I'm impressed—I don't think I'd be keeping my mind on my work with her flirting with me.*

"Dr. Satya Gupta, Senior Engineer." Dr. Gupta gave a courteous nod, his dark eyes studying Joe.

*A.J. called him right. Face like a prophet, eyes like magnets. He's got that* presence *thing going.*

"Dr. Wen Hsien Wu." Dr. Wu was a young, round-faced Chinese-American who resembled a youthful Buddha or an Asian cherub. He smiled and bowed slightly from his seated position.

*I think Jackie said Wu is the top contender for physician on board* Nike. *He must be hell on wheels to be that good at his age. He can't be much older than A.J.*

"Everyone, Dr. Joe Buckley, Senior Engineer at Ares." Joe was torn between a nod, a wave, and a bow. He wound up more or less doing all three at once, which probably looked incredibly stupid. Fortunately, no one laughed.

"Colonel Kenneth Hathaway, Acting Director, Project

*Nike*," General Deiderichs concluded. The name immediately brought Joe's memory in focus. The colonel was one of the best-known and most experienced astronauts in the U.S. space program. Joe had seen his photograph several times, although this was the first time they'd ever met in person.

The stocky Hathaway smiled at Joe and gestured for him to sit down. Joe realized he'd reached a seat, right across from A.J. and Jackie, but hadn't sat down yet. He did so quickly.

"Now that we are all introduced," the general continued, "let's get to business. I know most of you have some idea of the subject of this meeting, but in my opinion it will not hurt to go over it again, and this will bring our new members up to speed. Colonel, if you would?"

The general seated himself, and Hathaway took over. "As we all know, the ISMs—Independent Sensor Modules, what Mr. Baker calls his 'Faeries'—were released at a distance of slightly over one hundred and sixty kilometers from Phobos at 1600 hours local time on the 14th of this month. ISM-1, code-named Ariel, reached Phobos vicinity at 1745, the other three arriving an hour or so later. A survey to map possible water vapor outgassing sources from Phobos was begun as planned at 2100 hours. This survey indicated two potential sources for this outgassing, as seen here."

A 3-D projection appeared in the display at the center of the table, showing a false-color plot of vapor concentrations and likely emission points.

"Verifying the existence of native sources of water is deemed to be of great importance for the Phobos Base component of the *Nike* mission. Accordingly, at 0130 on the 15th, Ariel was directed to examine both locations to determine the possibility of tracing the source of the out-gassing material. The first location was a small crack in the surface of the moon, but the second proved to be a much larger fissure—sufficiently large to permit one of the ISMs to enter. As all other ISMs were functioning properly, Mr. Baker decided that the potential risk of losing one of the four was outweighed by the possibility of verifying the existence of water sources within the moon, and possibly discerning other important infor-mation about Phobos' structure and composition. Therefore, at 0335, Ariel descended into the interior of Phobos to search for the source of outgassing."

Joe noticed that even though no one else had been speaking, the room seemed to have gone even quieter. Whatever the others knew, they seemed to be almost holding their breaths.

"A little more than two hours later—to be precise, at 0552 local time—Independent Sensor Module-1, named Ariel, recorded this image."

The central display blanked, to be replaced with a large, detailed color image of a bronzish, three-sided plaque covered with strange symbols.

Joe just stared at the image for a moment. "What the hell is that?" he muttered.

"Precisely what we would like to know, Dr. Buckley," the general said bluntly.

"Well, in one sense we know exactly what it is," A.J. stated. "It's an artifact of a nonhuman civilization. Yeah, we don't know if it's an underground street sign, their equivalent of a historic marker like 'George Washington Alien slept here,' or a radiation warning. But the important thing is that we didn't put it there, and it's been there a really long time, and it's not natural."

Joe knew he sounded slow, but he couldn't help it. "Hold on. You found an alien artifact on *Phobos*?"

Dr. Wen Hsien Wu apparently shared his reaction. "I had known something unusual had been discovered in the survey, but *this* . . . General, why is this not in the news? It is not at all a matter for debate, as I see it. This is wonderful news! We are not alone! Why are we not broadcasting this image for all to see? And what other images have we acquired? Why—"

General Deiderichs raised his hand. "Dr. Wu, you are not alone in asking these questions. In fact, it is specifically to address these issues that we have called this meeting. Ms. Fathom?"

Madeline Fathom stood. "First, Dr. Wu, I'd like to make clear that in an ideal world, and in my own heart, I'm of your own opinion. I'd like nothing better than to throw the informational gates wide and let the world see it all. But this isn't an ideal world, and neither General Deiderichs nor myself are free to act just on what we feel."

She made a smooth, rippling gesture which Joe found jarringly familiar. After a moment, he recognized it as very similar to A.J.'s, when he was using a VRD display interface for controlling various peripherals. The display in the table's center faded to show a slowly-moving tunnel scene.

"The wonderful nature of this discovery, unfortunately, has become part of the problem. What we appear to have here is a fairly intact alien space installation. A.J. Baker, and others, are of the opinion that it's very unlikely any of the actual devices we may find there will be functional. However, many of them may be intact enough to be studied."

"And it wouldn't do to have just *anyone* studying such things, would it?" A.J.'s voice was heavy with sarcasm.

Fathom sighed. "Mr. Baker, I understand your hostility, but would you mind terribly much not directing it at me? Please? We're not making these decisions."

As A.J. opened his mouth, she interjected: "And if you make some smartass geek comment about 'just following orders' in a stupid German accent, I will actually get annoyed."

A.J.'s mouth snapped shut. Joe's estimate of the delicate-looking blonde woman shot upward. It wasn't easy to cut off A.J. at the pass, but she'd done it.

"The simple fact is that unless these aliens did everything exactly as we do, and never got past our own level of technology, the potential discoveries awaiting us in that base are revolutionary. We may not be at war with anyone, but we also have had many reasons to suspect the completely benign intentions of many other countries. Not to mention any number of paranational organizations. Therefore this project now falls under the category of a national security matter."

Joe shook his head. "Sorry, Ms. Fathom, but you know that's not going to work very long. You can't fake up the data that good. Hell, I got here because I knew something funny was up."

That unexpectedly brilliant smile flashed out again. "You're quite correct, Dr. Buckley. Some of the truth— most of it, I imagine—will be revealed immediately. But critical information must be controlled, and that is where

I come in. General Deiderichs will be directing the over-all operation, but I've been assigned to help sort the released information into categories we can release and those that will be kept restricted, at least until careful study has been concluded."

Joe nodded slowly. If done by someone who really understood how the different investigations of the projects were carried on, it just might work, at least for a while. There would be knowledge of the existence of the alien base, but the artifact analysis could take an indeterminate amount of time.

"We were debating how to contact Ares and discuss the situation, when Mr. Baker informed us that you were coming over here. While, in a way, we might have pre-ferred to talk to Glenn Friedet, the two of you actually constitute a considerable proportion of the 'guiding lights' of Ares. So we will at least discuss the basics with you, and then get into details with the rest of the main staff later. I think you can understand that, at this point, the government can no longer afford the risk of independent private flights in a potential security situation such as exists on Phobos."

# Chapter 18

Joe and A.J. both stood up. A.J. looked so threatening that General Deiderichs seemed about ready to rise from his own seat. To her credit, the diminutive security official did not so much as twitch.

"You are *not* saying what I think you're saying," A.J. snarled, before Joe could get out something similar. "I did not design and build the Faeries, map out Phobos, and walk through a fucking *fire storm* just to hand it over to the government to screw up. You can't stop us!"

"Mr. Baker, we most certainly *can* stop you; and if we have to, we will." Fathom's voice was calm and level. "But we would much rather work with you."

"And just how do you think that's going to happen? No offense to some of the people here, but NASA's brand of 'build the worst compromise we can think of' is exactly what we're trying to avoid."

Joe cut in to prevent A.J. from expressing something

in even stronger terms. "Ares' approach is completely contrary to NASA's, Ms. Fathom. And it shouldn't matter to you, anyway. Ares really, honestly, has no interest whatsoever in Phobos. If you want to declare it off limits, that's fine with us. We're going to Mars."

"How I wish it were that simple, Joe—can I call you Joe? That's a very nice argument if we look at it narrowly, but the government can't afford to do that. To be blunt, we have no idea where these aliens came from—or *come* from, since for all we know they're still around. Maybe from Mars itself. And even if they weren't, there's no reason they might not have settled Mars. At this point, we have to assume that Mars may also be a critical site for investigation, at least pending our full exploration of this base."

Joe opened his mouth to protest more, as did A.J., but neither of them could get a word out. The ludicrous idea that Mars—an entire planet whose surface area was equal to that of all land masses on Earth combined—was a 'site for investigation' simply beggared speech. Phobos itself was potentially huge, depending on how many aliens had lived there, and how many tunnels they'd carved over their time of residence. Putting Mars off limits because there might be something down there was like an Egyptologist insisting that no one visit North America because it happened to be on the same planet and might have vital Egyptian relics hidden on it . . . somewhere.

But it was equally clear that the decision had already been made—probably not by Fathom, or Deiderichs, but someone else. Fathom might even understand how ridiculous it was, but she wasn't about to say so.

"Well," he finally said, glaring at A.J. to keep him from

detonating. "Look, then, what the hell are you offering? From what I'm hearing, you're telling us to shut down."

"That, Joe, is because you and Mr. Baker didn't let me finish anything I was trying to say."

When the two blinked and looked slightly apologetic, she gave about a half-power smile and continued. "Gentlemen, Ares is in this thing already. And this is the real world, not an idiotic conspiracy theory novel. Even if the U.S. government *wanted* to, we couldn't make people like A.J. just disappear."

Again, the full-bore smile. Despite the animosity of the moment, Joe was a bit dazzled by the woman. And he couldn't help but notice the easy charm with which she'd just managed to segue into getting even A.J. on a first name basis.

"If you think the government manages the space program ineptly," Fathom continued, chuckling softly, "I can assure you that it manages conspiracies even worse. Or have you forgotten Watergate and—" She waved her hand, still smiling. "And all the other—what was that marvelous expression of yours, A.J.? Oh, yes. And all the other brilliant conspiracies built by the worst compromise the conspirators could think of, which have dazzled the American electorate over the decades. Not to mention turning two Presidents out of office."

That drew a laugh, even from A.J.

Fathom shook her head. "So, please relax. Yes, we're having a dispute. But let's keep the melodrama out of it. As I said, even if the government wanted to, we can't 'disappear' a single individual like Mr. Baker or Dr. Buckley—let alone the entire Ares Project. Not without producing a fire storm, for a certainty. We need your cooperation, people, not your antagonism. We can't let you keep going *exactly* as you were. But we can do something else."

She paused briefly. "Think, everyone. What is going to happen when this is announced?"

"Uproar from every quarter of the world," Joe said. Similar comments were heard around the table.

A.J., for once, didn't say anything, but his expression was that of someone having bitten into a chocolate-covered grasshopper and finding it didn't taste nearly as bad as he thought it would. His blue glare was fading—or perhaps sharpening—to a speculative stare.

"You are all touching on the initial reaction, but missing the practical point," Fathom said. "What will happen is that every nation with even a pretense to a space program will, as you say, 'want in' on the investigation. And to make sure that no one beats us there, I think you can rest assured that there will be a quite unprecedented increase in NASA's budget, a streamlining of its mandate, and an elimination of a great deal of the political wrangling that is normal business in this realm. We will not be sending a relatively few people to Phobos and Mars to demonstrate that we can beat private industry. We will be sending an investigative team to stake out the entirety of that moon and wring every tiny secret we can from the remains of that alien base. We will want, at the very least, to make a start at investigating the planet that they, evidently, found of interest as well. And we will be doing it as fast as we possibly can, with a virtually unlimited budget."

She smiled anew. "And as there is one other American organization that is already ready and able to prepare for landing on both Mars and Phobos, with trained and skilled personnel, we will naturally want to expend some of our budget in recruiting the assistance of the Ares Project."

Fathom turned to face A.J. squarely. "A.J., how would you like to go to Phobos yourself—on board a new, much bigger *Nike*?"

The expression on A.J.'s face almost made Joe laugh out loud. *So that's what someone looks like when the Devil offers them their heart's desire for that little, insignificant trifle of a soul.*

"You can't promise that." A.J.'s voice was weak.

"Not quite yet," Fathom conceded. "But I think we can if the new budgets we expect get passed. And if you keep giving us results like these"—she indicated the tunnel scene, where a closed, enigmatic doorway etched with unknown characters was just passing from view—"and can promise better on-site . . . I think you could bet on it."

She looked down the table. "Unless you have an objection to the idea, Colonel Hathaway?"

Hathaway had been quiet, just observing for the most part. Addressed directly, he shook his head. "In principle, no. It's true that A.J. Baker is no longer in prime physical condition, since the accident. But if, as you imply, we make *Nike* a much larger vessel with a larger crew—which means we can afford some redundancy in personnel— that shouldn't be a major consideration. Especially since his demonstrated skills clearly make him the best choice for sensor work."

"Very good." General Deiderichs spoke up, taking control once more. "Thank you, Ms. Fathom. Ladies, gentlemen, you now know the basic concept. The government recognizes this story will break, and break very soon.

When it does, we intend to pressure the legislature to give us the budget, priorities, and authority to proceed at maximum speed to assemble the hardware and personnel for a full-scale expeditionary mission to Phobos. We consider this to be of paramount concern for the security and interests of the United States and of the world at large. The Ares Project will provide its specific expertise in rapid and efficient independent missions to assist NASA, not only in designing *Nike* and her auxiliary systems, but in designing, assembling, and launching multiple supply missions for both Phobos and Mars destinations. Am I correct in assuming, Dr. Buckley, that with a sufficient budget you could prepare and launch a number of large-payload missions which would reach Mars within a year to a year and a half?"

"That would depend on how 'sufficient' the sufficient budget was," Joe said cautiously. "But if we make certain assumptions, and could hire adequate numbers of people, and have access to launch facilities without having to spend three months just getting the clearances . . . Yes, I think so."

Deiderichs nodded. "In a week or two we will arrange a meeting with yourself, Director Friedet, and your financial officer—Hank Dufresne, isn't it?—to determine the details of the contract work involved. By that time I believe we should have some reasonably firm numbers to work with."

*He's serious, all right. They've got this one planned out.* Joe now found himself regretting, a bit, his sarcastic thoughts about A.J. It turned out that he was no better at resisting temptation, when the Devil offered the spoon.

"In the meantime . . . Dr. Gupta. You and Ms. Secord will have to brief the rest of the engineering staff. It is my intention to send a crew of at least thirty, and possibly as many as fifty, people to Phobos. Can such a version of *Nike* be built?"

The sonorous, impressive voice replied immediately. "*Can* it be built? Undoubtedly. In fact, it has already been partially designed. The engineering department has often speculated on the need for larger vessels, and so such designs have been considered many times. There are tentative blueprints for ships twice the size, even ten times the size, of *Nike* as she currently stands. Is this not true, Ms. Secord?"

Jackie smiled. "Yep. Me and several of the guys worked out preliminaries for several *Nike*-based designs. A couple of them would be right around that size. With modern design software and no budget restrictions, I could get you a brand new set of blueprints good enough to start work on in a few weeks. But—"

Gupta took the cue as smoothly as if it had been rehearsed.

"—But, as our colleague Dr. Buckley says, whether it *will* be done depends on a great many things. So many assumptions which must be made to give you an answer. If, as you have implied, the launch is to take place approximately eighteen months from now . . ."

He frowned. "I must say that it can only be done—can *only* be done—if your promises become truth. If we must worry about the slowness of the bureaucracy, if we engineers must pass a dozen review boards for every new shelf design, then no. If these things change, then yes, I believe it will be done."

General Deiderichs gave his first smile, a tight but sincere little grin that flashed out and vanished. "I think you will find that bureaucratic roadblocks will begin disappearing very quickly, Doctor. The authority for this mission comes straight from the top, and for once there wasn't even any significant debate about it. As of now, priority requests for the Phobos Mission will override everything else. You can consider yourselves to be working for what will amount to a new Manhattan Project, though with some unavoidable public component to it. Assuming you agree?"

A wave of nods swept the room, ending with A.J.'s.

*They've reduced him to speechlessness! Will wonders never cease?*

Aloud, Joe said, "Conditional on the implied cooperation on NASA's end, yes. And conditional on Glenn and the rest going along with it. Me and A.J. may represent a large chunk of Ares, but it's not like we own it. I can't really see the rest of them turning this down, especially since I'd guess that if we did, Ares would just get shut down somehow. As long as you're not putting in an actual claim to Ares itself. We're a private concern, and we won't be absorbed into the government."

A quick glance flashed from the general to Fathom. Joe wasn't quite sure, but he *thought* that the blonde woman gave—not a nod, exactly, but a slight movement of the head indicating assent.

*Now that's interesting. If I did see that, the General was waiting on* Fathom's *approval? Good Lord. The woman can't be older than her mid-thirties. Where is her authority coming from?*

The exchange was all very quick. Others in the room might not have caught it, as several of them were obviously distracted by their own thoughts. In any case, the general's answer came smoothly enough.

"No need to worry, Dr. Buckley. NASA has been working with private companies since its inception. I am sure there will be no need to force you to abandon private industry status. I'm not sure we could do it legally, anyway, even if we wanted to. All we insist upon is that you have to agree to work within our security restrictions until such time as that's no longer necessary."

"Okay, then, I don't see a problem."

"Good." Deiderichs seemed to relax very slightly. "Well, ladies, gentlemen, I believe I've given you all more than enough to think about for the time being. Now, I'm afraid, I have a number of private meetings with various staff scheduled, and quite a few later on with members of Congress in the relevant committees. Ms. Fathom will be remaining here, as any new information will obviously be coming from this installation until further notice."

He rose from his chair. "Unless there is anything else at the moment, this meeting is concluded. Thank you all for your attention and assistance." He left, accompanied by Fathom.

A.J. still looked shell-shocked, until Jackie poked him. "Hey, A.J. Think about it. Now you'll get to design the sensor suite for the Nike. And ride a nuclear rocket to Mars."

"Yeah." A.J. was perking up, but there was still a wary look on his face. "So why am I still looking for the catch?"

"The catch," Hathaway said, getting up, "is that you'd better keep producing. Haven't you got some real work to do, A.J.?"

A.J. glanced at the corner of his virtual display and suddenly scrambled for the door.

"This is why I *hate* meetings!" trailed after him, as he ran out the doorway.

# Chapter 19

"Bracing calculations, check. Geometry, check. Force configuration, check."

A.J. glanced over all the parameters once more. He'd checked them a dozen times already, but he was still nervous. Three Faeries were about to try to pry open one of the doors, and if something went wrong, he could potentially be cut down to two ISMs—which wouldn't be able to transmit while exploring any distance inside the miniature moon, as at most they'd have only one other for a relay.

He'd told Jackie that he wasn't likely to lose the Faeries. That was true, in a sense, because just blowing the manipulator arms wouldn't be likely to cause trouble. The fact remained that prying on something in zero g carried other risks, especially if something broke. The sudden release of forces and fragments of broken prying arms flying around in close quarters could easily do damage to any of the Faeries. They had been built to survive launch and travel stresses, but only in specially-designed cradles in *Pirate*'s equipment bays.

Once he hit the transmit code on this one, there'd be no stopping it; the three little probes would follow their directions to the electronic letter. He ran another simulation. Too many unknowns. They might move the door, or break the Faeries, or anything in between.

At least he was sure there was something to find behind there. Despite the amazingly dispersive and absorptive characteristics of the door—and, apparently, the wall material on the other side—he had managed to gain an idea of the size and layout of the chamber beyond. Shadowy blobs hinted at other objects inside the oval room, which was about twenty-five meters long. He'd been able to get some idea of the composition of the door's exterior, which was an odd alloy of iron, copper, beryllium, and apparently mercury and silicon in small quantities. But the precise alloy wasn't known—and whatever was inside wasn't the same material. It might have a core of some sort of insulation, with the exterior clad in the aliens' version of armor plate.

"Well, are you going to just sit there all day, or are we going to get some action around here?" As usual, Diane's tone suggested a double entendre.

A.J. ignored it. "You wouldn't be in a hurry to push the button if it was several million bucks of *your* money. And if you'd spent months making the things."

Jackie looked up from her nearby workstation. As she was stuck at the command center until the news broke, Hathaway had set both Gupta and Jackie up with engineering design stations in the center. Gupta was currently off at the main engine facility, working with the others to determine if they wanted to make a larger engine design or just use several more like the prototype.

"Relax, A.J.," she said. "You've already gotten more than your money's worth out of them. I know they're like your babies, but do you want to wait another couple of years until we can get *Nike* out there to look?"

"No. Hell with it. All systems and calculations check. Implement Routine Prybar."

The "go" code shot out into the nonexistent ether, to stroll its leisurely way across the intervening millions of miles. Now that the decision was made, he relaxed, took a deep breath, and looked around. Suddenly he chuckled.

"What's funny, A.J.?"

"I wish I was in Hollywood."

Jackie looked puzzled. "Why?"

"Because in Hollywood, after I sent the 'go' command, we'd watch the results right away, and I'd have an emergency stop button on hand to keep things from going wrong."

"Video links at the speed of plot," Jackie chuckled, nodding sagely. "But it's just as well. If you were in Hollywood, you wouldn't use your emergency stop button in time. If something went wrong, the Faeries would go up in huge explosions—they're nuclear powered, remember. And if they *did* get in without mishap, an alien energy being would possess the probes and then download their commands to our computers and kill us all."

Diane's screen suddenly showed some animated robotic drones running through Phobos' corridors. "Resistance is futile—if less than one ohm" scrolled across the bottom as a subtitle.

"Hey, that's pretty good," A.J. said. "Did you do that just off the cuff?"

"Well, sorta. I had these little guys drawn up a while back, but I had to get the computer to kick in and draw the animations pretty quick, once the conversation turned in that direction."

"Cute. Well, it'll be a little bit more before we get telemetry back to show whether we've still got Faeries or if Peter Pan will need a new sidekick. So I'm going to run down and get me something to drink. Anyone else want something?"

"Coffee," Jackie said immediately.

"As if I couldn't have guessed. Diane?"

"Well, I'd *like* a Margarita, but I'll settle for a diet Coke."

"One coffee, one diet Margarita Coke. Got it."

A.J. jogged to the cafeteria; while he could've gotten the drinks nearer to hand, he wanted munchies too. About fifteen minutes later, he trotted back into the control room, balancing the drinks in one hand and a large plate of cheese nachos in the other.

"A.J.! You can't bring that in here!"

"That theory has been falsified, as I obviously *have* brought this in here. Here's your substitute Margarita." He put Jackie's coffee— dead black, no sugar—in front of her as Diane continued her protest.

"Well, you're not supposed to bring food into the center."

"If you read the rules," he retorted, sitting himself before his workstation again, "I think you'll find that you're not supposed to have drinks in the center, either. Which is a bigger problem around electronics than food, usually.

And it's one of those rules that I'll lay big odds was disobeyed about fifteen seconds after it was first enacted at the first computer workstation in history."

He gazed down cheerfully at his nachos. "I always clean up after myself, anyway."

"Aren't you supposed to be in training?" Jackie demanded. "That's like about a billion calories, mostly fat." She eyed the golden mass, sprinkled with deep green peppers, with a combination of clinical contempt and instinctive longing.

"I am indeed in training, but there's nothing wrong with my weight, thanks very much. I have an iron stomach and intend to keep it that way."

"Allow me to hope that you are right, A.J." Hathaway's voice came from behind them. "But I've known several guys with iron stomachs on the ground who spent their first time in real weightlessness fighting every second to keep from blowing their groceries all over the interior of the spacecraft."

"Well, I'm not a complete idiot. I don't plan to eat much before my first experience. Got a lot of other training to do first. Lots of suit practice."

A.J.'s conciliatory tone was then replaced by his usual theatrics. "Glad you could make it, Colonel! We're about to try to open up and see what's behind Door Number Three."

"Actually, Door Number D-11," Jackie corrected.

"Well, darn. Janice was always behind Door Number Three. D11 just has alien artifacts behind it."

"A.J., you're not old enough to remember that show," Hathaway snorted. "Hell, *I'm* not old enough to remember that show."

"Old shows never die. They live on in sound bites and cultural references for generations."

Movement showed on the screen. A.J. instantly focused all his attention on his VRD-enhanced display. "Grab a seat and don't spill your popcorn, ladies and gentlemen. It's showtime!"

The display showed four separate images in the separate quadrants. Three were image streams from their respective Faeries; the fourth was a constructed representation of the view of a hypothetical observer standing in the corridor, watching the three goggle-eyed metallic probes trying to open the ancient door.

"You people should appreciate just what's going into this show. Even with all the advances in the past few years, there's *severely* limited bandwidth available for Ariel to use in transmitting this back." A.J. watched tensely as the three probes slowly took their positions in the corridor, using their manipulator arms to brace themselves first.

"Can't be all *that* limited if you're sending us three streaming images," Diane pointed out. Then she frowned. "But . . . I know the bandwidth you specified. You *can't* be putting three image streams down that, not even with compression. Not even with the fact that we're using a much more capable relay satellite to handle the Earth transmissions directly."

"Not with *ordinary* compression, no. But what I'm doing here is not ordinary. There's an entire neurofuzzy expert system in each Faerie dedicated to smart compression, and I can specify methodologies if I need to. First, they take the main images and scans. Then they chop out all the stuff not in the immediate ROI except for a really general representation. Remember, in any given frame of video, very little usually changes; so you only need a small amount of data to represent it. Then, for people watching it, much lower resolution will do, so you can drop that. You can encode the picture even more by being able to have an encoded representation of the presented image concept. For instance, sending the image of the Faerie itself is a matter of just sending a listing of the current condition of the Faerie, something I can squeeze into very few bytes and then generate here based on the original design, with updates from later pics if needed. If we ever *need* the raw data, the Faeries can send that on demand later. They actually give me reminders to check data for importance before I erase it. Then I—never mind, here we go."

The three ISMs were now positioned in such a way that they were locked together, almost entangled but in a very carefully calculated manner. Each Faerie had two manipulator arms. Three of these, adjusted to maximum power, were hooked in the just-barelyaccessible crack where door and wall met. The vacuum deterioration of the seal had helped in that respect. Had that not happened, the manipulator arms would never have been able to get a significant grip on the door. The other three arms were configured to give the Faeries support, leverage, and stability, since in microgravity there was no assistance to be had from weight.

The three Faeries synchronized their systems as directed by A.J.'s programming, and then began to pull. For long moments, nothing happened. Indicators showed the stress on parts of the Faeries rising; then, passing normal limits, entering the danger zone.

A.J. was barely aware of the tension in his own arms.

His hands were literally white-knuckled as he gripped the console, lifting and pulling in sympathetic unison with his own creations.

Titania suddenly fired its chemical thrusters.

A.J. hissed. That was an attempt to utilize leverage and inertia to drastically increase the force on the door, for a brief moment. But he'd programmed that maneuver as a last-ditch effort, and the reason Titania had used it now wasn't immediately obvious to him.

The downward thrust pushed on the temporary structure formed by the Faeries in such a way as to use it as a fulcrum. Manipulator arms bowed alarmingly under the pressure.

Suddenly, the view from Rane spun crazily. The others followed suit, the emulation showing that something had broken and the three Faeries were trying to recover. Telltales blinked on.

"Damn! Lessee . . . Rane's broken both manipulators, must've gotten twisted around . . . One of Titania's still works . . . Oh, fu— farging hell, something banged into Tinkerbell's left lens!"

Rane's images steadied and she turned her cameras back. A piece of manipulator arm bounced lazily across the field of view. But the image also showed a yawning dark patch at the base of the door, fully two feet high. Large enough for a Faerie to pass through.

"Oh, yeah!" A.J.'s momentary annoyance and concern vanished. It would have been worth the loss of at least two Faeries to get that door open, in his view, and he hadn't actually lost any of them. All three were damaged, but none of them in a way that would render them useless or even tremendously impaired in their main function.

"Well, let's hope there's something in there worth looking at. I sure can't pull off that trick again. Knowing how these things go, we've probably just succeeded in breaking into the alien equivalent of the broom closet."

Rane was not able to retract or fold the remainder of its manipulator arms, meaning that it was much more likely to snag itself going through narrow spaces. Tinkerbell's loss of an imaging unit made it less effective for surveying.

That left Titania. Fortunately, the status indicators and a visual survey by the other ISMs showed that the non-functional arm was in fact completely missing—it had broken cleanly off at the joint connecting it to the Faerie's main body. There was nothing to prevent Titania from surveying the now-accessible room.

Nothing, that was, except the inevitable verification and programming delay engendered by the many millions of miles between Earth and Phobos. After Prybar had concluded, the change in the ISMs' status had been more than sufficient to require them to wait for instructions from A.J. on what to do next.

"Take a break, people," A.J. said, absently. "I'm going to be designating new instruction sets and getting the Faeries redistributed to maximize the bandwidth feed when I send in Titania. This intermission will probably run you about two and a half hours. If someone would like to thank me for producing this Oscar-winning film, they could grab me a couple of hotdogs with mustard and relish and a large OJ in an hour or so."

⌘          ⌘          ⌘

Two hours and forty-seven minutes later, A.J. sat back down at his workstation, having taken a quick bathroom break. He noticed a large number of new people had arrived to watch what was happening—some of the new scientists added to the project recently, and Madeline Fathom.

"The show should be starting any minute now, ladies and gentlemen. In . . . five, four, three, two, one . . . action!"

There was now only a single viewpoint, that of Titania, as the little ISM carefully maneuvered itself down and through the gap. It eased through and then activated its full-power lights.

There were faint gasps of indrawn breath throughout the room.

A.J. could not quite restrain another whoop of triumph. "*Not* a broom closet!"

"Closet, hell," Hathaway said in quiet awe. "That's a control room."

The large oval room was a study in curves and ramps and triangled paneling. Even though constructed by completely inhuman minds and manipulative members, the layout was something hauntingly familiar. A sort of dais, with scalloped indentations at the edge that must correspond to seating arrangements, was located in the center. Around the perimeter of the room, on the side opposite the door, there were a series of tripartite panels. They were clearly separated yet related in groups of three, each with what appeared to be some kind of display panel or viewing screen above the central of the three subpanels.

Other dark, indefinable shapes were barely visible, sharp-edged but confusing, casting eerie shadows on the walls behind them. Titania began its preprogrammed survey of the room, in a counterclockwise direction from the entrance—which, naturally, took the other shapes out of view.

"Damn! I flip a coin and it chooses the wrong direction."

"We'll get to that area eventually," Jackie pointed out reassuringly. "How long?"

"You can't survey the room too quickly, especially if you don't want to hit anything. I'd say it's another half hour before we get our second look. Getting other data in now and . . . Yes, it's what I thought. There's *something* in those walls that was messing with the readings earlier. They're all much clearer now."

A.J. was still not paying a great deal of attention to the other data. Like everyone else, he was watching the slow revelations of Titania as she carefully surveyed the great control room.

"Look at that," one of the newcomers whispered. "More symbols on those keyboard-type things."

"How do you know they're keyboards?" challenged another.

"I don't *know*. But if we assume this is a control room, then it stands to reason that these things are very likely to be something like a keyboard."

"Size argues that they must have been using a phonetic alphabet rather than one oriented to meaning, like ideograms," someone else put in.

"Unless they had developed a symbology that included a method of representing meaning."

"Well, it could be mathematical . . . But look there, that one. I think some of those symbols are the same ones on a couple of the plaques we've located in the corridors."

"Not just mathematical, then. Unless they discussed hallway-style directions in mathematical terms."

"The hallway signs don't have to be directions. They may have known directions instinctively. Perhaps they were reminders of significant equations . . ."

The discussion continued in low tones with the participants examining in detail the specific frames in question. The rest of the spectators continued to be glued to the new images flowing in from Phobos.

"There, that station, it's bigger," Jackie said. "And the ramp that leads up to it flattens out into almost a platform. It's got more than one of those display-type screens above it, too. A captain's station?"

"Could be," A.J. allowed. "Or chief researcher or engineer."

After a pause, he added: "Okay, people, here we go. We're getting back to a FOV that ought to show us those whatever-they-weres towards the far side."

The darkness lightened. The mysterious shapes began to clarify again. Something like a small, black-brown bush with a thick, jagged stem drifted by the imager.

"What the heck is that?" Diane wondered aloud.

Suddenly, sliding into view almost as though it had lunged from the left-hand side, a far larger shape loomed on the screen. Three long, sinuous projections extended towards Titania, with the glittering of something smooth and whitish showing between them. Behind these projections bulked a massive body extending several meters back into the darkness, shadows and light playing on it and hinting at more detail.

As Titania continued onward, the shape emerged more

clearly, coming into profile: an almost sluglike body, three
stout projections on the far end mirroring the longer ones
at the front.

"Holy mother of—" A.J. began.

"That's—" Jackie said.

"*Bemmie!*" they both finished simultaneously.

"Bemmie?" Hathaway repeated. "What the hell's a
bemmie?"

Madeline Fathom looked just as puzzled as Hathaway.
A.J. and Jackie turned to both of them, started talking at
once, and went through several cycles of "Okay, you tell
them, no, *you*, no, go ahead, you say it, no . . ." before
A.J. finally claimed the floor.

"Colonel, I think we have a new crew member for you.
Because,"

A.J. said with a wicked grin, "we know someone who's
*already* spent two years studying our aliens."

# Chapter 20

Helen Sutter stared around her in confusion. Now that she saw the buildings in front of her, she knew where she was. At various times, Jackie had sent her postcards with pictures of the installation—that part of it, at least, that wasn't restricted for security reasons. But it wasn't a location she'd ever really expected to be at, and she still had no idea of what she was doing here.

"Now that we've arrived," she said to the Marine next to her as they entered the NASA complex, "is someone finally going to tell me what the hell is going on?"

"The general will brief you very shortly, ma'am," the sergeant replied. "I'm not cleared to say anything about the situation at this time."

"Brief me?" she repeated incredulously.

This was surreal. The whole thing was like some kind of bad thriller script. She'd been sitting out at the dig, cataloging some of the fossils found in the past few days, when all of a sudden a huge military helicopter had come *whup-whup-whupping* over the ridge and landed so close to the camp that it damn near blew over the tents. From it had emerged an Air Force captain and this sergeant—Sergeant Ney—along with several other soldiers.

They'd told her they were there to pick her up, and made noises about national security. After she scanned their papers—which all looked very official, but weren't warrants and thus as far as she was concerned meant they had no hold on her whatsoever—she'd called Director Bonds. The museum director had informed her that he also had been contacted, that as far as he knew she wasn't in any trouble, but someone wanted to talk with her very, very badly and was apparently willing to pay for any inconvenience on anyone's part. She'd also gotten the impression that there was probably an implied, genteel threat on the other hand—that if she *didn't* go, the government might make things sticky for the museum.

So she'd gone, finding herself bundled politely into the chopper and flown out with Sergeant Ney—while the captain and the rest of the soldiers stayed behind, apparently to prevent anyone from calling out about her semi-abduction!

Sergeant Ney had been completely uncommunicative throughout the entire trip down here to New Mexico. And now here she was, at *NASA* of all places!

The sergeant stopped at a large door and gestured for her to enter. "The general is just inside, ma'am."

The room inside was a good-sized office, which had hastily been made over into the unnamed general's headquarters. It looked as if it had been used by a senior researcher up until maybe a few days or a week ago.

As she entered, the uniformed man behind the desk stood up and crossed the distance between them with a few quick strides.

"General Martin Deiderichs," he said, shaking her hand. "Welcome to NASA, Dr. Sutter. I apologize for the extremely urgent and I'm sure inconvenient way in which you were brought here. But once you see the situation, I think you'll understand."

She returned the handshake mechanically, but managed a reasonable smile. There was no point in being impolite. "Well, that will probably depend on the situation, General."

"No doubt, Doctor. You were brought in at the suggestion of some of the people currently on this project. The situation is . . ."

He seemed to be at a loss for words, for a moment. "I think it's probably just best to show you. Please, follow me."

Helen shrugged and did as he asked. At least it seemed as if this was neither a practical joke nor the result of some kind of terrible mistake she'd made. Though what would an Air Force general care about her mistakes at a paleontological dig, anyway?

After a short walk down a hallway, they entered a far larger room, one whose layout she recognized from many images: space mission control. At a centrally located screen ahead of her, she also recognized a tall, elegantly-dressed figure with slightly tousled salt-and-pepper hair.

She slowed involuntarily, then stepped forward. "Dr. Glendale!"

Nicholas Glendale almost jumped. His attention had been so riveted on the screen that he hadn't heard their approach. "Dr. Sutter— Helen, you've made it here. I arrived myself just two hours ago. Fortunately, I was in California when I got the summons."

"What, exactly, have I made it to?" she demanded. "And why in God's name is NASA summoning paleontologists in the first—"

Glendale stepped aside and around her, and with gentle pressure guided her to a seat before the console. "Please, Helen. Just take a look."

She looked.

She needed no one to tell her what the central object in the image was. She had done so many reconstructions, sketches, and 3-D models that no possible method of displaying it would have slowed her down for a moment.

*"Bemmie?"* she whispered.

No one said anything. Slowly, she became aware of the background to the image. Sharp-edged shadows falling across distorted-looking panels, everything oriented at odd angles as though a clumsy amateur photographer had been trying to take artistic pictures and failed. The viewpoint progressed around, staying focused on Bemmie, but revealing other things in the process. Walls of some kind of metal and rock. Those weird highlights and shadows on Bemmie and the background—they weren't like anything she'd ever visualized. Well, except . . .

A chill ran down her spine. She saw gooseflesh literally spring out across her forearms. This couldn't be a practical joke. But if it wasn't, then the only thing that could possibly, conceivably connect her, NASA, *Bemmius secordii*, and these images in front of her was—

"This is Phobos!" she blurted out.

"Correct, Dr. Sutter." Deiderichs' voice carried a

pleased tone. She got the impression he appreciated people who were quick on the uptake.

"I hadn't heard from A.J. in a while, but I knew . . ." She looked up at the general. "His Faeries found this inside the moon, didn't they?"

Deiderichs nodded. "Mr. Baker recognized Bemmie immediately, the moment he saw the thing. So did Ms. Secord."

She stared at the screen. It was still too much to grasp. "Bemmie . . . came from *Phobos*?"

"From somewhere in space, certainly," Nicholas Glendale said. "It couldn't possibly have evolved on Phobos itself, of course."

She turned to look at him, to find the famous grin even wider than normal.

"Helen, if I recall correctly I said that I'd have to change my position if you'd found a fossilized repeating shotgun. Instead, you had your friend go and find an entire base, complete with a second fossil. Not even that—a mummified body." He gave her a very old-fashioned little bow. "You were entirely, completely, and inarguably right in every particular. I cannot imagine the vindication you must feel— or will feel, when you finally grasp it all."

He turned to Deiderichs. "I am immensely honored that your people thought of bringing me on board. But I'm a bit old to be considering space travel. And in any event"—he pointed to Helen—"I really think Dr. Sutter is the only reasonable choice. She can now claim, with perfect accuracy, to be the world's first—and only— qualified xenopaleontologist."

He flashed the grin at Helen again. "Besides, I have a large helping of crow to consume, and a great deal of catching up to do on the work Helen did already."

"Space travel?" Helen repeated inanely.

General Deiderichs cleared his throat. "Yes, Dr. Sutter. We will want someone on the expedition which we are currently planning who can conduct what amount to autopsies and studies on bodies mummified for millions of years. And with your training and background, you may have other insights into things such as base designs and so on."

"*Me?* Go into space?" She flashed back to her childhood, staring at the moon and wondering what it was like. All the TV shows she'd seen, including some of the ones A.J. was so fond of. A dream that had been diverted when she found her first fossil in a nearby park.

"You're kidding. I'm too old."

"You had your fortieth birthday just a few months ago, Dr. Sutter. Popular mythology about daring young men and women aside, the fact is that forty is just about the right age for an astronaut. John Glenn was forty-one years old when he made his orbital flight; Yuri Gagarin, only a bit younger when he made his. Thirty-seven, as I recall. And Neil Armstrong was just two weeks short of his thirty-ninth birthday when he was the first man to set foot on the moon."

A smile came to Deiderichs' stern face that made him abruptly seem more human. "You certainly don't appear old, if you'll pardon me saying so. Had I not known otherwise, I would have thought you to be a woman in her mid-thirties. Furthermore, Doctor, we did a quick check of your medical records which are publicly available and you seem to be already in excellent condition. People who know you confirm that impression. 'Strong and stubborn as a mule' was the way Mr. Baker put it, as I recall." The smiled widened a bit. "I should add in fairness to Mr. Baker that he spent considerably more words assuring me that you didn't *look* like a mule."

Helen couldn't help but laugh. "Well, I hope so! *Him?* Comparing anyone else to a mule? He should talk!"

His face serious again, Deiderichs continued: "In short, unless a thorough and careful examination shows some hidden problems, there is no physical reason you cannot go into space. Unless you have some mental disability we don't know about. Perhaps claustrophobia?"

"What?" Helen shook her head, somewhat absent-mindedly. "No. Nor agoraphobia, either. *Space?*"

"Space indeed!" A.J.'s voice shouted from behind her. He'd just entered from the other side. "What's gonna be up, Doc, is *you.* Several million miles up. And me! And Jackie, and Joe!"

It was finally starting to penetrate, and for a moment Helen Sutter felt something that she hadn't since she was seven years old. Coming down the stairs on Christmas morning to see a vast expanse of wonders laid out before her and realizing that they really, truly, were all there for her.

But, no, it was something she hadn't felt even then, it was something most people only have in their imaginations. Helen's exhilaration didn't stem from childhood fancies of being an astronaut. Those had long ago faded away. It stemmed from her life as an adult. All those long hard years of work and study, now come to as triumphant a conclusion as anyone could wish for.

Bemmie really *had* come down from the skies sixty-five million years before and fought for his life beneath the crackling skies of a bolide impact. His people *had* watched the solar system from a great base built inside a twenty-mile-wide asteroid. And she herself would step foot inside the first alien structure ever discovered by mankind!

"Well," she said finally, her voice sounding almost conversationally inane in her own ears. "Where do I sign up?"

# PART IV: BLUEPRINTS

*Design, n: an outline, sketch, or plan, as of the form and structure of a work of art, an edifice, or a machine to be executed or constructed; the combination of details or features of a picture, building, etc.; a plan or project.*

# Chapter 21

"That's his missing hand."

"Yep. Though calling something with eighteen branches a 'hand' seems pretty weird to me."

"He'd say the same about a clumsy paw with only five branchings, I'm sure."

"Well, which one of us is sixty-five million years freeze-dried, and which one of us is sitting here still using his hands? Ha! Don't have an answer for that one, do you?"

"You're such a wiseguy, A.J." Helen studied the 3-D model, derived from multiple spectra of imaging combined. "I wasn't half-bad in my modeling."

"Taking into account water loss, damage, all the other good stuff, some of your reconstructions were damn near perfect. You couldn't get all the internals, but the externals are good. The colors would be more earthy, though."

"How can you get colors out of this? I'm not even sure if the external skin or whatever it is has just dehydrated or gone through a hell of a lot more changes in the time it's been here."

"Guesses, but pretty good ones. We have some idea of the chemical processes that go on in vacuum now, and I can run simulations. If I take the chemical constituents I can derive from my various sensors and run a simulation of what it would've looked like before sixty-five million years of space exposure, I get something with a sort of warm brown tint. Like good leather."

"Interesting. Still, with all the variables, I'd say it's more like a wild-assed guess."

"Give me half-assed, and you have a deal."

Helen snorted. "No one gets half my ass."

A.J. should have made another comment at that point, but he was silent instead. Giving him a sideways glance, Helen saw a rather dramatic blush just starting to recede.

*Well, now, that's cute. I guess a wiseass answer occurred to him that took him in a direction he wasn't ready to go.*

She paused mentally at that point. It dawned on her that she was skirting an area that *she* wasn't ready to go. She been working alongside A.J. for three days, ever since she'd agreed to participate in the planned expedition to Mars. Almost every waking hour, in fact. The experience, she now realized, had just driven home the impressions she had gotten in the two years since she'd first met the man.

*Don't kid yourself, woman. For whatever reasons—God only knows how and why it works—A.J. Baker really and truly turns you on.*

She shook her head slightly. She was *still* twelve years older than he was—always would be—and she was *still* not ready to go there. Probably never would be.

Before she could start blushing herself—at her age!—

she hurriedly went back to the subject at hand. "Are there any other rooms you can get into other than this one and the water room?"

A.J.'s tone seemed just a bit hurried, too. "A few, yeah. There's only one major room we haven't looked into yet. Its door is opened a little bit less than this one, but it was clearly jammed tight and no way we were going to lever it open. So now that we've done all the heavy work we can with the Faeries, I'll probably be trying to get one of them into that room. It might get stuck, though; it's going to be really, really tight. That's why I hadn't tried until now. And we've got a few more side corridors to go into first."

"What do you make of those things over there, that look like, oh, triangular plaques?"

A.J. studied the thirty or so glittering bronze-tinted plates that were piled in ages-old shallow drifts against the wall, probably due to Phobos' rotation. "My guess? Printouts of important data."

"Printouts? But they're metal. And they don't appear to be stamped or inscribed in any way. So why do you think they're printouts?"

"Hard to prove it right now, but on some wavelengths, just at the edge of maximum enhancement, I get hints of structure. Remember, these guys were sitting in a pretty limited environment here, so you gotta think about it. If they did prefer using hard copy, like we do, how're they going to do it? It'd be insane to bring along masses of paper, and it's not like you're going to be growing trees here. Or papyrus reeds. So you need something else.

"What would be ideal would be something sorta like an Etch-a-Sketch that doesn't go away at a shake but only at a specific signal. It'd be a physical display, but one you could use over and over again. And with a lot better resolution and control than an Etch-a-Sketch, of course."

Helen nodded. "Okay. But how would that work?"

"Remember when you first met me? My halo?"

"Yes. So?"

"Well, if you have miniature active agents like my sensor motes, only a lot smaller—real nanotech like they've been working on for years—you could make the surface of some object, like those plates, be composed of these agent-motes. They'd be networked together on the local level and could rearrange the surface physically to conform to whatever you wanted to display. Then, when you wanted to change the surface, you'd send another code to have them move around again. Properly designed, it could be pretty energy efficient. Everyone would be able to have a few of these little babies and they'd have permanent records without physical waste. If you ever really decided that a book or whatever wasn't needed any more, you just erase it."

He pondered a moment. "The things probably would scavenge power from transmissions in the air. You might even be beaming out some signal that was harmless to you and that didn't interfere with your other devices, just in order to keep 'em powered. Of course, once the power failed, the motes shut down. And by now, they're almost certainly vacuum-welded into a single mass. Not to mention that with sixty-five megayears having gone by since then, radiation probably hasn't done 'em any good either."

Helen thought about the bronze-colored tablets having a surface mutable as water, changing and freezing on command. It was a nice image, and it did make sense the way A.J. put it. But it was awfully speculative, based just on a faint trace of microstructure.

"Do you always jump to conclusions on that little evidence?"

"Well, yeah," he said, grinning a little sheepishly. "I like having a guess at anything I run into. Besides, I have a reputation to maintain." More seriously: "But they do seem to have a lot of the symbols on the keyboards and signs, and other things that might be sketches or something. So the tablets look a lot to me like sorta triangular clipboard type things, but they're also pretty much solid."

"I think I understand you," Helen said slowly. "Unless we postulate some odd religious requirement, it's hard to imagine they were spending their time carving or casting metal symbol-plates like this. It's not like they had to write in cuneiform. So you're saying that if they used these things as you're guessing, then obviously the tablets couldn't be as simple as they look."

"Right in one, Doc. Hey, here we go, the first stereo imaging of the interior of a Bemmie."

The combination of wavelengths the Faeries could scan in had given A.J. an extensive array of methods for analyzing the interior of just about anything. Helen didn't understand how it worked, but she knew that when A.J. was dealing with an organic, mummified target, he could tailor the approach for exactly that sort of object.

The image that materialized on-screen was a detailed, layered outline of structures down to a fraction of an inch in size, all done without having to touch the specimen. That was a good thing, too. It was quite possible that at least parts of the sixty-five-million-year-old Bemmie would disintegrate at a touch.

"There it is!"

The "it" Helen referred to was a large, three-lobed organ protected by the bony structure they had long since decided was effectively a skull combined with part of a rib cage—sort of a cephalothorax. The tripartite object bulged towards the front of Bemmie and extended back a considerable distance. Lines of tissue branched from it at regular intervals, and it swelled again about halfway down the body and then trailed off.

"Well, no one doubted Bemmie was smart," A.J. commented. "Still, that's a hell of a brain. Great for zombies, though. *Brrraiiiiins!*"

The idea of a Bemmie zombie was creepy, Helen thought, since they were actually looking at a mummified corpse. "Look at all these other organs. That must be the digestive tract. Right there at the mouth and going down—"

"How do you know that's not his respiratory system?"

Helen could tell that was just a contrarian question. But she answered anyway, tracing the complexities revealed with her eyes, trying to wring every last bit of information from the image.

"First, because the area it comes through has a number of structures that look like they were made for cutting and crushing—a mouth, just like we thought when we looked at the fossil. Second, because the structures trailing down here look an awful lot like flattened intestines. And, third, because I think *these* are his respiratory system."

A.J. looked at "these," which were a pair of structures extending from slitlike areas on each side of Bemmie. "Okay, yeah, I'd probably agree, at least at a first guess."

"You'd damn well better. Who's the professional reconstruction expert and who's the glorified photographer here?"

"Fine, lemme give you another daguerreotype for your collection."

Another view of Bemmie shimmered into view next to the first, this one done in different wavelengths.

"Oh, now there's some nice structure! That must be the equivalent of cartilage and connective tissue. Look how it layers along the shoehorns. Weird, it seems very heavily set, though. A lot more than I remember the limbs of the fossil being."

Helen gnawed on her lower lip for a few seconds. "I think I know what caused that. Drying out retracted the arms. I'll bet the extension and contraction tissue was pretty hydrophilic, even for living tissue."

"I dunno. Depends on the mechanism. As I recall, you've been arguing with yourself for the past couple of years on just how it managed the 'extend' part of that movement. Memory molecules, crystal structure, all that kind of thing."

He glanced back at the other view. "Getting back to the digestive and respiration systems, there's one area he was built better than us, if you're right. Bemmie never choked to death on a chicken bone. If they ate chickens. I wonder what he did eat? Was Bemmie vegetarian?"

"I severely doubt it, unless it was from personal conviction or ideology. His eating mechanism doesn't look all that much like ours at first glance, naturally. But my gut reaction—pardon the pun—looking at his, um, dentition, and the internal structure you've got here, is that Bemmie was an omnivore, like us."

"Just a guess though, right?"

"Yeah. An educated one, but still a guess. We don't have any idea what plants or their equivalent were like on his homeworld, or what other species existed besides themselves. But there are also these structures on the arms. I found some of them in our fossil Bemmie, but I couldn't be sure what they were. Looks like one of my guesses was right, however. They exist on the inside of the arms or tentacles in the front, and I'll bet the lumps of tissue under them indicate that they can be raised and lowered. Sort of like a cat's retractable claws."

"They do look kinda like claws. Or shark teeth even, or thorns."

"And where they're located indicates they were used to grab something and prevent it from moving away. And not gently, either. That looks to me like a predatory creature's design. Squid have some similar hooked structures on their tentacles. The length of the digestive system, though, is really over the top for something that's an obligate carnivore. At least here on Earth, the digestive tracts of meat eaters tend to be significantly less complex because, well, you're trying to convert meat into meat, rather than plants into meat."

"And that funnel sort of thing around the mouth. Like lips?"

"Yes, I think so. It's got more structure around it, though, from what I can tell. I'm not sure, but I think that it might not look so simple if it were still alive. Maybe not like pedipalps or other side organs, but not just a smooth funnel of tissue, either."

A.J. was studying other external features. "They didn't wear clothes, exactly, but they did have sort of harnesses and other things. I'll bet that's either jewelry or else some kind of communicator badge up there."

"Embedded in the skin? Well, I guess that tells us that they did have pretty tough skin."

"Not necessarily. After all, we get ears and other body parts pierced just for vanity. Still, at that size it probably did have pretty tough skin, like a rhino or elephant."

"Ugly things, weren't they?" Diane said from over their shoulders.

Helen opened her mouth to defend Bemmie reflexively, then grinned. "I *did* name him *Bemmius* for a reason, you know."

Diane frowned.

"From the old science fiction term, Diane," A.J. explained. "Bug-Eyed Monster, BEM."

Diane laughed at that, and smiled at A.J.

Helen wasn't surprised. She'd noticed already that when Diane acted just a bit clueless, it was whenever A.J. was nearby—and always about something A.J. could explain.

That annoyed her intensely, for some reason. Perhaps just the natural feminism of a woman in a man's profession. Or . . . She chewed on the problem for a moment, and was a little disturbed when she realized that the annoyance was something very old-fashioned. Archaic, even.

Pure and simple jealousy. *Argh!*

She shook it off. "Yes, I don't think I'd have wanted to meet Bemmie in a dark alley, to be honest."

"Or even in a lighted one," A.J. concurred. "He would've weighed in at, um—"

"Something over a ton," Helen supplied.

"—right, something over a ton, and had a hell of a reach

to boot. If you're right about those thorn things . . . Well, the thought gets ucky. He could do quite a number on you."

Diane winced. "And probably eat you afterwards."

"Doubtful," A.J. said. "If he could catch you in the first place— Bemmie was obviously not built for speed—he probably didn't have chemistry within light-years of ours. Couldn't eat us, anyway."

"You never know," Helen said, getting a surprised glance from A.J. "Preliminary analyses from the fossil site . . . well, it's hard to be certain, given all the time that's passed, bacteria, and so on. But it appears that Bemmie was based on DNA or RNA rather like our own. We eat an awful lot of things that aren't very closely related to us—mushrooms, for instance—and some of them are pretty darn nutritious. But I'd agree that there's a matter of more orders of magnitude involved in this probability."

"That argument didn't go over with you well a few years ago, Helen," Glendale pointed out from the consultant's station he'd been given at Helen's insistence. "What's a few orders of magnitude between friends?"

"Well, to turn your own argument back—and hope that I have to eat my words, so to speak, like you—if you can find a set of dinosaur bones with knife and fork marks on them, I'll agree that Bemmie's people could've found us tasty eating."

Glendale laughed. "Fair enough. And I agree, it's damned unlikely."

"I wonder if they were hostile or friendly types?" Diane mused. "I mean, if we'd been able to meet them."

"Maybe we still can," A.J. replied. "They certainly didn't come from this solar system."

Diane looked at him. "What? How can you be sure? Maybe they were Martians."

"Because—oh, let's let the expert explain." He glanced at astrophysicist Larry Conley. "Larry?"

The big, slightly portly scientist shook his head. "No way."

"But I thought Mars had tons of water way back then."

"Not that recently, Diane. Hundreds of millions of years—and please note the plural—back to maybe a billion or two. Mars wasn't much different in the age of the dinosaurs than it is now. And if Dr. Sutter's right, Bemmie started out aquatic, so . . . No. I doubt very much that even if we had magic space drives we could meet any of them today. It's been sixty-five million years, remember. If they still had any interest in this place, they'd not only have been here, they'd have taken everything over. No, by now, they've evolved into something completely different, or gone extinct altogether."

Despite the fact that he'd summoned the expert opinion himself, A.J. choked at it. "Hey, now, that's a couple of big-ass assumptions. I thought evolution stopped once we started controlling the environment."

Conley raised an eyebrow and ran his fingers through unruly dark hair—which, unfortunately for him, looked much more sloppy and less "artistic genius" than did A.J.'s mop.

"That's one theory—we came along, invented civilization, and when we found out about Darwin said 'oh, we won't be having any more of *that*!' But, as other people have pointed out, what we've really done is just created a new environment with new pressures. And even tiny, tiny pressures, over sixty-plus million years, will add up to one hell of a lot of change. And so far no civilization we've had has lasted recognizably more than a few thousand years. You want me to believe these aliens made one that lasted ten thousand times longer than that? I don't think so."

He pointed to the screen. "That shows they had not just intelligence, but curiosity and the energy and focus to want to go to other solar systems. I'd have to assume that they'd probably have completely colonized this solar system long before now. And we definitely would've found traces of an advanced civilization from even that far back. If they stayed on Earth at all, they only built a few relatively small bases. Otherwise we'd have found *something*."

"Still, I wonder what they would've been like. Maybe they were really peaceful types, having worked out all the crap that we still have to deal with. Crossing light-years of space would take a hell of a lot of work."

"Ah, the old 'more advanced and wiser civilization,' eh, A.J.?" Glendale's voice was amused. "I don't believe so, and I think your image there proves it."

"Huh?" A.J. glanced back at the image. "Um, he's kinda dead. And just because he wasn't a vegetarian doesn't prove anything. Dogs are carnivores, but they're pretty friendly most of the time. And if they overcame any violent impulses, like Helen said, they could all be vegetarians at this point. Well, at the point this guy got freeze-dried, anyway."

"They could indeed," Glendale conceded. "Yet not, I think, through being tremendously peaceful. Consider that object shown under the, ah, left arm. It wasn't easily visible in the earlier images, being so close and under the arm that it was in permanent shadow."

The object in question looked something like a large

laundry detergent bottle with the bottom cut off combined with a ridged bowling ball stuck on the end of a plunger, the handle of the plunger stuck through the bottleneck. It was made mostly of metal with some odd ceramic and possibly plasticlike bits and held by some kind of strap or holster affair with the open "bottom" end out. Rotating the model showed that the "plunger handle" was a hollow pipe or tube with fairly thick walls.

"My fossilized shotgun," Helen finally said, after a long silence.

"Well, I would say it is more of a pistol. Possibly also a shotgun in terms of its operation, but if I understand the nature of the cutouts on the side there, essentially what you have is a weapon intended to be used one-handed. If we may use the term broadly."

"So what?" A.J. demanded. "We knew they had weapons. That's no surprise. And the original Bemmie needed 'em, too. If he'd had a few friends with guns along, he might have gotten out alive."

Glendale smiled, a bit sadly. "A.J., you're quite right he needed one where he died. But our friend here— where was he?"

The sensor specialist froze for a moment, then sighed. "Yeah."

"Exactly. Our specimen is armed while in the control room of a base on an airless rock, uncountable miles from any possible hostile wild creatures. Why would he be carrying a weapon in such circumstances? It seems to me obvious that it was considered possible that he might need one, even there. One does not ship something across light years which one does not expect to need at some point. Now, it may be that he is something like a security officer, and that most of his people are not armed. But the need for such an officer still points to the potential for violent disagreements."

"It could be a symbolic weapon," Diane argued. "Marines still have dress swords, don't they?"

"Yes, but—correct me if I am wrong—I believe all such ceremonial weapons are associated with groups that on occasion must fight other people, yes?"

A.J. surveyed the Net. "Not quite all . . . But I won't argue, I'm convinced. Yeah, you don't generally carry weapons when you're a long way from anything that would ever require a weapon to deal with. So much for the enlightened peaceful aliens."

He shrugged. "Let's see if I can verify your guess, Dr. Glendale."

"Nicholas or Nick, please. *Not*—" He flashed a warning glance at Helen, but too late.

"—Nicky!" she interjected.

"Okay, Nick," A.J. acknowledged through a grin. "Let's take a look at the data on some other wavelengths. Peel away the layers of Bemmie to get at this thing here . . . hmm . . . enhance . . . nah, too coarse, let's try another . . . Ah, yeah, there we go. Damn, these guys used some funky materials! I think I can tell General Deiderichs and Madeline that, at the least, we can get some neat materials advancements out of this base."

Helen found the rapid transition of the security official from "Ms. Fathom," A.J.'s potential nemesis, to "Madeline" annoying also. She was quite sure that if Madeline Fathom had been male he would still be "Mr. Fathom" and A.J. wouldn't be at all concerned about whether he was pleased or not.

Jealous—again?? Stop this, Helen!

"What do you think of that?" A.J. demanded.

The main display showed a hugely enlarged version of the alien artifact, shadowy like an old-fashioned X-ray image. Inside the sculpted, ridged "bowling ball" were three well-defined hollows. Two showed nothing inside them, but the middle one was nearly full with hundreds, perhaps thousands, of tiny dots. Small lines ran from the empty hollows to the base of the hollow tube, which had some kind of complex mechanism at that point. The mechanism also connected, via a much larger opening, to the central hollow.

"Looks very interesting," said Glendale. "What exactly do you think we're seeing?"

"Well, the first important point is these little dots. If I blow one of them up a bit and check the scale, how large do you think they are?"

No one said anything for a moment. Then Helen smiled. "Four point six five millimeters?"

"On the nose."

"Ah, yes." Glendale nodded. "The mysterious 'pebbles' that Mike Jennings argued were cysts of some kind in several papers. Shotgun pellets, then?"

"Right. And these two chambers—they were using a binary propellant design, probably two liquids that have leaked away over the ages. This mechanism meters the amount of propellant and ammunition—I'll bet you could adjust it for volume of fire and so on. I suppose someone else might find another explanation, but I wouldn't bet on it. This is a *gun*. Nothing else I can think of that would fit."

Glendale looked at Helen. "And this verifies one of your other hypotheses, if I'm right."

"What? Oh, yes. We tend to use large single bullets rather than shotguns, but with the way Bemmie's muscles and skeleton connected, or rather didn't really connect, something like a shotgun would be a lot more devastating to them. So it makes sense that their side arms would also be based on shotgun designs. Unfortunately for poor Bemmie, an elephant gun or even a thirty-ought-six would have been a better choice for blowing away raptors. The shotgun hurt them and eventually killed them, but not fast enough."

"Neat," A.J. said. "I hadn't thought of that before. Guess I didn't read your papers carefully enough. Anyway, let's see what else we can get out of this before I have to go off to today's training session."

"Right!"

# Chapter 22

Helen gave vent to a mild curse as she realized her hammer had slid away from her. She leaned reflexively to get it and found herself floating away, scattering sample containers and her other tools in a slow-motion catastrophe across the room. "Oh, dammit, not again!"

The voice of Walter Myles, the microgravity operations training expert, spoke in her ear. "Sorry, Dr. Sutter, but you should be past simple mistakes like that. I'm not resetting it. You'll have to clean up and recover."

"Yes, I know. It's just so hard to remember."

"Well, ma'am, you have to learn somehow. Phobos has barely any gravity, around one two-thousandth that of Earth. That's enough to make things settle eventually, but from your point of view it might as well be nothing. Tidal effects are actually noticeable on that scale."

Helen didn't answer, as she already knew the numbers. The problem wasn't on the intellectual level, but the level of instinctive reflex. She was trying to retrain a body that had spent four decades in a one-g field to properly react in the almost total absence of gravity.

Helen checked herself against the far wall, absorbing the impact and grabbing one of the handholds spotted about the room. Thus secured, she was able to survey the situation and decide the best method to address the scattered clutter.

"You know, in the real situation, I'd have tools and things attached to me, right?"

"Correct, Doctor, but you'd also be in a real microgravity situation instead of a simulation. We would prefer that you learn to do your work well enough that you won't notice, nor care, whether the tools are attached to lanyards or not."

"Simulations are pretty damn impressive these days, though. I have to admit that I can't really tell I'm not on Phobos, except that if I concentrate I can tell up and down. But you confuse that by making 'up' be in the direction that it looks like one of the walls should be, instead of the ceiling."

In actuality, Helen was floating in a huge water tank inside the NASA training facility. The tools and such were, relatively speaking, real; but the exact way she perceived them, and the background against which the action took place, was all being generated for her inside the watertight spacesuit she had on. The spacesuit was also attached to actuators to assist her in moving in a fashion that would feel fairly close to the way real microgravity would feel—minus, as Helen had noted, the absence of an internal method for referencing up and down. That she'd get to experience later.

Having assessed the situation, Helen pulled a butter-fly net from the wall, where it had been held by a magnetic hanger arrangement, and launched herself slowly across the room. It took several minutes, but eventually she had rounded up everything except her pen.

"Where the hell did that get to?"

Myles being non-helpfully silent, Helen started another slow survey of the room.

Nothing.

*All right*, she thought, *let's reason this through. Which direction would it have been scattered in?*

She thought back, then looked carefully along the rather broad arc that it might have gone in.

Nothing.

Then she smacked herself in the head, or rather tried to. The spacesuit *thunked* obligingly. She called up the record of her mishap and replayed it in slow motion, watching the pen as it slowly, gracefully, somersaulted through the air.

And slowly, gracefully, somersaulted into the megayears-old ventilation duct.

There was only one appropriate response to that level of stupid accidental coincidence. "D'oh!" she grunted. "I suppose I am now the solar system's first interplanetary litterbug, as there's no way I'm getting that one back myself. Maybe A.J. would be able to send in a drone some-day."

"Well, not the first," Myles said, his tone amused. "Several other trainees have lost objects effectively permanently before. I will say that yours was the most elegant method for losing something on Phobos I've yet seen."

"Thanks. I think. Give me another pen and let me start this over."

"Certainly." The simulation shimmered out of existence, leaving a large tank with objects roughly coinciding with the Phobos control room layout set inside it. "Actually, go get yours back; it's over where the vent would be."

"Got it." Helen retrieved the pen and prepared to start the research simulation again.

*It's amazing how you can sweat so much in a climate-controlled spacesuit*, Helen mused later, as she finished toweling dry. *I hope we have a lot of thought put into creature comforts for this cruise. It's going to be a hell of a trip.*

At least the second half of the practice had gone well. If she could keep it up, she'd be ready to try real microgravity soon. They'd already tested her acceleration tolerance, which had been surprisingly high—at the same level, in fact, of trained fighter pilots. Only Colonel Hathaway had scored better.

She wasn't looking forward to weightlessness, though. A.J. had come back from his first experience looking about three shades paler. He hadn't quite lost his lunch, but apparently it had been a near thing. Still, he'd gotten over it and done his first orbital two weeks ago.

Joe, on the other hand, apparently hadn't even blinked when he first went weightless. Hopefully, Helen would have the same reaction.

That reminded her—Joe should be coming back from *his* first orbital flight soon. She checked the time. Yes, if she hurried she could be there for the landing.

She opened a voice channel to A.J. as she dressed. "Hey, A.J.!"

"What's up, Doc?"

"I'm going to go see Joe land. You coming?"

"I'm already on my way. Meet you there. Then we can all go out to eat before it's back to the salt mines."

"Sounds good to me."

She finished dressing, jogged down to the parking lot, and got in her car. She was careful to keep the windows rolled up as she exited. That wasn't to ward off the late autumn chill, it was to ward off reporters. Following the announcement of the discovery and the upgrading of both *Nike* and Ares, news crews were always hanging around the exits.

She let the window down after she passed the news people and headed for the landing strip, a couple of hours away. Her blond hair whipped in the breeze. The air was a little chilly, but the sensation felt *good* after all that time in a spacesuit.

She had a sudden vision of driving like this on Mars, the terraformed Mars that Ares envisioned. The New Mexico landscape she was driving through was even some-what similar to that on the Red Planet. *Now wouldn't that be cool? Well, not something I'll see, but maybe three generations from now.*

Eventually she pulled through the security gate, parked in the lot, and headed for the landing area. The vastness of the dry, dusty plain shimmered in the desert sun. The landing strip, a darker ruler-straight road built to a giant's scale, seemed to waver slightly. Off to the left, the control and support buildings threw sharp shadows against the hardened soil, but their somewhat illusory coolness wouldn't allow a good view of the landing. Instead, a long, open pavilion with chairs sat not far from the control area,

with a large flatscreen monitor installed in its own weather-
ized enclosure to one side to provide alerts and alternative
views of the landing.

About thirty people were there already. As Helen got
closer, she noticed that they seemed unusually quiet. Many
were standing, huddling closer to the monitor instead of
watching the sky.

"What's going on?"

"*Chinook* is in trouble," A.J. answered grimly.

*Chinook* was the orbital craft Joe had gone up in. "Oh,
no. What's wrong?"

"Not sure yet. They were getting funny responses from
the hydraulics, and then she went into reentry blackout.
We should've heard something by now, but . . ."

"Jesus." Helen knew what that meant. The likelihood
was that *Chinook* had disintegrated on its way down. Joe
would have known maybe a few moments of panic, and
then . . .

"*There she is!*"

Helen's head snapped up. High in the distance was a
pinpoint of white. It moved slowly and started growing as
she watched.

"Still no communications from *Chinook*," one of the
controllers said over the PA. "Craft is still roughly in
descent path in apparently controlled glide. Not on optimal approach."

"Mother of God," A.J. muttered, staring at something
only his VRD could show him. "*Chinook* is on fire!"

A moment later, A.J. tied in his enhanced feed from
the multiple cameras along the glide path to the publicly
visible screen that Helen and the others were watching.
Instead of just a tiny dot of an approaching object, *Chinook*

was an ominous daylight comet; a dot with a contrail of white, gray and black smoke, and tiny, grim flashes of flame-orange.

"We have a signal!"

A hiss of static on the PA was suddenly broken with a distorted but mostly comprehensible voice. "—trol, this is *Chinook*. We are in an emergency descent. Systems mal—"

A roar of interference obscured the signal. Then: "—arginally functional. Landing gear will not deploy. Re°*buzzz*° foam and emergency crews. Calling on suit radio. Do you copy?"

Helen recognized the voice as that of Major Bruce Irwin, the *Chinook*'s pilot. His Australian accent was unmistakable.

"Roger, *Chinook*, we copy. What is your fuel status, over?"

"Tried to dump remaining fuel, no go. Still have °*frrrz*° percent remaining. Fire hazard definite. Suspect exterior fire."

"Confirming exterior fire. Repeat, presence of fire visually confirmed. Can you land?"

Major Irwin's voice held a note of dry humor. "Control, I am positive we can land. Not sure if it will be a *good* landing, though. Must concentrate on that part. *Chinook* out."

"How the hell could he even joke about making a good landing? Obviously he won't." That came from Jackie Secord, standing on A.J.'s other side. Her hands were clenched tight to the back of the chair near her.

"He has to," Ken Hathaway said quietly. "The oldest and clearest definition of a good landing is one you can walk away from. And if he doesn't manage that with this . . ."

*Chinook* was much more clearly visible, streaming black smoke as it wobbled in towards the landing site. It was obvious that the craft was reacting sluggishly to controls, recovering from a tilt with an aching and frightening slowness.

"Come on, come on. . . " A.J. muttered. "You're almost there. Come on, almost there . . ."

*Chinook* was shedding velocity as well as altitude—that much, at least, was as everyone wanted it. The rumbling boom of its earlier transsonic passage echoed faintly across the desert.

"*Chinook* now three miles downrange, speed two-fifty-two and dropping—"

"Oh, *shit.*"

Something had finally come loose on the nose. Debris showered up and over, black smoke streaming across the cockpit. The damage spread as though pushed by the winds, and suddenly the cockpit seemed to disintegrate. Inky smoke spewed into the air and *Chinook* heeled slowly over, executing a dreamlike cartwheeling pirouette in the sky before thundering down to impact on its side, ironically directly in the center of the runway. The orbiter bounced up, spinning and shedding fragments of wing and tail everywhere, and the spectators dove for cover.

*Chinook*'s second landfall was squarely on the tail section, and with a whooshing roar it ignited in an orange-red-black fireball. Something had sheared through the fuel cells. Now nothing but a moving holocaust, the remains of *Chinook* seared their way down another several hundred yards of runway before shuddering to a flaming halt. Emergency vehicles, already scrambled, skidded to a halt around the wreckage and began trying to extinguish the blaze.

A.J.'s head was bowed, as was Jackie's. Helen tore her gaze from the blazing wreckage that had been bringing Joe Buckley home just moments before. As if she might find understanding and solace, somehow, she traced the trajectory of *Chinook* back along the trail of smoke.

·What was . . .

"A.J.? *A.J., Jackie, look!*"

A white dot showed in the air. As they watched, the dot descended and grew.

"Parachutes spotted," crackled from the speakers. "Visual confirmation that it is the ejection pod from *Chinook*."

Helen and A.J. were already sprinting towards the likely landing area, somewhat to the right as carried by the wind. The emergency vehicles passed them, of course, and by the time they arrived the ejection pod had landed and Bruce and Joe were emerging from it.

A.J. bulled his way through the EMTs. "Joe! *Joe!*"

Joe grinned, painfully. "I tried to tell them it was a no-smoking flight, but nobody listens to me."

# Chapter 23

Ken Hathaway's eyes widened a bit. "A radius of one hundred and forty-six meters—almost a thousand feet across?"

"Or more," Dr. Gupta said, nodding. "Half again as far across if we assume a rotation of once per minute. And farther across, *much* farther across, if we also wish to generate Earth gravity instead of merely something close to Martian."

The Air Force colonel scratched his head, looking doubtful. "A rotation of once every forty seconds or so still seems awfully slow. I'm sure we could spin up to considerably more than that and remain well within tensile safety limits. Look at what we can do with suspension bridges and all."

Gupta let Jackie field that one. "If it was just a matter of engineering, Ken, we could build it to be any size you want it to be. We could put you in what amounts to a washing machine or one of those carnival rotor things. But the problem is that a lot of people run into disorientation problems when they hit rotation over about two or three RPMs. For flights with small handpicked crews, you can ignore that problem to some extent. But our crew is much larger and is being selected for a much wider range of functions. Some of the members will be only marginally space-worthy."

"Tell me about it," Hathaway grunted, smiling rather crookedly. As an officer accustomed to the rigorous selection procedures of the military, he was still trying to get used to the much wider latitudes being applied to picking the *Nike*'s crew. No one who suffered from really critical medical problems was being accepted, true. But Ken felt the definition of "critical" had been stretched to the breaking point. There was one member of the crew who was sixty-three years old, and another who was at least forty pounds overweight.

Both of them, however, were also universally considered to be among the world's half-dozen top specialists at deciphering languages—and they were the only two who were willing to make the trip. So, aboard the *Nike* they would go, when the time came, whether the ship's captain was happy about it or not.

Jackie continued her explanation. "Now, we're not taking anyone who's a complete groundhog—they're going to have to be able to take acceleration and no gravity and all that—but Dr. Wu is firmly of the opinion that if we don't use slower rotation for our artificial gravity we will have problems with a significant portion of the crew. On the bright side, he's also firmly of the opinion that one-third gravity will be sufficient to maintain bone mass and prevent the other problems associated with long-term null-g situations. Ten years ago, we wouldn't have been able to be sure, but he says the most recent experiments have been consistent and clear and he's comfortable with a one-third gravity setting."

"Okay, okay. I agree, there's a lot to be said for a big ship. We should be able to make her pretty roomy, which God knows we're going to want. Still, even if I stop her from spinning, that's a hell of a lever arm I'm trying to turn with. Wouldn't want to break it off."

Jackie laughed. "Don't worry. The supports are designed to take anything you'll be able to dish out, even with the engines we're giving you. Here, take a look at our first main design model of *Nike*."

The 3-D imaging view lit up and, suspended in space, a model of Earth's first interplanetary ship materialized.

"Thank God for modern design technology," Ken mused, staring at the image before him.

"No kidding. Without state-of-the-art automatic modeling and simulation testing and expert design packages, plus actual years of in-orbit construction experience, we'd need years to reach a workable design."

Ken knew the truth of that. Many people didn't realize how difficult it was to design a new machine of any type. In the days before computers offered Computer Aided Design/Computer Assisted Modeling packages, design was a matter of physical construction of prototypes, testing of configurations, and iterations of these processes that could take years.

Even after the start of CAD/CAM in the late part of the twentieth century, the designs still had to be built multiple times and tested physically for a number of purposes. The computers back then simply weren't capable of modeling the full range of complex interactions the real world would throw at a device in a high-stress environment. That applied twice-over to spacecraft, which would have no safe harbor, no "side of the road" to pull over to, and which would be entering and exiting Earth's atmosphere under the greatest "environmental stress" imaginable. There was insufficient experience in the design of multiple types of space-suitable devices, in the assembly of spaceworthy habitats and vehicles, and related problems to permit the designers to make any useful assumptions.

In the past two decades, however, things had changed. Just as an old-style CAD/CAM package had permitted one person to equal the design production of a dozen or more old-style designers, modern CDM (Computer Design and Modeling) packages made one person trained in their use equal to a department of old CAD/CAM users, plus an entire testing lab. The modern CDM packages integrated modeling software equally advanced from its predecessors like MATLAB—capable of modeling and testing a designed part to a degree never before possible. Components were automatically checked for their capability to endure the stresses inherent in the design intent, while the designer continued the main design work based on broad conceptual designs. The specifics could be modified at will, and the entire design reworked to fit new specifications, all in a small fraction of the time earlier generations would have needed. With the firm empirical knowledge derived from thirty years of the International Space Station and its successors in orbit, such CDM packages now routinely produced new satellite designs, new living modules, and so on for space use in mere days—designs that worked.

Ken's hand reached out, tracing the ghostly outline of *Nike*. The main ship's body was one and a half times as long as her fully-opened span—about fourteen hundred feet. From slightly forward of the halfway point, a great wheellike ring encircled the ship, glittering with hints of both metal and transparent windows.

"That's the habitat area, of course," Ken said, pointing. "Do you realize how huge this thing is? I mean, good God, it must be nearly three thousand feet around!"

"We certainly do. And we'll all be discussing the logistics with everyone later. It can be done, though, with the priority that the government's put on it. The size is pretty much necessary, to give us room to operate in as well as to give us the gravity we need. We may be living in *Nike* for a year or more."

Jackie circled one area of the hab ring and a separate view zoomed up. As it did so, the ring seemed to fragment into multiple identical segments with the profile of a sort of squarish croissant pastry that was being slightly bent in the middle.

"The main structural elements here, and in the main body, are standardized units that lock together. The internals can be customized almost limitlessly around a set of standardized modular connection points. You'll have hallway sections that basically have nothing but empty space, and habitable sections that are in the center of a bunch of supplies like water which help with shielding. The same, as a rule, with labs, dining or rec areas—and all of them based on the same support and maintenance structure. The main body has its own standardized assembly parts. This allows us to crank out a lot of the ship from a relatively few assembly designs, then fill it up with what we need. The fuel areas, of course, are basically subdivided tanks."

Ken nodded, continuing his visual tour. To the rear of *Nike*, six great blocky assemblies, arranged in a pentagonal rosette with the sixth in the center, ended in the unmistakable vents of nuclear rockets. Front and back ended in smooth curves, the forward end coming to a graceful point. Colored areas indicated windows and sensor mountings.

"You've streamlined things along the front to back contours," Ken remarked absently. "Why? She's not going into atmosphere."

"Are you objecting to her appearance, Major?" Gupta's voice was slightly nettled. "Can an engineer not also have some appreciation of aesthetics?"

"Oh, no, no, not at all. She's beautiful. It's just . . ."

Gupta accepted Ken's backpedaling with a gracious nod. "Still, it cannot be argued that there is effort involved in such design and manufacture. Perhaps making the ship less streamlined would be cheaper and more swift. Yet, there are other considerations."

He nodded once more, to tell Jackie to continue. Gupta liked to distribute explanations among all his engineers, rather than be the sole source of information.

"Publicity," Jackie said. "This project is going to get rammed through no matter what people think, but the better we can make it look, the better it will go over. And the ship itself is going to be one of our biggest advertisements. We want everyone who's got a shred of imagination to be able to visualize themselves aboard her. And . . .

well, some of them would balk at a spaceship that looked like it was put together with an Erector set, even if it was perfectly safe and practical."

Ken looked up. "Believe me, I'm not complaining. That, my friends, is a *ship*. We've been sending out little rowboats up until now, but this time we are going in style. Does she have to be quite that large, and *can* she be that large—that is, can she be built that large fast enough?"

"Well, like we said, diameterwise the living quarters have to go out that far. The rest of the body is actually— relatively speaking— easy to build. It's going to be mostly storage space for equipment and consumables, and of course the main drive systems. Currently we have plans for one reusable orbiter/lander to be carried along, depending on our cargo capacity—we're going to want to bring a hell of a lot of instrumentation and analysis equipment to Phobos, so I don't know how much spare capacity we'll have."

She pointed to another part of the image. "The habitat ring will have some small attitude drives on it. The leverage advantage will allow you to adjust direction, or spin up the ship, efficiently from that point. But most of the drives, both main and secondary, will be on the main body. It's not something you can whip up in your garage, no, but the real complexities will be in designing the living spaces to hold the people, give us all lots of flexibility in what we see and do and where we can go during months in space. Even after we get to Phobos, it's going to be quite a while before we can live there. So I figure we've got to have living space that'll be comfortable for at least a year or two. Even with the rotation shuttle idea."

Ares' engineers, following up on their own designs, had

pointed out that once they got several return modules sitting on Mars, they could easily set them up to return to Phobos and then continue to Earth. That would make it possible to literally keep up a rotation of people on Phobos Base, with people spending a few months to a year on Phobos and then ending up back on Earth in a few months. The returning launches of supplies could be alternated with replacement personnel, keeping Phobos Base fully staffed.

This was a far preferable alternative than to have to use *Nike* to go back and forth. *Nike*'s vast power and resources were much more likely to be needed at Phobos. NASA had agreed with the basic concept, but added that the proper design approach should allow them to have reusable vessels which could act as orbital ferries. The first of these would be produced for *Nike* to take with her to Phobos; others would follow.

"Six engines? Are we talking about six like the prototype? Six million pounds of thrust?"

"And with a delta-vee of about twelve KPS."

"Holy . . ."

"That makes her mass ratio about four to one—3.89 and a smidge, actually," Jackie continued smugly. "Basically, if we take the trajectory we intend to, you'll be starting with about two KPS extra delta-vee. We wanted a lot of safety margin in there. Until we get safely established and the Ares processes kick in, there's no refueling for us."

"But why the hell so overpowered? I'd think a tenth that thrust would be enough. More than enough."

"Oh, undoubtedly." Jackie laughed. "It's overkill, sure—if our purpose was simply to move *Nike* from Point A to

Point B. But this is also another political maneuver to satisfy at least three different purposes."

"Three . . ." Ken studied the design. "I get it. The five exterior engines and reactors can be unshipped, can't they?"

"Give the man a cookie. Exactly. Take them all off and *Nike* still has one big-ass engine that's a bit of overkill, but a little extra power never hurt anyone. The NERVA fanboys and fangirls, of which I confess to being one, wanted to play around with possible nuclear rocket landers. With Mars' weaker gravity and no real environment to worry about, it's an ideal test location for things like that. More importantly, separate nuclear reactors of that size offer the chance to have a lot of power—and even redundant power—available on Mars or Phobos. It's also a showoff maneuver. *Nike* will be a powerful ship, and we can design the ship to take that level of stress."

"In addition," Gupta chimed in, "if one such engine is sufficient for a vessel such as *Nike*, consider: We have here the chance to get several such engines built and sent into space. But only now—*only* now. The political winds are fickle, are they not? If we already have the engines— nuclear engines, which are the sort most likely to cause fear and caution to delay the launch—it makes it much, *much* more likely that additional large interplanetary vessels will be built. Would it not be desirable to have *several Nikes*, *several* large research and exploration vessels, while we indeed have the chance?"

"I see. Very clever, Doctors. Build a really impressive ship and put in incentives to build more just like her." A broad grin spread across Ken's face as he contemplated the possibilities.

"Sooo . . . if I floor her, am I going to make everyone black out?"

Gupta's rich laugh rolled out. "Alas, I feel that this is *extremely* unlikely. We are using nuclear reactors, which have so very much shielding, and must have multiple redundancies and failsafes, and are taking so very, very many people and equipment . . . Were we using Orion, ah, then we could promise to give you accelerations of such magnitude. But I do not believe, even with our best efforts, that we could give you much more than a gravity or so, even when the vessel is nearly empty. Still, when you do, as you say, 'floor her,' I guarantee that it will be felt by all aboard, and felt for quite some time."

To a space engineer or astronaut, these were numbers that weren't seen in real life; they were fantasies. Oh, Ken knew that any science fiction buff could dream of a "reactionless" drive that allowed one to tool about the solar system as if driving a car. But in real life a "burn"— the firing of an engine—was measured in seconds, the change in speed in a few hundred meters per second, and the transition from one planet to another measured in many, many months.

To save weight and space, energy and thrust budgets were worked out to the greatest precision possible. A spacecraft was generally hoped to arrive at its destination with just a tiny bit of reserve left in its fuel tanks for final positioning, as every ounce of fuel taken to the destination was an ounce of payload wasted.

The "mass ratio" was perhaps the most telling statistic. It was the ratio of the mass of the fuelled ship compared to the mass of the "dry," or unfueled, ship. By way of comparison, a chemical-fueled ship with the same "delta-vee"—which meant the potential to change the velocity of the ship, the power to speed up and slow down, measured in absolute total speed change—of twelve kilometers per second would have a mass ratio of fourteen or more.

Colonel Hathaway was pretty sure his face now looked like that of a child at Christmas. Jackie and Gupta both smiled back at him.

"You seem to approve," Jackie said finally. "Then would you like to get into details? We've got a lot to cover in this overview."

"Yes, please!"

# Chapter 24

"It's been a few months, now. Still having no problems?" asked Hughes. The Director of the HIA leaned back a little further in his chair. Since the swivel chair was something of an antique, it creaked a bit ominously.

Madeline shook her head. "That would be putting it too optimistically. On the positive side, everyone associated with NASA for any length of time takes it for granted that someone will be assigned to do security. So having me show up was expected, even though I think they're still sometimes startled at the extent of my authority. But that's probably working in my favor. I have a pleasant personality and knowing they don't have to wade through the usual security-inquadruplicate suits them just fine."

Hughes smiled. " 'Pleasant personality.' So modest! Madeline, I believe I could drop you into a mob of devils in the Pit and you'd have them fawning all over you inside of a week. I assume the problems you're hinting at are coming from the non-NASA people. Of whom, unfortunately or not, we have a considerable influx. Many of them aren't even U.S. citizens, unlike the Ares crowd."

Madeline returned the smile. "Actually, the foreigners—so far, at least—are less cantankerous than some of the Ares people. A.J. Baker, in particular, has somewhat mystical notions concerning the spiritual essence of information."

"Ah, yes. The innate yearning for liberty possessed by data bytes. I've always wondered what Plato or Kant would make of that, from a philosophical standpoint."

"Plato would say that the actual information is a pale shadow of the Real Truth, so who cares if it gets suppressed? And if you can figure out two sentences of Kant, you're way ahead of me."

Hughes chuckled. "What about the other leading Ares figures? Friedet and Buckley, I mean."

"Friedet's practical enough. I've had no problems with him and don't foresee any. In any event, he won't be going on the voyage, so it almost doesn't matter. The real security problems will come after *Nike* reaches Phobos."

"True. That means Baker and Buckley. Baker is something of a given. I assume you've already figured out how to handle him if necessary."

Madeline nodded.

"And Buckley?"

"Joe?" Madeline considered. "He's less radical than his friend, but he's also the considered action sort. I think he's much more likely to follow along with rules so long as they don't violate some threshold of his, but if he decided to act would do so with a carefully worked-out plan. His apparent predisposition toward spectacular accidents appears to have made him more cautious when he does take action. Baker will act like the hero in a bad 'genius against wicked government' movie, which makes him easy to predict. I would actually be more concerned with Dr. Gupta."

"Due to foreign influence? Indian government ties?"

"Rather the opposite," Madeline contradicted. "He's certainly not someone who rejects his country of origin or its cultural traditions, but he seems firmly committed to his work and to the country he's become a naturalized citizen of since he emigrated. But his younger record is of a man with very techno-anarchistic leanings, and I do not think he has changed much in that regard. If he thinks information is being overcontrolled, he is not only capable of considering action, but as the chief designer and engineer of *Nike*, will be in a better position than just about anyone except possibly Baker to arrange information leakage without anyone catching him at it. Jackie Secord . . . I find her harder to read. Because of her longstanding and close association with Baker and Buckley, I have to keep her in mind as another potential risk. On the other hand, she's been with NASA for several years now and is accustomed to working under tight security restraints. And it's become clear to me that, at least on political issues, she doesn't share many of Baker and Buckley's attitudes. Especially Baker's."

"Do you think any of these people are security risks in general, or just risks of informational leaking?"

"Oh, the latter. I really don't think anyone on the project poses any sort of general security risk. The least enthusiastic people involved see it as a good job; the most enthusiastic are essentially religious about space travel.

The problem isn't patriotism; not even with Baker, notwithstanding his penchant for making outlandish remarks on the subject. It's simply that—like most scientists—they chafe at the idea of knowledge being locked up. That problem is compounded, of course, with those of the scientists who aren't even American to begin with."

"Yes, naturally. What about Glendale?"

Glendale's addition to the staff of the Project had been something of a surprise, given that Helen Sutter had taken the xenobiological slot. "I was concerned about him at first, sir. We have little leverage of any legal sort we could use on him, especially with his reputation and high visibility. But, fortunately, it looks like he will be remaining on Earth, which means that he won't get access to the raw data at all. He will probably continue to be the project's science liaison—a position he's admirably suited for and which allows him to directly participate without going into space. Which he may be physically questionable for, even if he wanted to go, simply because of his age."

"I trust *you* had no problems with qualifying?"

"No. My official tolerances are well within range. I did my own orbital this week, in fact."

"What sort of indications do we have on what we might expect out of the venture? Anything more concrete?"

"Several things. Some of the materials the aliens used are clearly superior to ours in a number of areas. We're trying some reverse engineering, but if it's microstructure more than composition that makes it work we probably won't be able to actually derive the formula by remote sensors. Baker is confident that we'll get better stealth and screening materials, at least. Possibly stronger alloys for some purposes, and a number of nano-technological hints which could be very useful. Their larger equipment he's not sure of. It will depend on how well we can study it without breaking something."

"What about the weapon?"

"The side arm was a disappointment. It isn't really all that different from our own weapons. But perhaps there are some things in which applying higher technology is mostly a waste."

She glanced through the notes showing in her VRD. "Overall, I would say that our original assessment holds. There is so much potential to learn in that base that we will almost certainly find *something* there which is of military significance. More likely many things."

The director sat up straight. "All right. All in all, everything sounds like it's going well, to me. Anything else to raise? Any other possible problems?"

"No, not that I can think of."

Madeline spent most of the flight back to Albuquerque staring out the window. Pointless, that, in a way, since night had already fallen and there was nothing much to see beyond the moon over cloud banks. But she found staring at nothing helped her focus her thoughts.

Doing her work while they were still here on Earth had been easy for her. It was going to be a lot harder in space. The most difficult task she'd face would be finding a method to arrange secure control as well as secure communications on a ship where there would be limited space, limited supplies, and every resource supposedly accounted for. That was going to require a number of tactics, all of which carried some element of risk.

She wasn't, of course, concerned about physical danger. Her mission wasn't likely to run into that level of threat. Even if it did, she had no doubt she could handle the matter. She was simply concerned at the risk of failure itself.

At first, she had thought it might turn out to be simple. The initial crew had all been American and, as such, subject to American laws. More important, in practice, was that half of them were military and the other half were civilians long accustomed to working in NASA's normal high-security environment. Unfortunately, with *Nike* being drastically enlarged, various political forces both at home and abroad had seen the opportunity to either enhance the international reputation of the United States or take advantage of it. Or both, for that matter.

Most of the expansion had involved bringing in scientists who were not in the least accustomed to considering security as an aspect of their work—a paleontologist, two linguists, several planetologists, and so on and so forth. Even many of the engineers added had been, from a NASA standpoint, outsiders. The military component of the crew was now fairly small—probably not more than one-fifth, when all was settled. Fortunately, those would all be Americans except for the Australian pilot, Bruce Irwin.

To make the situation still more difficult, a number of slots on the crew, about thirty percent, had been allotted to scientists or engineers to be selected from other countries. These people, obviously, were *not* subject to following the United States' rules and procedures with respect to security. Some of them, in fact, would be doing their level best to send as much information as possible back home.

That was only to be expected. But it made it impossible to cover the whole project with a blanket of secrecy. All the more so because these foreign nationals were, as a rule, well-acquainted with their colleagues from America. All of them would expect to carry on long, involved, and detailed conversations about anything and everything during the voyage and the later exploration.

Madeline had to find a way that she, personally, could control the communications from *Nike*—even in the face of considerable argument or resistance from other members of the crew. The worst part, she realized—with a sensation not far from shock—was that she didn't *want* to get into a quarrel. The problem was that these people weren't terrorists, spies, criminals—the sort that she usually dealt with. These people were astronauts and scientists and engineers, all of them trying to do their best. Their only potential failing was in a belief in a better world than really existed; one where you really *could* just tell everyone anything and there would be no political problems. A world where lunatic extremists wouldn't take advantage of new methods of destruction and blow people apart to make a statement.

But there *were* people like that. She almost shivered, remembering. Madeline knew that many of the HIA's other agents wondered— though they never asked—why she was so fanatical about her firearms and martial arts training, when her usual tactics on assignments were designed to minimize the chance of violence. A few of them probably guessed; and Director Hughes knew, of course.

She wasn't arming herself against the future, but against the past. She remembered being helpless and terrified.

She remembered being subject to the whims of someone powerful, capricious, and insane. She made herself dangerous to keep the nightmares at bay. Now, sometimes, in her dreams, when he came back, she wasn't a helpless child any more, and she could fight. But usually the nightmare only really ended when the helicopters landed and the gunshots went off, and the soldiers came and made her safe.

She looked at her reflection in the airplane window, suddenly-haunted eyes staring back. Madeline shook her head and forced the grim past away. She was no longer ruled by that, and her job was to stop things like it from ever happening again.

And maybe, if she was lucky, she wouldn't have to do anything drastic. Hopefully, the critical people would understand what she had to do, or at least go along with it. She knew she was good at being persuasive. That was the only thing, besides her attractive appearance, that she'd inherited from her biological parents.

The minute the plane taxied up to the gate, Madeline felt more cheerful. Whatever problems she'd run into, the truth was that she *liked* this assignment. Even, with a few exceptions, liked all the people she worked with.

Early the next morning, as was her usual practice, Madeline headed for the gym. To her surprise, A.J. was there already. While he was clearly a man in good condition, she'd figured he usually either worked out in his own rooms or at odd hours of the day. She'd never actually *seen* him doing anything requiring physical effort greater than lifting a bottle of soda.

Today, A.J. was dressed in a gi and running through katas. Off to the side, the physical trainer was watching with a well-educated eye. Sergeant Skonicki was also the NASA installation's martial arts expert.

While Madeline warmed up, she studied the blond imaging specialist's movements. His file had mentioned that he did some aikido and some Shotokan karate, although apparently he hadn't been attending formal classes in some years.

He was quite good, she thought. The smoothness of his movements, the precision of the strikes, blocks, and counters, were something a novice, or even someone of intermediate skill, wouldn't be able to emulate. He wasn't a true master, but the source of his evenly-muscled build was now evident.

A.J. finally noticed her watching him. "Hey, Madeline. What's up?"

"Just coming in for my own exercise. Got to keep in shape."

To his slight credit, A.J. managed to restrain some comment involving shapes. While Madeline was skeptical of classifying people into types, she couldn't help doing so in some cases. A.J. was clearly the type of young man easily distracted by pretty women. True, that was a large class of males, but A.J. was of the subclass "geek" which meant that he was perfectly safe for the woman to be around, aside from the annoyance factor. And, as a rule, could be easily manipulated into following said woman's directions.

*Sometimes it's just too easy,* she thought wryly. A.J. wasn't the type of man whom she found attractive. But keeping him distracted played perfectly into her plans.

She did feel slightly sorry for him, but not much. There were at least two other women on the *Nike* project who evidently *did* think he was their type, and he didn't appear blind to them either. So any damage to his ego would be temporary.

"You into the martial arts, too?" he asked.

"For a few years now, yes. Care to do some sparring?"

"Sure."

At that point, Joe and Helen entered. Joe had recovered quickly from his misadventures in *Chinook*, and was getting back up to his normal form. Seeing A.J. and Madeline facing off, he sighed. "A.J., I see you've still got it all wrong. The expression 'hit on the girls' is not supposed to be taken literally."

"Oh. I knew I kept confusing things." A.J. turned to Sergeant Skonicki. "You want to call it, Stash?"

"Sure." He cocked his head, considering. "Okay. Madeline, you're going to be *aka*; A.J., you are *shiro*. I'll be using Shotokan rules, sorta—I mean, we don't have an official setup here. That okay, Madeline?"

"I can live with it. What about throws and such?"

"I'll count those as full points, if either of you gets one. Try to avoid rude blows, but you can take whatever targets you think you see; we won't force you to just hit the chest. First to three points wins. We set?"

Skonicki waited for both to acknowledge him. "Okay. Enter the ring area, please. Bow to the judge. Bow to each other. Ready . . . *Hajime!*"

Maddie sidestepped, watching A.J. critically. He was smooth, but cautious. He wasn't stupid. He didn't come charging in thinking that his size would automatically be an advantage. It would be, used correctly, but men against smaller women often made the mistake of using it incorrectly.

A.J. was waiting for her to move. She had to come past his reach, which was quite noticeably greater than hers, in order to get to him. She stepped up and tried several combinations, but A.J. blocked and countered quite efficiently, nearly nailing her once.

Time for a different approach. If he was thinking in Shotokan mode, especially Kumite . . .

Suddenly Madeline dropped to the floor, extending her body outward and sweeping A.J.'s legs completely out from under him. "*Whoa!*" she heard Helen say involuntarily.

A.J. fell poorly, having been caught completely off-guard. She rolled and hit him with a (checked) elbow smash before he could gather his wits.

"*Yame! Aka*, first point!" Skonicki called out. "She suckered you on that one, A.J."

The imaging whiz nodded, getting to his feet. "She sure did."

The two bowed to each other again. "*Hajime!*"

This time A.J. came in for the attack, starting with a kick-punch kick combination. Madeline blocked them easily enough, but when she tried to turn the second kick into a catch-and-throw found that A.J. had anticipated the move and barely evaded having her head kicked.

She was getting his measure, now. One advantage she did *not* enjoy was chivalry. A.J. might be easily distracted by her good looks normally, but in the ring he apparently didn't care who you were or what you looked like. He wasn't pulling his punches any more than he had to, so to speak.

Fair enough. She spent the next few moments surviving a barrage of attacks, measuring his patterns. Then she slipped inside his guard and punched hard.

The result was that she found herself flipped around and landing hard despite a reflexive tuck and roll, and heard *Yame!* called out. "Ring out! *Shiro*, point!"

Some schools didn't do points for ring-outs, but she wasn't going to argue. In real life, if you could take control of your opponent enough to arrange a ring-out, you could probably arrange something more painful.

Once more they faced off. "One point all. *Hajime!*"

A.J. scored again, this time with a kick that concluded a five-attack string which was designed to trick the opponent into thinking it was a four-attack string. The impact staggered her back but didn't hurt much. A.J. clearly didn't mean to hurt anyone, and had good control.

The next face-off was critical. If A.J. scored again, he'd win. Madeline focused carefully this time, and the next flurry of blows ended when her high side kick rapped A.J. (gently) in the head.

"Last point. Good fight so far, people, let's have a good finish. *Hajime!*"

By then, they had gathered something of an audience. Ken Hathaway had come into the gym, along with half a dozen other people.

Madeline was pleased. *Perfect. I won't have to spread the story myself.*

The two combatants circled each other. Madeline knew precisely how skilled A.J. was now, and he'd definitely gotten a healthy respect for her at this point. Exploratory jabs and kicks, attempts at throws and holds, nothing quite getting through.

All right, time to finish this.

She let a slight opening show, let A.J. take it and

then dropped down to take out his legs with a different move.

But this time A.J. wasn't having any of that and his legs weren't there; one of them was in fact trying to deliver a foot to her face. She rolled gracefully away and blocked another kick and punch as she came to her feet, then drove in on the attack.

Once more the smooth, circular motion of aikido sent her sailing gracefully out of the ring.

"Ring out! *Shiro*, victory!"

A.J. and Maddie exchanged bows. He grinned at her. "That was a hell of a match. We have to do that again sometime!" His breathing was heavy and a slight whistling tone could be heard, but he wasn't exhausted yet. Despite the damage to his lungs, the man was in such good physical shape that he could maintain even something this strenuous for a fair period of time. A few more minutes of it, of course, would start taking a real toll.

"Definitely. I'll have to practice more, though. I didn't see that last one coming."

"Well, I am considered pretty fast. Still, that move relies on you coming in to me. You can avoid it if you watch carefully."

"I certainly will. You won't get me the same way twice."

A.J. laughed. "I wouldn't expect to."

"Well, I'd better get to my real exercises," Maddie said, sighing. "This was good, but I have to run through the boring routine."

Sergeant Skonicki came over to help her set up the weights. "Nice dive," he murmured.

"Top security," she murmured back. "Need to know—and you don't."

Skonicki chuckled. "See no evil, hear no evil, speak no evil, that's me. Though I would enjoy being there if he ever discovers what's what."

She shook her head. "Hopefully, this will all be a waste of effort."

# Chapter 25

"Is this really going to work, Dr. Friedet?"

The head of Ares Project shrugged. "It basically *has* to work, General Deiderichs. We're doing—by far—the largest construction project in space anyone's attempted. Without factories operating out there, we have to throw everything *up* there, and that's not an easy task. In fact, it's exceedingly hard, which is the reason that both NASA and Ares exist. In the past twenty years, we've added reusable first-stage heavy-lift vehicles and upped the cargo capacity of the shuttles. But the fact is that even if we ignore the fuel, we are trying to assemble a ship in orbit that masses two thousand tons. Fueled, *Nike* will mass nearly four times that. It's immense, General. So we need all the tricks we can get in order to get that much stuff into assembly orbit in time to meet your deadlines."

General Deiderichs nodded reluctantly. The schedule Glenn Friedet presented had been generated by Ares and

NASA's engineers working together to find a way to move that immense mass of "stuff" into space in as short a time as possible. Deiderichs found it a bit bemusing. Eight thousand tons was absolutely nothing on an Earthbound scale; freight trains carried that much. But then, trains could use seventy cars or more for a single trip. The situation for space was more like having to expend the same time, effort and money the railroads did per train—more, actually—except *your* trains could only move one boxcar load at a time.

"Basically," Joe added, "we're taking advantage of the one thing we have plenty of now. Money. We're preempting everything everyone else has even in other countries by paying penalty fees. Sometimes huge fees. We've got our own scramlaunchers, a few of the Shuttle-C mods, Europe's EUROLaunch-4, and Japan and China's launch capacity too. We're negotiating with India now, though they're not going to be able to add that much. Still, every little bit helps. Fortunately, pretty much everyone has reusable first-stage stuff these days, however they do it. So if you're willing to spend money like water, you can get respectable turnaround times."

"If I read this right, we're looking at something like eighty to a hundred flights." The general shook his head. "The logistics will be a nightmare."

"General, you knew this was going to get ugly when we started," Friedet said. "That limitation comes from the payload capacity on each ship. Even the big ones only manage to approach two hundred tons at a shot—and none of them actually reach that number. The average is more like one hundred and forty tons per launch."

Joe rubbed his chin. "The actual limitation is size, more

than mass. It'd be impossible to do this in any reasonable time if we were still limited to, say, things the size of the old Space Shuttle cargo bay. We'd have to send up some things in eight or ten separate pieces that would have to be put together, instead of two or three pieces. Some of our scramlaunchers can manage dimensions more than twice that now, which makes it—barely—doable, if we're really smart about what we ship so that we take maximum advantage of the payload capacity on each launch, and if we are ready to start assembling as soon as stuff gets up there."

"Still. That's an average of almost two launches per week. And assembling it will . . ." Deiderichs waved his hands, but Joe knew what he meant.

"Remote drones will be doing a lot of the assembly," Joe pointed out, "supervised on the ground and checked in orbit by experts. With A.J. and others helping to design the software that helps coordinate work like that— detecting the targets, translating the groundhog controller's directions into equivalents for space engineering, monitoring the assembly so that the drones can tell *before* they do something disastrous, projecting the feedback to the controllers so that they don't notice the time lag much, and so on—we can effectively have a far larger team in space. The first loads, of course, will be the manipulator drones."

Deiderichs winced. "I knew the idea was batted around for years, but we've only started to have good results with it, and there are so many debates about the designs. Are you going to get enough reliable drones for this kind of work?"

Ken Hathaway's face showed an interesting mixture of

chagrin and pride. "Baker's Faeries have been performing amazingly well in far worse, less controlled conditions, including their manipulative capabilities—which I thought were such a waste when he designed them. We're going with modified Faerie designs for a lot of the construction drones. Not so many sensors and other redundancies that were absolutely necessary for things operating a hundred million miles off, more power, a bit bulkier, stronger manipulators and additional tool units to perform the work. But they're based on designs that have now proven themselves under fire—even when abused to near destruction—and that makes it possible for us to produce quite a few of them fast. We figure another month and a half and we'll be starting real construction, now that we have a nucleus of a space dry dock already up there."

"Modern design approaches and our testing of materials helps out too," Friedet pointed out. "For many of the internal components which aren't major structural load-bearing elements, we've developed flexible molding approaches. What that means is that we can send up a few mold forms and tanks of solidifying foam material and create a whole bunch of things like interior partitions and furniture—without having to ship the things up, pack them with extra space, and all that."

General Deiderichs pursed his lips as he examined the schedule again. "I still don't see any way we'll make the original deadline."

"Probably not," conceded Joe. "But given that under normal circumstances this would've been something like a ten-year effort, falling behind by about three to five months isn't something to gripe about. You *have* to allow for some problems, some wiggle room, some testing and reworking. Once *Nike* launches, everyone on it is absolutely and one hundred percent dependent on everything in her working right. Even with redundancy. I know *you* understand this, General, but I'm not sure how clear it is to other people. You might be old enough to remember the *Columbia* disaster?"

Deiderichs nodded. "Yes. I remember it quite vividly."

"I don't remember it personally, but if you read the stuff from around that time, there were so many people trying to argue that they should have "done something"— gone to the International Space Station and waited for rescue, stayed in orbit until someone could get there, fixed the ship somehow, and so on. These people just didn't grasp that it wasn't like someone getting stranded on a mountain top or out at sea. To them, the ISS was in space, the shuttle was in space, so obviously the shuttle should be able to just go over to the ISS and wait for rescue. We know that it's not like that—that the *Columbia* simply, physically, could not *reach* the ISS from that orbit. All the other so-called solutions were just as impossible or impractical. I don't know if some of our enthusiastic funders grasp that once *Nike* is under way, there will be *nothing* man-made that can catch her, and absolutely no way for anyone to help if something goes wrong."

"You may well be right. I'll do my best to convey that to the President and the Cabinet when I present the current plans. Personally, I agree with everything you say. Three months off is nothing at all compared to what we're asking you to do. But I'm still going to have to make excuses to the guys who are writing all the checks, and some of them are peeved enough that they're being made to support this at all."

"And I have to go back to Gupta and Baker," Hathaway said, "and let them know if they should start or not. And remember what Gupta's going to say if the answer is 'wait.' "

"I do indeed. And I sympathize, Major Hathaway. Dr. Gupta is undoubtedly the right choice for the job, but I do not envy anyone trying to give him bad news." The general frowned for a moment. "Tell them to proceed with designs, but to order no actual construction until I get back with the authorization. Technically, I shouldn't even allow them to begin design work, but I'm willing to take that much on my own responsibility."

"I'll try to make them understand that, General," Hathaway said.

"And I'll get right to it." The general stood up. Much as he hated having to shuttle back and forth to Washington, the President and his top people preferred in-person meetings on matters of importance, despite all the technological advances in remote communication. And if he was going to be conveying news of mixed impact, he definitely wanted to be there physically.

He stopped a moment. "Oh, yes, I almost forgot." He signed a paper that had been lying on his desk, then placed it in its envelope. "Dr. Buckley, would you do me a favor and deliver this? Thank you." He strode out of the office.

Joe looked down at the envelope. "What . . .? Ken, it's addressed to you. Why the hell did he give it to me?"

Hathaway stared at the envelope as though it was a viper. "I think I know. *Damn.*"

"What?"

"The final selection for the command crew of *Nike* was being made sometime this week. You know General Steve

Goldman was campaigning hard for it. He's got space experience too, and a lot of connections."

"Oh. And Deiderichs didn't want to be here when you found out."

"Yeah." Hathaway sighed. "Well, might as well get it over with."

He took the envelope from Joe, opened it, and read:

"Kenneth B. Hathaway, Colonel . . . yadda . . . You are hereby informed that you have been . . ."

He trailed off, and then suddenly bellowed: "COMMANDING OFFICER OF THE UNITED STATES INTERPLANETARY SPACECRAFT *NIKE*!"

"Congratulations, you dreaming son of a bitch!" came Deiderichs' voice from the other side of the door, which opened to reveal the general grinning at them. He came over and shook Hathaway's hand, which seemed somewhat limp with shock. "Now get your team to finish building it. Hold on, though."

He reached into his desk. "Goldman was right about one thing. You do need the rank to command a mission as important as this one." He opened the case, revealing different emblems than those currently on Hathaway's uniform. "Congratulations again, Brigadier General Hathaway."

Hathaway was clearly having trouble keeping his voice under control. His eyes looked suspiciously shiny.

"I would have sworn they wanted Goldman," he said huskily.

Deiderichs looked at him for a moment, then nodded. "At first, they did—and so did I. But that was before I got here and had a chance to see the situation. I know better than to take a team with a commander they already listen to and trust, and replace him just because it might be politically expedient. If I went and got someone else, they'd have to spend a year just building the same rapport you have with your team now. If they can build one at all. Just do me a favor and prove that I made the right decision."

"Sir!" Hathaway saluted. The general returned the salute, nodded to the others, and walked out the door.

Ken finally came out of his daze. "I am going to go tell Gupta and A.J. and then I am going to go get a pass, and then I am going to go party like I have never partied before! And you're all invited!"

# Chapter 26

Helen glanced away from the handwaving explanation A.J. was giving, over to the nearby table where voices were rising angrily.

A.J. followed her gaze. One of the scientists—Dr. Mayhew, was it? Linguistics, anyway—was pointing to something, probably an image only she and her opponent in the debate could see. He was another linguist, a much older man by the name of . . .

A.J. keyed in a quick query and the VRD answered him.

*Right. Rich Skibow.* Ken's party was a major success, and it sounded like these two had been knocking back a few drinks before they got into their learned argument. As he hadn't been paying attention, he wasn't clear on what they were arguing about, but he could see that it was getting pretty heated.

And very annoying, he suddenly realized, as Helen

abruptly left the table to join the arguing linguists. He'd been enjoying her company very much, especially after their other dinner companions had deserted them at least temporarily for the sake of the dance floor. And now these loudmouthed specialists had to go and interrupt.

Not one to yield the battlefield, he followed Helen over.

"—identical symbols, I tell you!"

"No, no, no, not identical at all. Spacing over here, and—"

"Excuse me."

Rich Skibow and Jane Mayhew looked up irritably, but their expressions moderated when they saw Helen.

"Who—oh, Dr. Sutter."

Mayhew's face showed a sudden awareness of how loud they'd been getting. She pushed her prematurely graying brown hair out of her face with an embarrassed gesture. "I'm sorry. We didn't mean to disturb—"

"No problem at all. I heard part of the debate, and thought I might be able to help."

The two looked at each other doubtfully. A.J. could practically read their thoughts. *What would a paleontologist know about linguistics?*

Dr. Skibow shrugged. "Okay. Take a look."

The slender academic put his portable in the center of the table and it projected several images of various inscriptions found around the alien base on Phobos.

"Obviously, we don't have a lot to work with, but the aliens do seem to have used images something like we do. We've been trying to make some guesses as to meanings from location, image context, and things like that, and assigning tentative roles to various features seen in the writing. For instance, like us they seem to use spacing to separate groupings which may be words, sentences, or paragraphs. Which of those it is, however, is hard to know without having some idea of what the things are trying to say."

"Though at the moment we think the groups we see commonly separated are probably words," Mayhew added. "It seems unlikely you're going to put what amounts to three or four pages of text on things that we think are hallway signs, so these spaced groupings along the curves are probably words."

"The problem is that we've been coming across what looks like the same word used in situations that make no sense for the vague meaning we thought it might have."

Helen and A.J. studied the images for a while. The pictures were actually derived representations, cleaned out and with the "letters" and all other features outlined and marked up to make them clear. Helen tilted her head slightly as she gazed at the enigmatic symbols, then activated her own portable and put on her VRD. Soon thereafter, she brought up her own display, which gave her the same areas but from A.J.'s actual images, just enhanced slightly for better viewing.

"Take a look carefully at these now," she said. "Especially look at the different versions of the word."

At first no one said anything. A.J. didn't expect to notice anything significant, but the two linguists looked puzzled too.

Then, suddenly, Dr. Mayhew sat up straighter, a startled look on her face. "Rich, maybe she's onto something! Look. Here and here; and here and here."

A.J. followed her indications, and then it dawned on him. *Colors.* They'd often remarked on how even after all this time they could see colors on some things. The black and gold and other colors in the various texts found were perhaps the most clear-cut examples.

Dr. Skibow nodded. "Yes . . . that could be it. They may be using color as a modal change or something like it. How did you think of it, Dr. Sutter?"

"I recalled some of our original speculation, and it fit with the basic anatomical analysis I've been doing. Bemmie has a number of features roughly analogous to our cephalopods. In other ways, of course, his structure is more analogous to something like a crab. But one thing I'm sure of is that he evolved relatively recently from a water-dwelling species. His body shape is still awkward for land travel. In that respect, the way he's built reminds me of primitive amphibians—given that he started from a completely different *Bauplan*."

Seeing the frowns, she explained: " '*Bauplan*' means basic body shape. 'Body plan,' if you will. Bemmie's loco-motion must have involved a combination of slithering on his belly and 'walking' with his elbows to support his front weight. Then there's the skin structure we were looking at, right, A.J.?"

"Yeah—okay, yeah, I see. We've been finding a lot of skin cells that looked kinda funny for normal skin, but they could be for color control—chromatophores."

"It's been well established that squids and cuttlefish often use shifts in color to communicate. So I wondered if the color element was being neglected, which it was."

"Hmmm . . . Well, it does seem to divide things up more neatly," Skibow admitted. "But there still seem to be problems. Some things just don't seem to space prop-erly."

A.J. looked at the image he was indicating. It was one of the illustrated plates they'd found in the control room. He remembered that particular one rather clearly, because he'd been trying to analyze its structure.

"I think I can solve that. Give me a color that isn't being used, as far as you know, in any of the things you've seen so far."

Skibow and Mayhew looked at her other. "Pink," she suggested. Skibow nodded his agreement.

"Right. Pink it is." A.J. inserted *pink* into the color table, bound the variable, then transmitted to Helen's portable. "How about that?"

The two linguists stared at the new image. In some places, right where they were having difficulty resolving the relationship of the symbols, *new* symbols had suddenly appeared. Bright pink, but otherwise looking like many of the other symbols.

"Where the bloody hell did those come from?" Mayhew demanded. "Sure, that looks like it might make sense, but we can't just pull stuff out of our arses in order to make it work."

A.J. glanced at Helen. "Watson, you know my methods. I simply started with your own deduction."

Helen was thoughtful for a moment. "Elementary, my dear Holmes. We have no reason to think that Bemmie saw in precisely the same spectrum that we do. Ergo, you checked for symbols visible in something other than what *we* call 'visible light.' "

"Excellent, Watson, excellent. In point of fact, they appear to have seen somewhat higher into the spectrum than we do. That stuff's highly visible in the near-UV, but darn near invisible even at close inspection in visible."

He made a bow to the two and took Helen's arm. "I trust this resolves your little conundrum. We're going back to our table."

As they left, Skibow and Mayhew were once more discussing the symbols, but much more quietly and with no animosity.

After Helen and A.J. resumed their seats at their own table, she smiled at him. "That was very nice teamwork, A.J."

"Well, I had to do *something*. You were solving the whole problem on your own and that would really hurt my rep as the resident genius. It's really not fair anyway, that you should have all the brains *and* all the looks too."

She laughed quietly. "Yeah, right. Madeline and Jackie aren't losing any sleep over my competition in that arena, I assure you."

"That's bullshit, Helen!" A.J. blurted out, before he could think. "They probably aren't losing any sleep over it, sure. But that's just because they aren't playing in the same league you are."

The look she gave him brought home the fact there'd been a hell of a lot more emphasis in that line than he originally meant to put in. He was suddenly aware that his face felt very hot, but he managed to keep from looking away.

"I mean it," he said quietly. Then, not being able to help himself, swallowed.

Her expression was serious; at least she didn't think he was being funny. A.J. damned the lights in the place, or rather the lack thereof. He couldn't tell if she looked, maybe, like she was blushing too.

"A.J., are you making a pass at me?" she asked, just as quietly as he'd spoken.

His first impulse was to toss out his usual cavalier remark. Something inside him grabbed that impulse, slammed it to the ground, and beat it desperately into unconsciousness.

He dropped his gaze to the table, then looked back up. "Yes. Damn, yes. I . . . Okay, I know, I'm loudmouthed and arrogant and way too young for you and I'm sure if you wanted to have anything to do with me that way you'd have let me know a long time ago and Joe would probably have been a better choice if you wanted someone around my age and I'm sure there's plenty of other guys waiting in line anyhow but yes, I am, and I think you're gorgeous, did even when I first met you, but you're a lot more than gorgeous, you have like ten times the class of everyone else and . . ."

He was babbling. Babbling, babbling, babbling.

He clamped his mouth shut. Then, cleared his throat and said: "Anyway. Yes."

Instead of laughing, like he expected, Helen . . .

She *was* blushing. Even the dim lighting couldn't disguise it. The color in her cheeks made her look even more beautiful than usual.

Helen cleared her own throat. "A.J. . . ." she began, then stopped and looked aside. A rueful little smile came to her face. "I don't actually know what to say. How odd. I'm *never* at a loss for words."

He took a deep breath and squashed the part of his mind that had gone runaway on him. "You don't have to say anything, Helen. I know how stupid that was. You don't have to spare my feelings." He started to rise. "Look, I'll go—"

Her slender, tanned hand locked around his wrist and pulled him back down.

"Oh no, you don't, Mr. Baker." Her voice was a soft growl. Nothing at all like the even tone he was used to hearing.

"A.J., I don't . . ." She took a deep, slow breath. "Oh, baloney. I know exactly what to say. The truth is that I've always found you extremely attractive. It's just that I figured the age gap made for an insuperable barrier and so I shoved the notion out of my mind. I've kept it in a box under a tight lid for . . . what's it been? Two and half years, now."

Throughout, she'd still been looking aside. Now, her eyes came to meet his directly.

"I take it you *don't* find my age a problem?"

He started to make a wisecrack, but the same drill sergeant portion of his brain made the smartass do two thousand pushups in. . .

One second.

"No. Actually, it's . . . Well, to be honest, I think it's part of the attraction."

Seeing her cocked eyebrow, he sighed. "Look, Helen, I'm not stupid. I know I often act like a jerk. I don't even mean to, really. Well, not most of the time, anyway. It's just . . . I don't know. Defense mechanism. Whatever. But it never seems to bother you and I figured out a long time ago that's because you're old enough that you just don't care about stuff like that any more. If you ever did at all. So I can relax around you in a way that I almost never can around women my own age, unless they're just good buddies like Jackie."

He swallowed again. "And that's important to me. The thing is, no matter how much I act like the opposite— and it's mostly all talk—the truth is that I'm not a very casual person at all. No matter how I act. Not really about anything, and sure as hell not about, uh, well . . ."

"Sex. Love. Romance." The cool, relaxed, mature smile that A.J. treasured came to her face. "In whatever order," she added, waving her other hand breezily. Her right hand was still clamped around A.J.'s wrist.

"What the hell," she said, suddenly rising to her feet and half-dragging A.J. up from his chair. "Let's start with sex. And we'll see where it goes from there."

Their departure from the room did not go unnoticed. Joe and Jackie had followed the progress of the discussion between A.J. and Helen almost from the moment it began. They were sitting too far away to have heard any of the words. But the facial expressions and body language had made the subject matter obvious enough—even before Helen more or less hauled A.J. away. Not that he seemed in the least unwilling.

Joe drained his glass and set it down on the table with a solid *thunk*. "Well. It's about time, if anybody asks me."

For her part, Jackie bestowed a triumphant grin upon the other people at the table. "See?" she demanded. "I *told* you he wasn't my boyfriend."

# Chapter 27

Dr. Glendale, is it true that you will not be going on *Nike* yourself?"

"Dr. Glendale, is this mission really necessary?"

"Dr. Glendale, please tell us about the latest results! I understand progress is being made in translating the aliens' language!"

"Dr. Glendale—"

He raised his hands, flashing the smile he knew worked so well on camera. "Please, one at a time. This isn't my first press conference, even for this particular mission, and I know for sure it isn't yours."

"However," said Paul Morgan, "this *is* the first conference since any of the more concrete plans for *Nike* and her crew have been released. NASA's usually much more forthcoming than this, Doctor."

Morgan was the senior news correspondent present. There'd be no point in trying to evade him, even if Glendale wanted to.

"True enough, Paul. And please, everyone, call me Nick or Nicholas. I've been 'Doctor Glendaled' too much lately."

A patter of chuckles rippled through the large group of reporters.

"I know that all of you, especially the long-time space correspondents, are used to getting much better treatment. But there are all sorts of considerations ranging from national security to simple logistics that are involved here. To be frank, even I'm being kept busy enough that it's a bit of a stretch to take time and give interviews. And I'm by far the most superfluous person here."

He waved them into their chairs with a practiced gesture. "Before we go any further, though, would you please take your seats? Trying to answer questions from a mob of people standing around me is too much like being grilled by the police. I think. I've never actually been grilled by the police. But I am an expert on ancient predators. The velociraptors were pack hunters, you know. Surrounded their prey and tore them to shreds. Horrible business. Blood and guts everywhere."

That drew a louder round of chuckles, and the reporters started sitting down. Glendale was quite aware of his ability to "work" a group of people and guide them along the course he needed them to take, and was equally aware that this talent was one of the reasons he was now being the "front man" for the *Nike* project.

"Doc . . . er, Nicholas, tell me straight out: is this mission really necessary? And if it is, is the sheer *scale* of it necessary?" That came from Jake McNeil, a reporter for the generally antispace AccuNews Network.

"Jake, such a hard-hitting question right out of the gate?

Aren't you supposed to soften me up first?" Smiling, Glendale shook his head. "Why don't we get a bit more specific than that. Bring up the points of the mission that actually bother you—or, I suppose, bother your viewers, to be more accurate."

Privately, he doubted that the viewers of any given network thought any more alike than any other. But it was a common enough conceit that he'd use it as convenient.

"All right. We're getting tons of data already from Mr. Baker's probes. Why do we need to risk fifty people— fifty of our very best people, from all over the world—just to do what the probes can do perfectly well by themselves?"

"Unfortunately, Jake, your last clause makes an assumption I'm not willing to grant you. In fact, it's patently untrue. The probes are simply too limited. They're physically too small; unintelligent by themselves; limited in their equipment; and, most of all, incapable of adjusting themselves to new situations the way a human being can as a matter of course. A four-year-old child—for that matter, a toddler— can figure out in a split second how to get around an obstacle that will completely stump an automated probe if it's not specifically programmed to deal with it. And it can then take hours—*days*—before we can satisfactorily reprogram it from a distance.

"Certainly we could send more automated probes, but even today we simply do not have automated devices capable of the work that human beings can do in person. People like Helen Sutter and myself have careers for a reason, you know. It's simply not possible for an automated machine, even here on Earth, to perform a

paleontological excavation, or to unearth an ancient artifact without damaging it. We use such tools, but in the
end, it's still down to what we as human beings can manage to do. And this mission is the single greatest event in
the history of the human race, in my opinion. We are performing what amounts to both a paleontological and an
archaeological dig of an utterly unique character. We
*cannot* afford to screw this one up, to put it bluntly. We
need living, intelligent people on the spot, and we need
them to be experts in many fields. Why? Because we
haven't the faintest idea of what we might turn up while
exploring what appears to be a truly immense installation."

"Are you saying," Paul Morgan asked, "that the alien
base is even larger than you originally thought?"

"Yes, Paul. Another corridor was found behind one of
the remaining doors being investigated, and some of Mr.
Baker's sensor work shows indications of . . . Well, a lot
more 'stuff' for us to find. Our current thinking is that
this base is the size of a moderately large military
installation—which means that even with fifty people on
site it could take years to explore thoroughly. Probably
*will*, I should say, if we take any care at all in our investigations."

"Years?" Michelle Wright of MSNBC spoke up. "Is that
possible to do, Nicholas?"

"Oh, yes. We are already in the process of devising a
schedule of resupply and replacement flights. We should
be able to keep the Phobos operation supplied for several years, at least. That includes people being shuttled
to and from the Earth."

"This brings us back to the question of necessity and
potential waste, Nick," Jake said. "All right, I'll swallow

that you've got to have people on-site. I agree that no machine can do as good a job as a person in any situation that requires flexibility. But look at the *size* of *Nike* now. I'm not even sure we *can* build something that huge in space, let alone that we should."

"She is pretty large, I'll grant you—about four hundred and thirty meters long, and the habitat ring is almost three hundred meters across. But the diameter of that habitat ring is necessary."

"Why?"

Glendale wondered if McNeil was really that ignorant of basic scientific concepts. But whether or not he was, the question served nicely to make an explanation to the general public that wouldn't sound patronizing.

"You all understand, I'm sure, that we can't send people on such a months-long voyage through space under weightlessness." He waited just long enough for a little wave of nods from about half the reporters present. "People did not evolve in null-gravity or micro-gravity conditions. We need a certain amount of gravity to keep our bone structure from deteriorating, and prevent all the other problems that years of research on microgravity have shown us turn up in people who spend too much time weightless. And, alas"—here he smiled wryly—"we do not have any of the methods of generating artificial gravity that the movie industry does. So, the only method we can use is to spin the ship and substitute centrifugal force for gravity."

"I understand all that," McNeil said impatiently. "All the more reason, it seems to me, to use a *small* ship. It'd be easier to spin."

Glendale gave him that long, level stare that he'd perfected over the decades. First, on bumptious grad students; later, on even more bumptious reporters. It was a stare that managed to convey, without being precisely rude, that Glendale was momentarily stumped because the question was so inane that he had to grope to remember the answer. As if someone had asked him, *Dr. Glendale, how should one tie one's shoes?*

"Indeed." He cleared his throat. "Let me respond with a question of my own—addressed everyone here. How many of you like going to amusement parks?"

Hesitantly, there was a show of hands.

"Any of you dislike the rides? Like the teacup ones, or the rotor, or other spinning ones? Any of you really *hate* them?"

A number of the hands stayed up. Glendale nodded. "That's a pretty typical response. As it turns out, there's a sizable percentage of the human race that will get quite disoriented in something that spins faster than, oh, about two or three times a minute—let alone once every second or two. Now, as anyone who's been on those rides knows, how much force spin puts on you is directly related to how fast the thing spins and how far out from the center you are. If you want to have a given centrifugal force—say, equivalent to Mars' gravity of about one-third Earth's—and you want to rotate slowly—less than three times a minute—you have to be a very considerable distance out from the center. About one hundred and forty-six meters out, to be reasonably exact. If you wanted Earth-level gravity, well, you do the math. A lot farther out, meaning a lot larger ring. Luckily for us, experiments indicate that one-third gravity should be enough to prevent the problems."

"But even granting that width as necessary, what about

the rest of the ship?" asked another reporter.

"Well, a good deal of the interior of the main body is fuel storage. Remember, there are no filling stations along the way. *Nike* has an unfueled weight of almost two thousand tons—but she'll weigh almost *eight* thousand tons when we top off her tanks. The rest of the main body will have some considerable extra space, but who knows what she might be asked to carry once she reaches Phobos? And she will, of course, be carrying provisions for each person on board— which is quite a few tons per person, if you calculate it out. Not to mention scientific equipment of virtually every possible description, an SSTO lander—"

"A *what* lander?" That came from someone who was obviously not one of the regular correspondents.

"Sorry. 'SSTO' stands for 'single stage to orbit.' It refers to a lander that will be able to land on Mars with a mostly unpowered approach, and then take off back to orbit on its own, without needing a base station. Then, we have to carry construction equipment and supplies for making base areas on Phobos itself. And so on and so on and so on. You always need to remember that when you're a hundred million miles from Earth, you can't just send someone out to the nearest hardware store to get you that screwdriver you forgot to bring along. And these people will be out there for a year, at least, before they rotate back to Earth."

He fielded another question, from someone else.

After the reporter was done, Glendale shook his head. "Calling it a 'translation' is too strong a term. Our linguists are still not able to decipher the actual words of the alien language. But they are making progress in grasping how they wrote their language and some of its basic structure. To put it another way, they don't understand what the words mean, but they can now tell what's a word in the first place. According to Dr. Mayhew . . ."

# PART V: NIKE

Insight, n: a clear and often sudden understanding of a situation; often in the context of reaching a comprehension or solution to a problem which had previously appeared insoluble.

# Chapter 28

"Getting on close to two years, now," the director of the HIA mused, staring out the window. "I will say that this has been the smoothest operation you've ever run, Madeline."

She issued something that was a cross between a lady-like sniff of disdain and an outright snort. "That's because I'm working with a much higher class of clientele, so to speak. Compared to the usual run of lowlifes you stick me with."

He smiled, almost seraphically, and swiveled his chair back to face her. "I'm sure there's some saying regarding promises and rose gardens that applies here."

"It's helped—a great deal, I think—that A.J. Baker got involved with Helen Sutter."

Hughes cocked an eyebrow, inviting an elaboration.

"Helen's . . . Well, she's not happy about the security restrictions. Hard to blame her, since that's not something she's ever had to deal with in her profession. But she's a very level-headed sort of person, and I think she views the matter as not much different from the sort of practical limitations she's always faced. We're talking about a woman who'd make a damn good construction site foreman, if she ever had to start a new career."

Hughes grinned. "Is she still level-headed, after the blizzard of tabloid coverage?"

Madeline chuckled. "Oh, that's water off her back. She wouldn't pay any attention to it of any kind, if she didn't have to deal with the paparazzi. More precisely, if she didn't have to deal with Baker's reaction to them."

That brought an outright laugh from the director. A.J. Baker's scrapes with the paparazzi had become notorious. "But you think she's a good influence on him?"

"Certainly from our standpoint," Madeline replied. "Helen acts something like a coolant on a reactor, when it comes to A.J.'s public behavior. Well, leaving aside the paparazzi. Ever since they hooked up, I've had far fewer run-ins with him."

Hughes nodded. "Yes, I can see where she'd have that effect on the rambunctious young fellow. Part of the attraction she has for him, I imagine. I admit I can't quite figure out the flip side of that relationship."

"Why she's attracted to him?" Madeline shrugged. "I don't think that's hard to understand at all. Don't forget that almost all you ever hear about Baker from me are his . . . call them problem sides. But there are other things about the man—quite a few other things—that are very charming. I think that's especially important for someone like Helen, who's led a rather tightly regimented life because of the demands of her profession."

Hughes grunted softly. "Well. That's really none of our business, anyway. It's enough that she seems to have stifled his more anarchistic tendencies."

He sat up straight in his chair, placing his hands on the desk. "And . . . So. You'll be taking off day after tomorrow. Any last-minute issues we need to discuss?"

Madeline hesitated, for a moment. Then said: "Well, yes. Joe Buckley's become something of a problem."

The HIA director cocked an eyebrow. "How so? From the records, he's quite a bit less inclined toward the dramatic gesture than Baker. And that's your own assessment also, after eighteen months or so of working with him."

Madeline shook her head. "That's not what I meant. The problem is . . ." She took a slow breath and let it out. "The problem is that, as the months have gone by, I've found myself becoming attracted to him. Personally, I mean."

"Ah. Is the attraction reciprocated?"

"Yes. He's been very gentlemanly about it. No ogling— well, nothing obvious—and I think he's too intimidated by me to do anything beyond looking and thinking. He's a rather shy man when it comes to women, anyway. But . . . yes. It's pretty obvious."

"Obvious to you." Hughes' smile came back. "I think you often underestimate how much more perceptive you are about such things than most people, Madeline. Another by-product of your unfortunate childhood, I suspect."

Madeline shrugged. She was never comfortable talking about that subject, even with the very few people in the world who knew about it in the first place.

Hughes swiveled the chair and turned to look out the

window. After a few seconds, he said softly: "One of the reasons I'm very good at what I do is that I've never romanticized this work. In the end, for all its importance—some of the time, at least—it's still just a job. I've known very few people in my life who could be satisfied simply with their work. And I don't think you're one of them, Madeline, for all that you've tried so hard these past many years. And you're thirty-five years old now. Right about the age when dedicated single professionals start wondering what the rest of their life will look like. At the age of thirty, being a bachelor suits people like you just fine. By the age of forty . . . it has lost a great deal of its charm."

"Sir, you're my boss," she said, almost harshly. "Not my shrink."

He chuckled. "And you think there's that much difference, in *my* job? You might be surprised, Madeline, at the subject of many of the conversations I've had in this room with my agents. Especially my top agents, who've been at it for a long time. It's often a stressful life; almost always a rather lonely one."

He swiveled back to look at her squarely. "And I don't know anyone who has as much right and cause as you do to feel lonely."

"Sir—"

"Oh, hush. And save the 'sirs' for someone who cares about such stuff. Madeline, all I'm trying to say is that you are not, actually, superwoman. So if you find yourself getting seriously involved with him at some point, don't think it's the end of the world. It's not as if either of us thinks Buckley is an *enemy*, after all. He's a security risk only in the narrow sense that he might want to be able to talk openly about subjects we feel need to remain restricted. Just be rational about it, that's all. As rational as possible, at least—which is never easy, dealing with that subject."

She found herself biting off the instinctive retort. "I'd find a clearer explanation of that useful."

He shrugged. "I shouldn't think it's complicated. My advice? Do nothing, until the voyage begins. Thereafter, if you find the attraction remains, consider the fact that you will be in isolation from the rest of the human race for a period of at least two years. Quite possibly longer, in your case, since you may well not be rotating back as soon as most others will. So don't be an idiot. Yes, an involvement would certainly add a complicated and difficult curlicue to your work. But I think someone as capable as you are can manage to handle that, well enough. What I'm *sure* of is that trying to suppress your feelings under those circumstances will make you very squirrelly—and I have yet to meet a squirrel who makes a good security agent."

Madeline couldn't help but laugh. "Why do I think your answer would be considered sheer heresy by the heads of any other intelligence agency in the government?"

He smiled. "I'm sure it would. What I'm even surer of, however, is that not one of them has a tenure in office more than a third of mine—and precious few last even that long. Part of the reason is because they *do* romanticize the work."

Madeline's eyes almost crossed. " 'Romanticize'? That's hardly how I'd describe the way Davidson over at—"

"Of course, it is." The director's voice took on a very nasal tone. " 'My agents will give one hundred percent at all times. Anyone not ready for that—there's the door.' "

Madeline laughed. "Good imitation."

"It should be. I've had to listen to him talk, often enough. He's especially prone to giving that little speech to congressmen every time one of his agents gets fired for personal peccadilloes like padding the expense account—and usually gives the speech while he's junketing the congressmen and himself around on the taxpayer's dime. 'Romanticization,' Madeline, is just a way of covering the fact that we're all human by pretending they are and we aren't. Very satisfying to the ego, and very deleterious to our work. Why? Because we wouldn't be in business in the first place if people weren't all at least somewhat fallible. So I follow the old precept of setting a fox to catch a fox—and I don't pretend my fox is a virtuous vegetarian unlike all the others. Nor do I need them to be. A rational, reasonably self-controlled carnivore will do well enough. Better, in fact."

He stood up. "Enough saws from the old man, I think. Go forth, Maid Madeline, and smite the dragons. But note that I said 'Maid,' not 'Maiden.' " His accent thickened noticeably. "That's 'cause my mama didn't raise no fools."

Helen stared out the port. Her suborbital flights had shown her the Earth's curvature, but this flight was the first one where she could really *see* the Earth below her. The blue-brown-white sphere was familiar from images, of course. But it looked so completely different when you were in microgravity, looking down on it in real life.

"What's that?" A.J. said from her other side. He was looking ahead, and had been for fifteen minutes. "Is that . . . ?"

"Yes," Major Irwin confirmed. "That's *Nike*."

The tiny point of light grew, and expanded into a great structure that looked as if it had been made by a giant metal spider with a love for sharp angles. But in the center of that structure was a long, sleek, familiar shape. The fourteen hundred feet of *Nike* shone in the sun with white and silver highlights that picked out the details of every ridge and window.

Helen felt gooseflesh spring out over her arms as it truly, finally hit her that she was getting into an honest-to-God spaceship, one that could have flown straight out of any of the science fiction movies of the past seventy or eighty years. For a moment, she thought she could almost hear theme music playing.

A.J. took her hand in his. The clasp was easy and relaxed, almost unthinking—as was the little squeeze she gave him in return. After a year and a half together—the last six months of it no longer bothering to maintain separate apartments—their relationship had settled into something quite comfortable. Amazingly comfortable, Helen sometimes thought.

She chuckled softly. A.J. glanced at her.

"What's so funny?"

"I was just . . . oh, marveling, I guess, at how well we get along. Most of the time, anyway."

True love of his life or not—as A.J. insisted she was—his eyes were drawn back to *Nike* within two seconds.

Naturally. Helen didn't even sigh.

"Still pissed at me?" he asked.

By way of answer, she squeezed his hand again. "No. Not really. But I am glad we're not going to have to deal with paparazzi for a while."

Even as absorbed as he was in studying the *Nike,* A.J. had enough grace to flush. "Hey, look. I'm sorry I lost my temper, but even for paparazzi that guy—"

"I don't care. You should not have thrown him through a plate glass window. Especially *that* window."

A.J. winced. "Well, true enough. I still think the restaurant stiffed me on the cost of replacing it. But—ah—"

"But you weren't going to argue the point, seeing as how you were busy enough trying to keep criminal charges from being filed. Two days before takeoff."

A.J. would never flush for long. His grin was back. "Don't be silly." He jerked his chin forward, pointing to the *Nike.* "I knew I had a getaway. Talk about a fast horse out of Dodge!"

The surface-to-space shuttle *Hurricane* closed slowly with *Nike.* Very slowly, and very carefully. There'd be no slapdash or show-off approaches to what might be the most expensive object ever built by the hand of man, and was undoubtedly the most powerful vessel ever made. A.J. seemed constantly ready to jump out of his seat with impatience—a maneuver most strongly ill-advised in microgravity. But, finally, they could hear the transfer tunnel lock onto the external lock collar.

"We are docked with *Nike,*" came the pilot's voice. "All you passengers can unstrap now. Just be careful making your way out. One person at a time through the lock."

A.J. let Helen go first, even though his first impulse was quite clearly to launch himself in a single leap through the connecting lock. She found his attempts to be courteous at once gratifying and amusing. A.J.'s single-mindedness generally made him semioblivious to other people, even Helen. But when he *did* focus that capacity for concentration on her, he was just as intense as he always was. If nothing else, she thought wryly as she went through the lock, it made for great sex.

Ahead she saw the other airlock door open, and someone visible on the other side. As she passed through that lock, she saw that it was Ken Hathaway, upside-down and hanging from the floor. Realizing that the captain of a ship probably knew the orientation better than she did, she used the convenient handholds to rotate around and match him.

"Permission to come aboard?" she asked, grinning, in imitation of who knew how many scenes in movies.

He grinned back. "Permission granted. Welcome aboard *Nike*, Dr. Sutter! And A.J.," he added, as the sensor specialist squeezed in behind her.

"So how do you feel about being called Captain?" A.J. immediately demanded. "I know that in the Air Force that's pretty far down the totem pole compared to brigadier general."

"Well, it was a concession to the Navy. My training twinges occasionally, but . . ." Ken's eyes flicked back and forth, as if searching for hidden spies. "Don't tell anyone," he half-whispered, "but the truth is I agree with the squids. Here, anyway. Someone commanding a spaceship just *has* to be called Captain."

"It's not customary for the captain to be present whenever crew arrives, though, is it?" Helen asked.

"When they're important civilian crew, of course. Politics, you know. And when they're good friends, you show up anyway. Besides, I want to be the one to show off my ship. No one else except Jackie and Gupta get to do tour guide duty. They're the only others that can really call it *their* ship."

"Most of the others are already here, right?"

"Almost all. The Japanese astrogeological specialist, Dr. Ryu Sakai, is coming in tomorrow. Madeline Fathom will be coming up with him."

"And we get moving a couple days after that?"

"If all the tests show positive, A.J." Hathaway's grin came back. "And if the cops don't arrive to haul you away for assault and battery."

A.J. flushed again. "Hey, look, the guy practically shoved his camera into Helen's soup. Goddammit—"

He broke off. Jackie Secord had entered the chamber.

She was an arresting sight. Partly because she was floating straight at them, her face leading the way; partly because she was oriented at a ninety-degree angle; but, mostly, because of her grin. She reminded Helen of a shark, nearing its prey.

Jackie was holding something in her hand, which she brought forward and extended toward A.J.

"Oh, puh-*leeeeeze*, Mr. Baker, can I have your autograph?"

Helen looked down at the thing and burst into laughter. It was a copy of the front page of the tabloid in question. Half of it was a huge photograph of A.J., looking like an enraged skinny gorilla and glaring at the camera through the shattered window of a restaurant.

## A.J. in a Fury!
## His Love Nest With Helen Exposed!

"At least they finally dropped the headlines about you," she chortled.

Jackie rolled her eyes. "Thank God! Bad enough when

I was trying to convince the people who knew me that A.J. wasn't my boyfriend. Convincing half the world, with headlines like *Jackie Green-eyed With Jealousy . . .*"

She shook her head. "I think they had me on the brink of suicide for eight months straight. And, A.J., I *still* want your autograph."

"I don't have a pen," he grumbled. "And that's a terrible picture of me, anyway."

"I think it's pretty good, myself," Hathaway chimed in. He ignored A.J.'s glare and waved his hand toward the lock Jackie had come through. "But now—the tour!"

Having had her joke, Jackie folded up the copy and stuffed it into a pocket of her jumpsuit. She then added her handwave to Ken's. "You first, A.J."

As Helen followed him, she and Jackie exchanged a smile.

"Who woulda guessed, huh?" Jackie asked. "Bless you, Helen, for being the flypaper for the rest of us."

*I never would have guessed, that's for sure,* Helen mused. To her astonishment, in the year and a half since Glendale's press conference had made the Phobos expedition front page news, the crew of the *Nike* had become as famous as movie or rock stars. And—alas— it hadn't taken the tabloids more than a month to figure out that A.J. and Helen were the ideal target for their attentions.

A.J. claimed that was because of Helen's good looks. Helen herself thought that only accounted for—at most— two percent of the paparazzi's interest. Measured by any standard criteria, both Jackie Secord and Madeline Fathom were better-looking than Helen. Not to mention much younger.

No, most of the interest was in A.J. More precisely,

the fact that A.J. could be goaded into saying or doing something publicly that made splendid tabloid headlines. Which—

He had. Many times.

But it was all over now, thankfully. Whether or not the *Nike* was a fast horse out of Dodge, it was for sure and certain a refuge from the tabloids. And would be, for quite a long time.

So, Helen put aside all thoughts of smashed windows— not to mention an awkward photo of herself wearing, well, not much of anything—and concentrated on Ken's guided tour.

Hathaway was leading them down a long corridor, floating from handhold to handhold with a grace that Helen envied. She hoped she'd be able to get the hang of that soon. A.J. wasn't as good as Hathaway, but definitely better than she was.

"Here you're seeing some generic hallway," Hathaway said. "The habitat ring is made up of sixty sections a bit less than fifteen meters long, about ten meters thick, and thirty meters across. These sections come in two flavors: twenty of them have viewing areas, ports, on them— although they can be sealed off and shielded from behind— and the other forty have no such provisions. The sections all interlock together firmly and are connected to the main body by a sort of bicycle-spoke arrangement. At intervals there are also direct corridors connecting us to the main body."

It was a measure of A.J.'s excitement that he didn't make a single sarcastic remark to the effect that Hathaway was telling them stuff they already knew perfectly well. By now, Helen could have drawn a diagram of most sections of the ship, from memory alone. A.J. could probably draw a diagram and a schematic of the electrical system.

Somehow it didn't matter. Seeing the huge ship in person was a completely different experience than studying it in images and blueprints.

Hathaway snagged a handhold and brought himself to a halt before a door. Expertly, he evaded Helen and A.J. as they failed to grab other handholds and had to stop themselves some distance farther along and return.

"This is one of the cabins—the one we are assigning you, Helen, in fact. Or the two of you, if you want to share it. No paparazzi to pester you here, after all." His wide smile was replaced by a caricatured frown of disapproval. "Not that that stopped you, I noticed—*harrumph*—from living in sin back on Earth."

The "cabin" was actually a two-story apartment, with the bedroom and study upstairs, and living room and small dining room/kitchen downstairs. Multiple fastening loops, velcro pads, and other provisions were made for using the apartment in microgravity. But the construction was based on the fact that, most of the time, the ring would be providing one-third gravity, with "down" towards the outside of the ring.

"The furnishings can be moved around, partitions put in, and so on. The shapes aren't very variable—we only have two types of chairs, for instance—but we've tried to provide lots of options for layout. Basically, it's like very fancy Lego building blocks. You can turn and lock the units into standardized fasteners below, and there are utility hookups laid out in a standard grid pattern that you can take advantage of."

"Me?" Helen shook her head. "Not likely. I'm a pale-ontologist, not a plumber."

"Well, okay, one of the ship's engineers. You wouldn't want to try doing any of this without training—you hear that, A.J.?—and even with training you wouldn't do it alone. But within some pretty broad limits, you can have a custom living space. Before too long, I don't expect any two cabins to be the same. The engineers even set up mechanisms to make sure balance is maintained, if by some odd chance everyone on one side of the ring likes apartments crowded with lots of furnishings and every-one on the other side likes wide-open spaces."

Again, Helen ignored the fact that Ken was lecturing them on stuff they already knew. She just shook his head and murmured: "It's . . . *huge*. I never imagined it would seem this big. I mean, abstractly I knew the designs—but they didn't convey the sheer impact of the thing."

A.J. turned away from examining the kitchen setup. "We aren't Napoleonic-era sailors and we're not going to work well cramped into tiny living quarters for a year or more. We need space. And fortunately, space they could give us, since the ship had to be big anyway."

"Can we see the labs?" Helen asked.

Hathaway chuckled. "Have no fear, Dr. Sutter. About half the ring is living space. The other half is for working. We have everything on the ring from full networked infor-mation systems to paleontological, biological, chemical, nuclear, and engineering laboratories. Data is stored re-dundantly in another system in the main body, and we can send backups of critical data to Earth if we need to. We have integrated microfabrication setups for prototyping, tool design and repair, and so on."

Since Ken was clearly not going to be diverted from his determination to reiterate what they already knew, Helen decided it would be polite to indulge him.

"Main control is in the central body, right?"

"The bridge," Hathaway corrected her, clearly preferring the classic terminology. "Yes, it is indeed located in the forward section of *Nike*'s central body. We'll be visiting there too. Shall we go on?"

"Wow."

A.J. was simply staring around, grinning so widely that it looked like his face might split in two. "This is *so* cool."

Ken tried to look professionally proud, but that comment broke through the feeble attempt. He grinned back like a kid finding his dad had built him a three-story treehouse. "Yeah, isn't it?"

*Nike*'s bridge was arranged in a manner strongly reminiscent of many a fictional space vessel's. It was a long, egg-shaped compartment, with duty stations spaced around the perimeter, and a central dais with a command and control console and chair—a captain's chair, clearly— which could swivel to survey any of the duty stations.

Dominating the bridge, however, was the tremendous viewport, covering most of the "ceiling" area. A span of pure velvet blackness showed through in the dimmed interior lighting, sprinkled with stars and crisscrossed with the argent webwork of the dry dock facilities around *Nike*.

"That's . . . a hell of a window," Helen said finally. She realized she wasn't as familiar with this part of the ship's design. "Isn't that a weak point in the structure? At least for radiation shielding?"

"Not really. It looks like clear glass, but that's actually

transparent composite. It's coated with artificial diamond, and insulated with a foot and a half of optical aerogel with a high radiation shielding coefficient. The back section is similar but coated with an active-crystal matrix which can black it out—makes it reflective on the outside. And of course can be used to enhance anything you see through the port, or override it as a display, like a viewscreen. You actually have similar windows in your cabins; they just aren't open right now, so to speak. Because of the heating effects and the potential danger of people blinding themselves looking at the sun, we're keeping the window controls mostly to ourselves. We'll leave them open in the cabins whenever it's safe, once we're under way. You can always shut them off, though."

Helen waved her hand around the spacious bridge. "Let me guess. More political and publicity design compromises."

Hathaway nodded. "Not so much compromises as just overkill again. You could really run *Nike* from a single enclosed room, if you had to, with nobody at the controls. We don't really *need* a crew to fly this ship, although having one certainly acts as a failsafe. But . . . well, it just looks better this way. The public feels like they're getting their money's worth, and they ponied up a lot of it.

"The design *is* completely functional, too. You could in fact fly this ship on manual from the bridge, not that I'd ever want to see anyone try it. A.J., your station is right there." He pointed to a console area in the front and to the right.

As A.J. floated himself over to the indicated area, Hathaway added: "The equipment isn't a waste, either. Like almost everything else in the ship, it can either be used right where it sits or unshipped and brought down to Phobos."

"Hey, this thing already ties right in with my VRD!"

"Of course it does, A.J. They took the coding straight from your personal station at NASA."

"Neat! I don't even have to tweak it!"

Helen took another slow, admiring turn to examine the whole bridge. "I agree with you, Ken. It might be silly theatrical overkill in some ways—but this really *is* a ship. You can feel it."

"Yes, you can." Hathaway's gaze was focused out the huge viewport. "And she's about ready to fly."

# Chapter 29

Nicholas Glendale stood out on the landing field where, almost two years earlier, *Chinook* had crashed while trying to land. He wasn't here for a landing, however. He was gazing upward to see a launch.

It was chilly on the flat desert plain, now that the sun had gone down. All the more so because they were well into autumn. Glendale pulled his coat a bit tighter. The garment was cut thin and sharply angled, which was nice from a cosmetic viewpoint, since it emphasized his slender figure. But he missed the reassuring puffy bulk of the coats he remembered from his younger years, even if the aerogel insulation of his current one made it just as warm.

Back at NASA Control, the countdown had begun. He could hear the murmur of traffic between the ground and *Nike* in his ear, and if he wished, his VRD would display any of a dozen views of the great ship or the control center.

But for now he looked only with eyes. At an altitude of about two hundred miles, the fourteen-hundred-foot-long *Nike* stretched over 4.5 arc minutes—nearly a sixth of the width of the full moon. It was easy to spot coming over the horizon, if you knew where to look. Once it was up in the sky, of course, nobody could miss it.

Glendale knew where to look. He came out here often to watch her fly overhead.

He had never been interested in space travel, particularly. His own field fascinated him, and had since he was a teenager—the interaction of its personalities as much as the unearthing of ancient biological history. For whatever reason, paleontology had always seemed to attract some of the most colorful personalities ever to populate the halls of academia. Still did, for that matter.

Perhaps that very fact—having had no youthful fascination with space—had led to his current obsession.

"I was never inoculated against this," Glendale heard himself murmur. When a connection had finally been shown between Helen Sutter's problematica, *Bemmius secordii,* and Phobos, Glendale had been forced to really *look* at this utterly different field . . . and the space bug had bitten, hard.

It had not been easy, especially in the first few months after he'd realized he really *was* interested—intensely, passionately interested—in following the mystery of *Bemmius* to Phobos. For the first time in his life, Nicholas Glendale had found himself suffering—violently—from the hideous throes of professional jealousy.

Helen Sutter was, as he himself had said, the only correct choice for the mission. Not only did she already know far more about *Bemmius* than anyone else on Earth, but she was considerably younger than he was, at least as photogenic, and more athletic. Add to that the sudden romantic tie between her and the handsome young genius who had discovered the Phobos base—the tabloids had picked that up almost immediately—and only a complete idiot would try to bar her from the mission. The publicity alone would be worth millions in justifying the program to the public.

The fact had remained that Nicholas Glendale wasn't *that* old, he was well-known, respected, trusted—and, somewhat to his own surprise, he'd even passed the physical and psychological exams for space travel. Not with nearly as good a score as Helen or many of the other candidates, true, with regard to the physical tests. After all, he *was* sixty years old.

Still, physically, there was nothing to prevent him from going. Indeed, one of the members of the crew—the linguist, Rich Skibow— was sixty-three years old. Glendale had been astounded, and more than a little repelled, to find that he was actually entertaining thoughts of using his reputation and public leverage to force his way onto the crew. He had always detested scientists who tried to advance their personal goals over the needs of science, or over the metaphorical bodies of others. It was one of the reasons he had taken immense pleasure in dissecting that self-centered ass Pinchuk. Yet there he had been, thinking very similar selfish thoughts which would have, if indulged, resulted in shoving aside an undoubtedly more needed somebody off *Nike* just so he could joyride around the Solar System.

Coming up on visibility . . .

He glanced to the west, where *Nike* would soon appear,

her orbital direction giving her an apparent retrograde motion against the stars.

Not quite yet. A few more moments.

He had managed to get his new obsession under control, finally, and he didn't think anyone else had really noticed anything. Once he had forced himself to accept that he would not be going, at least on this first mission, he had thrown his new fascination some bones. Reading voluminously on space travel—he realized suddenly that he hadn't even glanced at a paleontological journal in three months— and slightly abusing his position and reputation to get himself some actual orbital time and a visit to *Nike*.

NASA had given themselves, and Glendale, one other special treat, however.

*There* she was! A glimmer, growing into a brighter light, as *Nike* continued her orbit. The countdown was now nearing its end. If all went well—if nothing happened to delay or stop the countdown, now in its last seconds— *Nike* would begin her departure from Earth by firing her engines just about precisely above Glendale's head.

She would not, of course, be driving straight towards Mars. Instead, she would be using multiple short burns to take a more economical route by exploiting the power of the Earth's gravity well, firing subsequently as she approached perigee and building velocity in a slingshot maneuver before heading on a transfer orbit to where Mars would be in about three months. She *was* going to be showing off what she could do upon arrival, however. The current plans were for her to do what amounted to a brute-force braking maneuver that would park her near Phobos with a single long burn.

Nicholas Glendale would not be on board *Nike*. But he would watch her leave.

"I see you, Helen!"

Near orbit and increased bandwidth allowed some personal channels. "All go so far," Helen responded. "Jesus, Nicholas, I'm nervous."

"No reason to be nervous. Excited, though, that's just fine."

"That, too. I wish you were coming with us, you know."

"Not as much as I do. Perhaps next trip."

"Goodbye, Nicholas."

"Goodbye—and good luck, Helen."

The voice of Ground Control echoed on another channel. "Thirty seconds to ignition."

"Main engines all show green. We are go for launch."

"Ignition in twenty seconds from . . . mark."

Glendale blinked hard and stared upward. The sparkling not-quite-dot was almost directly overhead now.

"Ten seconds. Nine. Eight. Seven. Six. Five. Four. Three. Two. One . . ."

*Nike* suddenly blazed brighter, six NERVA engines hurling superheated gases outward at a rate of tons per second. Nicholas knew that human eyes couldn't possibly see the effect of less than a quarter-g of acceleration on something already at orbital speeds, but his hindbrain insisted that the distant spacecraft had lunged forward eagerly and was already heading towards the horizon at an ever-increasing pace. He kept his eyes fixed on *Nike* as she silently accelerated on her journey to another world.

He couldn't say exactly at what point he could no longer quite see her. But when he finally admitted to himself that she was truly gone, he became aware of the tears streaming down his face.

Some of them were from keeping his eyes open too long.

# Chapter 30

"Gee," A.J. said, fighting to keep his face straight. "That's tough."

"I appreciate your attempt at diplomacy, A.J." Dr. Wu took another deep breath. The paleness of his skin didn't decrease, but the sheen of sweat seemed to be fading. "Even though the attempt is feeble and ineffective."

"It *is* kinda funny, though. After everything we went through, and now we're on our way and you—the doctor— are getting spacesick?"

Wen Hsien Wu grimaced, holding down his lunch apparently by force of pride. "I suppose if I were in your position I might find it amusing. As it is, I have a very hard time taking it that way."

"Seriously, anything I can do for you? I mean, this is really just a scratch, I'll take care of it myself."

"A bit more than a scratch, judging by the bleeding.

Yes, get me one of the blue pills from the container on the top right, marked 'Stabilese.' "

A.J. glanced in the indicated direction and floated himself over to the cabinet. "That's the antinausea drug?"

"One of them. This one works after the fact, unlike most. If I can keep it down for a few minutes."

A.J. got one of the pills out and handed it to the doctor. "Here you go. Look on the bright side. In a few more hours we'll be going to rotation mode. After that, we'll have about one-third gravity to work with."

"Yes." Wu swallowed the pill, seemed to turn slightly paler. Sweat broke out across his face again. Grimly he closed his eyes, then opened them quickly again to stare into the distance. A.J. said nothing, but handed the doctor one of the catcher bags in case his stomach won out.

Several more minutes went by. Slowly, color crept back into Wu's face, and he sighed with relief. "Well, I believe it is working. I still feel terrible, but not as badly as I did." He reached out. "Let me see that cut. Good lord, A.J., how did you manage to do that?"

"My reflexes are still on Earth. I was moving some of the equipment around in micrograv, got distracted, realized something was getting away from me, grabbed it, and lever action sorta whipped me around. Caught my arm on a bracket."

Wu shook his head. His hands shook slightly, too, but the instrument they held was still steady. "I think I can glue it together. I'd rather not have to go with stitches."

"Okay by me, Doc. I don't like needles myself."

A.J. noticed something about Wu as he carefully cleaned the wound and prepared to glue it together. To check on what he noticed, he flipped a bit of Fairy Dust onto the *Nike*'s doctor.

"There we go. Yes, that will do."

"You know the old saying, 'Physician, heal thyself'?" A.J. asked.

"Yes, of course. Why?"

"You'd better practice it. You aren't spacesick, or at least that's not all of your problems. You're running three degrees of fever."

Wu stared at him, then put his hand against A.J.'s forehead. "Yes, you feel cold. How stupid of me. I felt exactly the same as I had in the earlier training flights, so I just assumed . . . Well, stupid, as I said."

He frowned. "This isn't good, at all. We have a very confined population here. If a large proportion of us gets sick, operations will be severely curtailed."

"It's probably just a cold or a touch of flu, Doc. What's the big deal?"

"Flu still kills people on occasion, A.J. And when you have only fifty people and relatively little redundancy, even minor illnesses can have a major effect. I will have to issue an immediate warning." Wu shook his head. "At the very least, unless we're so fortunate as to have this be a strain that only I am vulnerable to, there will be an awful lot of miserable people here, for a while. And you don't even want to contemplate what could happen to someone who suddenly becomes sick while on EVA."

Picturing what would happen to someone who vomited while inside a spacesuit, A.J. was no longer amused.

Jackie stared, bleary-eyed, at the screen. She really didn't feel up to this, but Dr. Gupta was worse off. The deep voice was barely a whisper, and Dr. Wu—still looking rather dragged out from his own experience—had Gupta on IVs.

He wasn't the only one, either; by now over sixty percent of *Nike*'s crew had come down with the flu, and a few were in very bad shape. A.J. was the worst off. The infection had a respiratory phase as well as a gastrointestinal one, and the respiratory irritation had caused a violent sympathetic reaction from his already damaged lungs. The sensor specialist was in the small medical bay under constant observation. Wu thought A.J. was out of the woods, but it would be weeks before he'd be back to full strength. He barely had the energy to smile and exchange a few words with Helen when she visited.

Enough musing. Edwards was waiting for Jackie's instructions. "Okay. You'll have to unbolt the cover plate in front of you. It's held by four locking bolts with latches. The latches you can pop off with your screwdriver. Use a fifteen millimeter socket on the bolt heads."

"Understood. Fifteen millimeter. They all secured on the shaft?"

"Yes. Once you loosen them enough, you can swing all four out of the way. And they'll stay out of the way—there's a spring-loaded mechanism to keep them from flopping around."

"Roger that."

She closed her eyes and tried to convince herself the room wasn't really spinning. As the room really *was* spinning, at about two revolutions per minute, that was easier said than done. Tim Edwards was a good guy with a toolkit, but he wasn't an engineer. She'd have felt better about doing this job herself, if she'd been able to. But she still didn't dare get into a suit; and, unfortunately, all the other people who might have tried doing maintenance on the nuclear rocket engines were laid up.

Number Five engine had started having problems. The diagnostics pinpointed one of the valves involved in feeding reaction mass to the chamber. Fortunately, it was in a well-shielded area, because both she and Gupta wanted to replace the valve immediately and examine the old one to see what had gone wrong. If it was simply a defective part, fine. What they didn't want was to discover at the end of the trip that there was some underlying problem that had caused it to malfunction. By then, it might be too late to fix—and they'd need that engine for the braking maneuver.

"All bolts off, Jackie."

"Good." She forced her eyes to focus on the scene in front of her. "Okay, that panel was designed to swing up and out. It's on hinges, and there's a clip on the wall behind it which should keep it out of the way. Open her up."

Tim complied, slowly opening the access panel and locking it to the clip on the wall. "Got it."

"You should be seeing . . ." She trailed off, fighting to focus her memory. "There'll be three pipes in there. One has a bright red stripe on it, one a bright yellow, and one bright white."

"Yeah, you got it. Red, yellow, white."

"There should be two shutoff valve handles on each pipe. In between these shutoff valves are the control valve units."

"The shutoff valve handles are sort of like door handles, not like round spigot things, right?"

"Yes, that's right. They're open if they're in line with the pipe and closed if they're at right angles to the pipe.

All of them should be open right now."

"They are," Tim verified, after a short pause. "You want me to close them?"

"Just the ones for the feeder line. That's the white-painted pipe."

"Gotcha." A few seconds went by. "Damn, this bugger is— *whoa!*"

Tim Edwards flailed a bit on the screen and started floating away from *Nike*. Jackie reflexively gasped before common sense caught up with her reaction. Just at that point, Edwards' safety line brought him to a mostly-cushioned halt and he began a very slow drift back.

"I'm okay, I'm okay! Don't worry. The one valve was sticky and I had to push pretty hard. When it gave I over-compensated."

Jackie's heart was pounding and her stomach roiled. "Ugh. Don't do that again, please. When I worry I get sicker."

"I'll try. Okay, both of these are now at right angles to the pipe. You're sure I'm not going to end up glowing in the dark?"

"You've got a rad meter on you now. Your major danger is from space radiation, not from our engines. The quicker we get this done, the better off we'll be."

"Roger that. I have the valves shut off on the white-painted pipe. What do I do next?"

"Now we have to remove—"

She stopped, appalled. "Did you say *white*-painted?"

"Yes. That was the one you told me to shut off."

"Jesus, I'm completely out of it. Please reopen those valves. That's not the feeder for the reaction mass, it's the coolant."

"That's bad, isn't it?"

"Not under these circumstances, actually. We've already got it shut down. But it would have been in other circumstances, and in this case it would've meant you'd have wasted your trip out there. The one you want is the *yellow* pipe. I did say 'yellow' this time, didn't I?"

"Yellow, as in yellow-bellied. Um. Perhaps a poor choice of words, given the way I'm feeling right now. That's the one we want. Are you sure this time?"

"Yes. I'm sure. Yellow. Put the ones on the white pipe back in line, then turn off the ones on the yellow pipe."

"Roger." A few seconds passed. "All right, Jackie, the *yellow* pipe now has both valves in shutoff position, at right angles to the pipe. The *white* pipe's valves are both in line with the pipe."

"Very good." She focused on the situation at hand. "All right. That boxy-looking affair between the two shutoff valves is the control valve we're interested in. Please do a visual verification that the two units—the one you have with you, and the one we are about to remove—look the same."

"Confirmed," Tim's voice said shortly. "Allowing for the fact that I can't see all of the one that's currently in there."

"Don't worry. We'll have a couple of other checkpoints along the way. How are you holding up?"

"It's a little warm, but I can always duck a bit down to cool off. There's shade handy, and the suits are pretty good at keeping us cool."

"Just let me know if you start feeling even a little bit off. I don't want you getting sick out there in the middle of this. We can always leave Number Five shut down for a while, if we have to. It's not like we really need nuclear drive right now anyway."

"Don't worry, Jackie. I don't want to find myself spewing in my suit. Or just passing out from heat exhaustion, for that matter."

Jackie smiled wearily. "Okay, then. Let's go on to the next part. On the four corners facing you, there are bolts . . ."


"I think we're finally getting back to normal," Hathaway said. "A.J.'s moving around and trying to catch up on his work, and no one else seems in any danger. We're down to only twenty percent of the crew being ill, and all of them are in the recovery stage."

The time delay was quite noticeable now, with millions of miles separating the *Nike* from Earth after a couple of weeks spent en route. Finally, however, the image of Glendale smiled.

"That's good to hear, Ken. Everyone was very worried. So you don't think anything major has been impacted by the epidemic?"

"No, Nick. The only real problem was the need to replace the control valve on Number Five, and that was really more of an annoyance than a major issue. Tim Edwards performed admirably even though this wasn't at all his usual line of work, and Number Five has been tested and works just fine now. After taking apart the original valve, it appears that some of the bearings had suffered minor damage, possibly during manufacture, and after a short period of use the wear started to cause it to stick. We're testing all the others now and looking for signs indicating whether or not we might need to do other replacements, but so far it's all negative. The integrated distributed sensors are working fine."

After another long pause, Glendale nodded. "Good. The medical people are looking forward to your data. This is the first significant epidemic of any kind in space, so naturally it's of great interest. And all the other recent readings—radiation and so on—should accompany those."

"Don't worry, we've got tons of data to send and it's all been carefully arranged. Madeline—Ms. Fathom—has gone through the material and approved it, too."

"Well, then, we'll let you get back to work, Captain. Our best wishes to you and your people, and please let us know if there is anything we can do for you."

"Thanks much. I'll pass it on, though aside from the moral support you're already giving I don't think there's really much you could do. *Nike* out."

Ken sank back into a chair, feeling heavy despite the one-third gravity. The last two weeks had taught him the full meaning of the old phrase "weight of command." It had seemed that everything rested on his shoulders. He'd been sick himself, but had refused to impose on the heavily embattled medical staff—which consisted of Wu, Janice Ortega, Madeline Fathom and Helen Sutter. The last two were not officially part of the medical staff but they were the only two on board who had never caught the bug and had a pretty good knowledge of field medicine. That turned out to be especially true of Fathom. In fact, she'd volunteered to remain a regular assistant in the medical department, since her own duties as security officer wouldn't really take up much of her time until they arrived at Phobos.

Ken couldn't afford to be sick. As his staff dropped

like flies, he was the one who had to decide which of the increasingly small pool of healthy people filled which positions. No one else could really take the responsibility, and he wouldn't have given it up anyway. Even under these conditions . . . it was still his dream.

But a tiring dream. "System notification."

"Recording," the *Nike's* automatics replied.

"Captain is resting. Do not disturb except for emergencies."

"Notification posted. Expiration time?"

"Ten hours from now. Give me a wake-up call in eight hours."

"Wake-up call in eight hours. Understood."

"Thank you," he said reflexively as he moved towards his bunk..

"You are welcome, sir," *Nike* replied.

*It may not really understand anything*, Ken thought, as he lay down and closed his eyes. *But whoever did the programming understands very well.*

# Chapter 31

Joe cleared his throat. Then, cleared it again.

*I can't believe I'm even* thinking *about this.*

"Would you like to come in?" he asked, a bit gruffly.

"Said the spider to the fly?"

Joe managed a grin of sorts. "I don't have a parlor. Besides, I watched you and A.J. If I had any dishonorable intentions, I'd choose someone who couldn't break my arm just by looking at me funny."

The answering smile dazzled him, like it always did. "And you don't find that intimidating?"

"No. I don't."

"Good. A lot of men have a hard time with it. Especially because I'm so small."

Joe watched appreciatively as the diminutive security specialist entered his cabin, moving with the slightly bouncy gait that seemed favored in one-third gravity. Which, in the case of Madeline Fathom, he also found fascinating. As religiously as she exercised, her figure was on a par with her smile.

Once she was in, he closed the door. "I look at it this way. If we were in the Renaissance working for the Borgias, I'd be a poisoner rather than a swordsman. Safer—and I'd know what I was doing."

Madeline's smile came again. "That's for sure! Even here, forget the Renaissance—since you're the man who's in charge of seeing to it we can eat real food."

Food. Joe had always been a gourmet, but he'd never once in his life imagined that his interest and skill with food would lead to . . .

This. Whatever "this" turned out to be.

To Joe's considerable surprise, once the voyage started he'd found himself the focus of attention of several of *Nike's* unattached female personnel. At first, he'd been most interested in Diane, who was intelligent, skilled at her job, had a decent sense of humor—and was certainly good-looking.

Alas, Joe had one admitted obsession. The redheaded information expert had run afoul of it when she had put ketchup— *ketchup!*—on the sesame-marinated filet mignon which had been the dinner he'd selected for their second date. He hadn't said anything about it, of course, since he wasn't rude and it was her meal to eat as she chose. But from that moment forward, he'd lost any real interest in the woman.

Okay, sure, he was a snob about food. But he figured everyone had their own area they were screwy about. Might as well ask Queen Victoria to get the hots for a caveman.

Madeline, on the other hand . . .

She'd approached him after her shift's dinnertime, three weeks into the voyage, and asked him about the recipe for the chicken tikka masala. Initially, he'd taken it for nothing more than Fathom's invariant politeness. Despite the fact that her position in charge of security put her in potential conflict with almost everyone else on the crew, Madeline had actually become one of the *Nike*'s most popular people. Whether from her own temperament, or her training, or professional calculation—probably all three combined, Joe suspected— Madeline was just plain *nice* to people.

But it wasn't long before Joe realized that here was a woman who knew a great deal about cooking, and found the subject of real interest. A simple request for the recipe had become a conversation about cooking methods and preferences that caused him to be a half-hour late for his own shift.

By the time another month had gone by in *Nike*'s voyage, that initial conversation had turned into a regular series of such—and ones which ranged far afield from cooking. Joe had always thought that Madeline Fathom was very good-looking, of course. Just about everyone did. But as the weeks passed, he found himself increasingly attracted to the woman's personality.

True enough, the phrase *charming security official* still struck him as an oxymoron. But . . . Madeline Fathom was no longer an abstraction. Whatever reservations he had about her occupation, by now he was pretty well bowled over by the woman.

Tonight, as had become their daily habit, she'd accompanied him back to his cabin after dinner. Madeline's own cabin was not much farther along the ring. Finally, after several weeks of that ritual, Joe had worked up the nerve to invite her in.

"So what's playing at Cinema Joe?" Madeline asked, her hands on her hips as she surveyed the cabin.

"Entertainments old and new. What's your pleasure?"

"Movies suit me fine."

"Not into the fancy gaming?"

Madeline shook her head. "That's definitely A.J.'s territory, not mine." She hesitated fractionally. "I prefer to let someone else do the entertaining."

"Genre? Time frame?"

"Well . . . " The unexpected blush looked especially pretty. "I'm afraid I'm going to disappoint you."

"Unless you're about to profess a love for McDonald's cuisine, that would be impossible."

"Almost as bad. I like superhero movies, or anything where the good guys kick lots of butt and the bad guys are really bad." Madeline looked genuinely embarrassed.

Joe couldn't keep from laughing. "You're kidding! Usually that's the kind of thing the guys are supposed to like and the girl rolls her eyes at."

"Stop laughing!"

"Hey, I'm not. I may be a snob about food, but I'm no literary giant."

He flicked through his memory. "How about *Nemesis Factor*?" he suggested. It was one of his recent favorites, combining spy thriller with a super-martial-artist vigilante heroine.

"Oh, yes! I kept catching bits and pieces of that one, but never got a chance to see it."

The movie decided on, the two settled into the couch

to watch. Joe started the usual *male-on-a-first-date* fretting about *whether-andif-so-when* he should try to slide his arm around the woman involved. But Madeline cut the whole obnoxious business off at the pass. Casually, but firmly—the same way she carried out her professional duties—she took his hand and put his arm around her. Then, as if it was the most natural thing in the world to do, leaned into his chest and nestled her head on his shoulder.

It might, just possibly, have been the single most thrilling moment of Joe's life.

While Madeline made a very nice armful, once the movie started Joe found she was far too much of a fan to just sit back and watch. It was actually more like watching a movie with one of the guys. She practically jumped up and shouted when a particularly cool set of moves was used, and she'd occasionally heckle the bad guys while onscreen.

But when the main villain, Valmont DuChan, got his major scene—using his unnaturally charismatic appeal to gather followers in a cultlike organization to use terror tactics against the entire city— Madeline went quite uncharacteristically silent. She then excused herself to go to the bathroom, and didn't come back out for a while. When she did, Joe noted she seemed rather pale.

"Madeline, are you okay?"

"Sure, why wouldn't I be?" she responded, almost curtly. She sat back down and, to his delight, leaned back into him. But almost as soon as she did so, he realized just how tense she was. The body that had seemed so soft and feminine earlier now felt exactly like that of a very well-conditioned female athlete. Not quite as hard as a rock, but awfully close.

Not knowing what else to do, he started the movie again.

"Could we watch something else?" Madeline asked suddenly.

Joe stopped the movie and turned to her. "Sure, of course. But look . . . What's wrong? Did I do something to upset you?"

She looked startled. "No, of course not. It's just . . ." Her eyes shifted to the screen, with its frozen image of Valmont DuChan's face staring out with a fanatic's gaze.

"God, I can't believe this. I haven't had that stirred up in years." She closed her eyes and took a deep breath.

"Madeline, come on. Give."

She was silent for a long time. Joe resisted the impulse to say anything. He just sat there, quietly waiting with a questioning look on his face.

After what seemed like hours, she sighed and nestled into him again. Then she spoke, almost whispering in his ear.

"I'm an orphan, you know."

"No, I didn't. I'm sorry."

"I'm not sorry at all. My biological parents . . ." She glanced at the screen. "Shut it off, would you, please?"

After Joe did so, she closed her eyes again. "You know who the villain in that movie is modeled after, don't you?"

"Hmm? Well, yeah. Washington LaFayette, I assume."

"My parents were with LaFayette. Order of the Seventh."

"Oh, God." Joe couldn't think of anything else to say, his mind racing back to recall what he knew of one of the darkest events in American history.

Washington LaFayette, while still quite young, had

risen to prominence as a charismatic preacher and gotten himself elected to Congress. His handsome face was commonly shown in interviews, and he maintained the image of a reasonable and compassionate man, albeit perhaps excessively devout. After three terms in Congress he resigned, according to his claim, to devote himself fully to his ministry.

Image was all it was, however, for LaFayette was certifiably insane. In his private life, he was a radical "patriot" convinced that various "Un-American" forces serving the Anti-Christ were deliberately undermining the country through covert means. He built up an organization dedicated to "purifying" the country and "defending" it from these nebulous enemies.

Unfortunately, LaFayette was far more intelligent than most sociopaths. Even as his insanity grew, he was mostly able to conceal it, while tightening his grip on his own core group. LaFayette was able to gain total control over those most closely associated with him, who were divided into various "Orders," with the highest being "Order of the Seventh." They accepted everything he said and did, even when his personal habits as well as his political views became more and more extreme.

He designed a number of "purifiers"—his euphemism for targeted weapons of mass destruction—and was on the verge of actually beginning a strike against the most "contaminated" areas of America when one of the intelligence agencies finally realized what was going on. In a last-minute raid on LaFayette's compound, twelve officers of various enforcement agencies were killed and a number of others wounded. Four hundred and twenty-three of LaFayette's followers also died, the majority by suicide. LaFayette himself was shot before he could trigger the devices which would have destroyed the whole compound.

"Jesus. You couldn't have been much more than, what, eight?"

"I was nine." She looked up at the screen again, which was now dark. "Mike Dixon—the actor they chose—did an awfully good job. He even looks something like LaFayette."

A lot of things about Madeline Fathom that had always puzzled Joe now started making sense. "That's why you went into intelligence, isn't it, with a specialty in security? I wondered, since . . . well, you really don't seem the type."

She nodded. "They saved me. Killed him just before he killed all of us in the compound. My parents"—she spat the word out—"were ready to die with him. *Did* die with him, thank God, when they committed suicide. But they'd already stopped being anything like 'parents' to me by the time I was five. I knew they were grooming me to be one of LaFayette's so-called 'brides'—the bastard was partial to girls who'd just reached puberty—and I did everything in my power to avoid catching his attention. Which wasn't much. Fortunately, it was all over before that could happen."

The icy, calm way she spoke the words didn't seem to belong to a human voice at all. Joe groped, trying to imagine the self-control she must have started developing at an age that was normally the most carefree in a human being's life.

"I knew I couldn't fight him, that no one could fight him. But then the soldiers came, and they *did* fight him.

And they brought me somewhere safe. I told myself when I got older that I'd make sure that people like him couldn't hurt anyone ever again, and that I'd help the people that saved me. And . . . that's what I did. I was training for it by the time I was ten. Never had any other career I wanted."

She took a deep breath, and stood up suddenly. "Sorry that I ruined things. Look, can I take a rain check on the evening. Please?"

"Sure, of course."

She smiled. "Thanks, Joe. I like you an awful lot, just so you know. But . . . this kind of thing isn't easy for me."

Joe rose also. "You want me to walk you back to your cabin?"

She chuckled, a bit darkly. "I think I can manage, even if this is the rough part of town." .

"See you tomorrow, then?"

"Yes." She turned to go, stopped, and suddenly kissed him on the cheek. A moment later, she opened the door and slipped through, closing it behind her.

Joe stared at the door long after it closed, gently fingering the cheek she'd kissed.

"I will be good God-damned," he said finally.

As always in moments of stress or deep emotion, Joe's thoughts turned to food. Not eating it, but cooking it. Nothing relaxed him so much as working in the kitchen. Like most of the crew, wanting to enjoy the company and the conversations, he usually ate in the mess hall. But, needless to say, his kitchen was fully stocked.

The recipe he chose was a very tricky one. But that suited his mood—even more, his purpose.

Joe Buckley was not particularly experienced in the

business of falling in love. But he was very intelligent. Falling in love with Madeline Fathom was going to be a lot trickier than any recipe, so he'd better start warming up.

# Chapter 32

We are definitely making progress," Skibow said. "Oh, yes, quite a bit, thanks to you two," Dr. Mayhew agreed.

A.J. and Helen smiled together at that. They had rather warm feelings towards the linguists, who had catalyzed their relationship. "So do you want to share?"

"Well, of course, we do!" Dr. Mayhew said tartly. "Who wouldn't want to brag a bit?"

Her English accent gave her a schoolteacher air, especially with her prematurely gray hair pulled tightly back. "Take a seat and we'll give you a linguistic tour of what we've learned so far. We actually have some guesses as to the meaning of some words, which we'll get to in a bit."

"The first thing that strikes anyone when looking at these is that the writing is in curves, where we would use straight lines," Dr. Skibow began. "This seems to fit fairly well with the natural tendencies of Bemmie's manipulatory appendages and viewing arrangement. It's a bit more of a leap, however, to guess at the next level of structure. I believe we mentioned that we thought the various groupings of letters equate to words. This does rely on the assumption that the symbols are, like letters in English, basically phonetic in nature. That assumption, in turn, is based on the fact that so far we have found a very limited set of symbols used in what appear to be words—thirty-four, so far—plus a set of symbols we believe to be numerals in base nine. The very small number of symbols leads us to think they used an alphabet rather than a syllabary, although that's just a guess right now."

"For a short time," Mayhew picked up the narrative, "we thought that we had a larger set of words, and a rather confusing set thereof, than we did. However, one of the pattern-matching programs noticed that a lot of the words were mirror spellings of other words. After some comparison, we realized that our alien friends do at least one thing very differently from us. And by 'us' I mean *any* written human language. Where we write left to right or vice versa, they write outward from the *center*. The text in their approach is written something like this, if they were writing English."

She activated a display and wrote:

**xof nworb kciuq ehT Jumped over the lazy dog**

"So our initial survey would've had a total of nine words, when there's actually only eight unique words present, as 'the' appears twice. This method of writing brings up some very interesting questions as to just how our friends perceived things. Any human trying to read this way would start getting her brain scrambled pretty fast. Awfully dizzy, at least. In any case, we then were able to arrange a list of all the words and the order in which they appeared at any given point. That gave us a total starting vocabulary, if we could translate it, of about two thousand unique words from all sources, with a lot of those words being very common. Those are presumably the equivalents of 'the,' 'a,' and so on, but without knowing something of the actual meanings involved we're now getting out on the far fringe of guesswork.

"Once we had the clue of color to show us that we were in fact on the right track—and to bring up a whole bunch of symbols our visible-light images had missed—we attempted to assign meaning to some of the words based on context. If a word occurs in a particular context and not another, you can assume with at least some confidence that the change in context has something to do with the meaning of the word. Similarly, if you always see one word in conjunction with another word or symbol, you can guess that there is some strong relationship between the two."

"We have been going over the various 'noteplaques,' as we've decided to call them," Dr Skibow said, "and we hit some paydirt in the form of maps. Some of the maps we've been able to match up to known Solar System bodies, including Mars and at least a couple of the moons of Jupiter. Another one, we think, refers to Saturn and its moons."

Helen cocked an eyebrow. "You 'think'?"

Skibow shrugged. "Well, everything else matches quite well. But if that Bemmie map is accurate, Saturn had a moon about half the size of Titan, sixty-five million years ago. Which it certainly doesn't today."

"That's . . . possible," A.J. mused. "Even on the astronomical scale, sixty-five million years is a hefty stretch of time. An extrasolar body might have come into the system and yanked that moon out altogether. Or, for that matter, I've never been too satisfied with the current fashionable theory about what caused Saturn's rings." Somewhat grudgingly: "I admit, it's not my field of expertise."

Helen saw that Mayhew's plump face seemed to be undergoing a struggle of some sort, as if the linguist was trying to keep from laughing. When their eyes met, Helen smiled faintly, to show that she understood the source of the humor.

*A.J. Baker? Publicly confessing he doesn't know* everything?

For all of Mayhew's evident amusement, it was just as obvious that she wasn't irritated. People—including Helen—put up with A.J.'s unthinking intellectual arrogance, easily enough, because there was never anything mean-spirited about it. His attitudes didn't derive from personal competitiveness or a desire to belittle anyone else. They were just a side effect of the man's fascination with the universe.

Skibow continued. "We're hoping that in some of the other still-sealed rooms we'll get some more maps or similarly interpretable diagrams, because on the maps we found labels, just like we label our maps. We think we've got a handle on at least part of their system of measurement—on the large scale, anyway—and we're getting words out of it.

"Here's one. This word"—a series of Bemmian symbols shimmered in the display—"means crater, we're almost sure. That's because every time we find the equivalent spot on our maps, there's a crater right at that point. So far, at least."

"That'd mean an awful lot of repetitions of the word, across something like Mars."

Mayhew shook her head. "Not every crater is labeled, Helen— far from it. Only a few on each map. Presumably they were points of interest for our friends. Even on our astronomical maps we don't label every crater, only the larger ones. As these people were presumably actually landing on these bodies, I would therefore theorize that these were craters they landed on or had an interest in."

"Maybe not, though," A.J. countered. "Maybe the word isn't *crater*. Maybe it's *mine* or *quarry*."

Skibow raised an eyebrow. "Good point. It could, I suppose, also mean *colony*, if they were settling the area."

Helen made a face. "I see your problem. You're in the same position we were when we had the single arm-plate from Bemmie, trying to reconstruct something incredibly complex from almost no information at all."

"Yes. We hope that we can examine at least some of these craters and determine what it is about them that made them worth labeling. The puzzling part is that they certainly aren't the most spectacular and interesting craters. So perhaps A.J.'s guess is right: these are craters that had something interesting in them from a practical standpoint."

"Tell you what," A.J. said. "I'll have a couple of the Faeries pop away from Phobos for a bit and do some focused imaging and scanning on any of those craters that are in range. Combine that with the pretty heavy-duty info we already have on Mars, and I might at least be able to tell you something interesting about the ones you have labeled on the Mars maps. Do your maps cover all of Mars?"

"Oh, not even close," Skibow replied. "Perhaps twenty percent of the surface, and thirteen labeled craters in that area."

"Bring it up and let's see the equivalence on the surface."

The diagrams from the alien maps showed on the screen, and then faded. A map of Mars appeared, with part of what would be the tropical and subtropical portion of the northern hemisphere highlighted.

"Okay, I see. Yeah, I think the Faeries can get some decent images and ground penatrating radar shots on that, if the returns can be sorted out. I was getting some returns from Mars initially, but that doesn't mean that all parts of Mars will be equally good for GPR. The geometry might screw me up, too. But we'll see."

"Aren't you supposed to keep the Faeries researching Phobos?" Helen reminded him.

"I'm supposed to find out as much as I can about Phobos, the alien base, and anything else I can about Bemmie. These maps and the craters indicated are definitely related to Bemmie and his people. So I figure that if, by doing a little detective work, I can resolve our debate about just what they found interesting about those craters, I'll be just doing my job."

"True enough," Helen said. "I doubt anyone's going to argue with you anyway, not when you're basically our only source of on-hand investigation for the next couple of months."

"There are advantages to being virtually indispensable."
A.J. grinned.

"Which is why you shouldn't be scaring us by getting
so close to being dispensed with."

A.J. managed to keep his grin, but it faltered a bit. He'd
quietly admitted to Helen that his recent brush with death
had scared him, much more than his first, because this
one had taken slow days to close in on him. The fire and
explosion had been a few moments of pain and panic and
effort, and then he'd woken up with the worst behind
him. This time his own body had been slowly and inexorably shutting down, cutting off his air and energy.

"Yeah. Well, that's over, anyway. And we've taken a lot
of steps to keep anything like that from happening again."
He suddenly blinked and looked surprised.

"What is it?"

"Just remembered something I'd completely forgotten about while I was sick. I have to go talk to Ken."

"A problem?"

"Probably nothing, but he should know anyway." Helen
could tell that there was more to it, but obviously he preferred to keep the information to himself.

She didn't press him. Part of the reason she and A.J.
got along as well as they did was that they gave each
other a lot of room. One of the few things she'd found
amusing about the tabloids' obsession with her and A.J.
had been their constant predictions that the two of them
were on the verge of a breakup. In point of fact, their
relationship had been remarkably free of much in the
way of quarreling—quite unlike the marriage Helen had
gotten into for six miserable years when she'd been in
her twenties. The one and only photograph the tabloids

had ever published that seemed to show them yelling at each other—which they ran endlessly, of course— had actually been a shot of the two of them trying to sing.

Something which neither of them could do worth a damn, and had proven it that day to their mutual satisfaction. Helen would also allow that part of the reason the tabloids loved that photo was that it had been taken while they were vacationing in Florida and Helen's bikini had been . . . Well, a bikini.

A skimpy one, at that, even by bikini standards. Helen had only worn it because A.J. had bought it for her and insisted—and she had never worn it since.

"All right," she said, half-smiling at the memory. "I imagine we've taken up too much of your time, anyway. Dr. Mayhew, Dr. Skibow—"

"Jane and Rich, please," Jane Mayhew interrupted. "There's only fifty of us. It would be silly to stay so formal, even if I do keep falling back into my bloody lecture-room habits."

"No problem, Jane, Rich. We'll be moving on."

"Our pleasure, Helen. Drop by whenever you and A.J. feel like it. Who knows, you may solve our problems again."

"Well, you helped solve ours!" A.J. said, with a wink at Helen.


On their way out, Helen said with great dignity: "*We* didn't have a problem. *You* did."

A.J. smiled but didn't even try to make a rejoinder. Clearly, his mind was focused on whatever problem he was taking to Ken. There was as much point in badinage with A.J. when he was in that mind-set as there would be trying to swap jokes with a beaver making a dam—or a five-year-old child absorbed in watching a cartoon.

Oh, well. They'd *still* foiled the tabloids, hadn't they? A feat which, with some experience, Helen had come to rank right up there with taking the gold at the Olympics or deciphering the Maya script. Or winning the Trojan War.

And—although she'd disapproved at the time and still did— Helen couldn't deny that she wished she'd had a camera herself once. To capture the delightfully shocked expression on a paparazzi's face as A.J. sent him sailing through a window.

# Chapter 33

"And that's what I found."

Ken Hathaway felt a leaden weight sinking in the pit of his stomach, as he looked over the code and symbols A.J. was showing to him. "A back door?"

"Into the main controls. Covers the entire communications grid. I checked, and there's a similar one in the backup. Checked the rest of the systems—well, to make a long story short, someone has managed to compromise the entirety of our ship's systems. There's a back door into virtually everything on board that isn't completely standalone."

"How did you find this, and when?"

A.J. looked apologetic. "Actually, I found it a few weeks ago. Right when Doc Wu got sick, he told me how bad it might get, so I started trying to improve our automation. A lot of that being perceptual interpretation, I figured I could probably code it better than anyone else. I ran across a minor anomaly in the comm and sensor grid that led me to the first discovery, and then the others, until I realized that most of the ship must be like this. Then I got sick and . . . Well, forgot all about it until today."

With anyone else, Ken would have been furious. *How could you* forget *something like this?! For weeks?!*

But . . . That was just A.J.'s nature. The flip side of his ability to concentrate—downside, often enough—was that he could become oblivious to almost everything else.

"The reactor controls?" Ken had a horrid vision of someone having the ability to cause the entire ship to blow up or melt down.

"No, actually." A.J.'s face showed some puzzlement. "That's clean as a whistle. Oh, with some of the other back doors, whoever it is could probably get control of the engines and the reactor. But they'd be doing it through the standard interfaces aside from their initial system entry."

"Any guess as to the purpose of all these compromises? If they don't want to just kill us off, what do they want?" Ken rubbed his scalp. "I've got to call Fathom in on this. We're dealing here with her specialty."

A.J.'s jaws tightened. "That's exactly why you *shouldn't* call her in."

"Huh?" The captain of the *Nike* stared at the imaging and data processing specialist. "But she's already got authority to access pretty much anything she wants. She's in charge of security, for Pete's sake. Why would she have back doors hidden in the system?"

"Well, I like the woman, myself. I can't think of anybody who doesn't, really. But then—if you were a security heavy, wouldn't you rather that everyone liked you instead of being paranoid about you?"

Ken thought about it for a moment. "Okay, sure, of course I would. Still—"

"And if you were a security specialist working for the U.S. government, you'd be unhappy about the fact that political horse-trading has made something like thirty percent of the crew foreign nationals, wouldn't you?"

Ken snorted. "Security specialist, be damned. I'm just a soldier and *I'm* not happy about it. So . . . yeah, I see your point."

"And if—note that I say 'if'—you were the sort that felt that clamping a heavy security lid on things was the best policy if we found something really strategically useful, wouldn't you realize that the scientists aren't necessarily going to shut up on their own?"

Ken saw where this was going. "And if you did, you'd want a way to make sure that you could just *make* everyone shut up. Even if it meant overriding every system capable of communication on the entire ship."

"Yep. Especially since you'd have to be worried that even other Americans on board might prefer the 'information wants to be free' path. And that the kinda apolitical captain might back you up . . . and, then again, might not."

Ken set his jaws. "That's pure bullshit. I'm not into politics myself, that's true. And it's also true that all the years I've spent hobnobbing with you scientific types has made a lot of your attitudes about the free flow of information and knowledge rub off on me. But the fact remains—don't ever doubt it, A.J.—that I'm a professional officer serving in the military forces of the United States of America. Madeline Fathom is the duly-authorized representative of our government in charge of security here, and I *would* back her up any time she acted in that capacity. Regardless of whether I agreed with her or not."

A.J. shrugged. "Fine. But you think like a soldier. In my experience—thankfully limited—I really don't think security people have the same mentality at all. So whatever you might know you might do, they wouldn't necessarily think you would. If that twisted grammar makes any sense."

It made plenty of sense to Hathaway. A.J.'s analysis, now that Ken thought about it, was a lot more plausible than even the imaging and data expert knew. Unlike the rest of the crew, Brigadier General Hathaway had known General Deiderichs off and on for years. While the general hadn't told him much, the way in which he didn't say certain things was a clear warning: Madeline Fathom carried one hell of a lot of weight, possibly even more than Deiderichs himself.

That meant that whichever intelligence agency Fathom was working for—and Ken suspected it was the HIA, which had more clout than any of them when it wanted to use it—she had what amounted to a direct pipeline to the President. Which, in turn, meant that if the back doors A.J. had discovered did lead back to her, she had the legitimate authority to have them and to use them. That was true regardless of what Brigadier General Ken Hathaway thought personally about the mind-set involved and its readiness to use duplicitous methods.

*God forbid the right hand should ever tell the left hand what it's doing.* He remembered a wisecrack once made by a fellow Air Force officer: *The only difference between the nuts in security and the ones in lunatic asylums is that the security nuts insist their straightjackets have to have clearance and be stamped Top Secret.*

"What a mess," he muttered. "All right, A.J. I won't tell Fathom until you do an initial check to see if she's the one who's holding the back doors. If she is, then it's a moot point. You and I know, and we just forget about it. But if she *isn't* the one, then we've got a real problem with security and I'm bringing her in right away. And in the meantime, we don't tell anyone else. I'm willing to stretch things that far, but I'm not willing to spread this to anyone except Fathom."

A.J. nodded. "No sweat. If for no other reason, I don't want Joe to know. Not from me, anyway. You wanna talk about a mess."

Ken grimaced. To everyone else's surprise—and A.J.'s astonishment—Joe Buckley and Madeline Fathom were often seen together since the voyage had started. By now the two were, if not an item, at least one of the strongest candidates for becoming an item on board *Nike*. If they were wrong about Madeline, a very nice friendship—or something more—could be torpedoed with no justification. Or, if Joe reacted the other way, A.J. could find his best friend alienated from him.

"Right. In any event, we need to check all the other alternatives— and immediately. If Fathom's the one with the back doors, she has them on official authority. Which someone else *wouldn't*—and that would be an order of magnitude worse. We need to make sure, if we can, that that's not the case. In the meantime . . . Have you closed off any or all of the back doors?"

"Nary a one. But I've booby-trapped them. When someone activates one of them, I'll be able to catch 'em at it. And of course I can always override them now that I know what's going on. That's why you made me the DP head around here."

Ken gave A.J. a hard look, just short of an outright glare. "Understand something, A.J. If it does turn out that it's Fathom, I'll want you to remove the booby traps. I don't like the idea of her having those back doors, but what I don't like doesn't make any difference. She *is* in charge of security. But until we know one way or the other, keep them in place. If it's someone else, we do *not* want those back doors functional."

A.J. nodded, although Hathaway was quite sure that he had reservations. Reservations strong enough, in fact, that Ken would probably have problems with him if it did turn out to be Fathom.

But that was for a later day—which might never come.

In that respect, at least, A.J. obviously felt the same way he did. "Well," the imaging specialist said, "I just hope we never have to find out."

*So do I*, Madeline thought to herself as she shut off the recording. *So do I.*

Not that it would make a very big difference. She'd been expecting to hear that conversation, or one like it, right around now. A.J. was good, but he was only second-rate as a security specialist. More than good enough for basic civilian or low-level military stuff, to be sure, and he was probably a hell of a cracker if he wanted to be. But when you had the resources to draw on that Madeline did, a second-rater was only going to find what you wanted them to find.

Everything had to be a double blind whenever possible.

One of the best ways of defusing effective resistance was to convince your opponents that they were smarter than you were, always just a step ahead. In this case, she'd arranged for fairly well-hidden back doors to exist—while burying her real back doors far deeper inside the system. It was the same strategy she'd used with respect to her martial arts capability.

Not quite the same strategy, she reminded herself. It wouldn't do to underestimate A.J. Baker. Her martial arts skills were hers alone, while in this case she was only about as good as A.J. in her own right. Not even that, really, given a level playing field.

But this wasn't a level playing field, not even close. The HIA could tap the best people in the world when it came to this sort of work. All Madeline had had to do was arrange access for one of them to assist in the coding. He'd done the rest.

Bugging Hathaway's office had not been difficult. It had been trivially easy, in fact, since no one had been expecting surveillance equipment to be installed aboard *Nike*. The military people and scientists who made up the crew just didn't think in those terms.

Now she had to decide if she'd gotten all the use out of the monitors that she could reasonably expect, or whether she should leave them in place. The longer they sat there, the more chance there was that someone would spot them.

A.J. was, once more, the major threat there. He scattered his Fairy Dust almost randomly at times. And, unlike those in use in engineering and other departments, A.J.'s sensor motes were not merely cutting-edge but bleeding-edge, customized in both their software and sometimes even hardware aspects. In fact, she had to grudgingly admit that they outperformed even the supposedly top-of-the-line stuff she'd been supplied for this mission. If A.J. ever decided to start looking for other sensor motes, she'd be busted. Martial arts was his exercise and computer systems his sideline, but sensor systems and detecting things that were hidden was A.J. Baker's expertise. He was probably the best in the world at it. She knew without a shadow of a doubt that she could no more beat A.J. on that battlefield than he could beat her in an honest fight.

So the decision wasn't to be made casually. She'd gotten excellent intelligence from them so far. But was the chance of getting more such information worth the risk that A.J.—suspicions already aroused by finding the back doors—might decide to sweep the ship for other unauthorized activity?

"No," she answered herself aloud. She was already tap-dancing on land mines. The monitors she had in place to maintain surreptitious surveillance of *Nike*'s personnel were already stretching the letter of the law. Even the military members of the crew would be furious, if they found out. The civilian members would completely blow their stacks, negating at one stroke all of Madeline's long and careful work to build up their trust and cooperation.

There was no point in keeping around extra ways of detonating the mines if she didn't really need them. She sent out the signal which caused the motes to move into the air system and allow themselves to be filtered out with the rest of the dust.

Then, was surprised at the relief that swept over her. It was disconcerting to realize just how uncomfortable she'd become with her role in this mission. She hadn't

gotten the usual satisfaction seeing how neatly Ken and
A.J. had followed her script. It had been almost painful
to listen to them voicing their suspicions about her.

Jesus! I'm actually feeling guilty about this whole thing!

She shook her head and sighed. She still believed in
her mission, even if she'd slowly come to detest it from a
personal standpoint.

The worst aspect of the situation was that if she wanted
to avoid the eventual confrontation, she had to hope that
nothing particularly exciting or revelatory was discovered
on this trip. Which meant that either way things went,
her friends were going to end up disappointed—either in
what they found in Phobos, or in what they found in her.

And this was the first time in her life that Madeline
Fathom had had real friends.

Even possibly—she started to shy away from the
thought, but forced herself not to—a romantic involvement that went beyond a brief and casual sexual liaison.

Madeline couldn't conceal from herself that the worst
part of that whole conversation was the thought of them
telling Joe, and the relief she'd felt when they decided
not to tell anyone. For the first time in her life, she had
an impulse to just get it over with—go to Ken, tell him
the situation, and drop the whole thing in his lap. She sat
in the chair, feeling one-third of a gravity pulling on her
more heavily than anything she'd felt on Earth since she
was nine years old.

What am I going to do about Joe?

She had no answer. Or, at least, no answer she liked.

# Chapter 34

"All rotation stopped. Habitats secured and locked. All personnel report ready for acceleration."

"Understood." Captain Hathaway surveyed *Nike*'s bridge to make sure everyone was properly seated and strapped in. While they wouldn't be taking extreme acceleration, "up" and "down" would no longer be in their accustomed directions. And there would be varying levels of acceleration; enough to be anything from inconvenient to dangerous for the unwary.

He hit the PA button. "Attention all hands."

That sounded sort of pompous, but he couldn't resist. It also sounded proper.

"We are about to begin deceleration in our approach to orbit. After the main burn, there will likely be two or three minor burns to match us with Phobos and then bring us to rest with respect to it. Following that, work crews will begin preparations for landing. We expect to land the first people on Phobos sometime tomorrow or the day after. Unless there's an emergency, please do not move around until the main burn is completed. We don't want any accidents. We're all healthy and ready to get to work, and we don't need anything getting in the way of that."

The presence of a number of humans in the bridge area was more a security blanket and backup than anything else. The precise burn durations and vectors had been calculated and recalculated dozens of times, and were updated daily to account for any departure from the original assumptions. *Nike* knew exactly when to turn, exactly when to fire her mighty engines and for precisely how long. Unless something went wrong, neither Hathaway nor anyone else on board would have to lift a finger during the entire process.

The only expected partially-manual work when it came to flying *Nike* was going to be closing the distance with Phobos. The automatic orbit-matching was deliberately designed to leave a considerable distance between the ship and the little moon, just in case something did go wrong. Like the tiny Faeries before her, *Nike* would use ion drives to close the distance after matching the basic orbit.

Unlike the Faeries and *Pirate*, however, *Nike* had the fuel and power to match orbits through its own efforts, rather than requiring atmospheric braking. That was necessary, because the design challenges involved in making a spacecraft the size, shape, and complexity of *Nike* able to survive atmospheric braking were something to give even modern computers major, major headaches. Dr. Gupta didn't think it could be done at all, in the absence of science-fictional deflector shields or unobtainium hulls.

A faint vibration ran through the ship, and suddenly a deep-throated roar thundered through *Nike*. The nuclear engines had awakened for the first time in months. Six columns of nuclear-powered fire now blazed astern, pitting themselves against the miles-per-second momentum of the huge ship.

In space there was no sound. But vibration at that level transmitted itself through the main hull and reverberated in the atmosphere of the bridge. There was certainly sound in *Nike* herself. Ken was pressed back into the cushions of his seat at nearly half Earth-normal acceleration—which felt much greater to a body used to Martian levels of gravity after many weeks in space.

Displays showed the decrease in velocity, the approach of the vessel toward its intended orbit, Phobos approaching in simulation. Another showed the approach of *Nike* as seen from Phobos itself, a blaze of light from what had been something barely more than another star a moment before. A.J. had two of the Faeries positioned to record the entire approach and eventual landings for posterity.

The live view from a rear-facing boom camera, projected on the main window's active display, showed Phobos swelling. Starting at the size of a misshapen Luna from Earth, by now the moonlet was nearly twice that size.

The sharp gray-black shadowed surface suddenly looked menacing to Ken. Twenty kilometers was miniscule on the astronomical scale, but when compared to *Nike* it was immense. From that perspective, Phobos was a mass of rock nearly fifty times *Nike*'s length. It was a flying mountain the size of ten Everests mashed together, where an alien race had built a base—and had then died from an unknown catastrophe sixty-five million years before.

Perhaps Phobos had devoured them. The moonlet made Ken think of a gigantic sea beast, rising from the black depths.

He dismissed the grotesque notion. There were enough genuine hazards without inventing fantastical ones. "Engine status?"

"All engines showing green," Jackie answered. "Not that you needed to ask, really. If anything goes wrong, about a dozen alarms will scream their heads off."

"Will you at least let me *pretend* to be a real captain?"

"Aye aye, sir." Jackie got a false-solemn look on her face. "We're approaching the alien base, Captain. Should we raise shields?"

"Very funny. How are we tracking?"

"Well within tolerances. About four hundred seconds of burn left to go. Relative velocity has dropped below two point five kilometers per second."

The freight-train roar continued, the nuclear engines hurling more than three tons of fuel into space every second at an exhaust velocity of nearly twenty thousand miles per hour. Phobos was enormous and still swelling, now a hulking presence more than ten times wider than the Moon as seen from Earth. Even more than before, the satellite reminded Ken of a monster—with the five-mile-wide crater of Stickney being its single, glaring, off-center eye.

"How big is that going to get before we stop?" Ken wondered idly, trying not to sound at all nervous.

The problem with Phobos was that it was on a scale that the human mind could—just barely—grasp, as opposed to the Earth or the Moon. Something like that approaching touched a very primal chord.

"About seven point one six degrees—more than fourteen times wider than the Moon looks," A.J. answered, from his own console. "Being a hundred miles away is pretty far, sure, but that thing is twenty kilometers wide. It looks a hell of a lot bigger than it did in the photos back home, I can tell you that."

He turned his head and flashed Ken a wicked grin. "Lives up to its name *Fear*, doesn't it? Especially with that crater staring at us! Reminds me of some sort of gigantic Cyclops."

"Shut up, will you?" Hathaway growled. "I was *trying* not to think the same thing."

The blaze of *Nike* now covered measurable width on Rane's image; six separate tiny jets were visible.

"Sixty seconds left . . . thirty . . . ten . . . five, four, three, two, one, ze—"

The rockets cut off as Jackie was in mid word. Ken felt a momentary disorientation as free fall returned. Phobos loomed before them, but no longer did the barren miniature moon swell like a slowly inflating balloon.

"Relative speed with respect to Phobos?"

"Waiting on verification . . ." A.J. answered. "Okay, near zero. Very near zero. Let's just say that if we were staking *Nike* out in the yard like a dog, it'd be a week before she reached the end of her chain. Not bad for a shot across a hundred million miles. Starting closing calculations now."

Ken hit the intercom. "Ladies and gentlemen, we have stopped relative to Phobos. We have successfully completed the first interplanetary voyage in the history of mankind. Congratulations!"

He didn't need the intercom to hear the cheers.

# PART VI: PHOBOS

*Surmise, n: a matter of conjecture; an idea
or thought of something as being possible or
likely, often coming unexpectedly or by
surprise.*

# Chapter 35

"One . . . two . . . *three!*"

On three, Joe and Harry Ingram pulled hard on the levers, each held from moving by the bracing they were strapped into. Jobs like this could be done using automatic machinery, but automated drones were much better for doing the more controlled and predictable gruntwork of sealing, insulating, and making livable portions of Phobos. If human muscle and mechanical advantage couldn't do the job here, they could always use some of the fancier powered equipment.

No need, Joe saw with satisfaction, as the alien doorway ground partly open for the first time in over sixty million years. Ingram, who'd done more work of this sort than Joe, unsnapped part of his harness expertly and rotated his body around, shining a bright LED flashlight into the room.

"Clear on the near side, nothing in the way. Looks

interesting— not a duplicate of any of the other rooms we've seen so far. Let's get the door open a little further."

Joe nodded, noting to himself that it was a lot more comfortable doing stuff like this when you could use the best equipment. The Ares Project had planned on using the best spacesuit designs it could afford, of course, but when you are strapped for cash, what you can afford isn't the same thing as what a government agency with a top-level mandate and effectively unlimited credit can afford. The spacesuits worn by *Nike*'s personnel were lighter, thinner, tougher, more efficient, and more versatile than anything Ares could possibly have managed.

The suit's main advantages came from its incorporation of a carbon nanotube–derived fiber weave manufactured (at currently ruinous cost and mostly for military applications) by the Tayler Corporation. The "carbonan" reinforcement layers made the suits virtually impenetrable by any accident short of being struck by a meteor or shot by a heavy-duty firearm. The integrated electronics, "smart" sensors, recycling systems, and other bells and whistles had even forced A.J. to grudgingly admit that he couldn't have programmed their suits to be as effective; the integrated processor power simply wouldn't have been there.

Similar top-end designs were being tested by the military as powered battlefield armor. Due to a strong preference for saving power in space for other functions, however, there were no provisions for boosting the user's strength in the Tayler spacesuits. But there were ports to connect the suit to various other devices to control and even power them, as well as distributed sensors to track conditions around the wearer.

The suits were as well shielded as such mobile objects could reasonably be. The helmets were light and felt open, rather than cramped and claustrophobic as prior models had been. In addition, the suits incorporated an integrated exterior weave of electroactive pigments which varied the reflectivity of the exterior to assist in heating and cooling. Another layer of piezoelectrically-active fibers was able to stiffen the suit against detected impacts, distributing the force across the entire body of the wearer instead of permitting blunt trauma to be done to one area.

With the toughness of the suits a given, Joe and the rest of *Nike*'s crew were better able to concentrate on their jobs. It might not be quite as easy as working on something back home, given microgravity and other factors. Still, it was orders of magnitude easier than it would have been a couple of decades earlier.

Locked back in, Harry nodded to Joe and the two began working on getting the door to open wider.

"Hey, did anybody figure out why these doors got locked up?" Harry asked to the invisible audience at large. "I mean, it can't just have been the power loss—only idiots would design doors that couldn't be opened in case of power failure, at least for most of their base. And we've found things that look like manual opening mechanisms."

"Well," A.J. answered, "it's impossible to be sure until we find out exactly what caused the disaster. But based on models Dr. Sakai and some of the other people in the astrogeological specialties have done . . . you remember the lines on the side of Phobos?"

"Yeah," Joe said, adjusting the grip of the lever arms. "Fracture zones, right?"

"Yep. No one was sure how far down those things went,

or how intact—or not intact—Phobos was. The moonlet might have been just a ball of stone fragments that hadn't quite broken up. As it turns out the fracture zones aren't nearly that bad, but they are significant. If what happened to them involved a big explosion, or an impact, it might have shifted the geometry of the caverns slightly, changing angles just enough to cause the doors to lock up in their tracks."

"Makes sense," Joe said. "And with the seals shrinking through outgassing over the years, that would have given them enough space to move again. Okay, we're ready. Harry, let's open this thing up wide."

The door protested stubbornly, occasionally allowing the two to hear its dissatisfaction by transmitting a vibration through the equipment that sounded like a groan inside the suits. But, in a few minutes, the door was open wide enough for them to enter.

"Captain, we're going in now. And I think it's something new."

"Be careful."

"We will be. But, look, this place is dead. There's nothing dangerous here, aside from vacuum."

"That's what we *think*. Let's not assume."

"Right."

Joe drifted into the room cautiously after shining his own light around. The room was about average-sized, from what they'd seen so far. It was a bit over two meters at maximum height, which was too low for human comfort but still easy to move through. Fifteen meters long and about ten to twelve meters wide, the room's interior was clad in the metal-composite material they'd come to expect, with varicolored circles and lines on the walls that seemed to be a common theme.

Despite the similarities, though, it wasn't like anything they'd seen thus far. First, this room's long axis lay parallel to the corridor. They'd entered at one end, from the side. At the other end of the room was another door. That seemed to indicate a room bordering that side of the corridor but which had no direct entrance or exit in that wall, as they knew there weren't any other doors for quite some distance.

Secondly, the room was divided roughly in half down the center, by a low wall with a wide, flat top separating the two halves. On one end, the wall had a set of hinges of some sort. Behind this area was another set of doors and a small tripartite control panel similar to those found in the large control room and in a few other places.

A *Bemmius* mummy lay in that area, arms curled across each other and outward in what Helen currently considered a possibly instinctive defensive posture. "By doing that they protect the mouth, eye, and brain areas, and have those long, sharp hooklike structures pointing out towards any possible threat," she'd said. "This is rather like us throwing our arms up to protect our faces, or covering our heads with our arms in a falling rock area."

Judging by the number of *Bemmius* mummies found in that pose—which did not accord well with models of how a relaxed or a random death pose would look after mummification—it might well be that this was the equivalent of a person realizing he was doomed and ending up cowering in the corner.

"Look at his hands."

Joe nodded. The "hands," the complexly-divided portions of the quasi-tentacles that allowed *Bemmius* to use tools, showed signs of tremendous abuse. Some of the "fingers" were torn off and others were twisted and bent, showing that the internal structural plates were damaged or misaligned. Like others they had examined in the sealed rooms, this *Bemmius* had apparently tried to force the door open in a panic. A close examination showed that he had beaten and clawed at all three doors in the room, at some point during his imprisonment here.

"So, which door now?"

"Let's see what's behind the far door there. Until now, we haven't found any room that adjoins the corridor that doesn't have a door to it. I'm wondering why this one doesn't."

"Right." Joe floated back, gathered up the door opener that Gupta had designed while they were en route, and made his way back. He was careful in the microgravity not to let the heavy metal and composite structure get moving too fast. There might be almost no gravity, but the tool's mass was still the same.

"Have you seen the complaints from Earth about our exploration techniques?"

"Hey, they have a point," Harry said, floating at ease as he waited for Joe to get the opener in position. "If we were using these methods on, say, Egyptian tombs, we'd be lynched."

"Still, it's not like we're going to be letting in air to cause decay."

"No. But the proper archaeological—or paleontological, for that matter—approach would be to spend weeks slowly working away at methods to open them, recording each and every movement, and so on." He caught the door opener as it approached and gave Joe time to get set up to position the framework.

"Yeah," A.J. commented from whatever remote area he was working in, "but if the ancient Egyptian tombs had actually been built by space aliens, like some nutcases thought, and if we thought we might discover their tech inside, you can bet we'd be out there with backhoes and bulldozers and the namby-pamby archaeologists would be taking the back seat."

"No doubt," Joe concurred, "although I'd recommend you be a lot more diplomatic in the way you said that, if you were talking to Helen. I worked with her in the field for several summers, don't forget. And I can tell you that hell hath no fury like a bonedigger scorned."

A few minutes of setup and they were able to force this second door open, with a great deal of grunting.

"This one was a lot tougher," Joe finally gasped, relaxing in the restraint straps and waiting for his breathing to slow.

"Sure was," Harry said, almost as winded. "I wonder if—"

He did his unstrap-and-swing-around stunt again. "Well, that's interesting. This door's almost twice as thick as all the others."

A.J.'s voice broke in, pitched unnaturally low. "That leaves the question . . . was it so thick to keep something from breaking in—or is it that thick to prevent something from getting *out*?"

"Shut up, A.J.," Joe grumbled. "Being in these rooms with giant alien mummies is creepy enough without you tossing in B-movie paranoia."

"Fine, fine. Just don't go looking at any eggs in there, okay?"

"Thank you *so* much for reminding me of that image.

Get off the friggin' channel if you don't have anything useful to add."

Harry, ignoring the byplay, had unstrapped and was already into the next room. "Hey, now *this* is new."

Joe drew himself across the threshold and stopped to survey the new area. "Holy . . . You aren't kidding!"

The room was huge. Not quite the size of the monstrous room that had held the vast supplies of mud and water which the aliens had apparently favored, but still immense. The part that shared a wall with the corridor was a hundred meters long, and the room extended out from that wall twice as far. The ceiling height was about three meters—tall enough that Joe didn't feel his usual impulse to stoop. A sort of clear lane or corridor, about three meters wide, ran from the door they'd just entered across the entire width of the room. At intervals of a bit less than every three meters there were . . .

Booths, Joe guessed. Each booth had a low desk or something like it on the sides, with holes or depressions in it and other structures they'd already deduced were for holding things down in microgravity. These were pretty much universally present throughout the base, although in a number of areas it had seemed they were in positions indicating they weren't used much. That had led some eternal optimists in the crew to suggest that *Bemmius* had some form of artificial gravity. Joe doubted it; but, hey, nothing wrong with hoping.

The "booths" weren't enclosed, though. They were more like security gates at airports, Joe decided—two walls and a roof, giving you a semienclosed space about three or four meters long. That was much longer than any security gate a human being would need, of course.

But, adjusting for their greater size and the fact that their major axis was horizontal rather than vertical, just about right for a Bemmie.

You could just walk straight through from this side, down the long axis of the room to the far side. It was hard to make out details on that distant wall, but looking through the booth he thought he could see something on or against the wall directly aligned with the booth's opening. He checked a couple of others; yes, it seemed that there was something directly in line with each of the booths, way over on the far side of the room.

"Well, what have we found here?" Harry finally asked aloud.

"Looks like a bowling alley." That was Helen's voice. She must have tuned in to take a look. Joe gave silent thanks that she hadn't tuned in earlier, to hear—

"And I'll deal with *you* later, Mr. Baker. Conan the Barbarian, ha. You ever try using a bulldozer on one of *my* digs, you'll go out Conan the Castrati. As for you, Dr. Buckley, you ought to know by now that hell hath no fury like a bonedigger called a bonedigger."

Joe winced. Hastily, he focused on Helen's substantive remark. "Well, yeah, I suppose looked at from one way it does resemble a bowling alley. Sort of. But without any gravity worth talking about, you're not doing any bowling here."

"Close, and yet so far away." Hathaway's voice now broke in, clearly amused. "It's obvious y'all are civilians."

"What do you mean?" Joe and Helen asked, almost simultaneously.

Hathaway snorted. "People, *that* is a target range."

As soon as Hathaway said it, Joe felt like smacking his

forehead. Probably would have, if he hadn't been wearing the suit.

"Of course. That desk up front is where you'd go and pick up your gun for practice. The thicker door—and I'll bet this wall's a lot thicker too—keeps you from accidentally shooting through."

"Which means," Hathaway continued, his voice drawling speculatively, "that through the other door there might be an armory."

"Maybe. Well, yeah, certainly, in some sense, if the weapons are still there. But probably not military arms. I mean, you guys don't stock missiles and tank killers at the target range, right?"

"No, we don't. Still, it'd be interesting to see what they've got. I'd guess a variety of small arms, probably their equivalent of pistols, shotguns, and rifles."

Joe checked his telltales. "We've got plenty of air, and I don't feel a need to find a bathroom yet. How about it, Harry? You want to check?"

"You have to ask? This is the fun part of the expedition, like unwrapping presents at Christmas. Afterwards is when we get to the part where some assembly is required and we discover that batteries weren't included."

Harry started moving the opener toward the rear door. "We'll have to take a look at what they use as targets, too. We may be able to get a lot of used rounds out of there, which will give us ways to verify the characteristics of the weapons."

"Glendale was right," A.J. put in. "A bunch of peace nuts aren't going to have a training area like this—especially on a base where every resource had to be brought in from outside, and where most rooms had to be carved out of solid rock. Look at the size of the place. They could have had more than thirty people practicing at once, even as big as they were. That's a lot of people slinging lead—or whatever they used—and a hell of a lot of lead to sling. Lots of resources. These were not peaceful people."

Now Jackie's voice broke in. "That's at least one too many assumptions. They might have been peaceful enough, intrinsically— but had to deal with somebody or something else that wasn't. There's a difference between aggression and self-defense."

"Okay, guys, quiet down, let us work a bit here." Tough suits or not, Joe didn't want to be distracted by chatter while exerting a lot of force on small areas.

This door, however, refused to budge. After five minutes of trying, Joe and Harry sagged back in the harnesses. Or, at least, tried to—microgravity did not lend itself well to looking exhausted, whether you really were or not.

"Sorry, Captain, I be givin' her everything we got!" Joe said, in a fake Scots accent.

"Ken, I think we'll have to break out the cutters," A.J. suggested. "I've been going over their suits' sensor signals, and while they're nothing like as good as the Faeries', I can get some pretty good info from them. I think the armory door's locked, which makes sense. Would you leave it open all the time? And if the power died, our friend there couldn't have unlocked the doors."

"I agree," Hathaway stated. "Let's do it—but I'm not sure Joe and Harry are the right ones for the job. Guys?"

Joe, still panting a little, looked at Ingram. "What do you think, Harry?"

Ingram looked longingly at the door. "I'd like to try,

but we'd have to go back and get the stuff—and, being honest, I'm not trained in cutting tools for microgravity. Or even regular gravity. And stuff like that can cut our suits, so I don't think it'd be smart to play with it."

Reluctantly, Joe nodded.

"Don't give up quite yet, guys. If you can hang on for about ten minutes, I can have John Henry down there," A.J. offered.

John Henry was one of the heavy-duty drones. "Wasn't he working on securing parts of Phobos Hab Three?"

"His job's done for now. They won't need him for at least a few hours. Captain? How about it?"

"Let me check, A.J."

There was a pause while Hathaway verified with the work crews that the heavy-duty drone wouldn't be needed for a while. "Okay, go ahead. You've got a few hours at least."

Technically, Captain Hathaway didn't have to be involved in everything at this level but—like most of the crew—he wanted to see and watch everything going on. It would probably be several weeks before anyone started seeing this as a routine job.

"Shouldn't take too long. I get him down there and cut through the areas where the lock catches are engaged, maybe an hour or two tops, unless the stuff's a lot tougher than anything we've found so far. That might be true when we get to wherever they kept the big guns, if they had any. But I don't think it'll be the case here."

Joe took advantage of the delay to sip a bit of water and take a nibble of what he called "granola paste." The stuff was a tasty, if rather ugly-looking, snack he'd devised during the voyage. The stuff NASA provided them had offended every gourmet bone in Joe's body, once he tried it. He'd been quite sure he could come up with something better.

And so he had, with a little experimentation. His "granola paste" was just as easy to dispense from a tube as NASA's equivalent, yet had some real taste and even retained a little texture for chewing. People could eat it without feeling like they were eating baby food.

A while later, bright lights at the doorway announced the arrival of the squat, squarish work drone. Using both small jets and its own manipulators to move around, the remote was somewhat ominous in the way it made its entrance, seeming to climb through the doorway and drift forward.

"Okay, guys, stay clear. Electron-beam cutting is not something you want to be anywhere near."

"Roger that." Joe and Harry moved into the target range area. "Okay, we're plenty clear."

"Firing her up. John Henry, start drivin' that steel. Or those electrons, anyway."

A few minutes later, they heard A.J. grunt in what sounded a positive fashion.

"How's it going?"

"Cutting away. It's a little slow, but not too bad. You guys okay for another fifteen minutes or so? I think that'll do it for all the catches. This thing has three, near as I can tell."

Harry nodded, the motion easily visible through the mostly transparent helmet.

"We're both good, A.J. Go ahead."

It was only a bit longer than A.J.'s estimate when he gave the all-clear. "Give it a try."

After setting up the opener, the two looked at each other and then gave a pull. The door slid so suddenly that if they hadn't been strapped in, both would have been sent flying off through the nonexistent air.

"That did it, all right! Slid back almost as though it was still actually working. We're clear to enter."

As soon as the light flashed around the room's interior, Joe grinned.

"Captain, looks like our Bemmies were as fond as we were of different makes and models. Some of these look like the one the alien in the control room carried, but some of them are pretty different, allowing for the fact they've all got arrangements for being held by a *Bemmius*."

Joe drifted down the rows of racked weapons. One wall was devoted to rifle-style weapons. They had wider-flared bells at the ends, which Joe assumed were a three-"handed" grip and fire method.

"Damn, I wouldn't have wanted to go up against these guys," Harry murmured, looking down the barrel of a rifle. "That must be a two-centimeter bore. Maybe closer to three."

"No, you wouldn't," Helen concurred. "Greater mass and their construction make it fairly clear that with decent design they could hold and fire weapons of much greater caliber than we could."

"Some of these are personalized, I think," Joe said, focusing his light on what looked like swirls and patterns similar to the now-familiar *Bemmius* writing on the exposed surfaces of one of the handguns. "Maybe most of them, even. But the decorations faded or sublimed away in the millions of years since."

"Probably the side arms of the crew, kept safe when

not needed but still personal possessions," Hathaway guessed. "If so, we've found another similarity between us and them."

Joe had reached the next rack. These weapons had odd fins and protrusions along their length. He glanced down the barrel. "Hey, A.J., tell me what you think of this one."

John Henry drifted over, focusing sensors on the indicated weapon. "Well, well, well. That is no chemical propellant weapon."

"What? What have you found?" That was Madeline's voice breaking in, sounding unusually excited. "Sorry, but I *am* in intelligence, you know. New weapons, that's like my Pavlovian trigger."

"Looks like a gauss gun to me."

"Gauss gun?" Helen repeated.

"A gun that uses magnetic fields to accelerate a metallic projectile to high speeds," Hathaway explained. "Mass drivers and maglev trains work on the same basic principles."

"So the protrusions there are part of the acceleration design?"

"Probably. We'll have a lot of work to make sure. If it is, that does imply some advances in technology over us, unless it's a plug-in model. We'll have to see. Good work, Joe and Harry. Looks like we'll have something to really entertain the folks back home with. Not to mention some gadgets to get our engineers to chew on."

"That's code for 'okay, now get out of there before you mess anything up for the people who will want to record where everything was to the millimeter,' am I right?"

"Otherwise known as 'don't mess with the bone-diggers,'" came Helen's voice, darkly.

Hathaway laughed. "I'm so glad I don't have to translate for you. Besides, you've been out there a while. Time to come in."

"Right. Come on, Harry, we've got to lug this opener back. Unfortunately, A.J. didn't have the good sense to design John Henry like a pack mule."

# Chapter 36

"Too sparse for an archive."

"Ballocks," Jane Mayhew retorted. She shook her head vigorously—more so than was wise, actually, in a spacesuit. This was only the third time Mayhew had done an EVA outside of training, and she was still awkward at it. "Richard, we have no idea how many things they preferred to put on hard display, or their preferences in seating arrangements for groups or meeting places. We know those little pyramid things in the table were their equivalent of network connections, so accessing archives would be trivial."

Rich Skibow glanced around the room, studying the layout again. His more economical movements were partly a reflection of his personality, and partly due to his greater experience with working in spacesuits.

The wide, very long room had large, solid plaques on the walls— plaques which A.J. thought were bigger equivalents of the noteplaques found in the control room. A number of alien noteplaques were scattered about, with various diagrams and writing still preserved on their surfaces. Many of them rested on a very elongated table or desk, which had a number of the scalloped indentations they suspected were the equivalent of seating areas.

"A.J., would you quit grinning like a hyena?"

A.J. couldn't help it. The two linguists squabbled as though they'd been married for twenty years, and somehow after the one argument he associated the heated debates between them with good luck.

"Sorry, Rich." He tried to replace the smile with a serious look. "I agree with you, actually. Sorry, Jane."

"And why precisely, A.J.?"

"Well, if you look at things we've found so far, the Bemmies actually do seem to do things a lot like we do, allowing for the fact that they're three-handed, giant semi-land squids/giant crabs from hell. Their control room looks a lot like a control room, their shooting range looks a lot like a shooting range—and, to be honest, this looks a lot like a conference or briefing room. With the solid-display panels on the wall being for presentations."

He stared at what would be the head of the "table," if his guess was correct. The globe shape positioned there, etched with outlines and symbols, was mysteriously unrecognizable, quite unlike the others they'd seen.

Mayhew frowned. "I admit that would make sense with respect to these images"—she indicated the outlines on other wall displays which were clearly those of Mars' two hemispheres—"but what about that one?" She pointed to the same globe A.J. was wondering about.

"Their homeworld, maybe?" Rich proposed, after a

moment. "Maybe like a flag or something?"

A noise that sounded suspiciously like a giggle in their earphones startled all three.

"Not *their* homeworld," Helen's amused voice said. "*Our* home-world. That's a globe of the Earth."

"But it doesn't look anything like—"

A.J. broke off, as did the two linguists, who had started similar protests. A.J. was pretty sure his own face had the same shade of red on it as theirs did.

How embarrassing.

"Oh. Right. Sixty-five million years of continental drift."

"Very good, Mr. Baker." Dammit, that *was* a giggle!

More seriously, she continued: "That's Cretaceous-period Earth. I know that map almost as well as I know the modern one, given that we've never been able to map it completely." After a pause, she said quietly, "A.J, could you give me a close-up of that map?"

"Sure thing. Here you go."

"What is it, Helen?" Jane Mayhew asked.

"Just a minute, please. . . . Jane, Rich, would you take a look at the area to the middle right of center? There's a marking and some symbols there."

The two linguists squinted. Then Skibow nodded. "Yes, I see it. Those are the same symbols we've seen many times before—the ones we think mean 'crater' or something related to it."

There was a long silence. "I think I can tell you the subject of their last briefing."

The two scientists stared at each other. Captain Hathaway's voice broke in. "Now, hold on here. How could you possibly even guess that, Helen?"

"As near as I can tell, that symbol lies precisely on the

Chicxulub site. Where it was sixty-five million years ago,
I should say."

For a moment, no one got it. Then A.J. breathed, "Oh,
Lord."

"Of course!" Jane Mayhew said suddenly. "He died
*exactly* on the boundary, didn't he? You've told us how
that coincidence always bothered you, Helen. But it *wasn't*
a coincidence, was it?"

She looked around what they were now almost sure
had been an alien conference room. "That's what they
would have been discussing—the consequences of such
an immense impact on the biology of the most interesting world in the solar system. And they would have sent
some of their people down there to witness the events
firsthand. As far away as you found the fossil, they'd have
been in no immediate danger of being struck by the bolide
and its fragments. But they hadn't figured on the danger
posed by the local wildlife."

"Or maybe Bemmie just happened to be stuck down
there by accident," A.J. tossed in. "Engine malfunction,
whatever. That would still be enough to eliminate the
coincidence aspect that bothers Helen so much. I think
it's reasonable to assume they would have sent someone
down to make recordings before the impact—but couldn't
get away in time. And then the raptors got him."

He reached up to run his fingers through his hair, the
way he did sometimes when he was thinking. Banging his
hand into the helmet didn't seem as effective. "It's funny,
though . . ."

"What is?"

"I dunno, exactly. Just something nagging at me. I think
I'll go talk to Harry later and see if I can make sense out

of this little voice that's telling me I'm missing something."

"Well, let me know if you do," Helen said.

"You win, Rich," Jane said. "I agree that it's a briefing room. Now, let's get these little plates gathered up and see what we can get out of them!"

"Certainly, Dr. Mayhew." Rich grinned at her through his helmet and turned to assist in carefully collecting the many noteplaques.

Madeline sped down *Nike's* central passageway as fast as she dared. Unlike in the one-third gravity in the ring, she was now effectively weightless. Fortunately, after months of experience, she was moving pretty damn fast. Also fortunately, it was all happening here. If and when major analysis operations started being done on Phobos itself, she'd have a devil of a time monitoring it all.

Reaching the door to the bridge, she came to a halt with the help of the handholds and then entered.

No one looked around immediately. All of them were focused on the consoles in front of them.

"Goddam it," A.J. muttered, completely absorbed in the images his VRD was showing him. "Something is completely screwy in the code. I don't know what, but it's cycling back on itself. That's why we're getting no transmissions out."

"We could try going to another transmission system," Jackie suggested.

"They're all using the same basic control system, though," A.J. said absently. "Which means that the same fault might show up. What'd you do to trigger this, Barbara?"

"Nothing!" protested Barbara Meyers, the chemical

engineering analyst for the mission. "I've transmitted my reports a dozen times before; I do one every week. I've never had any problem."

"Well, something was different this time," Joe said impatiently.

Madeline sighed. This was about as bad a setup as she could have imagined. But there wasn't any choice.

"It was the content, not the procedure," she stated quietly.

All five heads in the bridge—belonging to Barbara Meyers, A.J., Joe, Jackie, and Captain Hathaway— whipped around. "What do you mean?" A.J. asked.

"Until now," Madeline said, keeping them all carefully in her view, "nothing of a really sensitive nature had been discovered or, at least, analyzed to the point that anyone intercepting the transmissions might be able to get anything useful from them of a military nature. However, Dr. Meyers was in the process of sending out a report containing a considerable amount of data on the chemical and structural analysis of the material found in the gauss weapons which she—and several others—believe is a room-temperature super-conductor. Such a material would have a great number of military applications as well as civilian ones, and is therefore classified."

"Then—" Barbara Meyer's face hardened. "Then you've disabled communications? You've been spying on what I send, when I send it?"

"You were told that official communications had to go through channels, and you have been blatantly ignoring the policy."

"Then I'm sincerely glad I have." Meyers' green eyes

narrowed. "If I'd been a good little girl, you'd have just quietly censored my reports and I'd be none the wiser, at least for a while."

"Yes, I would, if I'd thought it necessary. This *is* my responsibility and duty: maintain security."

Captain Hathaway seemed more puzzled than anything else. "A.J., I thought—"

"So did I." A.J. had a chagrined look on his face. "Obviously that was a ruse, a sort of decoy for me to find so that I wouldn't poke any deeper. But I don't think she's that much better than I am at this sort of thing, so it's something her agency rigged."

"You are quite correct, A.J." Madeline said, trying not to look at Joe. "I'm sorry. But it was a sort of lose-lose proposition here. The only way I wouldn't end up having to do this would be if we didn't find anything of great import."

"Well," Barbara said, "I happen to be a citizen of Australia, mate, not the bloody United States, so you can just sit on your security and twirl. I'm sendin' out my report one way or another."

"I'm afraid not. Captain Hathaway, I trust you will support your country's interests in this matter?"

Hathaway's face was grim. But his reply came with no hesitation. "Yes, of course. You have authority in this situation."

"Madeline, don't do this," Joe said quietly. She had to look at him, and it hurt. He was regarding her with a steady, sad gaze.

"Don't worry about it, Joe," A.J. said, getting up and walking toward the door. "There's nothing she can do to stop us in the long run. Hell, Doc,"—speaking to

Meyers—"I can put together a transmitter that'll get through directly, if I have to. So she's compromised the relay, that won't stop—"

"Do not go there, A.J.!" Madeline said sharply. "I'm quite capable of keeping you under observation. And while I'm not as good as you are at your specialty, I'm more than good enough to make sure I'll know if you try something like that. And if you insist, I'll have you arrested and confined. And sent back, as soon as shuttle service starts."

A.J. stared at her incredulously. "You wouldn't dare!"

"That's not a bluff, A.J. Ask the captain."

"She's got the authority, A.J. And if you go ahead, she can probably charge you with some kind of federal crime that'll land you in prison for a while."

Hathaway's voice was cold, as were his eyes looking at Madeline. Then he turned his head and bestowed the same cold gaze on A.J., who was staring at him in disbelief. "A.J., you'll have to let her decide what gets sent and what doesn't."

"The hell I will!" The blond imaging expert whirled on her, reaching out. "You listen to me, you—"

Her body was already in motion. She had been practicing moves both in microgravity and in one-third gravity, using both the *Nike*'s ring and hub, every day since the voyage began. Not that the outcome was ever in doubt, despite the fact that A.J. outmassed her almost two to one.

Arms met, one deflecting the other, catching, turning, pulling—

A.J. smashed hard against the wall. The grunt he gave was audible throughout the room. Then, to her surprise,

A.J. chuckled, albeit with some rather pained overtones. "Jesus H. Particular Christ on a pogo stick. You've been playing the game *that* deep?"

"I'm sorry. Really, I didn't want to do that. Or any of this."

"Then why are you, Madeline?" Joe asked gently, as she released A.J., who was dabbing at a cut lip. She tentatively handed the information expert a tissue, which he accepted without comment. Then she looked at Joe.

"Because not everyone is an angel, Joe, or even a decent imitation of a saint."

"Except our blessed government, of course."

"It tries, at least!" she said, keeping a tight leash on her voice. "As technology advances, Joe, it becomes easier and easier for smaller and smaller groups to become threats. There are software/hardware packages out there now allowing people to prototype new gadgets in their home for a few thousand dollars. And there's not a damn way to control what they make, despite all the tricks people have tried to build into the hardware and software. No matter how smart your security people are, the hackers and crackers are always just a little smarter. Hand them the blueprints and they make it. Do you think psychopaths and terrorists won't use anything they can get their hands on? Do you think every government out there is happy with ours? Have you studied history, or are you ready to repeat it? Create a new weapon, someone will use it eventually. Create a new technology, and one of the first things someone will do is figure out how it can be used to kill people. Of course our government isn't perfect, but your choice is to just let information run free. Well, information is a weapon. Perhaps the most powerful weapon of mass destruction ever invented. And I'm trying to keep those weapons out of the wrong hands for as long as I can. Because I know all about the 'wrong hands,' Joe."

Silently, she cursed herself. The last line showed her just how very personally involved she had gotten, how precariously weak her objectivity had become. She hadn't meant to refer to that at all, not even in private, let alone here. Only Joe would understand the reference, in the first place. It wasn't the sort of thing a professional should ever let slip. She hadn't made mistakes like that for years.

"You know this is going to break down the very minute shuttle service starts, right?" A.J. said finally, after a long silence.

She nodded. "Yes, I know. But a year or so lead will be much better than nothing."

A.J. glanced at Joe. She suddenly realized that A.J. trusted Joe's instincts more than his own—which meant he was in some ways a lot wiser than she'd given him credit for.

Joe looked over at Captain Hathaway, who was grimly silent, then tilted his head in a reluctant half-nod.

A.J. turned to Barbara. "Barb, we're going to all have to get together on this." Madeline tensed. "The situation sucks—and you can bet we'll all have something to say about it when we get home. But we can't afford to turn Phobos and *Nike* into war zones, and that's about what we'd have to do in order to stop her."

The glance he gave Madeline was half-angry and half-admiring. "She's *good*. I didn't realize until just now how very good she is. I guess we should feel kinda flattered, seeing as how they sent the female equivalent of James Bond out to watch us. She's been hiding a lot of what she can do, just to make sure she had a lot of reserves. What are we gonna do, shove her out the airlock? If she was crazy or something, well, we could lock her up, but she's just doing her job. If we fight her, yeah, we'll win. Here. But we've got to go home someday, and while you might just walk away, we won't."

Barbara stared at him for a few moments. "Bloody hell." She glared daggers at Madeline, then turned to the door. "I'll arrange the meeting."

She headed out, obviously to walk off her anger, stomping so hard that she bounced higher than intended and nearly hit her head on the doorframe.

Madeline let out her breath. Then she looked sharply at A.J., who was now leaning casually against the wall, still dabbing at his lip. "You're not going to try to play an end run against me, are you?"

"Naah. I thought about it, sure. But even though I'm better at some things than you are, I don't think I could pull it off. Technically, maybe, but not personally. And like I said to Barb, I'd have to live with it when I got home."

Madeline now looked at Jackie. The young engineer's gaze was certainly not friendly, but she didn't seem angry, either. More . . . intrigued, Madeline thought, than anything else.

"I could make something to send a message back. Between me and Dr. Gupta, we could make one that wouldn't even need the relay satellite, and you couldn't stop us, either."

"No, I couldn't."

Jackie cocked her head a bit. "Not even going to try?"

"What's the point? You and Gupta are the engineers

here, not me. I suppose if I was the security heavy some people find it comfortable to think I am, I could do something with blackmail; but that's not the way I work. I can't afford to damage the overall mission, either, don't forget. We need all the engineers and scientists we have to be working cooperatively. It's not like we'll get replacements any time soon."

The smile she gave Jackie was probably a little sad. "So I'll just have to rely on you not doing it because it wouldn't be very smart, in the long run."

Jackie nodded. "I can live with that." She headed for the exit. "Don't expect me at the meeting. I've got work to do."

After Jackie was gone, Madeline took a long, slow breath. Secord's attitude was a relief, from a professional standpoint. Trying to keep an engineer that skilled from circumventing her would have been almost impossible. And, unlike the voluble and undisciplined Baker, Secord was quite capable of carrying out a secret project and keeping it actually secret.

"Anyone else wish to vent their anger, or shall I expect it only at the meeting?"

"No," Ken Hathaway said in a tired voice that showed more than the usual trace of Southern drawl. "There won't be any more venting. And that's your captain speaking. If I have to, I'll impose military discipline on the ship. The truth is, if you hadn't turned A.J. into a damn good wallpaper imitation, I'd have had him tossed in the brig for laying a hand on you." He smiled wryly. "However . . . given the end result, it seems unnecessary. Not to mention that we're too damn busy to take time out to set up a brig in the first place. Somehow, the engineers forgot to include one in the design of the ship."

"Thank you, Captain. I do appreciate that."

He shrugged. "We'll get through this."

Joe headed for the door. She tried not to look like she wanted to say something to him, but he stopped anyway. "I understand," he said quietly, not looking at her. "But don't talk to me for a while."

"I disapprove of this very strongly, Miss Fathom," Gupta's voice rolled out. "The free exchange of information is absolutely critical to research of this nature. We have been chosen well, yes, but we are merely fifty, while on Earth there are billions. We are here to study the greatest mystery ever presented to mankind, and you want to hamper us at every turn."

"What I want, Dr. Gupta, is not at issue here. I have no choice or latitude in the matter. My directives are very clear. Discoveries of a potentially revolutionary military nature will be restricted in transmission to certain agencies, and to no others."

"You are being vague, Madeline—not like you at all," said Dr. Sakai. "To be precise, the 'certain agencies' you refer to are all agencies of the *United States*. I would remind you that a large percentage of the crew is not American and this is supposed to be an international expedition. Your country placed us here to give us access to these discoveries along with your own people."

"And you have no idea what a headache that gave us," Madeline said honestly. "Sometimes people outside the United States—and inside it, for that matter—make the mistake of thinking that there is a single, monolithic thing called the 'United States Government.' There is no such animal, beyond the formalities. It's an agglomeration of sometimes-allied, sometimes-opposed interests of all sorts and varieties with differing goals, ambitions, aims, and assigned responsibilities. The military and security groups wanted to keep *Nike* a purely American effort. The political groups had a very different set of priorities, and for those purposes decided to bring in some foreign nationals. They did not, however, see fit to change the security requirements. Squaring the circle being probably Washington's favorite pastime."

That brought a few chuckles. "The President sat firmly in the middle, as Presidents often do, and told both sides to follow their contradictory purposes. So here I am with a job I don't want to do, and that you don't want me to do, but that has to be done, and that is going to be done, and Captain Hathaway is backing me up on it."

"But this is idiotic!" Jane Mayhew's prim voice spoke up. "The political damage from not letting us talk will be potentially much worse than any temporary gain you'd make from this asinine so-called 'security.' We have no idea—neither do you—if our findings even indicate a room-temperature superconductor, much less how practical it would be to apply to military purposes. Whereas you can be *assured* that muzzling non-citizens of the U.S. will have definite repercussions." For a moment, her plump face looked startled. "Unless you're planning to arrange accidents for each of us, which I presume isn't in your agenda."

"God, no. This isn't a spy novel, it's a just typical political cluster-fu—ah, snafu. About as conspiratorial as kudzu, and just about as brainless."

Madeline drew a breath. "My job isn't to worry about the politics. My job is to control the flow of information, and I think it's an important job in this case. Don't underestimate yourselves—or play the hapless bumblers. The likelihood is that we *are* looking at such a superconductor, and given the track record of this group of scientists I'd say it's quite likely you'll discover at least enough about it to revolutionize that branch of science and technology. But leave all that aside. I'm not going to try to argue you into agreeing with me. Even if I could, it would take weeks."

"So," A. J. said from the front row, "what do you want us to do?"

"Not turn this into an all-out war," she said bluntly. "You'll be free to lodge all the complaints you want when we get back. I'm not going to stop you from doing research. I'm not going to try to prevent you from exchanging information with each other. I know that would be impossible and would destroy the effectiveness of the mission, even if it weren't. You send me the information you want to send out. Don't try to evade me or make new ways around it. I decide if and how to send it.

*"In the meantime,"* she held up her hand to forestall the rising mutters, "I will try to persuade my superiors— not General Deiderichs, but those who give me my orders—into reconsidering their position. But I will have absolutely no chance of doing that if you people don't cooperate to begin with. I know this business, people. It is what I have been doing for . . . well, a lot longer than I think most of you would believe. And one thing I know about the people I answer to is that if you push them hard, they push right back. If I can show them that you are cooperating but that there is a good and justifiable reason that continuing with my original mission will do

more harm than good, they may be amenable to redefining my mission parameters. But if while I'm trying to negotiate they find that *Nike* has sprung major leaks, they'll tell me to crack down hard, and we'll be in a much worse position than we are now."

She was putting every bit of persuasion she could into her tone. "Please, all of you. I don't like this any more than you do, and I know how much it grates on your ingrained habits and customs. But I need your cooperation, if not direct help, in finding the best possible compromise."

She fell silent. Saying anything more would be counterproductive.

Finally, Dr. Gupta rose. "As you say, Miss Fathom, this is a most unpleasant situation. Yet I am not entirely unfamiliar with the demands of politics. You have tried to be helpful in other areas. Though some here may doubt it, I believe you are trying to be honest with us now. For my part, then, I am willing to cooperate. In the end it will all come out, and so it is in your best interest to try to convince your superiors of the terribly grave mistake they are making."

There was a murmur at that. Madeline relaxed, though she didn't show it outwardly. Everyone respected Captain Hathaway, and there wasn't any doubt that A.J. and Helen, due to their unique connections with the mission, carried considerable weight also. But, in her estimate, the charismatic Dr. Gupta was now, politically speaking, the most important person on board. Although he was a nationalized U.S. citizen, his Indian origins made him something of a spokesman for the members of the crew who were from other countries.

"*K'so*," Dr. Sakai muttered. "*Saa*, let us all agree, then.

I, too, shall cooperate with you, Miss Fathom. It is not a pleasure, but I also see worse consequences from the continued argument."

"I don't believe this!" Barbara Meyer hissed. "We're going to let this fascist little—"

"*Enough*, Barb," Ken Hathaway said firmly. "Ms. Fathom hasn't been calling anyone names, so don't you start either." That was enough to forestall Meyer's gathering temper tantrum.

The Australian woman was still agitated, but she was also clearly a little embarrassed by her outburst.

A.J. stood. "You all know me, and you all know that I believe in censorship about as much as I believe in the Tooth Fairy. But I'm going to be working with Ms. Fathom on this one. Or, at least, not trying to work against her. Sure, I'm pissed. But we've still got a job to do here, and we're not going to get it done if we start playing 'Spy versus Spy.' I don't know about you people, but I came here to study Phobos and the resident aliens."

Helen nodded. Barbara looked like her face would crack from tension, then suddenly she shrugged. "Okay, fine. I'm in. Might as well all sink together. And you're right, A.J., I've got a lot to work on."

With that an invisible dam broke, and the murmurs were accepting, resigned, but no longer threatening and ugly. Madeline did relax visibly then, letting herself look smaller and more vulnerable. The group would be predisposed for the moment to look upon her as at least partially a fellow victim. It was even true, as far as it went.

"Thank you all," she said softly. "I will try to intrude upon you as little as possible."

She leaned back and let Hathaway take center stage,

giving the directions he had in mind to ensure proper information flow without violating Madeline's requirements.

Once, during the rest of the meeting, she looked at Joe. His eyes met hers, but only briefly. The expression on his face was as unreadable as a Bemmie noteplaque.

She'd won a victory, but it tasted like ashes in her mouth. A month had passed since she'd opened up her personal history to Joe. In the time that followed, they'd seen each other every day and spent many hours in conversation. No further physical contact had occurred. Madeline hadn't felt ready for it, and Joe had carefully respected her feelings. But, under the surface, she'd felt the attraction just growing and growing—and knew that it was reciprocated.

Just two days ago, she'd finally accepted that it had been the happiest month of her life. And now . . . It was over. For the first time since she was ten years old, Madeline Fathom wished she had a different profession.

# Chapter 37

"Ms. Fathom," A.J. said, "would you please join us in Phobos Conference Room?"

Madeline's voice replied a moment later. "With that level of formality, I suppose I must."

"I think you'll want to."

The past week had been uncomfortable for everyone. So far, no one had tried to get around the deal that had been struck at the meeting. But it was clear that many of them considered it to be a deal with the devil, and didn't go to any trouble to hide that attitude when Madeline was around. Room temperatures appeared to drop by ten degrees whenever she entered a room, with a few exceptions. Even those who appeared to have accepted the situation without particular rancor, like A.J., didn't seem inclined to let her off the hook she'd hung herself on.

And Joe was still avoiding her.

"On my way."

Fortunately she was already on Phobos. If she'd been on *Nike* it would've been a matter of hours to get there. She drifted down the newly sealed hallway towards the conference area.

Madeline raised an eyebrow as she entered, seeing not just A.J. but Captain Hathaway, Helen, Rich Skibow and Jane Mayhew sitting around the conference table. Hanging onto it, it might be better to say—the term "sitting" meant little in microgravity.

Helen gave her a smile. Somewhat to Madeline's surprise, since she knew that Helen's attitudes concerning intellectual secrecy were every bit as firm as those of most of the scientists, the paleontologist had been one of the very few members of the scientific staff on *Nike* who had been just as friendly to her since that meeting as she'd been before.

Madeline suspected that Helen's attitude stemmed from her own life's experience. *Us girls gotta stick together,* for lack of a better expression. The deep-seated, gut reaction of a woman who'd fought her way to the top in a male profession, seeing another woman in the same position come under pressure.

She'd even learned, from a somewhat amused Jackie Secord, that Helen had been so furious at A.J. when she learned of his behavior at the initial fracas that she'd verbally stripped his hide off—*too bad she didn't* BREAK *your fucking arm, you stinking bully!*—and then made him sleep on the couch for the next several days.

Madeline felt a little guilty about that. The truth was that A.J.'s grab at her had been more in the way of an angry reflex than a serious attempt to attack her. Madeline could have easily just fended it off. The real reason she'd chosen—as Ken Hathaway put it—to use A.J. for wallpaper hadn't been self-defense, it had been to make a point as forcefully as possible. So, readily, Madeline returned the smile. And, as she always did whenever Helen was around, felt more relaxed. ·

"Quite a grouping. What's so important?"

"We think we've made a discovery that rather changes our entire outlook on these people and what they were doing here," Jane said without preamble. "You will recall, I think, that in our attempts to translate the language of *Bemmius secordii* we found certain symbols and words which we believed to represent 'craters'?"

"Yes. I think by now I could even sketch the symbols. And you found that they'd already labeled the dinosaur-killer crater, too. Chix—whatever. I can never pronounce that name correctly."

"Yeah," A.J. said. "And, you know, that bothered me. For quite a while. The problem with it was a matter of the probabilities involved. Improbabilities, rather. First, look at the timing. If we're right, within days of the disaster that killed Bemmie and helped finish off the dinosaurs, something else hit this base—inside or outside—and killed off everyone inside, or at least a lot of someones. That's a pretty funky coincidence, isn't it?"

"Well, yes, but . . ."

"Wait up, there's more. Something about the whole situation bothered me, so I went to talk to our astrophysicists.

"These Bemmie guys crossed a hell of a lot of space to find this solar system, right? And they brought enough stuff with them to carve out bases in asteroids and apparently explore at least parts of two planets and other parts of the Solar System. Either they had some magic space-drive technology we don't even have the words for, or they used some kind of tech we can imagine. If the latter, the only methods we know of would require lots of energy. Lots and lots and *lots* of energy. Which means they'd be past masters of knowing how to 'watch the skies,' so to speak, for dangerous stuff."

A.J. loved dramatics, and Madeline didn't begrudge him the habit. So she waited patiently for him to get to the point. At least, with A.J., there almost always *was* a point. Eventually.

"So what the hell are the odds that they wouldn't see a friggin' asteroid long, long before it approached a planet they were studying? And that they also couldn't do something to stop it?"

Madeline frowned. "You're saying that either the impact shouldn't have happened, or that Bemmie shouldn't have been on the planet when it did hit."

"Bingo. And then we get to Joe and Harry's little room. Well, big room."

"The firing range?"

"Yes," Rich Skibow said. "Joe and the engineering department went over that area very carefully, given its potential for military significance. Since there wasn't all that much written material in the location, they didn't call me or Jane in for quite a while. But when they did, we noticed something immediately."

On the wall screen, a picture popped up of a storage bin. On the bin were a series of markings, ones that looked somehow familiar. Another bin or chute had other markings, some of them the same. One of the images from the back wall areas, downrange from the shooting booths, was shown; again, alien script, some of the markings identical to the other two.

Then the image of the Earth map appeared; at the crater site, among other markings, the same sequence.

"We no longer believe that this sequence of symbols represents a word meaning either 'crater' or 'site of interest,' " Jane Mayhew said. "Based on their occurrence on the firing range in the locations they were found and their association with certain objects, it is now our professional opinion that we have found a far superior and much more likely translation for this word.

"The word is *target*."

For a moment, Madeline couldn't quite take it in. "Target?"

Then it connected. "They were using asteroids as missiles! But what were they shooting *at*?" A thought suddenly occurred to her. "Hey, this may sound crazy, but could it be that it really was a literal 'dinosaur killer'—that some kind of dinosaur might have had a civilization and they were bombarding the planet?"

"Nice idea, and I thought of that one too," A.J. said. "But Helen says—"

"It's completely out of the question," Helen stated firmly. "For a number of reasons. The main one is that if a civilization large enough to be interesting or threatening to something like *Bemmius* existed on Earth at that time, we'd have found traces of it by now. Lots of traces. Consider the fact that we found traces of high tech around the original Bemmie, and he was just one fossil of one visiting technological race. I suppose a fantasy writer might be able to come up with some explanation as to how the entire fossil record could be wrong or missing *just* those critical pieces of data, but no paleontologist would believe it for an instant.

"Second, to wipe out such a civilization would almost certainly take a lot more than just one major bolide, unless it was something several orders of magnitude bigger than the Chicxulub impact. But there's only one 'target' symbol on Earth, although there are a considerable number on Mars and a few on other bodies around the Solar System."

Helen shook her head. "No, I'm not sure what they were shooting at, but it certainly wasn't a bunch of civilized dinosaurs."

"Do you think there might be traces around Chicxulub?" asked Jane.

A.J. shook his head doubtfully. "Dunno. I wouldn't think so, but then we don't know what the hell they were throwing asteroids at. Cthulhu and the Great Old Ones in R'lyeh? It's possible, I suppose, if whatever they were fighting was built really well. The impact might well have killed everyone off but left some pieces we could recognize if we're looking for them."

He stopped and waited expectantly.

Then she realized they were all staring at her, waiting.

Mentally she kicked herself. "Oh, I'm sorry. You're waiting for my approval. Please, go ahead, transmit this. It doesn't give away any useful technical details, which is all I'm officially assigned to watch for. And—who knows?—somebody might decide to go excavate Chi . . . Chick . . . Chicken Little. Whatever. Once you tell them."

"Chicxulub," Helen said, enunciating the syllables through a wide smile. "All right, Rich, Jane, we have a joint paper to write, as we're just about squarely in the middle of all our disciplines."

As Helen and the two linguists launched into a discussion of the projected paper, A.J. left the table and came over to Madeline.

"Thanks," he said quietly. "I figured there wouldn't be a problem, but you *did* stick yourself with the job of clearing everything."

"Yes, I did." She frowned. "Actually, I am concerned about this, although I see no reason to keep it secret. I've heard the arguments as to why we aren't going to meet *Bemmius* or any of his relatives, after all this time, and I'd presume all those arguments apply to any other species that were contemporaneous with them as well. But, still, I have to wonder—if they were fighting something that existed on more than one world at once, wouldn't that something else also be able to detect and stop things like that? And if so, how do you manage to hit them with falling rocks?"

"Yeah. That is a question. Maybe we'll get an answer when we look over the rest of the base and start sifting through the pieces that remain of the puzzle." A. J. shook his head. "Wouldn't that have been a hell of a fight to see?"

"It would," Madeline said quietly. "Pray that we don't."

She saw by the sudden widening of his eyes that he had abruptly made the connection to her job. "Yes, that is what I have to think about. Every day."

"You can't prevent scientific progress, though—or hide technology forever." His tone wasn't mocking, but serious. "In the end, people will find out anything you're trying to hide, and there's no way you can keep them from using it. You *do* realize that, don't you? Or do you actually believe that you can stuff the genie back into the bottle?"

"Yes. No. Most of the time, maybe and maybe not. And some days I'm not sure what I believe anymore. I'm sorry this whole situation exists, A.J., I really am. But I'm also very much afraid of what might happen to the world if certain things get out of control."

"Can't say I entirely blame you. Joe says you have good reasons, and I trust Joe. Speaking of which, go see him."

She looked away. "He told me not to speak to him. 'For a while,' he said. But since I don't know what that means, I thought I should let him decide."

"Yeah, I know. But . . ."

A.J. seemed torn. He started to reach for her arm, obviously to lead her out of the conference room. Then, drew it back sharply, as if he'd spotted a viper.

"Jesus!" she heard him hiss. "I lay so much as a finger on you, Helen will have my scalp."

A.J. turned the dramatic withdrawal of his hand into an equally dramatic gesture of invitation. "C'mon, Madeline, let's go somewhere else to talk. Ladies first."

As she preceded him out of the room, Madeline found herself in a good humor for the first time in days. Once they were in the corridor beyond, she looked at him over her shoulder.

"Did she *really* make you sleep on the couch?"

"Sure did. And let me tell you, even at one-third gravity that couch was lumpy."

"Good for her!"

A.J. smiled. "Funny. That's exactly what she said about you. We gotta veritable feminazi Waffen SS on this moon."

Madeline grinned at him. Despite their little brawl—if something so one-sided could be given the term—she liked A.J. Baker. And was glad to see that whatever animosity had existed seemed to have faded away.

He grinned back, although the look in his eyes had something of calculation in them. "Look, I'm sorry," he said quietly. "Helen's right and I was way out of line. Even if—"

For just an instant, he looked like a falsely-accused six-year-old boy. "I *still* think Helen's nuts to accuse me of trying to beat on a woman. I was just going to grab you by the shoulder, stop you. And besides . . ."

The calculation was back in his eyes. "I never had a chance, did I? Even if I had really been trying to get you."

"To be honest? Not a cold chance in hell."

"Didn't think so. What exactly are you, anyway? Seventh dan? Eighth dan? *Ninth* dan?"

Madeline shook her head. "The terms don't mean anything, in the schools I finished my training with. They weren't even schools, really. By the end I was learning one-on-one from the best senseis I could find, in whatever school—and none of them are people you'll ever see mentioned in the martial arts magazines. They pay no attention to that ranking business at all. They either decide to teach you, or they don't. The move I threw you into the wall with, I learned from a seventy-four-year-old Okinawan during the months I was on the island. Never mind what I was doing there. He was almost a hermit, having spent his whole life studying the art. Didn't speak a word of English or any other language I knew."

A.J. winced. "Oh, Lord. You're talking about a whole 'nother league, aren't you?"

"About as different as the major leagues are from double-A. The truth is, A.J., I'm about as far out on the bleeding edge of that skill as you are with your own specialty. Of course, with their greater strength, reach, and mass, there are some men in the world who could beat me in a fight. A handful of women, too. But you aren't one of them. Not even close, frankly."

She swallowed. "Ask Joe about it, if you want. Tell him I said it was okay. There's a reason that martial arts are an obsession for me. He knows what it is."

"Okay, I will. And, uh . . ."

Madeline smiled. "Oh, certainly. Since you're being such a gentleman about it, I'll let Helen know that I wasn't really in any danger of suffering from male chauvinist abuse."

"Thanks." There was silence, for a moment. Then Madeline swallowed again. "I think you were going to say something . . ."

"Yeah. Go talk to him. Now. Forget that 'in a while' business. He doesn't know what it means, either, and knowing Joe—which I do—by now he'll have convinced himself that if he approaches you he'll be rudely encroaching on the space he insisted you keep around you so that means he'd be acting like a jerk since he insisted on it in the first place and Joe can't stand the thought of being rude. The dummy. There are advantages, you know, to letting it all hang out the way I do."

Her eyes were almost crossed. "I understand what you're saying. But don't ever say that in front of a grammarian. That's the most twisted sentence I ever heard."

A.J. smiled, but it was a thin business. "There's one thing, though, Madeline. Joe's my best friend, and . . . dammit, don't you *play* with him."

She was genuinely shocked. " 'Play'? I don't—"

He waved his hand impatiently. "I didn't say it right. I

know you're not toying with him. That's not what I meant. What I meant was that I've never seen Joe get this hung up on a woman, and I've known him for a long time. And what that means is that nothing'll work unless you're willing to be as serious about it as he will. And I'm really not sure you can do that, Madeline. Or, to put it another way—being my usual crude self—will those unnamed and mysterious people you work for *let* you do that?"

"Oh." She started to make a quick response, but then forced herself to think about it.

"I don't know," she said finally. "But that's not really the issue. If I decide . . . They—he—can't really tell me what to do, and he knows it. If I decide, and he pushes me, I'll just quit."

" 'He'?"

"My boss. Never mind his identity. It doesn't matter, A.J., because this has never been a job for me anyway. Not really."

"Yeah, I understand. So what you're saying is that the real issue is what *you* decide to do."

"Yes."

Suddenly, he grinned as widely as Madeline had ever seen him do. "Well. That's a relief!" Again, her eyes were almost crossed. "Why? I never said *what* I would decide, A.J. I don't know myself yet."

The grin never faded. "Sure. Of course. That's what the whole complicated business is about in the first place. So what? Whether you and Joe work anything out is between the two of you, period. Maybe you will, maybe you won't. But that's all I wanted to know. That the only person inside of you is *you*. If you understand what I mean. Not somebody else, pulling the strings."

Her jaws tightened. "Nobody else *ever* pulls my strings."

"Oh, good. Well, that being the case—if you'll pardon me for taking the liberty—I guess it's okay for me to give you a push."

He reached out, planted his hands on her shoulders, turned her around, and gave her a little shove. Even as gentle as the motion was, with his much greater mass she found herself moving rather quickly down the hallway. Microgravity still seemed weird to her, sometimes.

"So go talk to him," his voice followed. "Now."

Madeline didn't quite follow his orders. First, because Joe was still on the *Nike*, so it took her several hours to get there. Second, because she made a brief stop at her own cabin.

When she left the cabin, she felt a bit like an idiot. There was something just plain ridiculous about a secret agent superspy carrying a hope chest. Of a sort.

# Chapter 38

Joe Buckley sat in his cabin, looking out at the stars, and at Phobos as the giant space rock moved in and out of view with *Nike*'s rotation. The new *Gourmet Illustrated Quarterly* glowed from his cabin display. Blinking in irritation, Joe pulled his attention from the eternal circling panorama and focused on the magazine. It dawned on him that he wasn't even sure where he'd left off. "Again. Damn."

He just didn't seem to find the recipes as interesting as he used to. Granted, he had a lot less opportunity to test things out on board *Nike*, even as well-equipped as the ship was. Still, he'd never found himself bored with reading new approaches or new ways to use the old ones.

With a sigh, he started flipping through his collection of movies and series. Madeline would've liked—

As soon as that thought intruded again, he gave a sound somewhere between a growl and a snort and stood up. A bit too fast, unfortunately. He bounced nearly three feet into the air, a mistake he hadn't made for months.

He considered going down to see how things were coming in engineering analysis. Room R-17 had contained what appeared to be a sort of vehicle, maybe a runabout or shuttle for *Bemmius*. Joe, Gupta, Jackie, and A.J. had been working on analyzing the thing from an engineering standpoint, using A.J.'s sensors and the engineering expertise of the others.

He was off-shift for another six hours, but it wasn't like he was getting anything accomplished here. He'd like to see what Mayhew and Skibow were up to, but he was temporarily *persona non grata* with the linguists ever since he'd gotten distracted for a moment while salvaging some noteplaques and banged one into the wall. The sixty-five-million-year-old artifact had practically exploded into powder and fragments. A.J. was trying to reconstruct what was on that plaque from the images the suit sensors had picked up incidentally. But it was taking a while as there hadn't been an in-depth scan of that one, and in some cases he was having to piece together components from partial images in various scenes at differing ranges, resolutions, and wavelengths. This was especially annoying to the two linguists as there was fairly good reason to believe that the noteplaque in question had included a map for part of Mars.

On the positive side, A.J. had pointed out, he and the rest of the physical sciences and engineering crew now had pieces of noteplaque to analyze without having to decide if they could afford to damage one. "You did that for us, Joe. Good work."

The door chimed.

Muttering something which was probably rude enough that it was a good thing no one else was there to hear it, Joe went to the door and opened it.

Madeline stood there, looking up at him with huge blue eyes. For a moment he just stared at her. Then he turned away. "Look, I'm not ready to talk right now. Please go."

After a moment, the door shut. He sighed and turned back to the case near the door, where he kept his spacesuit—and nearly ran over Madeline, who was standing just inside the door. "Madeline, what the hell—?"

The blonde security agent still hadn't said a word, but from behind her back she produced an enormous bouquet of flowers— roses, irises, daisies—and a box of chocolates.

The ironic inversion of the approach did not immediately strike Joe, as he was focused more on the utter impossibility of fresh flowers on board a ship nearly a hundred million miles from Earth.

"Where in the universe did those come from?" He reached out and took the bouquet.

Immediately he recognized that—as he should have assumed— the flowers were artificial. Yet he was still pretty sure that artificial flowers weren't among the cargo manifest for *Nike*. Atomic powered or not, every ounce of her cargo space had been allotted to useful things; even the decorative items brought on board had been selected for flexibility and long term use, not for casual ornamentation.

There was a faint perfume to the flowers, though not, as far as he could tell, that of any one flower. A scent Madeline sometimes wore, now that he thought of it. He studied the flowers more closely, still trying to make sense of their presence. At very close range, he could see they were handmade, and from the oddest things. Stems from sections of tie-down cable, petals from various types of shrink-wrap and packing seals . . .

He looked up slowly, incredulously. "You *made* these?"

"Yes," she said softly, almost shyly. "I know it's kind of silly, but— "

"How long did it take you to do this?"

"Not all that long. Well, about a week. I spent my off hours working on them."

"A week?" He glanced down at the chocolates. Those he knew were real, as he'd selected them himself. He also knew that on the Dessert Points scale that the crew had to abide by, that box represented about a full week's worth of desserts for Madeline—and she was someone who doted on chocolate.

He looked from the box to the flowers to her face. Her gaze was calm, serious . . . yet very intense.

"Why?" he asked, finally.

"There isn't a standard ritual to make amends to a man that I know of. Some things haven't changed much in a hundred years, despite all the other advances. But this gets my point across. Can I talk to you now?"

He gestured her further inside. "Sure, sure. Sit down. Um, have a chocolate."

"Not right now, thanks."

If she was turning down chocolate, she was serious. "Okay. Well . . . go ahead, talk. I'm kinda bad at this, and I wasn't ready."

Madeline settled herself into one of the chairs across from Joe's sofa, where Joe had sat down, and then looked into his eyes. "Joe, you've always known that I was an intelligence agent. This job was given to me the day A.J. discovered this base, and that job was to control information. An agent doesn't allow her personal feelings to affect her work. In fact, smart agents don't allow themselves to have personal feelings at all during a mission."

She gazed down at her hands, "I did, anyway, even though I knew it wasn't a good idea. But . . . oh, let's just say that mine is a lonely life. That didn't bother me for years. I'm still not sure why it started bothering me now. I think it's because all this time on the *Nike* project, especially since we left Earth, made me feel like I had something of a family. For the first time in my life, really."

Her shoulders seemed to twitch. "But whatever the reason, I did start having feelings for you that went way beyond anything an agent should have, for one of the people she is—I'll be blunt—assigned to watch over. I guess I'd hoped, somehow, I wouldn't have to do anything, so it would never get to be a problem." She shook her head. "A stupid hope. Either way it would have had a bad result—I have to intervene, and become the enemy, or I don't, because the entire mission finds nothing worthwhile.

"And that's what I don't want my life to be, Joe. Finding nothing worthwhile."

Joe stared at the small woman, trying to put his thoughts in order. As ever, Madeline was persuasive. Sincerity seemed to drip from every word. But Joe also knew that her professional skills made her a superb liar. A master of deceit, capable of convincing anyone that she was on their side, while she calmly worked against them. Or, if not against them, certainly not for them.

*Could* be a superb liar, he corrected himself. The ability

to do something didn't automatically mean it was exercised. And . . . did he really think she'd been lying to him all along? Or any of them, really?

*No.* He knew the answer the moment he asked himself the question.

He stood up and paced to the window, but ended up looking at her instead. "Madeline, I'm the kind of person who gets committed to things. And I guess what bothers me is that I don't know how I'd handle getting personally committed to someone who might well end up on the other side—the way I see it, anyway—of the life's work I've also committed myself to. You haven't gotten a response from your superiors yet, have you?"

She shook her head. "Nothing concrete, one way or the other yet. There must be considerable arguing going on."

"And what if they tell you to crack down?"

"Then I will. Unless what he—they—define as 'cracking down' goes beyond what I'm willing to do. In which case"—the brilliant smile came, in full flashing force—"I guess I'll be the first case of interplanetary unemployment. Maybe I can get a job washing bottles for the chemists."

The dazzling smile was a weapon, too, Joe understood. This was a woman who had devoted her life since she was a child to turning herself into a weapon—and in every way possible.

*Could* be a weapon, he reminded himself again. The fact that a good kitchen knife was kept sharp didn't automatically make it a weapon for murder. The problem was simply that a good knife *had* to be sharp, or it wasn't much use. Worse than that, actually. As an experienced chef, Joe knew full well that the most dangerous knife to the user was a dull one. It could slip when you applied the extra force you needed to make it work.

He stared out the window.

Phobos came. Phobos went.

Can I live with that?

Again, the answer came to him the moment he posed it.

Don't be stupid, Joe. And stop being so self-righteous, while you're at it. Every knife in your kitchen is as sharp as a razor.

He couldn't help but chuckle softly. "Leave it to a gourmet to fall in love with a razor blade," he murmured. "Serves me right for being such a snob."

"I'm sorry, I didn't hear that," Madeline said.

"Ah . . . never mind. I was just thinking to myself that if I insisted on a woman who didn't use ketchup on steak, I had a lot of nerve whining about the rest."

He turned and smiled at Madeline. The slight frown on her face made it clear she still didn't understand what he was talking about. No way she could, of course.

"Never mind. Let's just start with the basics. What do you want, Madeline? Concretely, I mean. Sorry, I know that doesn't sound very romantic. But I think like an engineer."

Her frown cleared immediately. "Oh, that's easy. I want to go back, Joe. At least for us. I want to sit down with you and talk food, watch bad action movies, and . . . whatever else we would do together. Even though I know my job isn't going to make that easy."

He looked at the flowers, which seemed to glow in the light of the cabin. She'd spent a week making them, using her ingenuity to design it out of completely unsuitable elements. Knowing, of course—God, the woman was sharp—the emotional impact it would have on him. Manipulating him, if he wanted to think about it that way.

And so what? Naturally she'd use the same skills she'd learned for her profession on a personal matter. Did Joe pretend he wasn't an engineer—forget everything he knew—whenever he repaired a personal item?

What was important was the end, not the means. She'd spent that time for herself, and for Joe, not for her mission. She did it because it was that important to her.

Finally, he felt something inside loosening, opening up almost like a flower itself.

"You know what?" he mused out loud. "I've been in absolutely rotten shape ever since this happened. My work's been crappy, I can't concentrate on recipes—hell, I can't even watch a damn movie because they keep reminding me of you. Like being a dull knife, myself. I don't think I can function without you around any more, Madeline."

She looked up at him with sparkling eyes, maybe a hint of tears. Probably something of an act there, too, but that didn't mean it wasn't sincere.

"So please stay here, eat my chocolate, and watch a movie with me. How's that sound? I have five hours before I go on shift."

"Sounds wonderful."

She sniffled happily, wiping her nose.

Naturally, it was a good sniffle. Even a great one.

"Finally," A.J. said to the uninhabited room around him.

He looked with justifiable pride at the image in front of him. It showed one of the noteplaques with a map of a section of Mars on it.

The thing to be proud of was that this particular plaque

did not exist any more—it was the one that Joe had accidentally wrecked a few days before. As they'd suspected, the plaque covered a part of Mars for which they had no other *Bemmius*-made maps, and was thus the only source of information about what Bemmie and friends had thought about this particular area.

He immediately set the system to processing the data on the plaque. "Hey, Rich, Jane," he called, his system patching into the communication net as he specified the people he wanted to talk to. "Got something for you."

"Don't tell me you actually got it back?"

"Jane, Jane, how could you ever doubt me? I said I could do it, didn't I? So let it be written; so let it be done!"

"So," Rich said, "is it Mars?"

"Yep. Looks to be a goodly section of the Valles Marineris. And I've got targets on it, too. Catalogue them as targets thirty-four, thirty-five, thirty-six, thirty-seven, thirty-eight, and thirty-nine."

"Nearly forty sites on Mars, more than on any other body we've found designated. They must have either been very interested in Mars, or had some reason to live there for a while."

"Well, I'm about to put all our target designees into my system and start seeing what correspondences I can find. I'll let you know if anything comes up."

"Thank you, A.J. Are you—ah, I see the file. Thanks again. We'll be studying this ourselves."

"My pleasure."

Turning back to the data, A.J. set up the simple general problem for the far more complex statistical analysis package: *find correspondences and anomalies in the data*. He had to do a lot less gruntwork than would have been needed decades before, when he would have had to explicitly enter not only the domains of "correspondences and anomalies" with considerable detail, but would also have had to explicitly point to what associated data would be needed. As currently set up, the system could make what amounted to "common sense" assumptions about both the domain and about what sort of data would be needed for this problem, and then go out and find that data on the network—or request the data, if it wasn't available.

He then went out to get a snack package, one of two he had allotted for the day. To his surprise, while he was choosing his snack, the system sent him a notation. This was way earlier than he'd expected anything.

"*Target 37 Anomaly. No Crater Corresponds.* Huh?"

As he walked back to his room, A.J. called up images of Mars and keyed them into the corresponding location for Target 37. "Well, I'll be damned. It's right. No crater. Other craters somewhat near it, but none of them anywhere close to a bull's-eye."

He wondered if he'd somehow screwed up his reconstruction. But a quick examination of the other targets—thirty-four through thirty-six, and thirty-eight and thirty-nine—showed that he hadn't. All of them had corresponding craters dead-on.

A.J. decided that he needed more information. It was possible that there was a crater there, which had just gotten filled in. It was, after all, at the bottom of an ancient watercourse. Maybe the impact had liquified fossil ice, the melted water filled in the crater, and then it got covered over by dust and whatnot.

"Dr. Sakai."

"Hai? A.J., what is it?"

"You're sort of in charge of the main orbital satellites. Can I steal one that's being used for areography?"

"Planet-facing? Yes, certainly. Which one?"

A.J. consulted the orbital schedules and the sensor resources for the satellites. All of them had been launched from *Nike* shortly after they arrived, along with Babel, the much larger and more powerful satellite that allowed them to communicate with all the satellites as well as Earth.

"I think MGS-Three. The Migs have the sensors I want and Three looks to be coming up on the right area soon."

"Understood. I will take MGS-Three off the active roster until you say otherwise."

There were advantages to being the guy everyone looked at as "Mr. Sensors." When you wanted something, they usually didn't object unless they were really using it at the time. MGS-Three would eventually go over all the same areas again, so it wasn't as though any data lost here couldn't be replicated later.

A.J. fired up the GPR and multi-and hyperspectral imaging arrays to their maximum resolution and detail settings. He wanted to get the best data he could on the target location, which was in the Melas Chasma area.

While he waited, he remembered that he'd promised to tell Jane and Rich as soon as he found something. "Yo, Jane! I found something. Or, rather, I didn't find something."

"Which exactly do you mean?" Jane responded, a bit nettled.

"I mean that Target 37 hasn't got a crater associated with it. Which means either they didn't shoot at that one, for some unknown reason, or the crater they made shooting it was obliterated later. I'm checking into that possibility right now."

"Really? That *is* interesting. We have over fifty targets found in the entire system and all of them have been associated with craters until now."

"I'll call you back once I get some more info from the Migs about that site."

"Please do! Anything unusual means more excitement."

"Don't want you getting overexcited. Maybe I'd better not call you."

"If you fail to call me as soon as you learn something, I shall complain to Helen about your cold, unfeeling heart. I shall also drop hints—very broad ones, I warn you!—that male chauvinism must be involved."

"Okay, okay, threat understood. Talk to you later."

An hour later, a mass of data streamed into his waiting analysis systems. Images in multiple spectra, hyperspectral data, ground-penetrating radar, filtered, spectroscopic, the works—so much data that MGS-Three had had to buffer the torrent and was still streaming it back to *Nike* several minutes after passing over the target site.

Finally the download was complete. "Time to start crunching. Give up your ancient secrets, I say! And reveal . . . well, probably nothing."

A.J. sat back and picked out a book from the rather large number still remaining on his *read someday* list. No matter what was found or not, it'd be a bit before the crunching gave an answer.

After an hour, he turned back to the VRD screen projected to his other side. "Let's see what—*Holy Mother of God.*"

Even with the resolution from modern orbital, the image wasn't particularly huge. And at the edges, it was fuzzy, worn-looking. But the angles, curves, and outline of the structure revealed beneath the floor of that section of Melas Chasma was as familiar as it was clearly not natural.

"All their base are belong to *me*," A.J. said, a huge grin starting to spread across his face. "I'm not telling anyone about *this* by remote call."

# PART VII: MARS

*Enlightenment, n: education that results in understanding and the spread of knowledge. Also, the attainment of true understanding beyond the physical into the spiritual reality.*

# Chapter 39

"A base on Mars?" Hathaway repeated, incredulously. "After sixty-five million years?"

"It's possible. Well, more than possible, because I've got the readings to prove it. They built really well, Mars doesn't have weather anything like ours, it's reasonably geologically stable, so if they were building well, yeah, lots of it could survive even after that time, especially if it was underground."

Madeline felt the pressure on her already. *Oh, great.* Another base—and the one on Phobos alone was more than enough to keep her constantly busy trying to balance the desires of the scientists on *Nike* and the political authorities back on Earth.

"But it will still be in worse condition than this one, correct?" Hathaway asked.

"Oh, for sure, Ken. At least the outer parts of it will. You can tell just by looking at the sensor returns that there are parts of it that just ain't what they used to be. But it looks to me like large chunks of it are apparently still pretty much intact—hard as it is for me to grasp how anything can stay that way over that length of time on a planetary surface. We are definitely going to get new construction tricks out of these guys, whatever else."

"I don't doubt it, A.J.," Hathaway said, "but I think investigating this new base can wait another few months, after all these millions of years. I'll check with NASA, of course, to see what they want us to do."

*Famous last words*, Madeline thought sourly, staring at the communication screen which had just gone dark after delivering NASA's instructions. They'd neglected a rather vital element of the puzzle, which NASA had cheerfully pointed out.

"Duh!" A.J. exclaimed, smacking his forehead. "Boy, are we a bunch of stupes. That base isn't one belonging to the same people. It belonged to their enemies, who might be entirely different cultures, creatures, whatever. NASA's right—which is a marvel in itself. We *have* to give that base a look, even if it's just a quick once-over, to see what it might have that's really different from this one."

For all his professed self-recrimination, A.J. was obviously delighted by the new prospect. Madeline, on the other hand, was trying not to scowl openly at the now-dead screen. She could tell that Hathaway was doing the same. Like her—and unlike A.J.—he had the sort of responsibilities that made this new development no joy to contemplate at all.

A.J. was oblivious to their concerns, of course. "Is this cool or what? We're actually going to *land on Mars*. I thought we wouldn't be doing that until the next trip. If then!"

Hathaway took a long, slow breath. "No help for it," Madeline thought she heard him mutter.

More loudly, he said: "We need a general conference. Jackie, please ask Joe and Helen to come to the bridge. We'll need both of them to give us an assessment of how feasible it will be to get to the ruins in the first place, without a major excavation that we don't have the tools for. Get both of the linguists, too. And Bruce Irwin, to be the pilot. And . . ."

"Ryu," A.J. suggested. "We'll need an areologist, for sure."

"Yes, and Dr. Sakai."

Jackie nodded and started speaking softly into the ship's communication system.


"Are you sending all of us?" Helen asked.

"Not on the first trip," Hathaway replied. "The lander just isn't big enough, given that we have to make room for the pressurized rover or there's no point sending anyone at all. The landing team will consist of yourself, A.J, Madeline, Rich Skibow—sorry, Jane, but he's better qualified on the physical end than you are—Dr. Sakai, Joe, and Bruce to pilot the lander. Helen, you'll be in charge."

Her eyes widened. "Why me?"

"I'd think it was obvious. This is basically a paleontological dig, and who's more qualified on *Nike* to be the boss of one? Bruce will be in command, of course, during the flight itself."

"That's fine," Jane Mayhew snapped. "But why is

Fathom going?" She was all but glaring at Madeline. "Do we really need a watchdog down there? Enough—I do *not* like this—to bump me off the expedition?"

Madeline gave her a smile. Not the full-bore one, just a serene little indication of innocence. "Don't be silly, Jane. Why would I go down *there* to play watchdog? All the communications from the Mars expedition will have to be relayed through *Nike* anyway. I can do my watchdog bit up here far better—and be enjoying my chocolates while I'm at it."

Mayhew looked suitably abashed. "Well. Yes. That's true."

Madeline now turned the smile on Hathaway. "Which does, however, bring up the question: why *am* I being included in the expedition?"

"Do you object?" Hathaway asked, gruffly.

"Officially? No, of course not. And speaking personally, I'd like to go, as a matter of fact. But I really don't see what special skills I bring to the task."

Hathaway looked at her for a long moment. "You don't, huh? Even you! Bunch of civilians."

His dark eyes swept around the table. "People, it may not have dawned on some of you yet that this trip will be *dangerous*—and dangerous in an up-close and personal way that the voyage here wasn't. If something had gone wrong with the *Nike,* the engineers would either have been able to fix it or they wouldn't. But, either way, there would have been no call for physical heroics."

"That's preposterous!" Mayhew blurted out. "Do you really think we'll encounter hostile Martians that require Ms. Fathom's martial arts skills to deal with?"

"That's not what I'm talking about, Jane—and you're

perfectly smart enough to know it." As even-tempered as he was, Hathaway was clearly restraining himself. "There are a thousand things that could go wrong down there. Any number of which could indeed require considerable physical exertion. So why is Madeline going, and you aren't?"

Because Madeline is in the best physical condition of any member of *Nike*'s crew, myself included, and you— since you've been blunt, Jane, so will I—are probably in the worst. You were forty pounds overweight when we started the voyage, and you've gained twelve pounds since. That's not because your diet hasn't been good—Joe sees to that—but because you have consistently refused to maintain the exercise regimen that Dr. Wu set up for everyone. He complained about it to me again just two days ago. He's starting to get worried that when you finally return to Earth you'll have real physical problems with Earth-normal gravity."

"Oh," Mayhew said, in a very small voice. Her pale, plump face was pink with embarrassment. "I've been very busy," she protested.

Hathaway shook his head. "Nobody thinks you're lazy, Jane." He glanced at A.J. "But in a lot of ways you're just like Wonderboy over here. You get so preoccupied with your work that you forget about everything else. Fortunately for him, A.J. developed good workout habits years ago, so he never slips too far. But you—"

He sighed. "I don't mean to hurt your feelings, Jane. Really, I don't. But I'm the commander of this expedition and I would simply be remiss in my duties if I let you go on this trip. I'm not too happy about sending Rich, to be honest, given his age. But we need a linguist and—being blunt again—he's in better physical condition than you are even though he's eighteen years older. He *does* stick to the exercise schedule."

Apparently not knowing where else to look, Mayhew gave her fellow linguist a look of appeal.

Skibow looked away for a moment. "I do wish you'd start exercising. I've begun worrying about your health myself. Not here, so much, in this low gravity. But once we get back . . ." His eyes came back to her, looking very warm. "I'd miss you, Jane. I really, really would."

After a moment, she smiled. "All right, then," she said. "I will."

Without looking away from Skibow, she said: "I withdraw my objection."

"Fine." Hathaway cocked an eye at Madeline. "Any further questions?"

She shook her head.

"Anybody?" The captain waited a moment and said, "Then let's get to it."


"Not to sound pessimistic and all, Ms. Fathom," Bruce said dryly, "but you do realize that no one's alive who's actually done a landing on Mars? Plenty of simulations and all, but believe you me, that's not the same thing."

"I do. I've also been doing the simulations. Since no one else has, I guess that makes me the copilot. God help us all. But you do have actual experience in reentry landings, Bruce, even though the atmosphere here is a lot thinner."

"Yes, I do. No, you don't." Irwin was looking at her very skeptically. "And why in God's name has a security specialist been practicing flying a spacecraft anyway?"

She grinned at him. "I like to learn new things. And I already know how to fly a plane."

He maintained the skeptical look.

"I do! Okay, a small one. And, uh, okay, not very well, I suppose. On the other hand—" She drew herself up stiffly. "Unlike you, *I've* never crashed any sort of aircraft, either."

Bruce snorted, and gave Joe a glance that was even more skeptical. "You've never been on a flight with our very own Typhoid Mary, either. Now you'll have your chance—don't say I didn't warn you."

"Hey!" Joe protested.

Irwin ignored him and went over to study the map spread across the table. "Where will we be landing?"

Helen pointed. "The base is located here, in the southern portion of the Valles Marineris named the Melas Chasma. If you look at this image"—she put up a photograph on the screen—"you can see that the Bemmie base is located about where this chevron-shaped white mark is, close to the edge of this secondary valley or canyon. There appear to be several flat areas not too far from it, well within range of the pressurized rover."

Bruce studied the image. "At first glance, you look to be right. But I'm going to go over it carefully with A.J., get him to do some models of the approach and all. We're going to have to do a powered landing at the end, since there's not enough atmosphere for a pure glide-and-land. May be able to set us down right close."

"I'll get cracking on those models for you, Bruce," A.J. said, standing up. "We've got a lot of work to do, and I still have to go over the reconfigurations for my Fairy Dust. I hadn't expected to be bringing any to Mars quite yet."

After A.J. left, Helen turned to the rest of them. "Jackie and Gupta are selecting the equipment to bring with us, Joe, but you need to make sure you're fully checked out on whatever's sent. You'll be our only engineer. Dr. Sakai, Dr. Skibow, please go over the equipment listings as they're generated and make sure we have everything we need."

Joe nodded. "The lander has quite a bit of capacity—fifty tons mass plus passengers—but the rover's going to eat up thirty-five of that. And I'd prefer that most of the equipment be able to fit into the rover's maximum carry of ten tons. We don't know how close Bruce will be able to land us or how far we'll have to carry stuff, and you can bet the excavation equipment will take a big bite out of that. Plus food, water, and all the other necessaries. So be selective about what you take, okay?"

Madeline was the only one not given an immediate task. After everyone else had left, leaving her alone on the bridge with Hathaway, she cocked her head at the captain.

"Tell me why, Ken. Do you *really* think there's much danger? I shouldn't think there would be, myself. The technology is all tested, we are all very well trained, and we've been operating here in space for months with no problems at all beyond piddly stuff."

He shrugged. "No, I don't. But who really knows? And *that's* why I want you there." He gazed for a moment at the entrance to the bridge, through which the others had recently departed. "Those are all fine and wonderful people, each in their own way. Jane Mayhew, too. But what they aren't—not one of them—are soldiers."

"Neither am I."

He gave her that dark-eyed stare. "Yes, you are, in the one criterion that matters the most. Danger is something you take for granted. Something you've trained for. Something you *expect*. Which they don't."

He looked up at the huge viewscreen, which now showed the great reddish orb of Mars. "Remember what it's named, Madeline. And remember that this planet destroyed more unmanned probes than all the other planets of the Solar System put together. They still make jokes about the Martian antispacecraft defense network. We'd be damned fools to assume that the first humans to land on the face of the god of war won't encounter any grief. And if they do, I want you down there. I'd go myself, but I can't."

She gazed up at the planet. It did look ominous, in point of fact. Mars always did.

"I understand. I'll leave you the codes before I go, Ken. In case something happens to me."

He turned his head to look at her. "You sure?"

"Yes. Three reasons. First, because I have to. It's possible, if you don't have the codes, that the program might malfunction and scramble all transmissions. It was designed by security freaks, don't forget. I don't really share that mind-set, but I understand it perfectly. 'When in doubt, suppress.' "

Ken's eyes widened a little. "Huh. I admit, I hadn't even thought of that."

"The second reason is that I trust you. If something happens to me, just continue monitoring the transmissions the way I have and use your own judgment as to what's okay to send and what isn't."

He nodded. Madeline was silent, for a while, her eyes never leaving Mars.

"And the third reason?"

"It will be an immense relief," she said quietly. "I'm *tired* of that burden."

She brought her eyes down and smiled suddenly. The full-bore Madeline smile that was hers alone.

"Instead, I got nothing to worry about except Martian monsters. For which—"

The fast set of katas she went through had Ken Hathaway howling within seconds.

"Take that, you nasty green thark!"

# Chapter 40

"SSTO *John Carter* ready for launch to Mars surface landing."

"All clear, *John Carter*. You may launch when ready, Bruce."

"Acknowledged. Stand by." Bruce Irwin looked into the screen showing his passengers. "Everyone ready? All strapped in? It'll be a couple of hours before we land, so get comfy."

"We're all ready, Bruce. Let's get this show on the road!"

"I didn't ask just you, A.J., now shut up. Everyone strapped in and ready?"

The others replied with various affirmatives.

"Right. I'll do my best, but it's a fair dinkum ride and no one's ever done this before. So it's probably going to get a mite bumpy, especially the last few minutes."

He switched back to the transmitter. "This is *John*

*Carter*, launching in thirty seconds. Locks disengaged. Bay doors open."

Bay doors on the side of *Nike*'s ring allowed *John Carter* to be launched by the simple expedient of using the ship's own rotation. The SSTO shuttle would slide along tracks until it reached the exit and then fly free. Once clear of *Nike*, Bruce would initiate a burn to set them in an orbital course for eventual deorbit and landing.

"Wheee!" A.J.'s voice came over the systems as he felt the slow, speeding, curved vibration of the shuttle's track-based launch. "Here we go, guys!"

He knew that Joe shared his excitement. It wasn't that there hadn't already been about a thousand wonders to appreciate, a million things to learn. But *this* was the real dream—the dream the accident had stolen from him, and that he'd been haunted with ever since they arrived: to set foot on the Red Planet itself.

"*John Carter* is now clear of *Nike*," Bruce stated. "Beginning orbital insertion for Melas Chasma landing site."

The orbital shift for this purpose wasn't huge, but had this been Earth they would have had to take considerably more time for the purpose—and probably used ion engines. However, *John Carter* could—barely—achieve single stage to orbit on Earth. Here, dealing with a gravity well only thirty-eight percent as powerful, it had deltavee to spare.

The rockets roared for a few seconds, pushing everyone into their seats with a force that felt immense. Glancing with concern at the telltales, A.J. saw to his surprise that it was only about two gravities.

"Damn, I'm out of shape," he heard himself say, his

voice slightly strained. "I thought we were doing four or five g's there."

"It does feel out of whack, doesn't it?" Bruce commented. "That's what months of soft living in a third gravity do to you. Don't worry, though. I'm not planning on anything more than three all the way down."

"I practice in the high-g rotor every week." Madeline's voice was serene. "It feels just fine to me."

"Thank you, Ms. Jane Bond. The rest of us have things to do rather than working on our mah-velous looks."

"Her looks don't need any work. And she puts as much time in the med department as anyone else does on their job."

"You, my friend, are prejudiced."

"You really should exercise in the high-g area more, though," Helen said. "You've been slacking off lately, A.J."

He took a deep breath and prevented himself from an instinctively defensive retort by biting his lip. "Yeah, I know. But you guys have been keeping me awful busy, you know."

Conversations drifted rather like *John Carter* for a while, as the shuttle headed for a particular point in time and space. "Okay, mates, can the chatter," Bruce finally said, as the time approached. "I'm about to take us down, and I don't need any distractions."

A.J. clamped his mouth shut.

"*Nike*, this is *John Carter*, we are about to begin deorbit burn."

"This is *Nike*, *John Carter*. You are about to begin deorbit burn, we copy."

"Burn starting in five, four, three, two, one—"

Once more the rockets roared, vibrating the shuttle with the power of contained explosions. The great red planet began to swell.

"Return all your trays to the upright position, please. We're about to experience a spot of turbulence."

"Breathe, A.J.," Helen said quietly.

He suddenly realized that he actually had *not* been breathing, as though he'd hold his breath the entire way down. "Jesus. But, well, Helen, this . . ."

"I know."

A faint vibration tickled at the edges of the senses, then grew. A keening whine began. Suddenly, for the first time since they'd arrived in orbit, Mars seemed to be *down* instead of *up* or *over there*. The pink-red-orange-brown surface was starting to look like a landscape instead of a globe.

*John Carter* was in the atmosphere now, its meteoric speed being slowed by friction that heated its outer shell, turning it to a glow which those on *Nike* could easily detect. Ionization cut out all exterior communications as the ship was briefly enveloped in a sheath of blazing fire. *John Carter* shuddered, Bruce preparing to take full control of the shuttle as they dropped to atmospheric speed.

*THUNK.*

"What was that?"

"Bloody hell."

"I said, what was that?" Madeline repeated, with more urgency. Sitting in the copilot's seat, she could see the telltales rising on Bruce's suit.

"Left wing extension buggered. And I'm getting poor response in the rest. Joe, no offense, mate, but this is the last bloody reentry I'm doing with you on board." Bruce's voice was light, but an undercurrent of tension made his words serious.

"*Shimatta*," Dr. Sakai said, calm resignation in the Japanese curse.

"What caused it?"

"Sorry, no way to tell right now. Bad parts, heating got to one of the joints, micrometeor, gremlins, the much-feared Martian Anti-Spacecraft System, take your pick. I gotta get us down in one piece first, then we can bloody well worry about the whys."

"You'll do it," Joe said.

"Mate, I didn't do it last time. We punched out, remember?"

"Well . . ."

"There's no ejection pod in *this* bird, I remind you," Bruce continued relentlessly, as if he found some peculiar solace in contemplating the worst. "Parachutes are no use in atmosphere this thin. I've got to put her down somehow so she doesn't completely come apart on us."

A.J. finally forced himself to grasp that they were in a genuine crisis. By reflex, he brought up all of the sensors and tied in.

"Look, we have—*damn*. Yeah, you're losing controls, Bruce. I can feed you some more data, though. *Nike*, this is *John Carter*, we have an emergency situation here. Clear everyone out of the satellite feeds, we need all the info we can get now."

"An emergen— Got you. Attention all personnel, this is the captain speaking. *John Carter* is having trouble. We need the entire satellite network cleared for the shuttle's use."

The remote communications started to synchronize. "Okay,"

A.J. said, "we're losing altitude faster, at least some. Best calculations . . . Bruce, you're going to have to make it a full powered landing. No way around it. We won't be able to make orbit again without refueling, but we can burn that bridge when we get to it."

"How much control will I have by then? Something's making this bird progressively harder to fly. Maybe a leak, or a slow fire, or something."

A.J. ran a couple of simulations as the numbers from the embedded sensors poured through the systems. "About half, I'd say. You'll have to land us with really sluggish controls. Think ahead of time. I'll give you a running calculation that'll cue you as to when to act to get things done."

"Right."

*John Carter* was now screaming down the center of Valles Marineris. The pink-orange sky set off the towering, darker cliffs to either side as the ground below swept past. The terrain was red, black-splotched, streaked with white—every color, really, now that they were close enough—all of it rough and smooth and mysteriously textured. It was an alien landscape that A.J. had modeled a thousand times. But this time it was real, flowing past a window instead of across a screen. Vibrating, blurry at times, but real, real, real. They were about to land on Mars!

No, he corrected himself, they were about to *crash-land* on Mars.

"Okay, Bruce, see the display?"

"Yes, I see her. When I reach the first border, there is my burn?"

"You got it. Bring some of our speed down and make

sure you get a feel for the controls before we really have to do it."

"Roger that." Bruce turned his head for a moment, and the transparent, wide-view sections of the helmet allowed them to see that his expression was calm. "Hold on, everyone. I'm afraid I can't quite keep my promise. We probably will go over three gees on this one, when I do the final burn. And it might get very shaky."

The rockets responded sluggishly, lagging their control directives by noticeable fractions of a second. "Blast. This is going to be a bloody lot of fun, trying to land her like I'm doing remote control from the blasted moon!"

"Remote . . . Hey, hold on!"

A.J. searched the archives . . . assembly . . . slave . . . predictive . . . tie in . . .

*Got it!* "Bruce, go opaque in your helmet."

"What? Mate, I need to see to guess some of this!"

"Trust me! I'm going to adjust the displays and your feedback through the suit just like we did for the ground engineers assembling *Nike*. Combining the predictions on the landing and the degradation of the controls. . . Well, it might not be absolutely perfect, but . . . "

"But a fair dinkum sight better than my trying to learn to play the game with my timing off. Right!"

Bruce's helmet went silvery. Immediately, A.J. knew, it would appear to him to go transparent again, showing him the controls, *John Carter*, even the others in the cabin. But this was a projection that was going to be off by just the right amount into the future to make things seem to react correctly.

"Mate, I hope you're leaving the computers enough power for me."

"I'm using the ones in the rover, brought them up by remote."

"Right. Okay, this is it."

*John Carter* was constantly trying to heel over to one side, like a car with a flat tire. That wasn't the real problem, though. Bruce could handle that. But they couldn't land flat like an aircraft. They were coming down considerably to the west of their original site, to make things worse. They were well over a hundred kilometers, maybe two or three, from Target 37. A flat landing would almost certainly run them into something they hadn't modeled well in the last couple of days.

A quick glance at the terrain below confirmed it. Bruce would have to blast back along their current vector; then, as their speed dropped, bring the *John Carter* vertical and land it on its tail. That was the way it was supposed to launch, of course—but that position was one they'd normally achieve after the regular landing was safely over. But with the controls degrading, his simulation had to keep updating how it did the model . . .

Bruce swore, as he saw his vision glitch. "Listen, mate, if it does that at the wrong time—!"

"I know, I know! But I can't help it, the model has to update if things change."

"Right. Okay, hold on. *Nike*, this is *John Carter*, we are about to make a landing. Please stand by. And if we don't make it. . . Goodbye, all, and it's been a hell of a ride. Give my love to Tammy back home."

They were all gripping the arms of their seats now, all except Bruce who wrestled with controls that were sluggish and less responsive than they'd been a few minutes before. The rockets thundered in the Martian atmosphere as they fought to slow *John Carter*'s headlong rush towards destruction.

A.J.'s eyes flicked around, taking in the instrument readings he could see. *Airspeed 350, altitude 1500 and dropping—holy SHIT that's a big rock, good thing we're past it—300kph, altitude 1000 meters . . . Dropping . . . oh, man, Bruce is good . . . altitude now 200 meters, speed dropping below 200kph . . . 100 meters . . . he's starting to bring us up . . . lateral speed 70, 60, 50—*

One of the rockets stopped responding entirely. *John Carter*, still inclined at a slight angle and moving over the ground sideways at a speed of about forty kilometers per hour, dipped downward. A.J.'s simulation had almost predicted the loss, but was off by a critical bit as there was no real data yet on just how the failures were progressing. Bruce fought for control, but A.J., living in the real world, watched helplessly as the momentary, uncontrolled drop brought the lander's tail assembly into contact with a boulder jutting from the soil of Mars.

The world spun as *John Carter* cartwheeled, bouncing impossibly in one-third gravity. Bruce tried to shut her down, but one rocket thrust for another critical half-second, spinning the ship along another axis.

The *John Carter* shrieked, groaned, and bellowed at its occupants as it tumbled. And then a tremendous impact brought silence and darkness to all within.

# Chapter 41

Jackie Secord sat at the communications station of *Nike*. Once more she played the final few seconds, the last voices recorded from

John Carter.

"Give my love to Tammy back home." An Australian accent, heavier than usual.

"—holy SHIT that's a big rock—" A. J., muttering under his breath, like he always does, not even aware sometimes he's doing it.

". . . please, please, please, hold together . . ."

Tears stung her eyes at the voice she'd known since she was a teenager, the voice that had taught her the difference between Triassic, Jurassic, and Cretaceous.

Can't make out the words, but that sharp murmur is Dr. Sakai. Praying, by the sound of it.

"Speed dropping below two hundred. Almost there, Bruce. You're doing great." Madeline Fathom, calm and unruffled, trying to keep anyone from panicking.

Nothing from Rich. I think he must've been holding his breath.

"Please, let her live, even if I don't make it." Joe, worrying about someone else to the end.

The tears came again, as the final moment arrived. A shrieking, shattering, crashing, banging noise, ending with a terrible silence.

"Come now, Jackie. There is nothing more to hear, nothing more except pain." The deep voice was startlingly gentle, as was the hand laid tentatively on her shoulder.

She shrugged Dr. Gupta's hand away.

"He's right, Jackie. It's been almost two hours."

"I'm not leaving!" she shouted, shooting to her feet and turning on Hathaway furiously. "I'm not!" The movement sent her drifting slowly towards the ceiling, as *Nike* was still turning and her spinning motion had detached her from the floor's grip surface. As the control room was near the center of *Nike*, it had less than a twentieth of a gravity—and that was focused in the wrong direction, towards the apparent ceiling.

The captain backed up a step when she spun. "Okay, okay. Stay there if you want to. But *please* stop playing the damn thing over, and over, and over. It's driving me insane."

Clumsily she bounced herself back to the seat. "I haven't played it that—"

"Yes, you have. You've been repeating it the entire time, ever since you sat down."

Jackie stared, eyes still blurred, at the digital readout. *He's right. I've been sitting in this chair for over an hour, playing it again and again.* She looked around, drawing a shuddering, tearful breath.

Three other people looked back at her with concern and their own shock and sorrow written clearly in their features. Dr. Gupta, dark eyes shadowed with pain over her loss and the loss of the others on *John Carter*. Jane Mayhew, looking decades older. Ken Hathaway, anger, frustration and resignation all warring for dominance.

"Sorry," she said quietly. "I know you all knew them too. But . . . we started this. Me, Helen, Joe, A.J." A fresh sting of pain threatened to bring tears back.

On the screen shimmered a horrid image of the twisted wreckage of *John Carter*, as it had been an hour ago before the last imaging satellite fell below the horizon. Her hand tugged at the chain around her neck, the one that held the smooth, shoehorn-shaped replica given to her by Helen just before the presentation.

Suddenly, the radio started talking. With an Australian accent.

"*Nike, Nike*, this is *John Carter*, repeat, *John Carter* calling *Nike*, come in please."

    * * *

*Why do I hurt so much?* Helen wondered, her mind still dazed. As she shook her head, she became aware that she was in a spacesuit.

*Spacesuit? Where . . .*

Realization struck, and she sat up suddenly. That was a mistake. Not only did she bang the suit's helmet on something, but her head, already aching, reacted to the jolt by throbbing its protest.

"*Ow.* A.J.? Joe? Hello, is anyone there?"

Slowly her eyes adjusted. Pinkish light filtered in through a hole in the mostly dust-covered front window. Before moving again, she checked the telltales. Her suit was undamaged, and apparently so was she. The reactive nature of the suit had possibly saved her life, and almost certainly prevented severe injuries. She hoped that the others had been so lucky.

It took considerable force to get her harness to unsnap. Cautiously, she got up.

"Oh, crikey. This wasn't worth the hangover I'm feeling."

"Bruce! You did it!"

"Did I?"

"Well, I'm walking away."

"Well, so you are. Maybe I am too."

"I'd rather have someone else do my walking, but I guess I will be too." A.J.'s voice brought inexpressible relief to her. She'd been afraid that the first lack of response meant there would be none at all.

Irwin finished unsnapping and leaned over to his copilot, checking her vitals. "Hey, Madeline, rise and shine!"

Poking at an unconscious martial artist might not be the brightest idea, Helen thought. She was about to voice that thought when Madeline demonstrated it by striking out and trying to roll away from the fuzzily seen figure looming over her. The roll was rather ineffective, as she was still locked in.

But she recuperated almost instantly. "Huh? Oh. Sorry, Bruce. Didn't mean to hit you."

"No problem, the suit kept you from hurting anything except my dignity."

"We're still alive. Everyone?"

"Not everyone." A.J.'s voice was suddenly utterly devoid of his usual humor. "Shit. I will *not* be sick in my suit."

Helen turned, and was instantly sorry she had. Dr. Ryu Sakai was pinned against the rear of the compartment by something—a support structure of *John Carter*, probably—that must have torn free in the last terrible impact, impaling or crushing his entire rib cage. The tough suit might have maintained some integrity, but there were limits to its protective capabilities. The astrogeological specialist was clearly dead.

"Jesus . . ." Rich Skibow spoke for the first time since the crash, tearing his way out of his restraining harness. "Oh, this is horrible."

It was then that Helen remembered that Joe had been sitting in front of Ryu Sakai. For a moment her heart seemed to stop. But . . . there was only one suit pinned to the wall with that hideous dark smear around it.

"Joe! Where's Joe?"

A.J. answered, obviously glad of something to distract him from the gruesome scene in the rear. "Ummm . . . Look, that beam ripped upward through the cabin. With that angle, it would've taken out the support column under Joe's chair. If we were still moving, he . . ."

A.J. trailed off. Helen followed his gaze.

Straight to the hole in the forward window. "Oh, no—"

She leaped toward the window and tripped. The wreck of the SSTO was leaning on something, inclined at an angle of about forty-five degrees both vertically and laterally. Scrambling in the light gravity, she made it to the hole and looked out.

*John Carter* rested atop a massive boulder five times its size. From her vantage point thirty meters above the rest of the terrain, she could make out a small, dark object more than a fifty meters off: Joe's seat, with a spacesuit still strapped into it.

"Joe! Joe!"

The figure moved. Joe raised an arm slowly and waved. Then said, shakily but firmly: "By the authority vested in me as a representative of the Ares Project and the first human being to set foot on Mars, I claim all the rights and privileges pertaining thereunto for the Project."

"Gah!" said Madeline.

"Hey, look, I'm sorry," Joe apologized, defensively. "I didn't know he was dead then."

" 'S'okay," Rich grunted. "I shouldn't have yelled at you. I'd have found it funny, any other time. I suppose it will be someday."

A.J. emitted a harsh little laugh, as he attached another cable to the support beam for their attempt to remove Ryu Sakai's body. "I will say that Madeline's face was worth seeing, when you opened up *that* can of worms."

Madeline didn't quite glare at him. She did glare at Joe. "You have absolutely no idea of the headaches this may cause, if your people insist on it."

Joe knew the dialogue focused on his unexpected claiming of Mars because none of them wanted to really think about the gruesome task ahead of them. He was still stuck in his seat, looking at *John Carter*'s red-dusted, ominous, shattered-looking hulk from fifty meters away. He had discovered upon attempting to get up that his leg was apparently broken, and Madeline had insisted he stay there until someone could get out and examine it.

The advice had become more serious when A.J.'s sensor analysis through the suit's onboard biometric monitors indicated that Joe might have a concussion also. He did feel rather detached, his head hurt, and he wanted to take a nap, which were not encouraging symptoms.

"I have some idea, yeah. But I don't know exactly how the legal ins and outs work, so I figured I'd play it safe. Let's face it, we're still a private concern and someday we'll be cut loose. If I'd fumbled this ball, everyone at Ares could've been completely screwed."

A.J.'s little laugh came again. "Have I mentioned that the two of you are redefining the expression 'odd couple'?"

"I can reach you, Mr. Baker."

"Enough. Pull, everyone," Rich said, straining at the beam.

There was a grating in Joe's earphones, then several grunts and a faint clanging noise. "That's got it. Poor Ryu."

"Has anyone tried raising *Nike*?"

"We will as soon as we get out of the wreck. Most of the systems are shut down right now."

Joe saw the others slowly emerge from the hole he'd made on his impromptu exit. Once more he was astonished that he was still alive. Either his suit had taken the impact with amazing resilience; or, more likely, the chair had spun as he went through the air and broken the window in front of him. He had no memory himself of the sequence of events involved. And then—which he also did not remember at all—the seat must have twisted around and absorbed most of the impact of his final Marsfall. However it had happened, he'd been incredibly lucky not only to survive, but with no injuries worse than a broken leg.

The five distant figures lowered a limp sixth to the dusty soil. "Rich, I know it doesn't mean much. But I think Ryu wouldn't mind being the first person buried on Mars."

Skibow was silent for so long that Joe was afraid he'd

angered the other man again. Rich and Dr. Sakai had been very close friends.

Then he heard a sigh. "Yeah. You're right. If he were alive, he'd probably be tickled pink."

Bruce's voice broke in. "I've got the radio working again."

For a moment all four people on the *Nike*'s bridge stared in disbelief. Then Jackie answered, her voice cracking with disbelieving joy. "Bruce? *You're all right!*"

"Well, yeah, it would seem so."

"Is everyone okay?" Ken Hathaway asked.

"I am afraid not, Captain," Madeline Fathom's voice responded. "Dr. Sakai did not survive the crash."

Jane, who had brightened immeasurably upon hearing Irwin's voice, closed her eyes and swallowed. She'd also been a good friend of the Japanese areologist.

Hathaway sighed. "Understood. I'll see to it his next of kin is informed, back on Earth. How is everyone else?"

"Joe Buckley has a broken leg—how bad we will determine shortly. He may also have a concussion. The rest of us seem to be healthy. But given that all of us apparently lost consciousness on impact, we must be alert for concussion as well."

"No 'apparently' about it, Madeline, unless you people have been awake for almost two hours."

"Not that long, no, although we have been active for some time. External links were being sent through *John Carter*'s systems and, as those were no longer active, we had to get out of the shuttle before we attempted contact again. Before doing so, we extricated Dr. Sakai from where he had been pinned. Perhaps we should have attempted contact earlier, but . . . We just couldn't leave him there."

"Yes, I understand. What condition is *John Carter* in? And the supplies and equipment on board?"

"The lander is . . . a wreck. I'm not even sure it could be repaired in a real dry dock. We certainly can't. As for the other, we simply don't know yet. We'll need a few hours, I think, before we can give you a solid assessment of the state of our equipment."

"All right. The main thing is that most of you are still alive. I can't tell you how relieved we are."

"Yes. Fathom out."

Jackie sagged back into the chair. *Alive. They're alive!*

Then she stood up so suddenly she almost separated from the deck again. "Okay. So they're alive. But now we have to figure out how to *keep* them that way."

Satya Gupta nodded. "Indeed, Ms. Secord, *indeed* that is our next order of business. They will need supplies, beyond any doubt. It is our job to devise some method to get those supplies to them."

Hathaway frowned. "*Can* you get anything to them? We don't have any other atmosphere capable vehicles. In fact, we have damn few things worth calling vehicles at all, except *Nike*—which certainly can't make a trip down."

"*Can* we?" Gupta's voice sounded almost offended. "Of course it can be done! We have almost limitless energy, we have all the equipment of *Nike*, and we have the knowledge with which to do it. It can be done. It will be done, for it *must* be done."

Jackie nodded. "There's got to be a way, Captain. Our only real enemy is time. It depends on how long they can hold out. When Madeline reports back . . . Well, if they're so bad off all they have is their suit resources, I don't know. But if they can manage even a week or two . . . We'll find a way to send them what they need if we have to get out there and *push* it to Mars!"

Madeline, a tiny figure against the hulking backdrop of *John Carter*, began moving towards Joe. "I'll check Joe. Helen, give me a hand, would you? You're the only one here besides myself who has much experience with field medicine. Then we have to assess our resources. Our prospects are chancy, I'm afraid."

Joe understood what she meant. *John Carter* was the expedition's only surface-to-space vehicle. If they couldn't survive on the surface of Mars for quite a while, there wasn't a thing anyone on *Nike* could do to save them. "We may all join Ryu Sakai soon enough," he muttered.

"Not if I can help it," Madeline said briskly. "I said 'chancy,' not 'dim.' On the positive side, only one of us is injured, our suits are all in working order, and the filters and rebreathers will give us considerable functioning time before we have to worry about running out of air. So we're not in immediate danger. The key thing is the rover. If we can just get the rover out of the wreck, I think we'll have an excellent chance."

She knelt beside Joe and probed his leg through the suit. "A.J., can you verify a fracture using the sensors we have?"

"No problem, with both your sensors and his." After a moment he said: "Yep. Clean break, but it's not lined up right. The suit can be forced into rigid mode in that area, though, so if you can manage to set the bone, I can trigger a splint."

"That means she's going to hurt me, right?"

Helen had arrived by then, and smiled down at him. "Look at it this way, Joe. We only hurt the ones we love."

"Listen, mates, keep the foreplay private."

Madeline ignored the byplay, as she considered the situation. "I need to make sure you're still when I do this, Joe. The low gravity may make that . . . interesting."

She glanced around. "Okay. Since you're still in the seat and still strapped down, we may as well use that as a harness. Hold tight onto the armrests. Hopefully your weight and the seat's will keep you still long enough. Helen, do your best to keep him steady. I'd suggest grabbing his shoulders."

Helen did so. Joe got his arms locked around the armrests. "Go ahead."

"Ready, A.J.?"

"Say the word."

"Trying . . . *now.*"

A blaze of white-hot pain stabbed up from the vicinity of his shin. Joe grunted or screamed, he wasn't sure which, but held on as the tension increased. He felt the chair quiver, and then suddenly felt something clamp firmly down the length of his leg.

"That's got it!" A.J. exclaimed. "Good work, Madeline. It's set and I've locked the splint down."

"How are you feeling, Joe?" There was concern in her voice now, unlike the flat and professional tone in which she'd spoken earlier.

"Be . . . all right, I think. Just let me rest a little, turn up the heat in my suit a bit, and get a drink. Minor shock, probably."

She brought up his biometric display on her suit HUD. "Yes. But you should be okay."

"I'll key an alarm in, just in case." A.J. said. "Joe, you just rest until you're sure you're up to moving."

"Don't worry, I'm not dumb. I'll sit here and admire the view."

A.J. paused. "Yeah. That's a hell of a view."

Sharply defined against the light pink of the horizon sky, only slightly softened by the distance, the five-kilometer-high walls of Valles Marineris reared their impenetrable bulk. It was the greatest canyon in the Solar System, and looked the part. The scalloped, gully-ridged sides demarcated an uncrossable barrier. Between the atmosphere-softened light and traces of dust or sand in the air, the distant surfaces seemed to have a dreamlike patina of lighter shades of rose and pearl.

Other, lesser ridges jutted at intervals like rocky knife edges, barring any direct route across the bottom of the mighty canyon. Dust and sand and rocks covered the floor of Valles Marineris, the latter mostly rounded from tumbling in the long-vanished waters and from millions of years of low-pressure sandblasting. Though the predominant colors were reds and pinks and oranges, there was a profusion of other colors, as well. White splashes on some areas; dark, almost black sands and gray-black rocks; a shocking glint of yellow, flashes of light from feldspar or quartz or mica. It was a wild, utterly untouched view, under an alien sky without a contrail or a cloud or any sign of life other than themselves. Joe felt it finally sinking in that he was actually, truly, and really on Mars, the first human being ever to touch the soil of the Red Planet.

He just hoped he wasn't about to end up the second person buried there.

# Chapter 42

Helen studied the generated imagery from the Fairy Dust A.J. had managed to insinuate into the stuck cargo hold area. "So the pin's twisted around and in the way?"

"Looks like it," Joe said, from his position now propped up against a boulder near the lander. "If we'd kept trying to slide it, we'd be at this forever. I think if we pull up and out a bit, though, we could get it to pop free, and then we could slide it the rest of the way."

"Once more Peter Pan saves the day," Madeline said.

"I'd object," A.J. said, "but the alternative is to be called Tinkerbell, I suppose. Why do you think I wanted my Fairy Dust with me? Even without a crash we would've had a hell of a lot of poking around to do. Sensor and comm nets are hard to come by out here, unless you can make them—which the Dust can."

"She was only kidding," Helen chided him. "Stop being defensive. I'd tell you to start acting your age, except I'm deathly afraid of the results. Now let's get to work, shall we?"

She and Madeline exchanged a quick grin. A.J. scowled a bit, but went to help Rich and Bruce without saying anything further.

The three men fitted the prybars Madeline had improvised from other parts of the wreck into the indicated locations and pulled. For a moment nothing happened, the weaker gravity of Mars making their pulls less effective than they would have been on Earth. But then a popping jolt told them the twisted lockpin had come loose, and with some more sustained effort the door slid open.

"Please be intact, please be intact, please be intact," A.J. muttered like a mantra as he dropped into the dark cargo bay. His helmet light activated and showed him the tilted bulk of the pressurized rover, still sitting in the middle of the bay.

"Well, first piece of good news. It seems to have stayed locked down. That gives us fair odds on it being intact."

"Take a look and check out the systems."

"I'm getting a response . . . Yeah, the processors are all running. Doing a diagnostic on *Thoat* now."

"Thoat?"

"What else would you call a steed we have to unload from a ship named the *John Carter*?"

"Well," Joe interjected, "Personally I'd rather ride *Dejah Thoris*."

A.J. choked. "Joe, I can't believe you said that."

"I'm trying to pretend he didn't," muttered Madeline. "Come on, Helen, let's get down there. Maybe in the rover we'll be out of junior-high-school-boy joke range."

She and Helen lowered themselves into the bay, with

Bruce following. A.J. already had lights starting to glow from the newly-named *Thoat*.

"And since everyone's having to go down to get to it," Joe continued cheerily, "I think you meant *Deep Thoat*."

Rich gave a startled snort. "I think that's quite enough out of you, Joe. Being charitable, I'll ascribe it to the pain-killers you took."

"You mean Joe thinks he's funnier when he's on drugs? That makes sense," A.J. said. The telltales came up. "All green! Well, except for fuel, as we weren't shipping her fueled up."

"Better check the fuelling hookups, then."

"Should be at the rear of the cargo bay."

"On my way." Madeline moved off in that direction, along with Helen and Bruce, as A.J. went up into the rover's cabin to see if anything inside had been shaken loose.

After a few moments clearing debris from the rear of the bay, A.J. heard a satisfied little sound from Madeline. "Got it! Scratches on the nozzle hookups, but they don't look to be badly damaged or out of shape."

"Then I'm opening up the fuel ports on the sides. Take the starboard one first."

"Understood. Helen, you and Bruce bring up the oxygen line. I have the methane."

The separate hoses were locked into place. "We are hooked up. Go, A.J."

"Starting . . . We have fuel flow! Ladies and gentlemen, we are in business!"

"Good. You finish prepping *Thoat* and the rest of us will figure out the best way to get it out of the bay. Joe? Can you tear yourself away from junior high locker room long enough to play engineer?"

"Sure, Madeline. I think you'll need to use *Thoat*'s winch. That's after we blow the side of the bay out."

"How will we do that?"

"Are you asking *me* about demolitions, Ms. Superspy?"

A.J. heard a chuckle from Madeline. "Yes, all right, I know something about it. Martian demolitions may require additional thought, however. The last thing I want to do is blow the entire lander up, with *Thoat* in it."

"Let me strongly approve of additional thought," A.J. interjected, "as I happen to be inside *Thoat* right now."

A light flickered. "Uh-oh."

"Mr. Baker, I do not like the sound of 'uh-oh.' "

"You shouldn't. Fuel flow decreasing . . . and . . . gone. We can't see underneath well enough, but I'd have to guess that when we crashed, the tanks got mostly shredded. Fortunately, we didn't end up with an earth-shattering kaboom. Mars-shattering kaboom, I should say. But only some of the gas in the last couple of cells stuck around."

"Have we got enough to get to Target 37?"

"Not a chance."


A.J. examined the telltales and had his systems run calculations. "Figuring that I have to make sure *Thoat* is fully charged up and then use some of the fuel to get out of the bay, I figure . . . Maybe thirty kilometers range; thirty-five, max. We got no more than a tenth full."

"How long will that keep us if we stay right here?"

"Generating power, keeping the heat going, refreshing the air . . . A couple of weeks, I guess. Hard to say, exactly."

"And when can we expect some kind of rescue attempt?"

"I really don't know. Joe? That's more up your alley."

"Not for several months, at the earliest. They might be able to get us some supplies with one or two orbital drops—if they can figure out how to cobble something together. But let's ask *Nike*. Gupta and Jackie are the ones who'd really know."

"Well, that's just bloody perfect," Bruce grumbled. He called Hathaway and explained the situation.

Jackie broke in. "We might be able to put together a lander using one of *Nike's* engines."

"A NERVA rocket lander? I suppose it might work. But you aren't getting that done any too quickly."

"Alas, no, Major Irwin," came Gupta's voice. "Even though we are well equipped for an expedition such as ours, creating a new vessel of that sort will take considerable effort. It was not planned for some time yet, and we shall be forced to improvise. A month, perhaps."

"No way we're lasting a month," A.J. said bluntly.

"We'll see if we can get at least some fuel down to you," Hathaway said. "I'm not sure, but there must be a way."

"Perhaps," Gupta mused. "Perhaps if we were to remove one of the auxiliary drives from the habitat ring, and—"

Something was nagging at Joe. Something he'd forgotten, something . . .

Could it be?

He tied into the system, bringing up the precise position of the crash. There. Closer than he'd thought, and just to the south.

"Yes! *Pirate!*"

⊠       ⊠       ⊠

A.J. felt his jaw drop as he realized what Joe was suggesting.

"You're kidding." He called up information he hadn't looked at in well over two years. "I will be completely damned. You're right, Joe! We practically ran *Pirate* over."

Hathaway's voice was incredulous. "Are you telling me that the same lander unit that originally dropped off the Faeries is in your vicinity, and might have fuel on board?"

"About thirty klicks from where we're sitting, Captain. We landed *Pirate* in Melas Chasma, after it dropped off the Faeries. Talk about a lucky coincidence!"

"I doubt if it was a coincidence," Joe said, his voice sounding distracted. A.J. knew the engineer was already starting to work through the practical aspects of their situation. "The Bemmies probably put their base there for the same reason we chose the site. Valles Marineris is the most spectacular area on Mars, except for maybe Olympus Mons and the Tharsis Plateau. Tricky to set down in, though—and Melas Chasma provides some of the few good landing areas in it."

That made sense. "And then all the stuff blew up after we found Bemmie on Phobos," A.J. mused, "and Ares got diverted into the *Nike* project. We just left *Pirate* waiting for takeoff. So she has never flown! If things held together, most of her fuel should still be there— and there was enough to take *Pirate* all the way back to Earth."

"There won't be that much left by now, A.J.," Joe cautioned, but he looked almost smug as he said it. A.J. could tell, from the expression, that his friend was finishing up his calculations and was pleased by the results. "Ares had to cut a lot of corners, with our budget—and one of the corners we cut was the fuel tanks. They were adequate for the purpose, but since we weren't planning to leave *Pirate* on the surface for very long, we didn't bother taking expensive measures to make sure they'd handle long-term storage under Martian conditions. By now, I'm pretty sure a lot of that fuel will be gone. Still—"

He looked up finally. "There's got to be enough left for what we need. If we take the hookup ends from here, I think . . . Yeah, we can adapt the connectors. All we've got to is *get* there, and we can fill up *Thoat* no problem. More than full, probably a couple of loads."

"I'll see if I can wake *Pirate* up," A.J. said.

"No. That's my job. You guys figure out how to get *Thoat* out of the lander. With my leg the way it is, I can't help with that anyway."

While the others started on that task, Joe called up the comm protocols, hooked to one of the satellites.

"Please still be working. I know we forgot about you, *Pirate*, but we need you now, more than the Project ever imagined."

SHOW STATUS. ALL SYSTEMS.

Suddenly a response showed. *Pirate* wasn't dead, at least.

Power Generation: 54%

Sensor Systems: Panoramic Imaging Unit: Green. Infrared Imaging Unit: Green

SOKAS Detector: No Signal

CANCEL. RETURN MODULE FUELING STATUS?

Refueling procedure completed.

Crossing his fingers and giving a little prayer, Joe sent the critical query.

DISPLAY REMAINING FUEL IN RETURN MODULE.

Fuel Remaining: 22476.3 combined total.

"YES!"

"I take it from your attempt to break our eardrums that this is good news?" Madeline asked.

"There's over twenty tons of fuel waiting for us. *Pirate's* still mostly running and ready."

"That was supposed to be an Earth Return Vehicle, Joe," Hathaway said. "Could you people possibly just take her back up here?"

"I'm afraid not. You have to remember that *Pirate* was unmanned. More a demo than anything else. Sure, she was meant to carry some payload back, but not with less than half her fuel remaining. And as long as she's been sitting here, I'm pretty sure she couldn't even make orbit any more. We didn't just cut corners on the fuel tanks, I'm afraid. A lot of her systems weren't designed for a long period of inactivity, especially not on a planetary surface."

He shook his head vigorously. "It doesn't matter anyway, Ken. Even if she was working perfectly, we couldn't do it. There's not enough empty space inside *Pirate* to fit one of us, even if we rip out nonessentials, much less all of us. And I'd hate to try riding her up perched on the outside."

Hathaway's sigh was audible. "No, that'd be insane. All right. It was just a thought. But can you survive on the surface for long enough?"

A.J. spoke up. "With that much fuel and resources? Yeah, sure. But if you guys can't figure out how to drop us food, it'll get pretty damn tight. Hopefully we can avoid 'Donner, party of five . . . Donner, party of four . . . Donner—' "

"That is *not* funny, A.J.!" Helen snapped. Joe could tell she was genuinely pissed. Wisely, A.J. busied himself with his work, keeping his head down.

After a short, pained silence, Helen spoke again. "Ken, leaving aside the way he put it, I'm afraid A.J. does have a point. What *are* the chances of getting us food? That's the one thing I can think of that there's no way we could jury-rig down here."

"We'll figure out some way to drop you supplies in the next few weeks," Hathaway said. "I just checked on the schedule, and the next lander is supposed to arrive here in three months. If you can survive that long, I think you'll be okay—even if we can't get you off the surface for some time after that. Yes?"

"Well, it'll be awfully cramped. But with the rover working and everything else . . . Yes, we can make it."

"We might have to strangle A.J. and Joe," Madeline put in, "just so we don't die from a concentration of toxic humor. But, otherwise, we can make it. I wintered over in Antarctica, once; six months in a shelter that wasn't much bigger than the rover, and was considerably less well-equipped. It wasn't any fun, but it can be done."

"What were you doing—"

"Don't ask."

"Ah . . . right. Okay, then, that's the plan."

"Not all of it," Helen countered. "I hate twiddling my thumbs, Ken. As long as we're going to be down here that long, we might as well get a good look at Target 37."

# Chapter 43

A.J. watched Madeline for the signal. The cable was now wound multiple times around a massive section of the nearby outcropping, with the other end connected to *Thoat*'s powerful electric winch. It had taken Madeline most of a day to figure out exactly how she wanted to blow the side of the lander, using some of the explosives they'd brought in case they needed them for excavating the ruins at Target 37. Everyone had been more than a little nervous—even Madeline, he suspected—when the charge was blown, but when the smoke cleared a large chunk had been taken out of the side of *John Carter* but virtually everything inside was untouched. Now, with the help of the winch, A.J. thought they could get *Thoat* out.

Madeline waved. "All set, A.J."

A.J. was acting as a spotter, observer, and advisor for Bruce. The Australian pilot was their best choice for driving *Thoat*, having practiced with it both in simulation and back on Earth. But this was going to be tricky even for someone with his experience. *Thoat* would emerge from the bay with over three meters of free drop beneath, and a heavily inclined surface of rock that could easily tip the rover if things got sticky. They had tried to use wreckage to make a ramp, but even in the one-third gravity Joe was uncertain about how well it would hold. And then, even if it did, there would still be the steep run down the huge inclined ridge before *Thoat* reached reasonably level ground.

If they could have set the winch cable on something towards the top of the ridge, that would have been better, but nothing on top provided reasonable purchase. However, if *Thoat* could survive the first few dozen yards down, it would pass the outcropping to which the winch cable was attached. From then on, it would be able to use the winch to slow itself down the rest of the way. Bruce had walked the route several times, visualizing the moves he'd have to make.

"Okay, everyone, make sure you're well clear. If anything goes wrong you'll want to be far, far away."

"Understood." Madeline and the others moved to the far side of the main ridge.

"Everyone's clear, Bruce. The cable's fastened. Snug it up."

The winch turned slowly, until increasing tension made the rover quiver. "Stop! You got it. Now, I'm trying to program the thing to keep the tension constant."

"Don't get too fancy on me, A.J. I don't need your gadget to yank on me at the wrong time. Maybe I should do the controlling."

"Do you think you can do it well enough along with all the other stuff you'll have to do?"

There was a moment's pause. "Blowed if I know for sure, but I guess you might have a point. Just make sure that it won't be pulling me if it's sideways on, right?"

"Got you. Limit of angular deflection. All right, whenever you're ready."

The thin air didn't transmit much sound, but a faint whine and rumble could be heard from *Thoat*. With a lurch, the rover moved up and forward, eating cable as it progressed steadily up the slope. "Keep coming, keep coming . . . almost to the edge . . . another few . . ."

Bruce gunned the engine and manually overrode the steady pressure of the winch, giving it a momentary full-strength pull. *Thoat* popped up out of its former prison. The front two pairs of wheels smashed down onto the inclined stone, while the rear wheels dropped with a ponderous crunch onto the makeshift ramp.

Which promptly shattered and collapsed.

*Thoat* slewed sideways and skidded, nearly tipping, as Bruce fought for control. The independently suspended wheels spun, trying to keep a grip, as the rover staggered drunkenly down the rocks. A.J.'s program had cut out completely as there was no predicting the angle at which *Thoat* might be.

The rover almost plummeted past the rock where the winch cable was attached, and at that point Bruce hit the winch controls again. The winch screamed protest at the abuse it was suddenly being asked to take, but the composite-metal cable held well. *Thoat* slowed and stopped, and then, carefully, began to make a rear-first descent down the steep slope.

A few moments later, the rover was on level ground. "Cooo-*eeee!* Now that was a ride, blokes!"

"I'm glad you enjoyed it," Madeline said dryly. "Let's hope we don't have to experience it again, however."

"No worries, once was enough. Let's get moving, shall we?"

"Shut her down for now. We want to load all the equipment we possibly can into her now."

"Right."

About two hours later, the last of the equipment that had not already been in *Thoat* was finally stowed. Then Rich turned to the others. "It's . . . time."

Helen nodded. "We probably won't be coming back this way, at least not for quite a while. And there's no point in bringing him with us."

The rocky soil was not tremendously hard-packed, and they had excavation tools already. Digging a hole did not take long.

"Do you want to say a few words, Rich?"

Skibow stood at the edge of the grave, looking down at the body. "Ryu Sakai was a good scientist and an even better friend. I'd known him since he was a visiting student at my university. I remember he once insisted that I try out for one of the musicals they had at the college, a production of *Little Shop of Horrors*. I got the part of the dentist and he got the part of Audrey II, the plant. That surprised me— all of us in the cast—because none of us had known what a good singing voice he had."

Skibow cleared his throat. "Ryu was always that way. One minute, looking like a professor and insisting on proper protocol; then, the next, startling you with some joke or new skill you had no idea he had. He used to do sleight of hand tricks in class . . ." Rich trailed off, then continued: "But he was always focused in the end on his career. That's why he was here, because there was never any question about following any path he could get to the other worlds he'd studied by remote. Ryu Sakai would have rather lived, of course. But he would also be honored to be the first man buried on another world. And he wouldn't want to hold us back."

He choked suddenly, then cut it off, sniffed back tears, and nodded. "He'd give us his blessing, I think."

"He certainly would, Rich," Jane's voice came softly. She'd been following the informal service from orbit. "He'd say: '*Saa*, let us waste no more time or fuel on me. I am no longer in need of it.'"

Rich's reaction was part laugh, part sob. "Yes. Yes, Jane, he would. And thank you for reminding me. So. Rest well, Ryu Sakai, under the sky and soil of Mars."

The others bowed their heads and waited a few moments. Then Rich picked up his shovel and began to fill in the grave. A few minutes later, it was done.

"And he has a hell of a tombstone," A.J. pointed out. "No one's moving *John Carter* from where it sits."

"No, I don't think they will," Helen said quietly. Then, shifting to a businesslike tone: "All right—everyone aboard. We're moving out."

That command necessitated first getting someone— Madeline, as it turned out—to load Joe in. She did it herself, to everyone's surprise—and Joe's voluble protest.

"Hey, be careful! You'll hurt yourself!"

"Don't be silly. In this gravity, you barely weigh seventy pounds."

The security specialist was such a small and very feminine-looking woman that people tended to forget how strong she was. The only one who didn't looked surprised was A.J.

Helen had to stifle a smile. *His* memories, of course, were considerably more vivid.

Once Joe was comfortably strapped in, the others quickly entered. To Helen's relief, *Thoat*'s interior proved to be much less cramped than she'd feared. When she said as much, Joe shook his head.

"Rover's probably too humdrum a term. Don't forget that *Thoat* was designed as a long-term Mars exploration vehicle. That means it isn't just a sort of planetary bus, but has to have living facilities aboard. It was by far the largest piece of equipment we brought with us from Earth, except for the SSTO."

Bruce verified the pressure was back up. The others lost no time in removing their helmets and suits.

"Cleanup is definitely the order of the day," Madeline said, moving to the rear. After a quick inspection of the sanitary facilities, she announced: "Well, it's adequate. But I miss our cabins more every minute."

"Too right," Bruce said. "But I'm in favor of anything that'll let us get a bit cleaner after more than two days in those glorified body stockings."

As Bruce set the rover in motion, following the path marked out clearly on the *Thoat*'s HUD, the others took turns using the miniature minimum-water cleaning facilities, and emptying the sanitary reservoirs of their suits into *Thoat*'s recycler.

※          ※          ※

"God, that feels good," Helen said, coming out last. "I know these are top-notch suits, but—"

"We're all agreed on the 'but,'" Madeline said firmly. "I also think that sentence works best unfinished."

"Amen," Rich concurred.

Joe had presented a problem, since his suit was also his splint. However, Madeline had been able to improvise a temporary splint; Joe held his leg carefully still while A.J. released the suit, Madeline applied the temporary, and then helped him remove the suit.

"A.J., maybe I should just leave that on?"

"Can't hurt. We'll probably have to be getting you in and out of your suit quite a few times over the next few weeks."

Madeline nodded. "I agree. We'll just have to make sure it fits right, and keep a close eye on it for a while."

Independent, wide, tall tires made *Thoat* a relatively smooth ride, given the rocky terrain they had to cross. The lesser gravity helped also, of course. Still, jolts were inevitable, and Joe was heard to curse more than once.

"Sorry, mate," Bruce apologized, after one especially big jolt. "Even with the best route there's still a bloody awful lot of rocks around."

"I'm going to put in a protest to the Martian Department of Transportation. The roads here are just terrible."

"Hey, they kept shooting us down before," A.J. pointed out wisely. "What makes you think they care?"

"Well, they better get used to it. It's payback for what they did to England back in the 1890s."

Ignoring the byplay, Helen sat down near Bruce. "How long until we get to *Pirate*?"

"Rate we're going? Say around ten in the morning

tomorrow, local time. I'm not pushing the girl over five KPH, even now while I can see well. It's going to be pitch dark out there when the sun sets, which is looking to be in a couple of hours."

"Now that you've had a bit of experience with the terrain, do you think we'll make it before the fuel runs out?"

Bruce shrugged, the motion visible though muted by the suit. "It's dicey. We're going to be right on the edge of our range. All we can do is hope."

# Chapter 44

*Thoat* grumbled its way over a large set of boulders, causing Joe to grumble in turn. Then the massive Martian rover crested the small ridge. A.J., who was currently sitting up front with Bruce, gave a whoop that almost deafened them.

"*Yeah!* Ahoy, me hearties, here be pirates!"

Helen moved up to take a look. In the distance, a kilometer or less away, squatted a blocky silhouette which she recognized from long-ago discussions with Joe and A.J. It was reassuringly familiar and, so to speak, very down to Earth in appearance. *Pirate* was a modification of the so-called "tuna can on a platform" design. It was neither elegant nor awe-inspiring, but looked exactly like what it was: a machine designed to do a job as efficiently and simply as possible.

She was flooded with relief. They were going to make it.

Joe voiced her thought. "Looks like we're going to make it, after all."

At that precise moment, *Thoat*'s engine gave a hiccup, and then died. The huge vehicle continued on for some distance, slowing all the while, its momentum only grudgingly yielding to the inevitable. It was assisted in this quixotic attempt by the gentle downward incline they were on.

Despite Bruce's best efforts, however, *Thoat* finally came to rest about half a kilometer from Pirate.

"I can't believe it," A.J. muttered. "Dammit, Joe, you had to go open your mouth!"

"Forget the superstitions," Helen said, though a small part of her had the same *blame Joe* thought. "It was physics we were up against. Not quite enough fuel."

"Now what do we do?" Rich asked. "I absolutely refuse to believe there's nothing we can do. Not when we could get out of this thing and walk over to *Pirate* in a few minutes."

Captain Hathaway's voice came over the ship-to-surface band. "*Thoat*, we see you have stopped short of the objective. What is the problem?"

"A day late and a dollar short on the fuel situation, Captain," Bruce replied. "We're trying to figure out what we can do at this juncture. I haven't got a clue, myself."

Helen's mind was a blank, also. But she noticed that Madeline was sitting perfectly still, her eyes closed. It looked almost as though she were asleep, but the faint wrinkle on her otherwise smooth forehead showed she was thinking.

"Bruce, how much cable is on the winch?" she asked.

"About a hundred meters, Madeline. Why?"

Joe understood immediately, with A.J. just half a second behind.

"Might work!"

"If we have enough juice," A.J. cautioned.

"Oh, right, there's a beauty of an idea!" Bruce said. "We haul ourselves towards *Pirate*, like the dying man crawling through the desert."

"Your simile is not particularly cheering, Bruce."

"Sorry, wasn't thinking."

"That's still a hell of a distance," Joe mused, his earlier enthusiasm fraying at the edges. "Will the batteries take it?"

A.J. was already checking. "I don't know. I'm calling up the data we had on power drain while we were using the winch to help lower *Thoat*. Practical data's always helpful. Hmm. Watts . . . battery capacity . . ."

A.J. ran the simulation several times. "Shit," he finally concluded.

"I take it the answer is 'no.'"

"'Fraid so, Madeline. Best-case gives us about two hundred and fifty meters before the batteries die or the winch does."

"The *winch*?" Joe protested. "That thing was designed to be good for months of expeditions!"

"Some of my sensors are giving nasty readings. I think when *Thoat* did that drop-and-stop trick, it might have damaged part of the winch."

"And I don't suppose we have two hundred and fifty meters of refueling hose," Helen sighed.

"Less than a tenth of that, actually," Bruce answered. "We're off by an order of magnitude."

Helen stared in frustration at the familiar shape of the

lander, so tantalizingly close yet impossibly far away. The
situation was ludicrous. They'd crossed a hundred million miles in a few months, and now couldn't reach another
ship that was not even a third of a mile away.

She suddenly realized what she'd been thinking.
*Another ship . . .*

"Joe," she said quietly, almost afraid to voice a question which might simply result in another punctured hope.
"*Pirate* is a rocket ship itself, right?"

"Yes, of course. How else would it—"

Suddenly he and A.J. looked at each other. "If
Mohammed cannot come to the mountain—"

"—then the mountain can damn well come to
Mohammed!" A.J. finished. He chewed on his lower lip.
"Theoretically, of course. Still, that *is* a landing and take-
off vehicle over there. If we reprogram the systems . . ."

"Going to be one hell of a little jump. Fine-tuning will
be the problem."

"That'll be my job. We'll need the whole area instru-
mented so we can watch performance, get her running
right. We'll only have one shot at this."

"Don't bring her down *too* close," Bruce cautioned.

"A hundred meters, I'd say," Joe responded, nodding.
"Well within range for the winch-crawling maneuver, but
far enough that if we're off by a bit we won't roast ourselves to death. Or drop *Pirate* right on top of us."

"Less than a four-hundred-meter hop." A.J. shook his
head, bemused. "Who'd have thought that the hardest
job we'd have to program on an interplanetary spacecraft
is getting it to go about one four-hundred-millionth of its
prior distance farther?"

He started checking his suit again before going out.

"Madeline, Rich, you guys come with me. We have to adjust some linkages on board *Pirate* and I have to play Tinkerbell all through the engines. Bring the tool kit."

"Don't need my help, A.J.? I turn a mean wrench."

"I know you do, Helen, but there's only so much room in *Pirate*. I only need two people, anyway. Next time you can take a turn doing my dirty work."

"She does that alread—"

"Kick him, Helen. On the broken leg."

The airlock cycled. After a moment, Helen could see the three figures making their way across the red-pink-orange sands.

Rich stopped at one point to examine a particularly light patch. "Poor Ryu. This is just what he would've been going nuts over. I think this is some kind of deposition, an evaporite, maybe a salt or something. Just one of the kinds of minerals colonists would need, and a hell of a clue to conditions here."

"He won't be forgotten, and the work won't be neglected," Helen said quietly. "Take a sample for the labs later, Rich. Let's get this job done first."

Back in his seat in the rover, A.J. watched the telltales climbing slowly. They'd done what they'd needed to do at *Pirate* and had returned a few minutes earlier.

"Navigation systems are up. We're not going to have all jets free, though; two years of crud blowing around seems to have fouled one. I've got compensation in the program for that. By the way, this work allows me to give a definite 'no frigging way' to the question of whether we could've gotten away using *Pirate*. She's deteriorated a fair amount. Takeoff-level thrusts just aren't in the picture. For that matter,

I don't think she'd even hold together for a full-scale take-off. Something critical would go in the middle of the burn."

"But you still think you can pull this off?" Madeline asked.

"Pretty sure. Not like we have much choice, anyway."

"You'll do it, mate," Bruce said, a bit too heartily. "It's just a little hop."

"True. But this ain't no kangaroo, either. 'Hops' are not really what it does." After checking a few more things, he said: "Bruce, I know you didn't have any direct training in this, but I'd feel real good about it if you'd stand by on controls to override. Just in case something blows."

"No worries, mate, I'm right here. Been running your little simulator the past couple of hours. Doubt I'll be needed, though."

Joe checked the readings also and recalculated the trajectory they would need. Then had Jackie and Gupta check it all again from *Nike*.

"You are cutting it fine indeed, very fine," Gupta pronounced. "But, as you say, you have no choice. Jackie and I both check you, and *Nike* herself concurs. Good luck."

"Thanks." A.J. took a deep breath. It was more than a little ironic, he thought, that the most critical mission *Pirate* had ever been given required only a fraction of the capabilities it had originally been designed for—and it still might not make it, because that specific task hadn't been anticipated. You really couldn't ask for a better demonstration of the inherent limits of unmanned spacecraft.

He, along with many others, had been advancing that argument for years—and, now, he might well prove his point in the worst way possible. By dying.

"Here goes."

Inside *Pirate*, long-dormant pumps whirred to life. Despite the attenuation of the Martian atmosphere near *Pirate* there was still the sound of continuous thunder as the multiton test lander launched itself into the sky at a very slight angle. It rose up, seeming to float atop a cushion of near-invisible flame, and then cut off thrust. The passengers of *Thoat* watched, transfixed, as the ship that was their single hope of survival drifted upwards, then downwards, on a path that would bring it near enough to reach.

Fire flared again from the rockets to cushion the fall and prevent the relatively delicate lander from cracking itself like an egg. One of the jets sputtered. Bruce nearly took control, but saw the jet catch again. A.J's program was already compensating.

Fifty meters, forty, thirty . . . At an altitude of two meters, the rockets cut off, and the lander settled gently to the ground.

Tension vanished into elation as A.J. once more nearly leaped from his seat. "*Yes!* Distance from *Thoat* is now . . . eighty-seven point two meters."

Bruce was practically chortling. "That's great! We can hook the winch cable right to *Pirate* and draw ourselves alongside."

"And," Madeline added, just as gleefully, "Joe and I have figured out a working coupler for our two hose systems. The fuel will be flowing in minutes, after we get these two together."

"Then let's not waste any more time," Helen said, getting up. "I'm going out to get that winch cable strung."

"Coming with you!" A.J. was up now, also.

"Most of us are coming," Madeline said. "If you remember the pain it was stringing the cable the last time . . ."

"Oh, yeah. I guess we leave Joe and Bruce."

"Living in the lap of luxury as we are, mates. See you whenever you slaves are done."

With four of them working to drag the cable and fasten it to *Pirate*, the job didn't take very long. The winch, despite some worries, did not fail on the way, and Madeline and Joe's coupling scheme worked.

So, a few hours after *Pirate* had made its extremely short flight, Bruce leaned back and grinned at Joe sitting next to him. "*Thoat*'s right happy now. Fuel's coming in and it ain't gonna stop until she's full up."

The engineer didn't answer, as he was busy with further designs and computations.

"What's up, Joe?"

"Figuring out how we can separate one of the fuel tanks from *Pirate* and store it on or in *Thoat* somehow. It'd be silly to try to refuel by driving back out here, and I don't know whether *Pirate* will survive a longer hop. So if we can drag some extra fuel along somehow . . ."

"Makes sense. Certainly worth looking into while we wait."

By the time the *Thoat* was refueled, Joe was satisfied. "Okay, it's going to be uncomfortable on the ride over to Target 37, but if we clear most of the equipment out of the cargo bay we can put one of the fuel tanks in there. We'll have to live with a lot of clutter for the next couple of days, I'm afraid."

"That's way better than leaving fuel a hundred

kilometers behind us," Helen stated. "We'll do it. Good work, everyone."

She leaned back in her seat, feeling the tension draining out of her. "Well, whaddaya know? It looks like we might actually survive long enough to—"

"Don't say it, Helen! Don't say it!"

# Chapter 45

Gupta shook his head. "Too risky, Jackie, too risky by far. We have no opportunity for second attempts in this." He continued to study the design, but he was clearly more worried now than he had been when they first confronted the challenge. A workable solution was proving more difficult to find than he'd expected.

Jackie was just as discouraged. The problem wasn't getting something to deorbit. Gupta's original idea was sound enough, in that respect. They could unship one of the ion drives on the habitat ring and use its small but steady thrust to drop just about anything out of orbit in a few days.

The problem was the actual reentry—more precisely, surviving the impact with the ground. Parachutes were just not all that useful. They'd provide some deceleration, of course, but not nearly enough. The thickness of the Martian atmosphere was less than two percent that of Earth's.

True, most of what they intended to drop wasn't particularly sensitive to shock. But there was still a difference between an impact at twenty kilometers per hour and one at four hundred KPH. A critical difference, generally known as "crash and burn."

"What about reentry itself? How's the design there?"

Gupta's dark eyes brightened. "There we are in excellent shape. The simulations show that we have sufficient materials to make some quite large aeroshells, especially if we sacrifice some of the aerogel insulation to this important project."

"That's no problem," Jackie said, nodding. "Take it from the right places and we'll hardly notice. When you say 'quite large,' are you sure . . ."

"*Very* sure."

"Okay, just checking. I mean, we're not dropping a little rover onto the surface. We need to send them stuff measured in tons."

"I am aware that I am old and perhaps appear decrepit in your eyes, Ms. Secord, but I do not forget such simple points." Gupta's words were grave, but there was a spark of humor in his eyes.

Jackie smiled. "You're not all *that* old, Satya. And don't forget that young little me with the still-perfect neurons is the one who forgot the difference between white pipes and yellow pipes."

She turned back to the simulations. "Damn. It all comes down to . . . well, to coming down. We can get it out of orbit, and get it through the atmosphere, but we can't land it intact. Are you sure the rockets won't work?"

"No, I am not sure. But that is precisely the problem. They may work well. However, they may fail at some point, and if they fail at the wrong point . . ." He sighed. "I can guarantee a firing of a simple rocket for a short time, but this will not be so simple. There will not be time for extensive testing; perhaps only one, very small, preliminary design to be test-landed before we must land the supplies for real. A vehicle to be landed by rocket needs fine control, especially if we have no time for long prototyping. But we lack the resources of people and materiel to, as one might say, throw money at the problem, and if that control fails . . ."

"Yeah. Maybe we need to put in another call to Earth, bounce some ideas off of them, see what they . . ." She trailed off.

A poke brought her back to awareness. "Jackie? What is it? You stopped talking. Have you an idea?"

"Almost, I think. But I'm trying to figure out what it is."

What was it? Something about what I just said. Talk to other people. Bounce ideas off them—

Bounce?

The idea was at once so obvious and absurd that she burst out laughing. "I've got it, Doctor! It'll take a lot of the lining fabric in some of the holds, a hell of a lot of sealant, some carbonan reinforcement— probably have to rip some suits up for it—but we can do it!"

Gupta looked at her, one eyebrow raised in an expression of expectant amusement. "And, what, precisely, is it that we can do?"

"The third Titan probe! And what was it, um, *Mars Surveyor*? Cosmic bubblewrap, Doctor! We'll surround the thing with airbags and *bounce* it to a safe landing!"

The dignified engineer stared at her for a long moment.

Then, startlingly, gave a high-pitched whoop and swung her around. "Yes! Yes indeed, yes! That is exactly the sort of thing we need! Design it well, design it strong, and it almost *cannot* fail. With a few rockets— of the simple sort—yes, Jackie! That will work!"

"Defacing the environment of Mars, sure enough," Joe stated, with all the grim satisfaction of a Cassandra. "I now have proof that we are conscienceless exploiters of this helpless planet."

Madeline smiled. "I demand to see your evidence, tree-hugger."

"Behold, o closet robber-baron." Her HUD lit up with images from *Thoat*'s rear-facing cameras.

"Oh, wow," she said involuntarily. *Thoat* was crossing a flat area that looked dark gray from ground level, making its closest approach to the looming wall of the Valles Marineris. The cliffs here jutted out in a spur that *Thoat* had to skirt on its way to Target 37. The great towering ridge, scarcely a kilometer distant, threw back the sun's light diffusely, making the entire region brighter except for the dark sands.

But where *Thoat*'s wide-treaded wheels had dug in, bright salmon-red-orange ridges and scalloped lines marred the ground. "Wow," she repeated.

"Interesting," Helen said. "That dark stuff is just a thin coating on the surface, it looks like. Maybe airborne dust from something else?"

"Or there could be alternating layers—maybe seasonal."

"True. Maybe the next expedition—you know, one that doesn't crash—will be able to look at it and figure it out."

"I'm sure there will be a lot of expeditions," Madeline said. She looked out the forward port. As usual, Bruce was driving, focusing most of his attention on the nearby features so as not to run into any surprises.

She raised her gaze, looking farther out. "What is *that*?"

The others looked up.

"Bugger me," Bruce said calmly.

A towering yellowish column swirled in the distance, huge, misty, threatening. As they watched, they could see it was approaching. Dust roiled about its base.

"That looks like a tornado!" The tension in Helen's voice was that of someone who had more than once found themselves in Tornado Alley during peak season.

"Sort of," A.J. said, his eyes viewing the scene through satellite and sensors. "It's a dust devil. Peak wind speed of this one appears to be about one hundred and eighty kilometers per hour, and she's about five kilometers high."

"A hundred and eighty kilometers per hour?" Bruce said. "Bloody hell."

Madeline felt the same way. Winds that fast could—

Both Joe and A.J. started laughing.

"What the hell's so funny?" Bruce demanded. Madeline glared questioningly at the two former Ares members— then at Rich, as he joined in the laughs. All of a sudden, Bruce started laughing also.

Madeline looked at Helen. "Maybe it's a male thing. You know, driving toward certain death? Like their idiot ancestors used to charge into battle naked, to show they weren't afraid."

That caused A.J., who had been about to say something, to laugh again. "Sorry, sorry, but—look, we're on *Mars*. The air pressure out there is less than a fiftieth of

Earth's. That's how dense—or thin, rather—it is compared to our atmosphere. And it's how dense a fluid material is that really determines how hard it's going to hit you. Look at water: if you immerse yourself in water and even weigh yourself down with lead, just try standing against a current of a few kilometers an hour."

"Oh." Madeline felt foolish. She had a vague memory of reading something about this in one of the dozens of books and papers she'd studied during their training for the mission.

Helen stared out the port. "So what you're saying is that you could walk right out there into that thing and it'd feel like being in . . . "

Joe did the calculations for her. "About a sixteen kilometer per hour wind back home. A nice breeze, and that's about it. With a bunch of dust."

"So it's no threat?"

"None at all, not to *Thoat*. In fact, we should have all our sensors going as we drive through it. Might learn something. Though I'd slow down a bit in the fog."

"Don't need to teach me my business, mate. I don't drive faster when I can see less, rest assured."

Madeline still felt an involuntary tension as the swirling vortex approached. Towering as high as the canyon walls and spinning at over a hundred miles per hour, it did not seem harmless at all but a looming, elemental threat.

Then *Thoat* was plunging into the maelstrom. She thought she felt a faint vibration, and there was a slight hissing noise. But aside from the sight of the dirty yellowish haze streaming by and obscuring their normal vision, the huge rover simply ignored the formidable-looking dust devil.

A faint, almost subliminal flicker made her jump. "What's that?"

Bruce and A.J. leaned forward. "Hey! That's cool." Deep purplish light shimmered, barely at the level of visibility, on the few sharper edges on *Thoat's* nose. The violet light brightened and seemed to leap from one of the short sensor antennas toward the ground several times.

"Cool, fine, but what is it, and is it dangerous?" Madeline was a bit nettled by the uninformative reaction. Her instinct was that anything you didn't understand could be dangerous, so you needed to understand it fast.

"Corona discharge," Joe answered. "Mars' atmosphere is almost as thin as the pressure inside a neon light tube. Close enough that if you build up electrical charges, they'll jump long distances. It's not dangerous to us, though. The rover's insulated, and when you go through the lock those handgrips you're required to hold make sure that if you did build up a charge outside, it gets equalized. But it could be a pain in other ways. Also might give us some other phenomena to see later."

Momentarily they broke back into sunlight, looking up at a slice of bright pinkish sky surrounded by the spinning sand clouds. Madeline was not the only one to exhale in relief.

Somewhere in the middle of that, without her remembering having done so, she discovered that her hand was holding Joe's. It was the first time there'd ever been any physical contact between them in public. Even in private, there hadn't been much, since their reconciliation. For reasons that were still obscure to her, Madeline had not been willing to move quickly, in that regard.

Fortunately, Joe hadn't pushed the issue. Madeline

wasn't sure why, since it certainly wasn't a lack of sexual attraction. As the days had passed and she'd gotten to know him better, she'd decided that the explanation was very simple. Joe was smart enough to know that he wasn't smart about things like that, so he was willing to let her take the lead and set the pace.

She felt very warm, for a moment, and gave Joe's hand a squeeze.

Then they reentered the storm.

"It sure looks impressive," A.J. said. "But it's just a bunch of hot air."

Helen slapped him playfully.

"Sorry, I didn't mean to shock you. I was just trying to make a comment about current events."

"Okay, that's enough," Joe said sternly. "Give him his discharge."

Madeline snatched her hand away. "God help us! Helen, we're doomed. Months of this, we're facing! Their jokes were bad enough, but now—*puns, too*?" She almost wailed the last two words.

Helen shook her head gloomily. "I know. We'll just have to breeze through it."

Ignoring the aghast look on Madeline's face, the paleontologist leaned forward and asked Bruce: "How far have we got to go?"

"We're in the home stretch, luv. Judging from the maps and all, we've got about fifty klicks left and we're knocking on the front door."

"So we'll be there sometime tomorrow?"

"Right around six, local time."

"Then day after tomorrow we'll be looking for the base."

"As long as we don't get in any more trouble. Keep your fingers crossed."

Madeline almost did cross her fingers, even though she was generally even more sarcastic about superstition than Helen was. But there really wasn't any reason to do so, that she could see, even if she were so inclined. Since their desperate juggling of rockets and fuel back at *Pirate*, they hadn't encountered any significant problems. The accurate intelligence from both ground and orbital sensors allowed Bruce to follow a carefully plotted course with minimal major obstacles. All he had to do was make sure he didn't run them into a gully or a too-big rock, and he was more than good enough to manage that even on the slightly hairier parts of the trip so far.

She decided a celebration was in order. "Then I say if we do make it all intact, we open one of Joe's special dinners and throw ourselves a party. It's been one hell of a trip, and we're going to be living pretty frugally for the next few months."

"I'm up for that," Joe agreed cheerfully. He took advantage of the thaw to snaggle Madeline's hand back.

His concussion had apparently had no lasting effects, fortunately. He no longer suffered from excessive sleepiness or dizziness, and the leg was already showing some signs of healing. Dr. Wu was a bit concerned about how strong the bone would wind up being, since it would be healing in one-third gravity throughout. But, obviously, there wasn't anything that could be done about that. At least Joe would be contributing to science in the process, being the first human bone injury healing in low gravity conditions.

"I think that's got a unanimous 'yes' vote coming, Madeline," A.J. said. "Especially from those of us who're going to be working lots of overtime."

"Then put it on your social calendars. First official rest day on Mars."

"I hope I can find a date."

"Oy, don't taunt those of us who know we won't get one," grumbled Bruce.

"Don't complain; you're a flyboy. Your problem's trying to get away from them."

"Right. Tell that to Tammy, would you? Make sure you do so from a distance. She throws a mean skillet."

A couple of hours later, darkness forced Bruce to stop for the night, still not far from the kilometers-high wall of the Valles Marineris. "Time for a bit of dinner, and then the last run tomorrow."

Joe distributed their strictly limited rations—enough to live on, not enough to get full on—and they ate. Madeline was deliberately slow in her eating. She wanted to give her body the maximum chance to realize that, yes, it really was getting fed, even if it wasn't getting as much as she'd like.

Joe had finished already and was looking out the south-facing port. Suddenly, he stiffened. "Hey, Bruce, kill the lights."

"Why? What's up, mate?"

"Just do it."

A chill ran down Madeline's spine. What did he see? There couldn't be anything out there that cared about lights.

Could there?

Reflexively, the hand she still had free went to where, in times past, she'd have kept a gun.

If she had one now, which she didn't—and a fat lot of good it would do even if she did. Was she going to shoot through the port, with nothing out there but very, very thin air, almost all of it carbon dioxide?

The lights went out and they were plunged into pitch blackness, only a faint glow to the west marking where the sun had gone down.

"What is it, Joe? What'd you see?" A. J. demanded. The tone of his voice showed that he, too, found the situation unsettling. "There's nothing out there!"

"Not quite. Take a look."

As her eyes adapted to the darkness, Madeline suddenly realized that it was not totally dark through the port. A phantom glow shimmered in the distance; then, seemed to move toward them.

"Holy . . ." she breathed, and heard some of the others mutter something similar.

"What the hell *is* it?" asked Helen tensely.

But Joe's answer seemed simply fascinated. "Look carefully."

Now Madeline could see several glows, like immensely tall distant columns, flickering faintly with a violet radiance.

*Violet . . .?*

"It's like the dust devil. But what's moving at this time of night?"

There was a sound of a hand smacking a forehead. "Dust falls! Of course! Dammit, Joe, don't scare us like that!"

Now that A.J. had named it, Madeline could see that

the motion wasn't really toward them. That had just been an optical illusion, partly brought on by nervousness. Instead, it was a downward flow; a gentle and impossibly slow water-falling motion.

"A.J., if you let your imagination run away with you, I can't help it. There's nothing alive on Mars. Well, maybe some bacteria somewhere, but that's it. The dust falls through the air and picks up charge just like we did, and discharges it during the fall. No ghosts involved, just physics."

Joe's voice suddenly dropped an octave. "Although . . . There *is* the legend of Old Bemmie, who wanders these canyons in search of his missing tentacles . . ."

Children. That's what they are, overgrown children. Why am I falling in love with him? Why is Helen in love with that other juvenile delinquent?

Finding no logical answer, she sighed and continued staring out at the ethereal glow in the distance.

"Not ghosts," she said. "Fairies."

"That's a good name," A.J. said, seriously. "*The Faerie Falls of Mars.*"

"Logged," Bruce said a moment later. "First tourist attraction to take anyone to see, I'd say. A beauty, that is."

They watched for a while in silence, as Mars put on a show for its first visitors in sixty-five million years.

# Chapter 46

They arrived in the vicinity of Target 37 right around the time Bruce predicted, but the next several days had to be devoted to unloading the rover and setting up a base camp before they could even think about searching for the alien ruins. The most pressing business was to bury the extra fuel tank they'd brought from *Pirate* in order to provide the container with insulation and keep leakage down. They'd probably lose some of the fuel to outgassing, no matter what they did, but this way the loss would be minimal.

Once the fuel was hooked up to *Thoat*'s generators, they were assured of months of refrigeration and compression. Hopefully, they'd be rescued before they had to return to *Pirate* for more fuel.

Even more hopefully, the extra fuel they'd brought from *Pirate* would never be needed at all, much less a return trip to the lander. It would simply remain there as an emergency backup. As soon as the fuel tank was buried, they started setting up the most critical pieces of equipment they'd been carrying in the rover—the reactors initially developed by Ares Project which would use Martian raw materials to manufacture the water and oxygen they'd need, along with providing them with a self-sustaining fuel supply in the form of methane.

The reactors they'd brought with them, of course, were considerably more sophisticated—not to mention expensive—than the "Ruth, Ferris, Porky, and Ethyl" prototypes originally built by Project Ares. After NASA had more or less absorbed Ares into the drive to reach Mars as soon as possible, the powers that be at NASA had wisely decided to simply adopt Ares' designs rather than start from scratch. But, with the money NASA had available to throw at the problem, by the time *Nike* left orbit the reactors it carried on board were at least three generations more advanced than the originals.

Within two days, the reactors were up and running with no hitches—and all six of the humans on Mars heaved a collective sigh of relief. So, just as heartfelt, did the crew of the *Nike*. Whatever happened now, so long as *Nike* could figure out a way to provide them with food, the people stranded on Mars could survive indefinitely.

The next task was to set up the "bubbles." Those were the aerogel-insulated hemispherical tents that would provide them with far more living space than they'd had aboard the rover. They'd continue using *Thoat*'s kitchen and sanitary facilities, of course, since the bubbles had no cooking provisions at all and "toilets" that were essentially just very high-tech chamber pots. But they'd have far more room and, even more importantly, personal privacy.

Finally, they removed the rest of the equipment and supplies and stored them in the bubbles. Only then, after working like beavers for five days after arrival, did they enjoy the little party they'd promised themselves.

By that time, *Nike* was relaying down what seemed to be a veritable avalanche of congratulatory messages from Earth. Most of them were not even from people and organizations directly connected to the space program.

After reading one message, sent by the faculty and student body of a university in a Chinese city that Helen had never even heard of, it dawned on her that they were famous. And not "famous" as in "tabloid meat."

Famous.

When she said as much to Ken Hathaway, in one of their conversations, the brigadier general just laughed.

"Are you kidding? Helen, I don't think you have any idea. The crash-landing of *John Carter* and your subsequent trek to safety at Target 37 has been the lead story in every media outlet on the planet since it happened. NASA tells me they think more people in the U.S. are watching the news about it every night than watched the Super Bowl."

"You're kidding." She stared at the screen, an empty feeling starting to come to her stomach.

Famous . . . *Really* famous . . .

"Nope, not kidding in the least. We're only sending down a smidgeon of the messages that are pouring in."

*God help me. The tabloids were bad enough.*

She had a sudden nightmare image of herself trying to conduct a dig somewhere in Montana—with a crowd of spectators surrounding the site.

"I'm a *paleontologist*," she half-wailed. "How will I be able to keep doing my work?"

"Um. Well, as to that . . . I can tell you, for sure, that at least you won't have to worry about collecting a salary any more. I haven't sent them down, since it seems pointless at the moment. But I can tell you that what looks to be every major garment manufacturer in the world is engaged in a bidding war to get you to be their spokesman. Last I saw, the top offer was fifteen million dollars."

He paused, momentarily. "Well, 'spokes*woman*,' I guess I should say. Emphasis definitely on the gender. Seeing as how the main interest seems to be—"

"Nooo—"

She *did* wail, that time—and felt her stomach fly south for the winter.

"Yup. Their new projected lines of swimwear."

"I'm almost forty-three years old, for God's sake!"

"Yup," Ken's cheery voice continued, relentlessly. "I guess that explains why—near as I can tell—every cosmetics company in the world launched their equivalent of World War Three too. Women entering into middle age are apparently the biggest clientele for cosmetics, at least measured in terms of the money they spend—and you just became the poster girl for all half a billion of them. Last I heard, the cosmetic companies' bids were up to—hold on, I'll check with Jackie—"

He was back in seconds. "Eighteen and a half million, she says. She asks me to pass on that she recommends the offer that wants to market the stuff under the title 'Helen of Mars.' I do agree with her that they came up with the niftiest slogan: *the face that launched the greatest ship of all.*"

"I'll kill her," Helen snarled. "And you're next!"

"Under the circumstances, that's a pretty idle threat,"

Ken pointed out, as cheerily as ever. "Jackie also wants to know what you'd like for your birthday coming up. She warns you she can't afford anything fancy, even if you are on the verge of becoming richer than Croesus."

"I want a cave in a desert somewhere!" Helen half-shouted. "Where I might get my privacy back!"

Ken laughed again. "Why bother? Just stay on Mars."

Helen's eyed widened.

And widened. Her stomach paused in its headlong flight.

She looked at A.J. He was sitting nearby in the rover, obviously doing his level best to keep from laughing himself.

His level best wasn't nearly good enough, so far as she was concerned. "One chuckle out of you," she hissed, "and you can look forward to a completely celibate stay on Mars."

That sobered him up, some. The threat wasn't idle, either. Not since they'd set up the bubbles and had some personal space again.

"Wouldn't think of it," he managed to get out.

*"Good."* After a moment, though, her glare started fading. "What do you think, A.J. Is it possible?"

He shrugged. "Maybe. It's certainly feasible, from a technical standpoint. The real question—what else is new?—will be the funding. At a guess, I'd say that depends mostly on what we find—or don't find—at Target 37. If there's a real dig to be done there . . . You know what I mean. A major one."

"A real dig," she mused. "A major dig. Major digs take *years . . .*"

Somewhere far to the south, Helen's stomach wheeled around and start flapping back.

⊠     ⊠     ⊠

Since A.J. managed to keep from chuckling—barely—Helen didn't carry out her threat that night. Rather the opposite, in fact.

"I love you," she murmured, contently exhausted and lying sprawled across him. "Would you stay here with me?"

"Don't ask silly questions. I came here looking for one dream, and found two. Of course I will."

She could feel a suspicious rumble, with her palm spread across his bare chest. "What's so funny?"

He was practically choking, now.

"What's so funny?"

"Well, I just got to thinking about funding. And it occurred to me—"

"You even finish that sentence, mister—!"

"Let's see what we can find," Helen said. "And stop whining, Joe. Paleontologists always start work at the crack of dawn, you know that. It's not my fault—"

She broke off abruptly, realizing she might be treading onto delicate ground.

Joe wouldn't be coming with them, naturally, with his leg broken. He and Bruce and Rich would stay behind in the camp and finish setting it up, while the other three started scouting for Target 37.

Helen had decided to leave Bruce and Rich behind also, because neither of them had any skills that would be of particular use in this initial scouting expedition. A.J. was coming along for his sensor expertise, which would almost certainly be needed to find ruins that were sixty-five-million years old. Helen, of course, was the only one except Joe with real experience at this work. Finally, she'd chosen Madeline

because three would be safer, and Helen had a great deal of
confidence in the security official's general competence.

So there was really no reason for Joe to be up this early.
Helen assumed that Madeline had woken him up when
she arose. Which wouldn't have been hard to do, since
she'd been sleeping with him.

Madeline Fathom had apparently decided that their
safe arrival here was an omen, or a signal—or whatever it
was that mattered to her Inner Self, which Helen still
found somewhat mysterious. As soon as they'd started
erecting the bubbles, she'd quietly and matter-of-factly
explained that she and Joe would share one, so they only
needed to put up four instead of five for living quarters.

The look on Joe's face when she'd made that announcement had been . . . priceless. It was blindingly obvious
that it had come as a surprise to him, too.

The look on his face this morning, on the other hand,
was that subtle, hard-to-define-but-unmistakable expression that characterized civilized men trying to suppress
their cruder impulses. A combination of smugness and
exultation kept under tight restraint, so that the barbarian within didn't start leaping about the landscape and
shouting "Boy, did I *score* last night!"

But he also looked inexpressibly happy, so Helen for-
gave him his male sins. When all was said and done, she
approved of Joe Buckley. Very highly.

"It's not *my* fault," Madeline said, smiling that million-
dollar smile. "He insisted I wake him up before we left. I
felt bad about it, since I didn't let him sleep much in the
first place. Broken leg be damned, he got no mercy from
me last night."

Okay, then. *Not* delicate ground.

⊠        ⊠        ⊠

Putting on his helmet, A.J. glanced over at Joe in admiration. One of the things he'd always liked the most about his friend was his very solid ego. It just didn't seem to faze Joe at all that he'd gotten himself a woman who could probably outdo him in almost anything except engineering and cooking—and maybe not the cooking. At this point, A.J. wouldn't really be surprised to discover that Madeline Fathom was a Cordon Bleu graduate, on top of everything else. She seemed to pull out new skills the way a magician pulled rabbits out of a hat.

"A.J.?"

He suddenly became aware that Helen was speaking to him. "Huh?"

"I said, are you ready? What's up?"

"Just thinking, taking up too many processing cycles to detect your inquiry. Sorry, yes, I'm set. Got it all ready."

The three of them stepped into *Thoat*'s airlock and cycled out onto the Martian soil. A.J. took a deep breath, as though he were stepping outside a mountain cabin and breathing in the air. The magnificent view called for some such gesture.

The orbital pictures had shown the area of Target 37 as being near, or even right below, a whitish chevron-shaped marking next to a small gully or canyon on the floor of the Melas Chasma area. Such images are deceptive, however. A.J. was struck again by just how deceptive they were as he glanced to his right.

There, about a quarter of a kilometer distant, was the edge of the so-called gully.

The term was a little ridiculous, he thought. The sheer scale of Valles Marineris warranted calling it a gully, perhaps, but on Earth it would be a canyon in its own right. More than three kilometers across at its widest, it ran a curved, slightly zigzag course for more than thirty klicks before petering out. Even here, where it narrowed drastically, it was several hundred meters wide and hundreds deep, red-pink-gray rock walls plunging down into a shadowed crease in the immensity of Mariner's Valley.

As they had been the first humans to reach the gully, they felt they had the right to name it. And since they'd done so through the services of the huge rover, they'd unanimously decided to name it "Thoat Canyon." Barring any official objections later, of course; but, under the circumstances, that was hardly likely.

The lighter soil, not so clearly whitish up close, had strong concentrations of salts in it. For reasons that were unclear to A.J., that news had been very exciting to the areologists on *Nike* and presumably on Earth. Small rises and cliffs surrounded the area to the north, where A.J. was facing, and to the left. *Thoat* had needed to round the southern part of its eponymous canyon and drive northwest to reach their current position, and he could see their tracks still visible in the sands to the south. The wind would undoubtedly erase them eventually, but for the moment he suspected that most of their course across Mars could be traced from orbit with a good enough telescope.

"Where are we going?" Madeline inquired. "You were running your sensors most of the night, right?"

A.J. sighed. "Much as I hate to admit it, I am at least partially defeated at the moment. You know how some of the weird alloys and composites the Bemmies had on Phobos kept messing with my sensors, from GPR on through just about everything else? Well, there's one big-ass chunk of this base that seems to be made out of that same stuff. I can't see anything past it—which means on the other side of the base, under it, and partly to the sides. And I can't drive *Thoat* around to check from different positions, obviously."

"So you got nothing?"

"I didn't say *that*. I just didn't get nearly as much as I hoped to get, and there's nothing that looks tremendously promising. We'll have to scout around the base perimeter—which is pretty darn big— for the next few days with portable units, if we want to get data on the rest of the area. I can say this much: if we're going to find entrances, that ridge"—he pointed to the fifty-meter-high cliff half a kilometer away—"is our best bet. Remember how we found the entrance to Phobos Base? Well, the same problem we faced on Phobos is here, only about a million times worse. Any opening that was standing on regular open ground will have filled in completely. I'm not sure if you can get solid rock out of just wind-blown stuff settling. But, if you can, after sixty-plus million years any openings that got filled in might be rock by now. Even if not, they'll have been completely buried eons ago. So, just like on Phobos, we have to look for caves or cracks that might have stayed open that long."

Helen nodded. "Makes sense. We do have one thing in our favor, too. Mars is geologically stable, compared to Earth. There's almost nowhere on Earth you could go which would have a chance of retaining any geological structures that old. Especially not things like caves and tunnels. But Mars has less gravity to collapse things, a lot fewer earthquakes, and—so far as we know, at least—no mechanism like plate tectonics to refurbish the surface every few hundred million years."

"Pretty much," Joe agreed, having been listening in. "It looks like it tried to go for that model around the time Olympus Mons got started. But without the ability to keep a liquid mantle, that was doomed to failure."

"The ridge it is, then." Madeline set off, the other two following. Close on A.J.'s heels came one of the two automated equipment and sensor rover carts they'd brought with them. Land-bound equivalents of the Faeries, essentially. It was loaded with portable GPS and other sensor equipment, plus rock-climbing gear.

"Back off a bit, Willis," he told it. Willis obediently fell back a meter or so farther, making A.J. feel less crowded.

Fifty meters was nothing compared to the main cliffs of Valles Marineris visible in the distance. But, up close, they were still formidable walls of red-gray stone, fissured and seamed, covered with the dust of years beyond count that sifted slowly down the rock face.

"Here's a hole big enough," A.J. said. He shone a light down. "Seems to go a fair distance, too."

After crawling into it for several meters, however, he learned the rough-floored tunnel narrowed to nothing. "Dry hole. Well, I didn't expect to find it right away."

"A.J., Madeline and I will keep looking for good possibilities in this rock face," Helen said. "You're wasting your skills doing that. Anyone can crawl into holes. See what you can get on GPR and your other gadgets."

"You got it."

A.J. began removing the equipment from Willis and setting it up. At least in this new location he'd have a different angle on the base and might get some shots at areas that had been completely obscured before.

Unfortunately, his repertoire was relatively limited here. The surface was heavily covered by drifting dust, so using acoustics would be basically useless. The Fairy Dust wouldn't help here, really. GPR and related RF approaches were pretty much all he could use without the ability to bore into bedrock. He could use a synthetic-aperture type approach to increase resolution and sensitivity, though, if he moved the GPR setup.

For the next several minutes he was busy reconfiguring Willis and setting the GPR unit firmly on the little rover. "There, that's got it. How are you people coming?"

"Lots of little holes and big holes," came Helen's slightly breathless voice. "But nothing promising, so far. You?"

"About to start getting us some more data." He started Willis and the GPR unit running. For the next hour he paced the sensor platform as it sent regular pulses into the Martian soil and bedrock, recorded the returns, and sent them to *Thoat*'s main systems to analyze. He could, of course, have had *Nike* do the analysis—with the satellite network, they were never out of communication with the interplanetary vessel—but he liked doing things with what he had. And this analysis wasn't particularly difficult.

It was, however, increasingly disappointing. The more the returns came in and were processed, the more clearly the base on this side was delineated. And the less and less likely it became that there were, or ever had been, any entrances—natural or *Bemmius*-made—in this area.

Finally he shook his head. "Ladies, give it up. There's nothing to find here."

"Damn," said Madeline without rancor. "I was hoping we could find something fairly quickly—because I certainly don't like the idea of trying to dig our way down to the thing. Well, we still have more perimeter to check. Maybe tomorrow."

She started making her way down the backside of the ridge, which sloped much less steeply on that side.

It wasn't until a few moments later that it registered on A.J. that Helen hadn't responded. For a moment he almost panicked, until he saw that she was at the top of the ridge, looking outward. Maybe just admiring the view. It'd be a while—a long while—before any of them started taking that view for granted. Compared to Valles Marineris, the Grand Canyon in Arizona was a ditch.

"Helen, you okay?"

"Hmmm?" Her voice sounded distracted. He could almost see her expression; it was the one she wore when she almost had a problem solved. "A.J., what do your GPR scans say about the geology?"

"Geology? Well, I'm not an expert, but basically, um, we've got the top layer of crap, something that I guess might be sorta-sandstone under the dust and debris, then a bunch of denser stone, and something else under that. The sorta-sandstone isn't very thick, the denser stone is thicker—maybe fifty to a hundred meters total in this area, though I get vague indications it tends to be even thicker off to the west. The denser stone makes it real hard to see through past that, and I have to be honest that I wasn't using stuff that would look down past twenty to fifty meters anyway. Any tunnels we're looking for have to come nearer the surface than that. Why?"

She turned and gazed off towards the west, then back

to the east. "Where were the close orbital photos of this area?" A moment later: "Yes, those are the ones. Thanks."

For a few more minutes there was silence. Then she said briskly, "We're looking in the wrong area. We want the east side."

"Over at Thoat Canyon, you mean?"

"Exactly. But it's not a canyon."

"Huh? Then what is it?"

Helen's voice was growing more excited and animated as she worked her way back down to his level. "I think it's the biggest damn sinkhole I've ever seen in my life. Look at the pictures again."

A.J. called up the images. The gash in the Martian landscape, now that he studied it more carefully, did have the folded, crumpled look of something that had collapsed from below. "But aren't most sinkholes round?"

"Generally, yes, but there are reasons it might not be. The way things sit in this region, and the shape of that collapsed area . . . What I think we have here is a collapse of a cavern which had a thin roof of volcanic basalt over it. The basalt is thicker in this area, but thinned drastically over there. That was at the edge of the flow, or some area that for some reason didn't get covered as well."

"A cavern . . . *thirty kilometers long?*"

"A network of them, maybe. Plus the gravity's so much less. Damn, I wish Ryu were still here. He'd know."

"Well, we can bounce this up to *Nike* and see what the experts have to say."

It wasn't long before Chad Baird, one of the planetographers, was on the radio with them.

"Quite possible. What you may have there is an area

that used to have fossil ice in it. The ice slowly—over a period of millions of years—sublimed away and percolated through the rock above. It would refreeze in the upper layers, weakening them, then evaporate away again when things warmed up. Eventually there would be a huge empty space and weakened rock to give way during one of the infrequent major Martian quakes."

"And if the cap stayed intact here, and was thicker . . . Is it possible there could be some ice left under this area?"

"There could be, Helen, yes. With a large deposit underground, and a relatively impermeable basalt cap on top . . . Yes, there could be."

A.J. saw where this was going. "Good call, Helen. That's real good."

"You get it, then? Our best chance for any entrance is obviously on the wall of Thoat Canyon near the base, and the base is here almost certainly because somewhere down here they found water—which they needed even more than we do."

"Joe was right, then," A.J. mused. "It was no coincidence at all that *Pirate* wound up so close. That's one of the things we in Ares were looking for, too—water. And we decided to look here because Valles Marineris gets you deeper into the surface of Mars than anywhere else on the planet."

He was getting excited, now. "And if there is such an opening, I might be able to find it the same way we found the one on Phobos."

"Exactly. If there's any connection to fossil ice, any opening will show a higher water concentration."

A.J. found himself grinning in anticipation. "Let me get back to *Thoat* and do some work. We just might find our way in after all!"

# Chapter 47

Helen's heart pounded as she was slowly lowered down the side of the three-hundred-meter cliff. "How much farther?"

"About fifty meters," A.J. answered. "Don't worry, I'm already here. Me and Madeline will pull you in."

Her hunch had been right. A.J.'s sensors, concentrated in the area along the rim of Thoat Canyon for several hundred yards, had in a day or so pinpointed three sources of excess water vapor, one of them clearly larger than the others. Lowering Willis via *Thoat*'s winch, A.J. had found an opening nearly three meters high and almost that wide.

Although well-suited for open ground exploration, Willis was not designed for a spelunking expedition. There was no way around it but that they would have to take the risks themselves.

The fact that it was her idea and that she was the closest thing they had left to a geologist did little to comfort

Helen on the way down. A three-hundred-meter drop would be fatal even in Mars' thirty-eight percent gravity. It was possible her suit might save her from instant death, but that sudden stop at the bottom would almost certainly leave her in critical condition—and with no medical facilities around to speak of, that would be even worse than immediate death.

However, she made it without incident. The other two pulled her inside and tied off the cable to a rock a few feet into the cave. It was with considerable relief that she felt her boots once more on solid stone. "All right, let's see what we have."

"Let's get these spare oxygen tanks set up first," A.J. said. "If an emergency comes and we wind up needing them, we don't want to be fumbling around."

That took only a minute. "Okay. Helen, I think you and Madeline should lead the way. I'll be leaving a trail of bread crumbs."

A.J.'s "bread crumbs" were small sensor and radio relays, which would permit them to continue to talk to the others even if they got quite a ways underground. That was necessary, if for no other reason than that Ken Hathaway had invoked his captain's authority and flatly forbidden them to go underground unless they could maintain communications.

It was a good idea anyway, leaving communications aside. Helen had some experience with exploring caves, and it turned out Madeline had even more. (For the usual non-reason: *Spent five weeks, once, with a group of fanatic spelunkers. No, don't ask why. It's still classified.*) Both of them knew how easy it was to get disoriented underground, with no lights beyond what they brought with them. But if they did get lost, A.J.'s bread crumbs would guide them out.

The tall opening in reddish-black stone slanted sharply downwards after the first few meters. It did not change much in size for quite a while, however, as the little party continued following it. After about sixty meters, the tunnel mostly leveled out and continued deeper into the cliff, towards the base.

"Dropping first relay," A.J. stated.

The walls of the tunnel were rough, showing no sign of intelligent shaping that Helen could detect. That didn't necessarily mean anything, of course. It did a dogleg to the left and then curved towards the southeast.

"That isn't very promising," she remarked, as it clearly took them away from the base.

"Don't start complaining yet," A.J. said. "I'm still picking up water concentration."

"Full stop!" Madeline said from just ahead. Cautiously, they moved up at her signal to take a look.

The tunnel seemed to end here, until they got close and saw that what happened was that the tunnel itself had been essentially beheaded. A short bit of it remained ahead of them, while at their feet a wide crack dropped vertically into the depths. It was two meters across and much longer than that. From their current vantage point, they couldn't tell how much longer.

Madeline shone her light down the crack. There seemed to be a floor, over a hundred meters down. "Good enough, I think. Helen?"

The paleontologist agreed. "Yes, we'll make the descent. One at a time. I think you should go first, A. J., then me. Madeline, you bring up the rear since I think

you're our best climber in case something goes wrong."
She cocked her head. "Am I right?"

"Probably. I spent some time on the Matterhorn, once."

Seeing Helen's eyes roll in her helmet, Madeline protested: "Hey, it was just for the fun of it! I was on vacation,
and I rather enjoy danger sports."

Now A.J. was rolling his eyes.

"It's true!" Madeline insisted. "The only top secret
involved is how I managed to evade the attentions of Swiss
males with too much testosterone and too little common
sense. That's still classified. My boss is real big on contingency planning. If Switzerland ever drops her neutrality
and becomes a U.S. ally, he thinks I might have to go in
and establish the security for their chocolate recipes."

Chuckling, A.J. dropped another bread crumb and
began to lay out the climbing gear, while Madeline and
Helen judged where best to put the pitons.

The descent was made quickly. Getting back up would
be a bit more tedious, but they had a powered ascender
device that would be able to bring at least one person up
to the top. From there, with muscles on top and bottom
working against low gravity, they should have no problem
getting the other two out.

The crack became much broader as they went down.
Once they were at the bottom, they could see that it had
gone from two meters across to at least thirty meters. The
length was still impossible to determine.

There were no fewer than three tunnels exiting nearby.
A.J. set his sensors in each one and after several minutes
declared that he couldn't tell which way to go. The water
vapor concentration in each was roughly equal, at least to
the limit of what he could analyze at this point.

"Which way is the base?" Helen asked.

Seeing A.J. point, she nodded at the exit closest to that direction.

"Then let's try this one."

"Works for me."

Narrower than the others, this passage required them to go single file and watch their heads. It twisted and turned and A.J. used three more bread-crumb relays.

"How many of those do you have left?"

"Forty-five. Believe me, I came prepared, especially after my experiences with that 'block out everything but gravity' stuff on Phobos."

"It appears to be widening," Madeline said. Once again, she was in the lead. "I think I see a larger area in front of us."

They emerged into a cavern and shone their lights around. "Oh, my God," Helen breathed.

They were now probably three hundred meters down, below the floor of Thoat Canyon by a considerable distance. The cavern loomed above them, its ceiling nearly fifty meters above their heads and its sides disappearing into the darkness beyond the reach of their lights.

But it wasn't the impressive sides that caught their attention. It was the diamond-bright sparkle from above, where pure white shimmering crystals hung from every point, where long stalactites glittered like diamonds, where other surfaces were coated with a luxurious white fur.

"Ice," A.J. pronounced.

Helen found herself almost unable to speak for a moment. Partly because the faint worry that they might run out of water if the reactors malfunctioned had now vanished. But, mostly, just because the fairylandlike sparkle was visually stunning.

After a while, though, she began thinking of the puzzle involved, and its possible implications. "How could there be that much water here? In this atmosphere? Could any fossil deposit have lasted this long with direct openings to the outside?"

"Might not have to," Chad Baird's voice broke in. Apparently the scientist had been listening to their transmissions. "One of the major theories—still being debated, but it's got strong support—is that Mars actually has a water table. Clearly it used to have a huge amount of water, and the theory is that a lot of it remains underground, maybe a kilometer or two. If so, what you may have is one, two, or three different interacting layers of water transport depending on depth, temperature, pressure, and some other less important factors. In that case, what might be happening here is that the fossil ice sublimes, gets redeposited in the caverns you've reached, and is at least partially replenished by water vapor percolating up through the soil beneath. Remember, you're way down below the general level of the ground there in the Valles. So if there is a water table, you're a lot closer to it. And with what you're seeing, that sounds more likely than ever."

Helen nodded, still staring. "And if sublimation and redeposition is keeping these structures around in this volume, there must be a fair amount of water farther down here."

A.J.'s enthusiasm came to the fore. "Let's find that base!"

Across the cavern they walked, cautiously. After they

found many signs of impacts, they kept a wary eye on the inverted faerie realm above, in case one of the ageless decorations decided to become a slow-motion plummeting missile.

It was Madeline who spotted the path that led upward in the direction of the base. It looked strange, as if it were made of melted wax or something similar. None of them could decide if it had been created by nature or intelligence.

Surprisingly, A.J. held out for natural causes. "We know there were aliens about so we tend to think everything weird is their doing. But I'm betting that Mars itself has got more weird saved up for us than Bemmie could have cooked up in the short time he was here. Maybe it's something left over from the era when Mars had lots of running water."

"Doubtful," Baird commented. "A lot of the rocks involved in water deposition are, themselves, fairly heavy with water content. They tend to disintegrate in this kind of atmosphere as they dehydrate. But you have basalt over the top of the area, so it's possible that you're looking at something caused by volcanic action eons ago."

The steep path, if that's what it was and not some kind of lava-flow or other natural channel, took considerable time and effort to climb. Finally, they stood at the top and looked down a tunnel about the same size as the last one. Helen eyed the ceiling suspiciously; there were signs of cracking at intervals along the way.

And then they rounded the corner and found the door.

The construction of the doorway was similar to those found in Phobos base, but clearly not identical. A.J. sent back high-resolution pictures in all spectra to *Thoat*. Inside the rover, Joe studied the doorway and other structures partially visible around the door before they disappeared into the rock at either side. He looked at them both in normal imagery and the more esoteric, partial imagery A.J.'s sensors could extract out of the stubbornly shielded material.

"It's not the same," he said finally, "but it looks like the same kind of technology was involved. That's the best way I can put it. It doesn't differ from the Phobos designs nearly as much as those do from ours. It's more like the difference between Egyptian and Greco-Roman architecture."

"So you think it's the same species, in other words." There was a note of disappointment in Madeline's voice.

"That'd be jumping to conclusions," Helen said. "I can think of other possibilities. To name one, this could have been built by a different species—including a hostile species—but one which had been in contact with the Bemmies long enough for their technological methods to have gotten largely shared. The way that, nowadays, an office building in Tokyo or New Delhi doesn't look that much different from one in New York or Barcelona. For that matter, if aliens had examined the Japanese planes that fought at the battle of Midway, they'd have had a hard time seeing much difference from the American ones."

"True," A.J. said, "provided the two species were physically similar enough. Even if we shared technology with Bemmie, there's still no way we'd design a lot of things the way they do. Or vice versa. That door's quite a bit taller than I'd expect a Bemmie door to be, for instance. Although it could've been a small cargo door, I suppose."

"How about getting it open?" Madeline asked.

"Brute-force it," Joe proposed. "You don't want to try anything involving arc-cutting in there."

"Why . . . oh."

" 'Oh' is right, A.J. You want to find out what it's like to be on the inside of a giant neon light tube? At the least you'd probably fry your electronics, and at the worst you'd fry yourself. The pressure's slightly higher down there, but I don't know that it would make enough difference—and we sure don't want you to be the experimental guinea pigs. No way around it. You'll have to come back here and get some of the excavation equipment."

A.J. sighed. "Oh, now that's going to be fun. Even with the low gravity."

"Well, you could just come back and forget about it, and we all just sit around swapping jokes until the rescue shuttles get here in a couple months."

"I do not think so," Helen said firmly. "Okay, guys, let's head back. Tomorrow is going to be a big day."

Madeline's voice was resigned. "More like tomorrow and the day after, at least. I've done operations like this before—don't ask where or why—and I think you're underestimating the difficulty we're going to have getting that equipment down here."

Helen thought the security specialist was probably right. But she didn't really care. She was bound and determined to get into the base. If that meant dragging equipment deep into Martian caverns, well, it couldn't be that much worse than setting up a major dig.

She led the way, as they left, already working on the problem. "We'll need to set up a field camp and supply area for this operation. We don't want to have to travel all

the way back to *Thoat* and main camp whenever we run
short of a few items. The exotic location aside, this isn't
fundamentally much different from any major dig. When
you're out in the badlands, you don't hop in a vehicle and
drive off every time someone's thirsty and wants a soda."

"Yeah, sure. But at least you didn't have to worry about
bringing your own air supply."

"Shut up, A.J.," Madeline growled. "Besides, even that's
really no big deal. I once spent four weeks in a camp so
high up in the Himalayas we had to haul in oxygen. It was
a pain, but not that bad."

She didn't start laughing until A.J. was choking audibly.
"Just kidding. I didn't really spend four weeks on the
slopes of Mt. Everest."

"Well, praise be for small favors," A.J. muttered.

"It was only eleven days—and it was on the slopes of
Denali in Alaska, not Everest in Nepal, and it wasn't so
high up that we needed oxygen tanks very often. I won't
tell you which slope, though. That's still classified because
my boss thinks someday the Athabascan Indians might—"

"I don't want to hear it, Madeline!"

# Chapter 48

"Okay, people," Joe said, several days later. "I think your best bet is to use the 'ripper' on the door."

He and Bruce were the only ones remaining topside. With the alien base discovered and the strong possibility of new writing being found inside, Rich was now on site with Madeline, A.J., and Helen. Joe hated being left behind, especially since as an engineer the alien base no doubt held as many exciting possibilities for him as it did for anyone else. But dragging a broken-legged man through tunnels didn't appeal either to the others or even to the broken-legged man himself.

Helen felt sorry for him, but at least it kept him in the safer area. She didn't feel very confident about the safety of these underground mazes, no matter how placid Mars' geology was supposed to be.

Neither, to her dismay, did Chad Baird. "Be very careful down there, Helen," he'd said. "Yes, Mars is geologically stable compared to Earth. But that's just an average, on a planetary scale. Any *particular* spot on Mars might be far more dangerous than most places on Earth. And while I'm fascinated by what you've found down there, I really don't like the looks of it, from an explorer's standpoint. Whatever the mechanism is that created those ice caverns, it has to be a fairly active one or the ice wouldn't still be there at all. And now you'll be introducing a new disturbance. So be careful."

Unfortunately, A.J. had been there to hear the conversation. For two days thereafter, he'd gone around periodically intoning lines from an old science fiction movie: *Be afraid. Be very afraid.*

Joe thought it was funny.

Joe would.

So, Helen had insisted on delaying the operation until they could put whatever supports and braces they could design and make in that last run of tunnel that had cracks in the roof.

It wasn't much, since their material supplies were limited. Mars gave up no wood for timbering, of course. But at least they had a comparatively secure route from the door to their field camp and supply dump. They'd set that up at the base of "Melted Way," the odd path that led up from the large cavern.

Madeline and A.J. dragged the "ripper" towards the alien door. Unlike the sort of rolling-valve doors found on Phobos, this door seemed to be designed to split in the center and slide up and to the side. This made the "ripper," a bastard descendant of a forklift and the jaws of life and a few other gadgets, ideal for the job. It could insert its pair of flattened-tine lever arms into the crack in the door and pull it apart by main force, assuming the door wasn't stronger than a bank vault.

A.J. positioned the lever arms above and below the area where he believed there was a sort of bolt or other fastener according to his sensors. Then, he and Madeline braced the ripper—which he'd promptly nicknamed "Jack"—solidly against the rock walls with its built-in extensible supports.

"Okay, everyone clear back. We don't want to take any chances on being hit by something if either the door or Jack breaks."

No one debated that. All four of them returned to the top of Melted Way before A.J. sent the command.

"Okay, Jack—let 'er rip!"

They were able to watch the operation on a screen, from sensors left on site. The fuel-cell-powered ripper hummed, and there was a sudden screeching noise audible all the way down the corridor as the lever arms inserted themselves forcibly into the narrow crack between the door valves. The humming abruptly dropped in pitch and became louder as it began to force the doors open.

A.J. watched telltales on the sensors rising. The stress built up, started to edge towards the caution zone. *"Stop."*

"No go?" Madeline asked.

"Bah. I have not yet begun to fight. I just don't necessarily see that I have to do it in one pull. Repetition and overstrain, that's the key. The same way you break a piece of metal by continually bending it back and forth. I'm betting that after umpteen million years, even that alien material is subject to being fatigued."

At A.J.'s direction, the ripper began a series of sudden,

very high power pulls, none of which lasted long enough
to endanger the machine. The ripper also began moving
the tines up and down and trying to twist them, exerting
force along most of the length of the opening.

Then A.J. ordered it to give another long pull.

With a suddenness that caused them all to jump, the
door split wide open. The ripper emitted another high-
pitched whine before shutting down.

"We're in!" A.J. announced exultantly.

Once they arrived at the door, they moved the ripper
out of the way and retracted its supports. Then, slowly,
they entered the alien base.

A gray-white chamber about ten meters wide greeted
them, with another door directly opposite the one they
had forced. This one was of a single piece, a sort of flat-
bottomed circle, and seemed to open inward, towards the
interior of the base. A wide construction that looked rather
like a helicopter rotor whose two blades had been dented
on alternate sides with sledgehammers stood out from
the center of the door.

"That's a locking valve," Madeline said decisively. "Like
the ones on some submarine doors, except it's much bigger."

"Don't tell me," A.J. grumbled. "You've spent time on
submarines, too."

He raised his hand abruptly. "I know, I know. It's still
classified because your boss thinks someday he might need
to take our new ally the Sultan of Cumquat deep-sea
fishing. I don't need to know the details, however. That's
because I agree with you. This is an airlock, and that's
why it opens inward. If someone left the outer door open,
you can pull all you want and it'll still be held shut by the
higher pressure in the base."

"I think you're right, A.J.," Rich said, pointing. "Those markings look the same as those we've found near airlock doors on the Phobos base."

Helen's trained instincts as a paleontologist were leaning her toward the same conclusion. The locking valve had confused her until Madeline identified it, because it was out of human scale. But now she could see that the bladelike extensions were well positioned for the long manipulating arms of a *Bemmius*.

"Yes. I think this was a Bemmie base, too, not that of a different species. If Rich is right, they even used the same language."

"Not necessarily," Skibow cautioned. "There are a lot of subtleties in the way Bemmie script works that Jane and I are unsure about. We'll still very much groping our way, from a cultural distance far greater than any we face dealing with a human language. Even there, don't forget that to someone unfamiliar with any of them, the way Chinese and Japanese and Korean are written all look quite similar, even though they're not very similar at all."

He moved closer and scrutinized the markings. "I should have said that the markings here look similar, not the same. They might be identical, but that would take closer examination. And keep in mind that even the markings on airlocks in Phobos aren't always identical, either."

"Okay, Rich, caution noted," Helen said. "But, more and more, I'm thinking that Bemmie was quite similar to us in many respects, whatever the differences elsewhere. One of those similarities—if we're right—being the fact that they didn't always get along with each other any more than we do."

Madeline, meanwhile, had been studying the lever

arms. "If this works anything like ours, it's mechanical, and probably a sort of turning lever or screw arrangement. Did they have a preferred direction? Clockwise or counterclockwise, I mean."

Helen shook her head. "Not that I've ever been able to determine. Rich? A.J.? Any opinion?"

A.J. shook his head. So did Rich.

"May as well just try one, then, and see what happens," Madeline said. "Experiments-R-Us. Let's start with clockwise. Rich and A.J., why don't you go over to the one on the right and lean down on it. You both weigh more than I do, so you'll get more leverage. Meanwhile, I'll pull up on the other one."

"Damn lady weightlifter." But A.J. went over to the lever she was pointing to.

"Don't be silly, A.J.," Madeline said sweetly. "I'm quite sure you could lift a much heavier weight than I could, so small a woman am I."

She sounded about as sincere as a praying mantis extolling the culinary virtues of broccoli. Helen almost laughed out loud. "What do you want me to do, Madeline? Give you a hand?"

"No. Just stand there and watch. I have a feeling we're going to need an observer to let us know if we've moved it at all. Otherwise we could wind up straining at it for hours, not knowing."

Once they were in position, Helen gave the signal. A.J. and Rich essentially jumped on the right side while Madeline pulled upward on the left.

To their surprise, the handle moved grudgingly about ten degrees before it stopped. "Maybe that's got it!"

The door, however, would not open. A.J. inserted Fairy

Dust around the rim and determined that some sort of bolts were retracted.

"But something else is blocking the entrance and keeping the door from swinging open. We'll have to push it in."

That called for reconfiguring the ripper into a device more like a short, fuel-cell-powered battering ram. After about twenty minutes, the ripper started pounding regularly on the door.

"You do realize that we are to Arean archaeology what Indiana Jones would have been in real life," Rich commented dryly. "You watch, Helen—future generations of our colleagues will call us looting barbarians."

Helen smiled. "Yes, I can see it now. 'Helen the Hun' and 'Skibow the Scalper.'"

She shrugged, a bit uncomfortably. "It rubs me the wrong way, too, being honest. But . . . what can we do? On Earth we have the luxury of unlimited air when we want to get into an ancient ruin."

"True enough," Madeline said. "Even digging in Antarctica was a picnic compared to this."

A.J. would never leave well enough alone. "Why were you *digging* in Antarctica? Never mind, never mind. Still a deep, dark secret."

"Well, the name is, but that's just to protect the family from publicity. Not the fact. I was trying to find a corpse. It was all very anticlimactic, in the end. I was called in because the guy who disappeared knew a lot of classified information. But there turned out to be no foreign skullduggery involved at all. Not a terrorist in sight. The damn fool just got drunk and wandered off too far. You really, really, really don't want to do that in Antarctica."

There was a sudden crunching, tinkling noise, and the inner air-lock door ground inward an inch and a half. On the next blow, it moved six inches, and the next caused the door to swing almost fully open, amid a sound like a cement mixer filled with champagne glasses. With nothing left in its way, Jack the Ripper shut down.

White dust drifted smokily in their lights. As it settled, they could see that the corridor beyond was coated with ice.

"They were hooked to a water source, all right," A.J. said, quite unnecessarily. "Well, let's take a look-see."

After he and Skibow moved the ripper to the side, all four of them started cautiously down the icy tunnel. Helen and A.J. were in the lead, with Rich coming next and Madeline bringing up the rear.

"The ice starts off incredibly thick on the ceiling," Helen reported. "Two meters thick, at a guess. Fortunately the roof is much higher than I'd expect with Bemmie construction. I think that's because, from the looks of it once the ice starts thinning out, this was originally a natural formation that they just took advantage of. The ice starts tapering two thirds of the way through, and is gone completely about fifteen meters from the end. The roof here is just rock. The walls are sort of gray colored, with the floors almost black."

"I see another door," Rich said. "It looks like it has a plaque with the same airlock markings."

Madeline came last, walking down the ice-coated corridor carefully, to keep from slipping. She was quite a ways behind them because she'd stopped to study the wall at one point.

The ceiling collapsed.

❊        ❊        ❊

To Madeline, time seemed to freeze. The fact that the great slabs of ice fell more slowly than they would have on Earth just made the coming doom a bit more protracted. Even three eighths of a ton, multiplied by untold tons, is a crushing weight.

If time seemed frozen, her brain wasn't.

She saw A.J., Rich, and Helen ahead of her—facing the wrong way, and too far in any case to be able to reverse direction and escape. They were now almost at the far end of the tunnel.

They weren't in immediate danger, because Madeline could now see that only the central area of the tunnel was caving in. That was the part right above her.

She glanced back and saw that she had no time to make it out herself, even if the supports beyond the tunnel held and the entire cave system didn't come down. And even if she could, the other three would be trapped.

She might—barely—be able to race to shelter with them at the far end, assuming she didn't slip on the treacherous footing. But that would just leave all four of them trapped.

With not much oxygen left, only the water in their small sip tanks, and no food. And only Bruce and Joe—and him with a broken leg—to try and get them out. With, even leaving aside the fact they'd have asphyxiated by then, not more than forty hours they could count on the suits remaining powered. Once the batteries were dead, they'd freeze within minutes.

In the very short time it took her to finish that assessment, the slabs had come more than halfway down. There was only one possible chance left, slim as it might be. She took a step forward, stopped, planted her legs, extended her arms at what she guessed was the best angle, and braced herself.

The ice arrived.

A moaning, grumbling noise echoed through the tunnel. A.J. spun to see the roof coming down, seeming to break in two directly above Madeline's head.

A ghostly blast of white-red dust filled the corridor. A.J. felt himself dragged backward by Helen, away from the collapse. The two of them tripped over something. They fell to the floor and lay there, expecting to see the roof come down on top of them also.

"Madeline! A.J.! Helen!" Joe's voice came faintly over the radio. "Are you all right? What's happening down there?"

Dust fogged the air so thickly that A.J. felt an impulse to cough or hold his breath, despite the fact that none of it could possibly get to him. His voice was strained when he answered.

"Cave-in, Joe. Me and Helen seem to be okay." The rumbling had faded away. The ceiling in this far area of the tunnel seemed solid enough. He looked at Helen, who blinked wide-eyed back at him. For a moment the two just held each other. He saw Rich picking himself up. He was apparently what they'd tripped over. "Rich is okay too."

"What about Madeline?"

It was starting to sink in. "Jesus . . . She was smack in the middle of the tunnel when it came down."

He heard a choking sound from Joe, a sound filled with so much pain that it caused his own eyes to sting. "I'm going to take a look, Joe. We really don't know anything yet."

Despite that attempt at reassurance, A.J. had no real hope that Madeline was still alive, as he groped his way toward where she'd been. Ice dust still drifted thick as smoke in a burning building in the corridor. He couldn't see anything, although he could sense Helen and Rich following him.

"I can't see anything at all yet. Place is filled with ice dust. Some rock dust too, looks like. Hold on . . ."

He could now make out vague dark shapes in the beam of his light. "Clearing up slowly. Probably all blocked, but I'll get as close as—"

He broke off sharply. Just stared, wide-eyed.

Helen and Rich came up beside him. "Holy . . ." Rich started to say, but trailed off, unable to finish.

Helen said nothing at all. Just shook her head, back and forth, like a metronome.

Finally, A.J. cleared his throat, very loudly. "I swear, I swear, I swear. I will never again made a wisecrack about Supergirl."

Madeline stood in the center of the corridor, her arms stretched up and out to either side at perhaps a sixty-degree angle. Her hands held up two huge slabs of ice which, in turn, prevented most of the ice above from erasing the entire corridor like a bubble from a wad of dough.

They heard a gasp from her. Now that the ice dust was clearing away, A.J. could see that Madeline's eyes looked as wide as his felt.

"W-what do you know . . ." she said shakily. "It worked. For now, anyway."

"What? *What* worked? How the hell are you holding up all that? Dammit, you're *not that strong*. Three-eighths gravity be damned. No human being who ever lived is that strong!"

By the end, he was almost screeching. A.J. realized he sounded half-hysterical; relief, terror, incomprehension all mingled in his high-pitched demand. Somewhere in the background, but not really grasping the words, he could hear Joe hollering words that combined relief and demands for a coherent report.

"No, I'm not." Madeline took a slow breath, settling her own nerves. "But I thought the suit might be."

The dazzling Fathom smile came. Even shining through her faceplate, it seemed to light up the whole tunnel. "I remembered what you did with Joe, after he broke his leg."

Enlightenment burst over A.J. "Mother of God. You made your whole suit go to rigid impact mode and lock that way. With mostly carbonan components . . . yeah, it could work. Genius. Pure effing genius."

He finally understood, now, why Hathaway had been so insistent that Madeline accompany them.

False modesty aside, A.J. knew he was extraordinarily intelligent. Something of a genius, in many ways. But his mind groped to imagine the combination of foresight, quick thinking, and instantaneous reaction that had enabled Madeline to do what she'd done.

A.J. knew he'd never have been able to do it himself, if he'd been in her position. He'd have been nothing more than a smear in the ice.

In the end, brains were only a part of it—and a small part at that. The universe that had shaped Madeline Fathom was just a completely different one than had shaped A.J. Baker.

Whatever residual animosity he still had regarding Madeline's role in the expedition finally vanished. She was what she was—but she was all of it. You couldn't pick and choose what you liked.

"The good and the bad and the ugly," he murmured.

It was a package deal. And—on Mars, all things considered—one hell of a good package. It had kept them all alive, when they'd otherwise surely have been dead.

He must have murmured louder than he thought.

"Thank you, I guess. Joe doesn't think I'm ugly, though, so poop on you."

Impossibly, her smile brightened. "Now, A.J.—if you don't mind—I'd like to be able to unlock the suit and put my arms down someday. This is going to get very uncomfortable, after a while."

"We're on it." The hollering over the radio finally registered. "Hey, Joe, calm down, will you? She's alive and smarter than we are."

"*Thank God*. Thank God. Madeline—"

"It's okay, Joe. I'm fine, really I am. It was scary for a minute, but if the cave back of us is okay, we're going to be just fine."

"I want you back here right away."

"Don't be silly, Joe. If I unlock the suit, we'll be trapped—and it's going to take Helen and A.J. and Rich quite some time to substitute some other sort of bracing. So just hold your horses."

While the rest of them were preoccupied with Madeline's situation, Rich had passed gingerly through the "Madeline Arch" and gone to check conditions at the opening of the tunnel.

"I think we're okay," he said, coming back. "The bracing

held. In fact, as near as I can tell, the roof out there is just fine. I thought at first that the roof had caved in because of a Marsquake, but I think it was just the localized effects of the strain the ripper put on this area near the door we forced. Why it worked that way, I have no idea."

Chad Baird spoke over the radio. "Underground structures can be very quirky. In fact, that's exactly what I was worried about." His voice sounded a little shaky, too. "What kills most people in mining operations is not the big dramatic explosions and cave-ins and floodings that make the national news. Those are awfully rare, at least when proper safety precautions are taken. But coal miners and hard-rock miners still get killed, year after year, in ones and twos—because a piece of the roof came loose and fell on them."

He paused a moment, as if checking something. "I can tell you for sure and certain there's been no Marsquake in that area. Our sensors would have picked it up. So I'm almost positive Rich is right. I hate to say it, but it was your own activities that weakened the roof."

"Gotcha," said A.J. "On the bright side, we've got some good titles for new movies. *Indiana Jones Had It Coming.*"

Joe chimed in, almost giggling with relief. "*Lara Crusht, Tomb Raider No More.*"

"Hey, that's good. The sequel to follow: *The Mummy*—"

"SHUT UP!" Helen and Madeline shouted simultaneously.

"Please," added Rich.

A.J. choked off the rest. Then: "Ah, right. Let's get Madeline out of her new job as a roof column. Joe, switch from movie fan mode to engineer mode, will you? This is going to be tricky, since we don't have much in the way of material to make supports from."

⚜        ⚜        ⚜

With three of them working together, it took about four hours to get sufficient bracing jacked into place to let Madeline relax her suit. Most of the "bracing," unfortunately, was nothing fancier than moving pieces of ice and a few loose rocks into what they hoped was a supportive structure.

None of them were very happy with the results, when it was done. The "support structure" looked more like a pile of rubble than anything else. But at least, at Joe's suggestion, they'd been able to carefully position the ripper in such a way as to serve as a more substantial brace for what seemed to be the shakiest area.

That done, at Madeline's insistence, the others cleared the corridor. Then she unlocked the suit and, slowly and gingerly, lowered her arms.

But there was no sign of movement from the roof, except a very slight slippage that Jack the Ripper's tines kept from moving more than a few inches. Almost tiptoeing her way, Madeline came out of the corridor. Once safely outside, she started wiggling her arms to get them working again. Four hours holding her hands over her head, even in low gravity and with the suit doing the actual load-bearing, had not done pleasant things to her blood circulation.

"Not so bad, really," she assured them. "I've done worse in other places."

Helen suddenly hugged her. A moment later, A.J. and Rich joined in. For about a minute, the four people were clutched in a spacesuited huddle far beneath the surface of Mars, all of them shaking a little as the reaction finally set in.

❈     ❈     ❈

Madeline finally broke it up. "Come on, guys. I appreciate it—I really, really do—but we've still got work ahead of us."

"Not now!" Joe's voice almost shouted. Then, more calmly: "Seriously. Helen, I'm not going to tell you what to do, but—"

"No problem, Joe. I've got no intention of continuing our investigation today. We all need a rest. Even if we didn't, our oxygen reserves are too low to do anything more than come out."

Startled a bit—he hadn't thought to check in a while—A.J. took the readings. "You're right about that."

"Are you going to be okay?" Joe asked, concern coming back into his voice.

"Relax, willya?" said A.J. "We've got plenty left to make our way out—even leaving aside the emergency tanks we left at the bottom of the cliff. But Helen's right. We don't want to fool around with anything else today. If another emergency happened, we'd be truly and royally screwed."

For all that Helen's intellect told her they were doing the right thing, all of her emotions and professional instincts pulled her in the other direction. They were on the verge—the verge, damnation!—of what might prove to be another extraordinary discovery. Now that the ice dust had completely settled, she could easily see that beckoning door at the other end of the tunnel where they'd almost died.

She shook her head, firmly, and turned to follow the others as they headed toward the surface.

A.J. made a wisecrack once they reached Melted Way. For once, Helen thought it was appropriate. Sort of. "Hey, look at it this way. Live to loot another day."

# Chapter 49

In the event, exploring the Bemmie base had to be postponed for some time. Captain Hathaway was adamant that means of securing the unstable roof areas had to be put in place first.

"We came *that* close to losing two thirds of our people down there," he stated forcefully. "No way will I permit that risk to be taken again, until I'm satisfied that we've dealt with the problem. That's final, Helen, so don't even bother arguing about it."

In truth, Helen wasn't really inclined to argue anyway. Much as part of her desperately wanted to get into that base, that part was easily disciplined by the very experienced boss of many field digs.

A.J. took a bit of stifling, of course. But, by now, Helen was the acknowledged world expert—champion of the entire Solar System, in fact—at the Art and Science of Stifling A.J. Baker. Admittedly, she had the advantage of being able to use a means of coercion not available to anyone else.

The problem then became . . .

How?


"It's ridiculous!" A.J. snarled. "We've managed to cross interplanetary space using umpteen forms of cutting-edge technology. And now we're stumped because we don't have any—"

He spat out the last two words as if they were the foulest profanity: "—*stupid wood.*"

Joe was almost as frustrated, but he couldn't help grinning. "Well, the phrase was always 'with jacks and timbers,—' "

"I don't want to hear it!"

" '—and without timbers the rest means jack.' "

A.J. glared at him, refusing to crack a smile over the feeble pun. Joe spread his hands. "What do you want me to say? It's just a fact. Old-fashioned and 'stupid' as it may be, wood is still the best material for a jillion purposes. Shoring up shaky tunnels being one of them."

"Fine." A.J. shifted the glare to Bruce Irwin. "Get on the radio and tell Hathaway to send us down some pine tree seeds. Or bulbs— whatever the stupid things grow from. We'll set up a greenhouse somehow and plant them and sit back and wait one or two hundred years until we've got some timber."

"Pine grows quite a bit faster than that, actually," Helen said, sweetly. "You're confusing it with some of the hardwoods. In ten years—fifteen, tops—I think we'd have a harvestable crop."

"Great." A.J. was practically grinding his teeth.

"Well . . ." Joe mused, "we could use iron too, in a pinch. Hold on, let me do the figures . . ."

"Cut it out, Joe!" A.J.'s glare looked to be fixed on his face permanently. "It'd take just as long to build an iron industry from scratch. That Ferris-descended reactor we've got wasn't designed to crank out I-beams—and you know it."

Jackie came to the rescue.

"Don't start denuding all the Martian forests yet," she said breezily, in their next radio exchange. "We think we've figured out a solution, and we'll be sending it down to you as part of Operation Care Package."

"What is it?" A.J. asked eagerly.

"Not telling. It's a surprise present for Helen. Don't forget what day it is that Care Package'll be bouncing down to you." There was a slight pause. "Uh, A.J., you *didn't* forget, did you?"

They were all in the rover, listening. A.J. suddenly realized that Helen's eyes were on him.

Very, very beady eyes.

Fortunately, A.J. pulled back from the brink of disaster. "Of course not!" He turned and gave Helen his most winning smile. "Happy birthday, darling."

Her return smile was a very cool sort of thing. "I think he was saved by the bell, Jackie."

They heard a feminine-sounding snort coming over the radio. Then: "Anyway, I'm not telling since you don't need to know yet. You'll find out in three days."

"Just try to aim it well, please," Helen said. "We don't want it to bounce so far that *Thoat* can't reach it."

"We'll do our best," Hathaway answered. "But you'd

rather have to hike a bit than have this thing bounce on top of you, I can guarantee it. It sure 'nuff ain't going to be light."

"Point. Well, let's all keep our fingers crossed, Captain."

"I'm crossing everything I got two of," Hathaway assured her.

The ion drive was not meant for speed, of course, so despite the low orbit of Phobos it was not the next day, nor the next, but the day after that when all six of the crash survivors assembled to look for the first sign of what might be their relief, and quite possibly salvation. Food was every bit as short on Mars as trees were.

Helen stared into the bright pinkish sky, trying to calculate where Care Package would first appear. Since she was facing west, and Care Package was due to make its crash-landing somewhat to the south, that would be to her left . . .

She realized suddenly that she was being silly and instructed her HUD to display the location in the sky where she ought to be looking.

"Cheating, eh?" A.J.'s voice came.

"Are you saying you're actually not using a gadget to do your work for you, Mr. Baker?" Madeline asked.

"Only some of my work. I'm trying to figure out the angles based on the images from above. I like testing my gut instincts sometimes."

"We'll see how well you do, then."

"This is *Nike*, Mars Base One. Care Package is steady on reentry now, and should become visible to you very soon. So far all shows green."

"Understood, *Nike*. We're all hoping."

"*There!*" Helen felt a touch of pride that she'd spotted it first. A tiny black dot, barely visible in the pinkish haze, moving toward them, far to the west and slightly south. It grew bigger as they watched.

Much bigger.

"That sucker's getting kinda close . . . " Joe muttered.

"You said you didn't want it too far away," Jackie said in their ears.

"Well, yeah, but too close and she may bounce right into Thoat Canyon. We'll have a hell of a time getting it then!"

"Have faith, Dr. Buckley, have faith," came Gupta's sonorous voice. "We have checked our calculations most carefully."

Care Package screamed down to Mars—literally screamed, from the sound produced by the aeroshell— only a few kilometers to the west and south of *Thoat*. Barely a hundred meters up, Care Package blew the remaining portion of her aeroshell and released the parachute, revealing the balloonlike airbags surrounding the precious cargo. Her first impact blasted black and red sands high into the thin air with a smacking sound incongruously soft and distant and then kicked her, spinning, back into the air, rising fifty, sixty meters before arcing back down, to hit again, and bounce, and hit and bounce again.

"Jesus, is she going to stop?" A.J. asked nervously. "She's heading right for the edge!"

"That would suck," Joe said bluntly.

The bounces were getting shallower and quicker, even in Mars' feeble gravity. Suddenly, Care Package wasn't so much bouncing as rolling, throwing dust aside as it slowed itself through friction with the previously untouched sands. Helen held her breath as Care Package continued its journey, slowing, slowing, until it rolled to a stop a kilometer and a half to the south and slightly east of Mars Base One, no more than two hundred meters from the edge of Thoat Canyon.

"*Yeah!*" she heard herself shout involuntarily. "Package delivered safely!"

"Now that," Jackie said with satisfaction, "is a landing."

"Bah," A.J. said. "I betcha *we* bounced farther. And we didn't have balloons, either."

Helen's birthday present was there, too, just as Jackie had promised.

"Oh, swell," Helen complained. " 'Some assembly required.' "

"Look on the bright side," Jackie countered. "At least you don't need any batteries that weren't included."

A.J.'s attitude was mixed. On the one hand, he was delighted to have the means to create a safe entry into the Bemmie base. On the other, he found the means themselves contemptible.

"I can't believe this. I was expecting some sort of high-tech wizardry from you people."

"Do not be childish, Mr. Baker," said Gupta. "In many respects, the ways of our grandfathers are still best."

"Still. We're going to *stuff* our way there. How undignified."

✖      ✖      ✖

Undignified it might have been, but it worked. The half-shredded portions of the airbags that had enabled Care Package to survive the landing, when properly positioned and braced by the package's structural pieces, did a fine job of filling the tunnels so tightly that there was no chance of any further roof collapses. They left a passage just big enough to allow them to get through along with whatever drones they needed.

That still left the problem of the ice cavern, of course. The interior of the cavern was so immense that not even a hundred Care Package shells could possibly have filled it up.

But, to everyone's relief, Chad Baird pronounced that the cavern's size provided enough of a safety margin in itself.

"Look, even though it's probably a recent formation in geological terms, the emphasis is on the word 'geological.' On the scale of human lifetimes, that cavern is very old. It's been there for millennia, certainly. So, barring one of the very rare major Marsquakes, I can't see any likelihood that the cavern itself will collapse. The real danger is much more prosaic—those chunks of ice that it periodically drops on the floor below, as the stalactites shed some of their weight."

"And how do you propose they protect themselves against *that*?" Hathaway demanded. "I don't care if— theoretically—assuming the right position with the suits locked in rigid impact mode would shield someone well enough. Just because it worked for Madeline once doesn't mean it'll work every time."

"Don't need to," replied Baird calmly. "Ken, stop fretting for a moment and just *think*. Like a soldier, if you will. The ceiling of that cavern averages forty-five meters above the floor, and in no place they'd be passing through is it lower than thirty-five meters. In Martian gravity . . ."

"Oh." Hathaway cleared his throat. "Spotters, you're saying."

"Right. Unless a whole section of stalactites sheds at once—and that's not the way it normally works—all they have to do is pass through the cavern one at a time, with the rest keeping an eye on the ceiling to warn the person below if anything's coming loose. As slowly as any dangerous piece of ice will fall on Mars, with that much distance to travel, they can easily be out of harm's way by the time it lands."

There was silence on the radio, for a moment. Everyone listening in *Thoat* had their fingers figuratively crossed.

"Okay," the captain finally said. "It's a sloppier solution than I'd like, but . . . At least we won't be risking more than one person at a time."

"Just because we've used *one* low-tech solution for making the corridors safer doesn't mean we should suddenly go backwards in time, people." A.J. spoke up. "Spotting things is not a job for people. It's a job for machines. Smart sensors. I can tweak the sensors in the suits to watch for such events and display the alert, and even show you which way to go to escape. And unlike people, the sensors won't get distracted, sleepy, or fail to look the right direction at the wrong time."

Hathaway grunted assent. "Okay, that's a better solution. Go to it, people."

❊     ❊     ❊

Three hours later, they were finally back to the second door. This time, all six members of the party were there. None of them wanted to miss this moment.

Impatiently, they waited while A.J. and Joe brought up and positioned Jack the Ripper, in case they needed the drone's services.

They didn't. The door opened almost as smoothly as if it had just been closed an hour earlier.

They passed through into the interior of the alien base on Mars.

Ten minutes of silence later, Madeline spoke the first "Oh my God" of the day. The three words would be echoed by all six beings who saw the installation for the first time in sixty-five million years, again and again, as the day passed.

Finally, their oxygen running as close to the margin as Helen dared, they returned to *Thoat*.

"Well?" Ken asked.

"Jackpot," was A.J.'s reply.

Helen's was more dignified. For a while.

"Captain Hathaway, we have uncovered an alien installation which, though most of it is in the state of ruin you'd expect from planetary as opposed to vacuum conditions, is still in good enough condition to be studied and investigated for . . . oh . . .

*"The place is HUGE, Ken! Way way way way way bigger than the base on Phobos! We'll be digging for years! I'll be working here till I croak of old age! Ha!"*

"You'll need funding," he pointed out, mildly.

"No sweat. Tell Jackie—no, ask Satya, he's the best horse-trader I know beneath that solemn exterior—to start jacking up those bids. The only condition—*ha!*—is that they have to send a photographer to Mars. No way I'm letting those paparazzi get near me. And whoever cosmetics companies use. Professional sniffers, whatever. Hound dogs, for all I care. *I love this place!*"

# Chapter 50

Three weeks later, Helen was as enthusiastic as ever. Except for Rich, however, the spirits of the other members of the party had dropped some.

Not much. Just the inevitable amount that would affect anyone who, unlike a field paleontologist or a linguist, didn't regard excruciatingly patient study to be the quintessence of professional pleasure.

"It's pretty run-down," A.J. grumbled one evening over their communal dinner in *Thoat*. "Yes, I know that's to be expected. Even as well as the Bemmies built and even with Mars' atmosphere and stable geology, sixty-five million years is sixty-five million years."

"On Earth, not one percent of this would have survived," Helen pointed out.

A.J. half-glared at her. Not because he disagreed, but simply at the insufferably cheery way she said it. "I know," Helen added, grinning at him. "What do you expect from a grubby bonedigger, o ye high tech wizard?"

A.J.'s good spirits returned, within seconds. However much the state of decay of the ruins at Melas Chasma frustrated his professional desire for the sort of things he could investigate thoroughly with his methods, as he'd been able to on Phobos, the personal side of his life was as good as he could ask for. He loved Helen, at any time. Helen in the best mood he'd ever seen her—day after day after day—was a pure delight to be with.

The dinner finished, Helen kicked off a general discussion. "I've come to the conclusion that this base isn't at all like the one on Phobos. But I'd like everyone else's assessment."

"Agreed," Madeline said. "But I don't know if you're seeing the same things I am. What are you seeing?"

"Well, the most obvious is that this base was fully intact. All the damage we're seeing is from time passing. There was no damage from bombardment or weapons of any kind, as far as we can see."

Helen took a bite of the small fruit ration bar that constituted dessert. "We've found no *Bemmius* corpses here—or corpses of any kind. Plenty of noteplaques, but all of them neatly stored away, not scattered like they were on Phobos. Everything here is neat, in order, and a lot of it is completely empty. Like a house someone just put up for sale. They evacuated this place at their leisure, either well before or well after the bombardment. What are you seeing?"

"Layout and design," Joe said promptly. Rich and A.J. nodded.

"The purpose of the bases was entirely different," Joe amplified. "The design of the one on Phobos, as far as

I'm concerned, is clearly military. We've found firing
ranges, tons of hand weapons, indications that much larger
weaponry was once in place, rooms that are hard to cate-
gorize as anything other than barracks, so on and so forth."

A.J. picked up the thread. "By contrast, down here . . .
Well, it's really hard to analyze some things, since they
have—as you say— stripped a lot of the equipment out.
Something the Phobos residents apparently never had a
chance to do. But from the wiring, pipes, layout of rooms,
and other things, it looks to me—and most of the engineers up on *Nike* agree—that this was more of a research
institution."

"What about the Vault?" Rich asked.

"That is a puzzle," Joe said. "One that we'll have to
solve. If we can figure out how to get into it."

The "Vault" was located near the center of the base, from
what Helen and A.J. had been able to ascertain so far about
the base's layout. It was a huge structure that was made of
the most stubbornly tough materials the Bemmies—or
whoever had built the base—had owned, supported by
massive reinforcing columns three times thicker than any
support members in the rest of the base, and sealed off
from it with only one connecting corridor and doorway.

The Vault was so clearly separate and massive as to be
intimidating as well as mystifying. There was even some
evidence around the doorway, based on slight irregula-
rities of the nearby walls and floor, that over the past
sixty-five million years the miniscule geologic activity of
Mars had moved the rest of the base slightly while not
affecting the Vault. The doorway in question didn't just
look like a vault door, either—it appeared to actually *be* a
vault door, in terms of thickness and toughness. In point

of fact, there was considerable debate about whether to call it a door, at all. There was no sign of ordinary opening mechanisms, although the seam where it fit into the tube-like entrance hall for the Vault was clear enough.

"It's as though they sealed the door shut with no intention of ever opening it again," Madeline mused.

" 'And so,' " A.J. said in a sepulchral voice, " 'they placed a seal upon the Tomb and all manner of enchantments, that that which lay within would never again—' "

"Shut up, A.J.!" came a chorus of voices.

"You know . . ." Rich said after a moment. "A.J. might be onto something this time."

"Huh?"

Rich laughed. "I don't mean that some nameless eldritch horror lies beyond the door. I mean that it might literally be a tomb. Like a pyramid, you know. What if whoever they were had a sort of religious structure to their civilization, and one of their leaders died here?"

"But wouldn't that be awfully wasteful?" Joe objected. "Would that make sense for a civilization this advanced?"

"At the time," Rich countered, "Egypt was probably the most advanced civilization in the world. And you're trying to make sense of things based on our point of view. Sure, so far, it does look as if the Bemmies were rather like us, in many ways. But we don't know for sure that the Bemmies built this base, although the ergonomics of what's left does look rather appropriate for their species. And even if it was built by them, we don't know what their culture was like. If they were having a war—which all those crater targets damn well seem to indicate—it might have been religious in nature. Anyway, it's just a thought."

Madeline looked at one of the images of the enigmatic

sealed entrance which were lying on the table. "Well, there's only one way to find out."

Joe smiled. "That's my delicate lady love. Her favorite word. *Boom.*"

Despite A.J.'s occasional references to *Things Man Was Not Meant To Know*—Joe's witticisms were even worse— Madeline and A.J. spent the next few days trying to figure out the best way to get through the doorway. In the end, sure enough, the only workable method they could think of involved one form or another of demolitions.

That was something they approached reluctantly— especially Madeline, despite Joe's wisecrack. The concepts of high explosives and underground exploration did not generally combine well, and Madeline knew a lot more about both subjects than anyone else on Mars did.

However, there was little doubt that they were in fact going to give it a try, since they couldn't figure out any other way to accomplish the task. The Vault represented a huge unexplored area of the base and potentially the most valuable one. If it were a tomb of the sort Rich had speculated about, one of the most common features of such tombs on Earth was that they were filled with all manner of valuables and items meant to accompany the owner to their afterlife.

Joe did suggest that it might be their dump, especially for radioactive waste, but even that might provide valuable clues to their technology and society. In any event, after sixty-five million years all the high-level radioactives would have decayed away. Their suits would provide more than adequate protection if that turned out to be the case.

❊    ❊    ❊

"Charges set. I'm coming down." Madeline's voice was calm and businesslike, showing none of the tension Joe knew she must be feeling. If something went wrong, she could collapse enough of the base to make the Vault unreachable for years, if ever.

Having finally been able to come along again after more than a month convalescing, Joe watched the opening at the top of Melted Way for her small suited figure to appear. For safety, they would trigger the detonation from outside the Ice Cavern, making sure that even if the worst-case scenario happened, none of them would be caught in it.

A few minutes later, he saw Madeline making her way down the path, and went to meet her at the bottom. His leg ached slightly and was still in a cast below the knee, but at least it was now functioning.

"How many did you set?"

"Five. I see no point in trying this halfway. Those alloys, composites, whatever they are, they're just tough as hell. Either I can blow that door, or I can't. If I did it right, it shouldn't make much difference in the risk as to whether I used one charge or all five."

"Still," A.J. said, "five? We just want to blow the door off, not vaporize it."

Madeline peered into the distance and spotted him waiting at the other side of the cavern. "Actually, I just want the door gone. If it's in one piece or a thousand isn't critical, as long as I don't damage too much behind it."

"I just hope you got your designs right."

"I checked them several times," Madeline said. "And the more I looked at that door, the more sure I was that I was going to need all of them."

The explosives had been designed as shaped charges, with geometry and backing to direct virtually all of their force along the door seam. With incendiary materials—basically thermite, that venerable mix of iron oxide and aluminum which burned at over twenty-five hundred degrees centigrade, and would do so even underwater or in Mars' almost nonexistent atmosphere—to hopefully continue the cutting, burning through anything that remained.

Madeline insisted that Joe cross the cavern first, while she and A.J. served as his spotters. Then she scurried across herself. By now, crossing the cavern was almost routine. Experience had shown them that the stalactites only dropped pieces on rare occasions. They still maintained the spotting system, but no one had ever actually had to use it to avoid being struck.

They would trigger off the charges from the relative security of the floor of the rock crevice. Hathaway had almost insisted that they return aboveground altogether, but eventually they'd talked him out of it. The climb up the crevice was the slowest and most arduous part of the trip.

Fortunately, Chad Baird had sided with them in the dispute.

"That's all rock, Captain, with no ice or loose material to be shaken down. The charges Madeline set aren't *that* big—and there's all that empty space in the cavern to absorb what little shock waves get transmitted through the thin air. They'll be safe enough there."

Grudgingly, Hathaway had finally agreed. So, now, everyone was waiting on the crevice floor.

"Ready?" Joe asked. At the acknowledgements, he glanced at his display. "Okay, Madeline. Set it off."

The image of the Vault's sealed door, transmitted down A.J.'s line of bread-crumb transceivers, abruptly fuzzed and vanished in a fog of smoke and dust. Through the veil, five blazingly blue-white smears of light could dimly be made out, the incendiaries continuing their work. Joe imagined he heard a faint thud, but knew it had to be his imagination. The smoke became thick, but the most important thing about the image was that it continued to exist.

"No collapse. None of my sensors are showing any sign of movement, either," A.J. reported with satisfaction. "Let's head on up. By the time we get there, it should be done."

"No, let's wait until it's finished," Helen said. "I don't want to listen to Ken hollering at me afterward."

"There's no point in rushing, anyway," Madeline chimed in. "The wreckage will stay very hot for a while, and these suits were definitely not made to take steel-melting temperatures. Keep an eye on things in IR and make sure you don't touch anything without the right tools."

"Don't teach your grandfather how to use sensors," A.J. retorted. "I can see better in three spectra at once than you can in one. And I understand it all."

"To understand is not to act. I've seen you act without thinking. That was my caution."

"She's right, A.J.," Joe said.

"Well, *of course* you're on her side."

"I don't recall being the one who decided to run into burning buildings with nothing but balls, a blanket, and a VRD."

"Okay, okay. I get the point. I'll wait until I'm told it's safe before grabbing anything."

Eventually, Helen gave the signal. "Come along, people," said Madeline. "And everyone take your chunk of ice."

Even Bruce was there this time. It had become clear that aside from certain areas—which were now braced—it was reasonably safe to be underground here, and no one wanted to be left out of the chance to enter the Vault for the first time.

The smoke had mostly settled and was flowing away through the base, many of its components being heavier than anything the thin Martian atmosphere could support. By the time they finally reached the Vault, the air was almost clear. The sealed door still smoldered and glowed in places.

Madeline took her block of ice and motioned everyone to the side. Then, very gingerly, holding it only by her fingertips, pressed the ice block into one of the holes.

Steam blasted out, accompanied by high-pitched crackling, hissing noises. Madeline held the ice steady but made no effort to push it harder into the hole.

As her chunk melted away, the others methodically repeated the process, using thermal shock to hopefully finish the job of weakening the door—and, incidentally, cooling it to a workable temperature.

The cautious and methodical approach had been dictated by Joe. To something of his satisfaction, it was A.J. who graphically demonstrated why it was the right method. A.J. pressed his first chunk of ice into its hole with vigor and determination. The chunk of ice was blown out of the hole almost on contact, ripping itself out of the sensor expert's hands and continuing on, a hurtling twenty-kilo missile that could have hurt someone, if it hit the wrong way.

"Okay, Joe, you were right. That would have been bad."

"Damn right it would, Mr. Seat-of-the-Pants."

Finally Joe decided they'd done all they could, and they began attaching cables to the door. Most of the door appeared to have been eaten through, according to A.J.'s Fairy Dust examination, and the remainder of the seal area was cracked.

Jack the Ripper was once more reconfigured, this time to a winch configuration. A block and tackle had been rigged using cable of the same composition that *Thoat*'s winch used, and Jack was braced and locked to one of the main support columns. Even with bracing methods and mechanical advantage, the cable was far stronger; Jack would break long before the cable would.

It was something of an anticlimax that after all that preparation, the Vault door moved almost as soon as Jack started pulling. Within a minute, the heavy drone had dragged it open far enough to allow the little party to enter the area it had formerly sealed off.

"I guess you do know your explosives," Joe said. "But then, I always knew you were dynamite."

Madeline actually *giggled*.

"Why is it," A.J. complained, "that you tolerate *his* stupid jokes?"

But Madeline ignored him, since she was already passing through the door. The interior of the tunnel beyond was a pearl-gray color, almost nacreous, smooth and seemingly unmarked by the immense span of years. Twenty meters farther down, the tunnel ended in a door, with the widely-separated lever arm design they had seen before.

Madeline reached it first. Obviously not really expecting any positive result, she gave a small tug upward on the left-hand crossbar.

The valve lock handle spun smoothly, as though it had been checked and oiled only yesterday. The other arm nearly clipped A.J., who jumped back with a startled exclamation. Madeline had stepped back herself, not having expected any movement at all. When nothing untoward happened, she moved forward and gently turned the lock still further clockwise, until it finally stopped after three full revolutions. They'd learned from experience that the Bemmies opened and closed things in the opposite directly that people generally used.

Cautiously, she pushed inward. The massive door, well over two meters high and wide and, as they could see as it opened, half a meter thick, swung back without effort or protest.

"Sixty-five million years," A.J. almost whispered. "And it opens like someone was just here minutes ago. What the hell is this?"

Madeline entered first, flashing her light around. "Looks like a sort of rotunda with—"

Her words cut off in a shriek of unrestrained terror.

Madeline nearly dove out of the doorway. The others backed away hurriedly also—all the faster because Madeline was normally unflappable. Anything that could frighten *her* that badly . . .

"Madeline, what was it?" Joe asked. A.J. had yanked the door shut and spun the lock the other way. The people listening in from *Nike* began asking what had happened with the common morbid mixture of worry and excitement that such events tend to produce.

Madeline's breathing slowed, and suddenly she started to laugh. More questions began to flood the link. Madeline stopped laughing long enough to choke out: "Hush up, everybody. It just took me by surprise, that's all."

She took a deep breath and looked over at Helen. "You go in first. You deserve to, I think. Don't worry—it's safe."

Uncertainly, Helen went to the great door, reopened it, and entered. Her light moved slowly around the room. Suddenly, she gasped. But, forewarned, she didn't come running out or scream the way Madeline had. She just stood there, mostly out of sight half behind the door.

Joe and A.J. followed. At first, all they could see was Helen, her face inside the mostly-transparent helmet staring in what looked like almost religious rapture. For a moment, they forgot why they had come, seeing tears starting from her eyes. And then, as they turned, they could see what she was staring at. Both of them cursed and stepped back, almost in unison; but they, too, were unable to take their eyes from the sight before them.

Towering above them, no more than fifteen meters away, rearing meters high under the ceiling of the immense room, the monster seemed poised in the moment of attack. Its hide was banded in shades of green and brown and black, the camouflage of a predator. Behind a gaping maw more than a meter long filled with teeth as long as a man's hand, the eyes seemed to blaze with hunger.

*Tyrannosaurus rex* snarled soundlessly, motionlessly, at the first beings to look upon him in sixty-five million years.

The others came in slowly. Bruce and Rich, warned by their reactions, didn't jump back, but couldn't restrain their own quiet curses of disbelief.

"A.J.," Helen said quietly, "is it . . . is it . . .?" She reached up to wipe the tears from her eyes, until her hand encountered the helmet.

A.J., called back from his own stunned amazement, directed his sensors at the looming creature. After a while, he said: "Yes, indeed it is. A mummy, not a model, deliberately mounted and preserved. Before we opened that door it might have been pure nitrogen or some other inert gas in here. I'll know for sure once I analyze the readings."

"But . . . *why*?" Madeline asked. "Why in the world would you devote so much of your effort to seal away samples of Earth's life-forms on some other planet—and that planet not your own? I mean, I could understand making a museum or something on your own world, but this was sealed off!"

Rich was standing stock-still. None of the others noticed until they heard him breathe ". . . could it *be*?"

Then he was moving purposefully around the room, flashing his light here and there. A *Bemmius* flashed into view, this one brightly colored and not dull like the mummies discovered on Phobos, sealed behind some kind of transparent material. Rich's light disregarded that, came to an opening in the wall across from them. Without pause, he entered that corridor, then came to another door. The others were now following him, Helen trailing and staring back at the tyrannosaur as though it might vanish.

"Rich, what's up?" Joe demanded, puzzled. "What are you looking for?"

When there was no answer, Joe realized that Richard Skibow was focused so completely on what he was doing that he probably hadn't even heard the question. The door in front of Rich swung inward, and Rich almost lunged through, flashing his light around the short corridor. Then he stopped, and slowly, almost reverently, reached out, touching a shining transparent surface behind which . . .

Joe would have scratched his head, if he hadn't been wearing a suit. *What's this stuff?* he wondered. Behind the window—that was all he could call it—was a series of objects, with symbols in the Bemmie language above each group.

"What is it, Rich?"

"Not a tomb," Richard said finally, his voice almost a whisper. It held the same near rapture that Helen's had a moment before. "What else have we done, when we seal things away forever?"

He didn't wait for their reply. "A time capsule. A time capsule— with a Rosetta Stone sealed within." He pointed to the first object, a single oval stone. Over it, a symbol. The next section held two oval stones, and another symbol. The next section, three oval stones. Joe understood suddenly.

Rich turned and pointed down the corridor; the next door had symbols on it and a different kind of handle. "And a simple key to make you able to tell when you've learned what is here, and then move on."

His voice rose in excitement. "Jane? Jane, this is it! *They've left us their language!*"

# Chapter 51

"Well, okay," Rich said cheerfully over dinner four days later, "so I didn't get it quite right. It *is* a Rosetta Stone. Jane and I are now quite sure of it. Even if we still can't read any of the inscriptions, we can discern enough to see that they are in at least seven very different scripts, maybe eight or nine—we're still arguing about that— which wasn't true on Phobos or anywhere else we've found writing here in Melas Chasma. But they didn't leave it for us. Why should they? We weren't even a gleam in some proto-lemur's eye yet. They left it for other Bemmies. And since they apparently didn't know which group of Bemmies might come, or when, they left the messages in a representative language of what both Jane and I think were all of their major language groups."

He slurped down another spoonful of the evening's entree and swallowed appreciatively. "Joe, my heartfelt congratulations. How you manage to turn that stuff they sent down into meals like this is a mystery."

Joe inclined his head toward Madeline, sitting next to him in the rover. "Thank her, not me. That's one of her bouillabaisse recipes."

Helen's eyes widened. She'd been savoring the meal as much as Rich had. "*One* of them?"

"Yup. I've got seven others that I know by heart. Of course, I'll have to juggle the ingredients a lot. Even up on *Nike*, they don't have everything I'd need to do them full justice."

While others had been talking about the meal, A.J. had been staring pensively out of one of *Thoat*'s ports. There was nothing to see out there, of course, now that night had fallen. The Martian starblaze that was such a splendor when standing outside at night—one of the few benefits of the planet's thin atmosphere—was mostly filtered by the port.

Joe finally spotted his friend's preoccupation. "A penny for your thoughts."

The imaging specialist shook his head. "You don't want 'em, Joe. Trust me, you don't."

The bleak tone in his voice was startling. *A.J. Baker, depressed and melancholy*, was something of an oxymoron. Conversation at the table stopped and everyone swiveled their heads to stare at him.

"What's the problem?"

A.J. finally turned away from the port. "If Rich and Jane are right—and I'm not arguing the point—then consider the implications. Take that spaceship model we found yesterday, that's gotten us so excited."

That had been the most exciting find of all, at least for everyone except Rich and Helen. In one of the rooms had been a two-meter long-model of what was obviously a Bemmie spacecraft. Two meters *across*, it would be better to say—because the ship was designed something like a tuna can tapering toward the rim.

The model had been very detailed, far too much so to be simply a symbolic representation. Most exciting of all, therefore, had been the fact that, even after long and close examination, nothing that could possibly be a venturi or any sort of exhaust system or mechanism had been found on it. Whatever drive the aliens had used, it worked on some principle completely different from rockets of any kind. Apparently, however it worked, the Bemmies had possessed the long-fabled reactionless drive of many science fiction stories.

Madeline grimaced slightly. Spotting the expression, Joe gave her hand a little squeeze under the table. For Madeline—at the moment, at least—the discovery of that model was more a source of vexation than excitement. They still hadn't transmitted the news up to the *Nike*, after she'd asked them to wait until she could consider all the security implications.

By now, with the request coming from Madeline, not even A.J. was inclined to argue the matter. Whatever low opinion A.J. held of security policies in general, it no longer spilled onto Madeline Fathom. If that's what she wanted, that's what she would get. No quarrels, no questions asked.

"Explain, A.J.," Helen said.

"The question we were wondering about has just been answered, I think. Whatever drive they were using, and however different it so obviously is from our rocket propulsion systems—Jesus, a *reactionless* drive!—it's still not a faster-than-light drive. Can't be, or they wouldn't have devoted that much time, labor and resources to creating a time vault and left messages written in many languages. Even went so far as to seal it up in inert gasses."

Joe's eyes widened. "Oh." Then, a moment later: "Damn."

" 'Damn' is right," A.J. echoed, sighing. "Our highest hopes just got torpedoed. They didn't have a faster-than-light drive."

Madeline looked back and forth from Joe to A.J. "You're sure?"

Helen answered. "It makes sense, Madeline. I should have thought of it myself. Would have, if"—she flashed a little smile—"I hadn't gotten so preoccupied with all those mummies and models."

She gave A.J. and Joe an apologetic shrug. "Look, guys, I'm sorry. But, for me, this place is *already* my highest hope. It would be for any paleontologist, at least one specializing in the late Mesozoic." Her voice lowered, became almost a whisper. "After all these years, we finally get to see what they *really* looked like. No more guessing from skeletons and bones. *Tyrannosaurus, triceratops,* three species of duckbills—there's even a good sampling of sea life."

A.J. and Joe nodded. Bruce Irwin chuckled. "I think they forgive you your sins, Helen. Grudgingly." That brought a little round of laughs, lightening the atmosphere. But Madeline stubbornly returned to the point.

"I still want it explained." She hesitated. "Guys, I *need* it explained. Clearly. Clearly enough that even a national security adviser who isn't the sharpest pencil in the—ah, never mind—that even political types in the highest places can understand."

"Okay, Madeline, here it is." A.J. shifted forward in his seat, leaning on the table with his weight on his forearms. "That vault was *designed* to last for millions of years. *Millions,* not thousands."

"You're sure?"

"Yes," Joe chimed in. "A.J. and I could prove it with some work, if we concentrated on analyzing the materials, construction, and so on and so forth. But we don't really need to. Any engineer will understand the point. Even given the Bemmies' superior construction methods and materials, nobody except gods could slap together something that would last sixty-five million years under planetary conditions. For Pete's sake, they even designed those main supporting pillars to handle geologic shifts."

"Ah." Madeline leaned forward, matching A.J.'s arms-on-table posture. "I get it. Phobos could be an accident. That base survived because it was in vacuum, not to mention microgravity. The Vault can't be an accident."

"No. Mind you, I'm not saying they planned for *sixty-five* million years. I suspect they didn't. But they planned for millions, maybe a few tens of millions." A.J. glanced at Helen. "Somebody like Nick Glendale who specializes in probability analysis could demonstrate it, I'm pretty sure, just from the math alone."

"I'll ask him to, in fact," Helen said. "Once you and Joe put together the basic data."

"Millions of years . . ." Madeline said softly. "Millions . . . Okay, I get your point. If the Bemmies had a faster-than-light drive, there'd be no reason to create such a vault. Even with all of them dead in this solar system, they'd expect some other Bemmies to come along much sooner than that."

"Yep. They could travel between the stars, but even for them it was a slow business."

"A haphazard one, too," Rich said. He ran fingers through his thinning hair. "Without an FTL drive, there'd be no way to maintain any sort of transsolar political unity of any kind. It'd be hard enough to do, even with one. However the Bemmies were organized, politically, it would have started fragmenting the moment they spread beyond their home system. Give it a few millennia, certainly tens of millennia, and even the records would start getting lost. As if Shelley's poem *Ozymandias* was repeated over and over again, in one star system after another."

Helen had always loved that poem, to the point where she'd committed it to memory. She recited the closing lines now: *"My name is Ozymandias, King of Kings, Look on my Works, ye Mighty, and despair! Nothing beside remains. Round the decay Of that colossal Wreck, boundless and bare The lone and level sands stretch far away."*

Silence filled *Thoat*, for a time, as they contemplated an alien civilization spreading across star systems over an immense span of time—and losing its memory as it went. The thought was majestic and melancholy at the same time.

Helen herself broke the silence. "I understand. They'd have no reason to expect any other Bemmies to come into our solar system at any given time."

"No, they wouldn't," Joe agreed. "A reactionless drive isn't magic. All it does is make *sublight* interstellar travel possible, where it really isn't with any kind of rocket drive."

"Why not?" Rich asked.

"Because you're basically driving yourself—any kind of rocket, chemical or nuclear-power, it doesn't matter—by throwing exhaust out the back end. That means the farther and longer you want to go, the more fuel you need to bring with you—but the more fuel you carry, the harder it is to increase your speed. We engineers call it the rocket equation, and it's been a paradox for us since the beginning of the space age."

"Simply put," A.J. elaborated, "the best speed a rocket can reach—relative to the velocity of the exhaust that's driving you forward—is proportional to the natural logarithm of the percentage of mass left after all the fuel is consumed." -

Seeing the linguist's cross-eyed look, Joe chuckled. "Let me put it more simply still, Rich. Could you cross the Atlantic in a small boat with an outboard engine? Assume for a moment that the ocean is as still as a pond, and there are no weather problems. Just look at it as a straight fuel-and-engine problem."

"Well . . . no, not really. Oh, I suppose you could eventually get across—assuming, like you said, that we ignored the real conditions of an ocean. But, jeez, it'd take forever."

"Why?"

"Well, it's obvious. To keep the engine going, you'd have to haul a great big damn barge full of gas, and how fast could you possibly go if . . . Oh. I see."

"Yup. Welcome to the rocket equation. On Earth, on the oceans, we can get by just by making the ships big enough. That works, well enough, with speeds that low. But it really doesn't work, if you're trying to cross stellar distances with a rocket drive. That's because the mass ratio problem gets progressively worse, the faster you go. And with distances like that, you have to go very fast, or you'll spend . . . Oh, with chemical fuels, it would take thousands of years just to reach Alpha Centauri—and you'd need a fuel tank about the size of the Moon. Nuclear drives are better, but not that much better."

"What you're saying, in short," Helen came in, "is that a reactionless drive is the equivalent of using sails to cross the ocean. However the Bemmie system worked, they were able to use some sort of energy that they didn't need to carry with them."

"Right. Or, at least, carry just enough fuel to keep whatever the engines were running. But they wouldn't be blowing most of the fuel out the back end. Their drive would still be slow—meaning sublight speeds, even if it was much faster than rockets. But not so slow or with such handicaps that it couldn't be done at all."

He waved a hand, stifling A.J. "Yeah, yeah, I know. Bussard ramjets. But that's just an engineer's daydream, so far as anyone knows. Obviously, the Bemmies never took that route. Why bother, when you have a drive that detours the whole fuel problem altogether?"

Joe had been thinking about it further, even while he talked. With the earlier dream of an FTL drive so rudely shattered by A.J.'s cold logic, a number of other things about the model of the Bemmie spacecraft they'd found in the Vault were starting to make sense.

"I'm willing to bet it wasn't even that fast a drive," he mused. "I hate to say it, but now that I look on that model in the cold light of day, that almost flying-saucer design makes a lot of sense. They *spun* it, I'll betcha. Because they needed centrifugal force to substitute for gravity just as much as we do."

A.J.'s eyed widened. Unfortunately, there had been no scale provided—that humans could read, anyway—to give any sense of how big the ship modeled actually was. "*That* big?"

"Why not? Sure, with that modified tuna can design it'd outmass *Nike* by an order of magnitude. At least. Even assuming it was no bigger—an assumption we have no reason to make. And so what? With a reactionless drive, mass doesn't really mean that much, if you've got the time to make the trip in the first place. And there are a lot of advantages to a big ship, especially for long trips."

He considered the problem, for a few seconds. "I'm also willing to bet that, leaving the issue of propulsion aside, their drive worked more or less along the same principles as our ion drives, in other respects. A very low acceleration—much too low to provide artificial gravity itself, which is why you have to spin the ship—but one you can sustain for a long time. So you *could* cross interstellar distances. But it'd take an awfully long time. Maybe even require generation ships, although . . . "

A.J. shook his head. "Not if you can keep the acceleration constant. Still, you're talking trips measured in years, maybe decades— and that's just to cross between nearby stars."

"Yep. Alas. Bye-bye that daydream."

Madeline sat up straight. "Put together a short summary of all that, would you? Or, rather—Joe, you do it. A.J. has to concentrate on solving Rich's little problem. If he can."

The imaging specialist sat up even straighter. "If I *can*? Ha! O ye of little faith, watch—"

Madeline smiled at Helen. "See how I cheered him up?"

❈      ❈      ❈

The next morning, A.J. was scrutinizing Rich Skibow's "little problem."

It wasn't all that little, actually, speaking physically.

"You're sure? That'd be one hell of a big book. Using the term loosely."

"Well, Jane and I aren't *sure*. But, yes, we're almost positive that has to be *the* Rosetta Stone. More precisely, the key to getting at any of them." He waved a hand, backward. "The one I thought was a Rosetta Stone when we first entered turns out to be just one of dozens like it. They've all got that multiple-script feature, but Jane and I think *this* thing is the key to unlocking the puzzle. Insofar as it can be unlocked at all, anyway. Since none of these has a script in a language we know—obviously— they aren't really the same thing as a Rosetta Stone. But it's as close as we'll ever come. Just having a number of languages for comparison will help us a lot—especially because I'm pretty sure this thing is what amounts to a superdictionary."

After Rich finished, A.J. went back to scrutinizing the object. The item in question rested in a case that, from the looks of it, had at one time also been sealed in inert gases. Here, though, the passage of millions of years had taken its toll. However it had happened, one corner of the case had cracked. The crack wasn't much, but it was enough for whatever gas had filled the case to have leaked out long since.

Of course, the case itself had still been in the inert atmosphere that had filled the entire Vault. But the simple fact that the Bemmies had taken the trouble to seal it separately indicated how critical they'd apparently considered the item it contained.

The item itself was a little more than a third of a meter across, composed apparently of mostly manufactured diamond plated over a substrate of their composite with maybe platinum as a coating, since it was shiny like a mirror. A circular mirror with a polychromatic reflective surface; A.J. thought it looked rather like a giant DVD surfaced with faceted crystals.

After studying the thing carefully for a few minutes, A.J. turned back to Rich. "Okay, I'm pretty sure your guess is right. If so, what we have here is something like a digital data disc. They took advantage of refractive tricks to allow them several layers to write on with different wavelengths. They're probably using a binary encoding— that's at least reasonable—but their coding table I'm going to have to figure out . . . hmmm . . . "

He looked back at the item he'd tentatively labeled a data disc. "Looks like it's all here, though. The problem is that we haven't got a reader for it. And whatever readers they might have had—which we haven't found yet, and may never—they wouldn't work by now, anyway. Bemmie super construction notwithstanding, nothing that relies in any way on moving parts is still going to be functional after sixty-five million years. At least, nothing on that level of precision; the door mechanism worked, but that's several orders of magnitude cruder and works on what amounts to brute force. So the question becomes, are we smart enough to build a gadget that will substitute?"

"Are you?"

A.J. frowned. "Of course I'm smart enough. Well. I think. But here I don't have the stuff I'd need. I need emitters in just the right wavelengths—tunable, mind you—I need control circuitry, I need a way to spin the sucker and get the timing right, yada yada yada. And you can bet I'll have to experiment with it a lot, because we're bound to stumble across some obvious, critical, need-to-know information that we don't know, like: 'well, *of course* the files are all encoded with three primes.' If I was on Earth I could whip together some kind of test-bed, but here I'd have to cannibalize something, especially for the moving parts."

"So you can't do it?" Jane said in a disappointed tone. She was following the discussion from the *Nike*, using relays established by the bread crumbs that A.J. now had scattered throughout the Vault.

"Stop jumping on me! I know you're excited about this, both of you, but hell, you're asking me . . . Well, it'd be like going back to the 1970s and handing someone a DVD. Even if you told them about it, they might not have the gadgets to read it with, and they'd sure need to think about it. Especially if you left out something about how, oh, MPEG encoding worked. I have to assume these guys gave me all the critical info, but they could have dropped the ball anywhere along the line." A.J. frowned. "I'll think about it for a bit."

He left the inner area and went back, musing on the problem. He found Helen carefully going over the scaly hide of a velociraptor of some kind. A *Deinonychus*, he thought, although he wasn't sure.

"What's up, sweetheart?"

She jumped. "Don't startle me like that." She pointed to the raptor mummy. "Look close."

He did so, studying the hide in the area she indicated

with his usual eye to detail. "Oh, those little depressed markings?"

"Yes. I think those are marks of some kind of parasite—a louse or something. I'm hoping I can find one intact, or at least some pieces left in the scales. The problem with these being preserved is that someone cleaned them up which eliminates all that kind of thing."

"Listen to you! You're complaining about someone having left you perfectly preserved dinosaurs to work on!"

Helen laughed and hugged him suddenly. The spacesuits eliminated the sensuousness of the embrace, but A.J. still found the gesture heartwarming.

"Yeah, pretty ungrateful, aren't I?" She looked back at the dinosaur. "And that's what brought us together, too."

He grinned. "I remember. I came out there to give you a look at your dinosaurs through the rock, and then you guys almost killed me for faking the scan."

"Well, you can't blame us. You *were* showing off. Mr. 'Look, I have a halo!' "

"Okay, I'm no angel, but—"

He froze.

# Chapter 52

After a while, he became aware that Helen was poking him.

"A.J.? Answer me! You just cut off there and—"

He made a sharp gesture with his hand and she went quiet; he was glad she could recognize the signs. The idea was there and it was a hell of an idea. It seemed like it could work . . .

"It would work," he muttered to himself, "if I can pull it off. Not easy . . . cross talk . . . network topology . . . emitters, yeah, but how much will I need? Power supply for the whole thing, higher constant use than design . . . but with *Nike* to help . . ."

He suddenly gave a whoop, picked Helen up and spun her around. In Mars' gravity, this caused them to spin out of control— fortunately for continued harmony, not into the raptor mummy— and over in what might have been an embarrassing position if they hadn't both been wearing spacesuits.

"*Yes!* Thank you, thank you, you are gorgeous and brilliant and just plain always say the right thing at the right time!"

She was laughing. "You nut. What is this all about?"

A.J. rose, giving a hand to Helen at the same time. "You and old fangface there and a few reminiscences. I can do it, Helen!"

He felt the grin just about splitting his face from ear to ear. "I know how to decode that damn disc! Screw Earth, I don't even need to go back to *Nike*, I just need her bandwidth and some design work that we can do right here!"

"Joe! Hey, Joe, you and me have got some detective work to do." As A.J. and the Tayler Corporation had programmed, the smart suit recognized when the wearer spoke a name in such a way as to indicate "connect me with this person" and opened an appropriate channel. Not waiting for Joe's response, A.J. continued marshaling his resources. "Yo, Jackie!"

"Ms. Secord is sleeping at the moment," came an automated reply. "If this is an emergency—"

"Not really, no. Is Dr. Gupta there?"

The unmistakable sonorous voice answered in a moment. "Yes, I am here. A.J.? What is it that you need? No emergency, I hope?"

"No, just a hell of a job. I'm going to need a lot of the processing capacity of *Nike* dedicated to running an ad-hoc network with, um. . . a few billion individual nodes."

To his credit, Dr. Gupta's reaction was only slightly delayed. "That is indeed a formidable task, especially if as I suspect you will be passing data through the network for analysis. You will have the protocols for us and the specifications on what functions you will need? And when exactly this will be needed?"

"Oh, you can bet on my having the exact code for you. When? Ah . . . let's say the day after tomorrow. I've got some engineering work to do down here with Joe. I just want you guys to make sure that I'll have the system clear for me then."

"It shall be done, assuming that the captain approves. What is the reason for this interesting task?"

"Getting that disc Rich found a couple of days ago to spill its guts so Rich and Jane can really go to town."

"Ah. In that case I cannot see any reason why you would not have access to virtually all of our processing capacity at the time you specify."

"Didn't think so. A.J. out."

He started for the exit. "Joe! You coming?"

"Yeah, yeah, I'm coming. Remember that Mr. Gimpy is slower than you are. Mind telling me exactly what it is we have to tinker together out of duct tape and WD-40?"

"Sure, won't take a minute."

Joe had a lot of questions and comments that changed the design somewhat. But by the time they got back to *Thoat* and the tools they needed, the basic design was already visible in their HUDs.

"Not too hard. Yeah, A.J., we can do that in a day."

It actually took ten hours and seventeen minutes.

A.J. carefully unpacked the device from the container he'd used to carry it all the way from the surface to the innermost sanctum of the Vault. He placed it on the polished, flat surface that was clearly a desk or table and, despite millions of years of waiting, seemed to be just as solid as the day it was made.

"It's showtime."

Rich looked at the thing in bemusement. "Just what *is* it? It looks like something you and Joe dreamed up with a box of metal Tinkertoys and a few electronic lab kits."

The object was about half a meter across, a square framework of slender metal tubes or thick wires with a carefully arranged clamping device in the center, and round black cases at the corners. Wires trailed from it to connect to a fuel cell.

"That," A.J. said, as he gingerly extracted the precious disc from its case, "is the support and supply framework for the device that's going to read this old book-on-disc for you."

"Ah . . . there's no reader or anything on that framework," Rich pointed out, as A.J. clamped the disc carefully into the holder. "And that clamp won't let the disc spin, which seems almost certain to be the way it was read."

"There will be, and it doesn't have to spin," A.J. replied confidently. "Just watch."

And with that, he took the entire bag of Fairy Dust he'd brought with him and upended it onto the framework, disc, and all.

In that large a mass, the dust-sized, motile sensor motes looked more like liquid graphite than dust, but unlike any liquid, the mass stopped flowing long before it could spill off the table. Eerily, the stuff began to move upward, spreading first along all the structural supports of the framework, and then filling in the gaps, and covering the entire surface of the alien disc.

"You know, I'm not sure anyone's ever used this many

smart-dust motes before in one application. Hell, Dust-Storm freaked when I told them before we left how many of my custom motes I was going to need to take with me. They'd never done a single run that large before. But I sure as hell wasn't getting caught short way out here, and now I'm real, real glad I didn't. I'm still offloading a lot of the housekeeping and data analysis tasks off to *Nike*, except for the ones that just have to be done local."

Rich had backed up a bit. He clearly found the oily, alien flowing motion unnerving.

"Relax, Rich. I know it looks funky, but I'm pretty sure it's not going to become an alien intellect and suck out all our brains."

"Ha, ha." Rich came closer. "So how are you getting around the need to spin the thing?"

"I'm scanning it in various wavelengths as indicated, and if I can manage to get down to the resolution we need—that's the tricky part, and why I'm using a lot of capacity—we can basically replicate each layer of the disc and emulate spinning it by reading the data directly, if you see what I mean."

Rich's eyebrows rose inside his helmet. "Yes . . . yes, I think I do see. But do you really need so many to just read it?"

"Yeah, because if the initial data I got from scanning the disc is right, they've encoded the data just a little bit too fine for our regular sensors to pick up. So I have to pull off a major enhancement trick. Image enhancement really relies on the fact that you can increase the information content of your data through more resolution in space and time, and that with very small shifts in the perspective from which your data is accumulated, you can often derive much more data which is hidden within your apparently too-coarse data stream. You can average out noise, you can take pictures from multiple sequential perspectives and see how things change at borderline points . . . Oh, there's about a million and one ways to do it."

He gazed with great satisfaction on the Fairy Dust now covering the alien artifact. "I've coated the surface of that thing with over a billion sensors, all examining the surface as closely as they can, and the sensors are shifting points of view slowly as they record the data. By the time they've done a ten-times-redundant scan—sometime late tomorrow evening—*Nike* will be able to shift her work from maintaining the network to doing serious, serious number crunching—using everything from simple image enhancement with interpolation all the way to synth aperture and a whole bunch of other approaches to get that hidden info out."

He checked some telltales on his HUD; everything okay so far. "Assuming the Fairy Dust network holds out. What I'm doing here is way off the beaten path. Those little black boxes at the corners are RF transmitters supplying the power to the Fairy Dust, on a frequency which shouldn't mess with the rest of the work too much. But, basically, what I'm doing to these little guys is running them on overdrive for a whole day. Way out of spec. Theoretically they should be able to do it, but . . . " He shrugged. "If it works, though, you guys get to do your work making a full-scale translation protocol, and together we just might read this thing before we even leave Mars!"

⌘     ⌘     ⌘

Ken Hathaway's expression on *Thoat*'s screen was solemn, as he looked at Madeline.

"You're sure?"

"Yes, Ken, I'm sure. Just pass along the transmission to Earth exactly as I send it up to you."

"I'll be glad to—"

"No. First, because there's no reason for your name to be on it anywhere. Mine is enough for the authorization. Second, because I see no reason in the world that we need to sink two careers here." She gave Hathaway a very warm smile. "Thanks, Ken. I appreciate the offer, I really do. But there's still no point to it. For the record, you heard nothing, saw nothing, said nothing. Just-Following-Orders-Hathaway, that's you."

He looked away, seeming to swallow a bit. "Okay."

"Hey, look on the bright side. It's not as if they can actually have me shot." Now she gave him the great gleaming Fathom smile. "We didn't bring any guns down here with us. Security issues, you know?"

That got a laugh, at least.

"Sending now, Captain Hathaway."

To her surprise, Joe was waiting for her when she came out of the rover. She'd deliberately timed the transmission for a period when everyone would be occupied elsewhere.

"Joe? What're you—"

"You just sent it, didn't you?" He cleared his throat so noisily it was quite audible over the radio. "Whatever it was you decided to clear, I mean."

She could feel her expression going blank. "Yes. I did."

"Yeah, I figured that was what you were so tense about, the past day or so."

She hadn't thought he'd noticed. The knowledge that he had warmed her, at a moment when she felt very cold. So much so, that she almost explained.

But . . .

No. Let it be on my head alone.

"Okay," Joe said. "I just wanted to know because . . ."

He was acting, for all the world, like a high school boy trying to work up the nerve to ask a girl on a date. More precisely, the way a geek acts when he's trying to work up the nerve to ask out the high school head cheerleader. Even in the suit, Madeline could see him fidgeting.

She almost burst into laughter. "Joe, what's on your mind?"

As if by sheer force of will, she could see him settling down. "Sorry. It's just . . ."

His head turned for a moment, looking across the Martian landscape. Madeline's gaze followed his. The sight was a splendid one. The sun was beginning to set over the far distant rim of Valles Marineris, casting lengthening shadows over the crimson-pinksalmon landscape. The colors always seemed at their richest, then.

Still not looking at her, he reached into one of the pouches of his suit and brought out something. Quite small, whatever it was, completely hidden in his glove.

"When A.J. told me he was making one of these up for Helen— last night, he told me—I asked him to make me one. Real quick, so I'd have it in time."

"In time for what? And what is it, anyway?"

Finally, he looked at her. His glove opened up. Nestled in the palm was a ring. The band itself was some sort of utilitarian metal. But the stone set in it was a shimmering, multicolored brilliance like nothing Madeline had ever seen.

"I wanted to ask you before I knew what the message was you sent. Just . . . Well, so you'd know. That it wasn't any kind of condition, I mean. Whatever decision you made is okay with me. Even if I don't agree with it."

Her eyes were still riveted on the ring, and . . . whatever it was glimmering in its center.

"We don't have any diamonds, of course," Joe said apologetically. "And no way to get any, for . . . God, who knows how long? I don't think there are any on *Nike*, either, except for industrial use. And those are . . . well. Not pretty."

"Joe, it's beautiful," she whispered. Her mind was trying to grapple with the real issue, but kept getting distracted by the mystery. "But what *is* it?"

"A.J. showing off, what else? He told me he could do it." Joe picked the ring out of the palm of the glove with his other hand and held it up. "It is gorgeous, isn't it? Prettier than diamonds, if you ask me. Of course, you'll have to get it recharged periodically, which you wouldn't have to with real stones."

Her eyes widened.

"Yup. What a show-off, huh? Genuine 24-carat solid Fairy Dust."

"Yes," she said firmly. Then, she shook her head. "I'm not talking about A.J. Yes, he's a show-off. Who cares?"

She looked up from the ring, to Joe, to the landscape. Her vision got worse as it went, from the tears watering them.

"Damn, there are things I hate about spacesuits," she muttered. "Can't wipe your eyes, can't blow your nose. Yes, Joe Buckley, I will marry you."

⌘        ⌘        ⌘

A while later, she added: "And that's another thing. Hugging in a spacesuit is a pain, and kissing's impossible."

Joe laughed. And laughed. Never once letting her go.

"I warn you," she whispered, as close to his ear as she could get. "You'll have to be the only breadwinner, for a while. I'm pretty sure your bride-to-be is about to become unemployed."

"Who cares?"

"Well. And you may have to visit me in prison, too. I don't *think* that's likely, but . . ."

Finally, he pulled back. "Like that, huh?"

" 'Fraid so. And, yes, I understand and appreciate the fact— believe me, I do—that you didn't wait to know before you proposed. But you might want to reconsider now that—"

"Oh, bullshit." Joe keyed the general band used by *Thoat*'s company. "Hey, A.J.! Madeline thinks she might have to take it on the lam, in a few months. That be enough time for us to figure out how to make our getaway into the badlands of Valles Marineris?"

The answer came immediately. "Sure. Biggest badlands in the Solar System, too."

# Chapter 53

The director of the Homeland Investigation Authority stared out of the window. At a distance, he could see a little stretch of the Potomac River.

The sight of the river was soothing. A little reminder, if he needed it, that politicians and bureaucrats came and went—not exempting himself, even if his tenure had been much longer than usual—but the nation remained.

Throughout, half his mind—but no more than that—remained attentive to the continuing prattle coming from the National Security Adviser. The rest of his mind was busy recalling every NSA who'd passed through Washington in the years that Hughes had sat in the director's office. Had *any* of them been quite the unmitigated ass that Jensen was?

The answer kept coming up: *no*. Close, in one or two cases, but no cigar.

"—charges of treason not out of the question, I tell you!"

Enough was enough. He'd listened politely, now, for well over fifteen minutes.

"That is perhaps the silliest statement I've ever heard in this office, George—and I've heard quite a few."

He swiveled his chair to look at the NSA sitting on the couch some distance away. Jensen had insisted on the couch, as usual. This time, though, Hughes had insisted on remaining at his desk.

"The charge of treason is a very specific one, whose parameters are clearly spelled out in the Constitution. You couldn't find a shyster anywhere—not even in this town, not even in the Justice Department—who'd agree to bring that charge against Madeline Fathom. They'd be afraid of being disbarred for incompetence."

*A pity we can't do the same for NSAs.* But he left that unsaid.

"George," he continued, "if you do so much as try to charge her with violating this or that security law—oh, you could certainly find something, we've got so many of them—you'd still come out of it on the short end of the stick. 'Short end' as in—"

He held up his pudgy hand, with only a millimeter or two separating the tips of his thumb and forefinger. "—you'll be clutching the itty-bit tip fighting desperately for your political survival, while Fathom uses the great big meaty part of it to club you silly. Well . . . not her, personally. She'd stay out of it, directly. If I know Madeline—and I do—she won't even make any statements to the press. Doesn't matter. The media will beat you to death."

He leaned forward, plucked a small stack of magazines from the top of his desk, and flicked them over to the coffee table.

Hughes had been a pretty good basketball player in his youth, until the certain knowledge that he'd never be taller than five and a half feet put paid to that ambition. All but one of the magazines landed squarely on the table. Even that one landed face up on the carpet.

Madeline Fathom's face up, to be precise. That was *Celebrities Today,* which, as usual, had gone for a full-face glamor shot. Most of the other magazines, being news magazines, had run a different picture—the image taken by A.J. Baker's recorders as he'd first found Madeline in the collapse of the ice tunnel.

"She was on the cover of half the magazines in America, that week. With 'America's Supergirl' as the banner in most of them. She's better known to the public than you are these days, George, and—I guarantee you this much—one hell of a lot more popular."

He chuckled heavily and added, in an exaggerated Southern drawl, "A popular security agent, if that don't beat all! Created one heck of a problem for us, o' course. The HIA's been flooded with applications since, at least half of them girls about to graduate from high school. Betcha that a few months from now, 'Madeline' will be the most popular name for newborn girl babies. Give you ten-to-one odds."

Jensen was staring at the magazines as he might stare at so many venomous snakes set loose from a cage.

"Face facts," Hughes said coldly. "Start with the fact that she's way smarter than you think. There was not a *single* military secret in that entire transmission. Not one. That was her assignment. Defined in precise and narrow terms, I admit, but that's exactly how a hostile press will define it—and what are you going to say? Much less charge her with? 'She failed to read our minds properly'?"

"Who *cares*, Andy?" Jensen exploded, half-rising from the couch. He was so agitated he lapsed into profanity, something he normally avoided. "The whole fucking transmission's a violation of national security! She told the whole world everything, God damn it!"

Now, he did rise fully to his feet, and dramatically started counting off on his fingers.

"Start with item one. The whole world now knows that such a thing as a reactionless drive is possible. Which means that every relevant university lab and research institute in the world—not just ours—will be kicking into high gear to figure out how to make one.

"Item two. The whole world now knows that we've found the key to translating the Bemmie language."

Almost—not quite—he sneered at Hughes. "So big deal if it'll take years to decipher that key, assuming the linguists are right—and who's to say *they* haven't been compromised? One of them is a foreign national, you know."

" 'Compromised,' " Hughes drawled, again exaggerating his accent, as if he couldn't help do so while savoring the word. In the dialect of Washingtonese favored by Jensen and his type, that translated as: *can't be certain to get with the program in every jot and particular.*

He sat up straighter and went back to his usual manner of speech, which had only a trace left of his Mississippi rural origins. "Yes, one of the linguists is a foreigner, indeed. A citizen of our well-known archenemy, Great Britain. The only country, let me remind you, to ever invade the United States—and who's to say their conduct for the past two centuries hasn't just been a ploy to get us to lower our guard so they can do it again?"

"This is no time for jokes, Andy!"

"Who's joking?" He twisted his head slightly, gesturing in the direction of the Pentagon. "You and I both know perfectly well that somewhere buried over there are plans for repelling a British invasion— and invading them, for that matter. They're called 'contingency plans' and we've got them for just about everything. A surgical strike at Antarctica's penguins, I imagine, if that's ever needed. And so what? Nobody in their right mind really expects them to be used— just like nobody in their right mind really thinks Ms. Jane Mayhew is Mata Hari. Including *you*, so don't give me lectures about telling jokes. And will you please sit down? As short as I am and as tall as you are, you're giving my neck a crick having to look up at you."

After a moment, Jensen did so, his long and angular body folding up on the couch like a collapsing pile of sticks.

"What a *nightmare*," he hissed, closing his eyes and rubbing them. "It's the combination that makes it such a mess. A reactionless drive in the abstract would be one thing. Such a drive *and* the possibility we might someday be able to interpret what might be blueprints for building it has every nation in the world hollering bloody murder. All of them are now insisting that the United States has to open up the space program and give everyone equal access to Melas Chasma. The Central African Republic, Mongolia, Paraguay, you name it."

He lowered his hand and stared gloomily at the opposite wall. "Those we can brush off, of course. But the Chinese and even the Europeans are every bit as adamant, and . . ."

"Those we can't. Or, if we did, wouldn't do any good. I've seen the intelligence. If they really put their money where their mouth is, the Europeans can build a *Nike* or its equivalent inside of three years. It'd take the Chinese longer, but not that much. The Indians could eventually manage it, too—possibly even the Brazilians—although that would take a couple of decades or so."

He swiveled his head to look out of the window again. The Potomac settled him down, as always. That very same river had flowed there, after all, more than two centuries earlier when the British burned the capital. Hughes' long career, if nothing else, had convinced him that most political uproars were a lot of sound and fury, signifying nothing once a few years went by.

"And then what?" he mused. "Do we instruct our people on Mars and Phobos—that mighty military host—to fend them off with . . . I'm not sure what. I believe Captain Hathaway has a few pistols stashed away somewhere, in the event he ever had to suppress a mutiny."

"The President—just this morning—sent down orders to start building three more *Nike*-class ships," Jensen growled. "We can get them functional before anyone else can assemble even one equivalent ship up there, and I can assure you—"

"Yes, yes, they'll be armed to the teeth. And—again—so what? Do you really propose to start a new world war over this?"

He turned his head back to look at Jensen. "Well. *Do* you?"

"Don't be absurd!"

"I'm *not* being absurd. 'Absurd' is a word you apply to a threat that everyone knows is empty. Which that threat is—and the Europeans and the Chinese will say so openly.

The Europeans will probably be polite about it. Formally speaking, at least."

His hand started moving through the pile of papers on his desk, looking for one of them. "It's a done deal, George. My own recommendation—yes, I know it's out of my area—is that you recommend to the President that we be Mr. Nice Guy about the whole thing. Offer to set up a joint space program. In the real world, once their feathers get unruffled, the Europeans and Chinese will let us basically manage it. If for no other reason, because they won't want to sink the money into creating their own full-scale alternative. So we wind up with a messy compromise but still one that isn't out of control."

He found the paper he was looking for and took it in his hand. Then, waited.

Jensen gave the innocent wall the benefit of his glare for another minute or so. "Very well. But whatever else— I want that woman fired. *Fired,* do you hear?"

The Jensens of the world were *so* predictable. Hughes grunted, a bit amused, and held up the paper in his hand.

"Don't need to fire her. This is her offer of resignation. She sent that as a coda to the main transmission."

Jensen stared at him. "She *resigned?*"

"I didn't say that. I said she *offered* to resign." He glanced down at the paper. "To quote her exact words: . . . in the event that would prove helpful to either you or the administration. I would, of course, respect the terms of my confidentiality agreement.'"

Jensen's narrow face looked almost like a blade. "She *knew.* How else explain that offer? This was no innocent girl fumbling a job too big for her."

"Of course, she knew. I told you she was one of my

three top agents. I don't pick 'em—sure as hell don't pro-
mote 'em as fast as I promoted her—unless they're smart
as a whip. And Fathom is something of a real genius at
this work."

" 'Genius.' " Jensen's lip curled. "You have a strange
definition of the term, Andy."

He unfolded his body and rose to his feet. "Very well.
Tell her the resignation is accepted—make sure you stress
the penalties attached to violating the confidentiality
agreement—and we'll let it go at that. I'll so recommend
to the President. In the meantime, we'll want you—"

He broke off, seeing Hughes shaking his head.

"Not 'me,' George. Whatever it is you want, you'll need
to discuss it with my successor."

The Director of the HIA leaned back in his chair, clasp-
ing his hands over his belly. "You can inform the President
he'll have my resignation on his desk tomorrow as well."

Jensen stared at him. As the seconds passed, his eyes
grew wider and wider. So did his mouth.

"I will, of course, respect my confidentiality agreement
also. But I do remind you—sorry, George, but it's the
law—that any such agreement is superceded in the event
Congress launches an investigation. Which"—he smiled,
very thinly—"I imagine they probably will."

Jensen shook his head abruptly, as if to clear it of
fuzziness. "Andy . . . nobody is asking *you*—"

"Be quiet," Hughes said. All the simmering anger he'd
felt at the current administration since it came into office
finally surfaced, although his tone of voice remained soft-
spoken. "I am sick and tired of people who think the
phrase 'national security' is just another way of saying
'what suits us, because it's politically convenient at the

moment.' I didn't survive more than twenty years in this office because I let whoever the current occupant of the White House was dictate to me my responsibilities. That's the reason Congress and the public have put up with me for so long. I'm the anti-J. Edgar Hoover, if you will, in that respect. Everybody makes jokes about the President's legal plumbers and the buck vanishing here, but nobody takes it all that seriously—because they trust me, enough at least, not to allow the HIA to get pulled into those games. I've proved it before, in a crunch, and I'm quite willing to prove it again."

He unfolded his hands and pointed a forefinger at the Security Advisor. It was a very short, stubby finger, to be sure. But it still bore an uncanny resemblance to a cannon.

"The real problem here isn't Fathom. It's that—as usual—you people insisted on having your cake and eating it too. If you wanted Fathom to clamp down full and tight security, you only had to instruct her to do so. Of course, that would have produced a political firestorm, once the word got out publicly. Even here at home, much less abroad. So, instead, you relied on her to interpret your inner desires properly. So that if something went wrong, you could—as usual—blame the flunky in the field for whatever mess you found in your lap."

He returned his hand to its comfortable clasp over his belly. "Clean up your own messes. I do not and have never allowed one of my agents to serve as a sacrificial lamb or a scapegoat for an administration's convenience. You fucked it up, you fix it."

Hughes used profanity even more rarely than Jensen did. And Jensen knew that, since he wasn't actually stupid.

"What . . ."

"I suggest you recommend to the President that he take Fathom's *fait accompli* as established and preexisting policy—the thought of doing otherwise never occurred to him once and you can practically see the butter not melting in his mouth—and we go from there. I'll send her a private message making clear that she stretched it as far as she could. Coming from me, she'll accept that. Thereafter—"

He shrugged. "It ain't the end of the world, George. Just another complicated situation that we live with from one day to the next. Like we've been doing for a long time now. The world gets a reasonably open space program that they feel part of, and don't feel too threatened by, and we can still buy ourselves a year or two—won't ever be longer than that, don't kid yourself—in the event the people at Melas Chasma ever do turn up any real military secrets. '*C'est la vie,*' as our off-and-on French friends say."

Jensen was trying to glare at Hughes, but . . . was obviously finding the task difficult. As several of his predecessors had discovered over the years, the country boy from Mississippi was impervious to such efforts. Mississippi was ancient history. Hughes had been in Washington and survived its feuds longer than just about anyone. One of the other common jokes in the capital was his nickname. *Devil Anse Hughes.*

"All right, then, keep her if you insist. But send out a replacement as soon as—*what?* You won't even give me *that* much?"

Hughes stopped shaking his head. "George, for Pete's sake. *Think.* Or if you won't, then trust my assessment of the situation. Now that Fathom's gotten what she wanted—"

"Which was *what*? What *did* that bitch—" he broke off, seeing the Director's glare. Andy Hughes glared even less often than he used cuss words.

"Not in this room, George. Not ever. Way I was brought up, we don't call a lady a bitch. Sure as hell not a lady like Madeline Fathom. She's been places and done things that would have—"

He broke off himself. *Pearls before swine, and all that.*

He leaned forward, putting his hands on the desk. "What did she want? Exactly what she's going to get. You still don't understand, do you?"

Then, wearily: "Ah, never mind. My recommendation to the President is that we leave the existing agent in place. Seeing as how— this is not rocket science—one of the *other* side effects of her transmission is that she'll now have all those cantankerous scientists out there eating out of her hand. Thirty percent of whom, I remind you, are foreign nationals—and one hundred percent of whom are among the top scientists in the world and will be about as easy to keep squelched as herding cats. Genius-grade cats, to make things worse. If there's anyone who can do it— well enough, anyway—it'll be Madeline Fathom."

"Oh."

"Yeah. 'Oh.' Live with it, George. Just live with it." He looked at his watch. "You'd best get back, since you'll be having a new crisis coming down the pike."

"What are you talking about?"

"Oh, I figure right around . . ." He glanced at the watch again. "Now, I'd say, it will finally be registering on every CEO of every major aerospace, oil and auto company— probably the railroads, too—that a reactionless drive might upset their applecarts. They'll be flooding the

President with calls demanding to know what he intends to do about that dire threat to national security."

He managed to say it without a trace of sarcasm. A waste of effort, really, since by the time he was finished the National Security Advisor was already out the door.

# Chapter 54

Three days later, after watching the latest news transmission sent down from *Nike*, A.J. shook his head. "Jeez, who woulda guessed? It never occurred to me that transmission of yours would stir up such a hornet's nest. Honestly, I thought you and Joe were joking about taking it on the lam."

By then, Helen and Bruce had finished clearing the table of the dining ware and cleaning it. That was always an obnoxious chore, given the water regimen in *Thoat*, and thus one that was scrupulously and fairly rotated. The task done, they returned to the table.

"What is your situation?" Helen asked quietly. "I mean . . .?"

Madeline waggled her hand back and forth. "Not too bad, all things considered. Think of me as skating on very thin ice—but I'm an excellent skater, if I say so myself, and I've got a great pair of skates." She reached out and patted the interior wall of the rover. "Bless *Thoat*. And all the rest. It's just awfully hard—especially in Washington—to skin alive Ye Heroine of Ye Day. Even if half of them are sharpening the knives and would like nothing better."

She lowered the hand and patted the table with it. "Anyway. Here I am and here I'll stay. For a veddy veddy long time, I imagine. The director made it pretty clear that as long as I stayed out here he could cover my ass—even keep me in charge—but if I ever returned . . ."

She shrugged. "That's fine with me. This is the best assignment I've ever had or could hope to have. The work is fascinating and important, I like almost all the people around me—boy, is that a change from my usual situation—and . . ."

She lifted her hand, admiring the ring. Across from her, as if by involuntary reflex, Helen held up her own hand, which had an identical one on the ring finger. Except that no Fairy Dust ring would ever be identical, the way the motes shimmered and shifted their colors.

"I'm even getting a husband out of the deal." Sighing softly, happily, she leaned against Joe sitting next to her and nestled her head into his shoulder. His arm came around to hug her close.

"Well, you've got guts, lady," A.J. said. "Of course, I've known that for a long time. But I have to admit I never expected you to go against the grain like that."

Madeline raised her head a little and gave A.J. a serene smile. "What? You think I did it because I've gotten converted to your libertarian viewpoint? 'Information wanna be fwee' and all that twaddle. Ha! Dream on, Mr. Baker. I did it for the same reason I do everything professionally. I'm a security officer and I saw a major threat to national security. I grant you, that required me to meddle with issues of policy that I wouldn't normally stick my nose in. But . . . the situation was unusual. The threat involved was potentially the worst our nation has ever faced."

"National security? Worst threat?" It was obvious from the expression on A.J.'s face that he had no idea what she was talking about.

Madeline lifted herself up from the comfortable embrace. "Tell you what. How about we forego the usual word games after dinner—and the lousy jokes—and go outside a bit early? There's something I'd like to show you all out there, that I think would make what I did more sensible to you. Well, maybe. But we'd be putting on the damn suits anyway, before too long, to go to bed."

"Suits me," said Helen. "I'm getting sick of playing Ghost and Botticelli anyway. Whatever possessed us not to tell Jackie to include a deck of cards in Care Package?"

"Well, *I* thought of it," insisted Madeline. She gave Joe and A.J. the saccharine smile they so detested. "But I knew our engineers would get offended if I suggested they couldn't just *make* something that simple."

Joe chuckled. "Hey, look. No wood, no paper. No paper, no cardboard. There are limits to ingenuity, when you run up against Grandpa and his stubborn ways. But Jackie says she'll include a deck in the next package."

Rich Skibow had been unusually silent since the meal began. Now, he cleared his throat. "Uh . . . actually, I was going to ask all of you if you'd be willing to leave early, anyway. I, uh, have a personal communication I need to make."

Everyone stared at him. The elderly linguist seemed to flush a little. "If you don't mind."

"No, of course we don't," said Helen, using her boss-of-the-dig tone. "Everybody, up. Let's go outside and see whatever Madeline wants to show us, and give Rich some privacy."

A few minutes later—putting on even those state-of-the-art spacesuits was never a quick affair—all five of them came out of the rover and took a few steps to get out onto open ground. Above them, with only the horizon blocked off by the dark mass of the cliffs of Valles Marineris, the Martian starblaze was its usual glory.

"D'you think . . ." mused A.J.

"Oh, I'd say so," Helen chuckled. "As you've pointed out yourself any number of times, they bicker like an old married couple anyway. So why not get all the benefits, too?" More briskly, in the boss-of-the-dig tone: "But it's none of our business, until and unless Rich wants to talk about it. So. What did you want to show us, Madeline?"

"That." Madeline pointed up, to the stars. "I'd like each of you to tell me what you see there."

That took another few minutes, once she got them going. The phrases used were sometimes prosaic, some-time poetical. The words "wonder" and "awe" came and went like people passing through the revolving door of a busy office.

When they were done, Madeline nodded. "That's about what I thought. Not one of you—not once—used any of the words I'd use. Words like 'fear' and 'terror.' "

She gazed up, silent for a moment. "You want to know what I see—and have seen, every time I've looked at the stars, since we arrived at Phobos and first learned the truth? I see a cold, frightening, hostile universe. A universe that once sent an alien species into our solar system, who, for whatever reasons—which we still don't know and may never—fought a war that almost destroyed our planet and did destroy most of its advanced life-forms."

"Jeez, Madeline," A.J. started to protest, "that was—"

"Sixty-five million years ago. Yes, I know—and don't think I haven't taken great comfort in the knowledge. Because what it means to me is that I think we've still got plenty of time to prepare, if we use the time wisely. But ask yourself, A.J.—or Helen, rather, since she's the expert—how long is sixty-five million years? Really? Measured on a geological scale, or a galactic one?"

Helen pursed her lips. "Well . . . it's not *short*. Not even for paleontologists or geologists. Not even for astronomers, really, although for them it's starting to get into the small change area. Still . . . yes, I see your point. It's about one tenth of the time since complex life first began emerging on Earth in the Cambrian Explosion. And a still smaller portion of the time since the galaxy formed."

"Right. So who's to say it can't happen again? In fact, is almost *bound* to happen again—hopefully later rather than sooner; but eventually, no matter what."

The sight of everyone staring at her made Madeline chuckle. At night, in their suits, their eyes looked very beady indeed.

"Yeah, sure, I know it's a paranoid way of looking at things. Folks, that's what I *do*. Security. In a way, I guess, you could say that's what I am."

By now, they all knew her personal history. She felt herself shiver, slightly. "Not since I was a child have I ever been able to forget that the universe produces Washington LaFayettes just as surely and just as inexorably as

it produces butterflies and buttercups. So it's my job—
my life, if you will—to keep an eye out for them."

Silence, for a minute or so. Then A.J. said: "Now, I
see. Jesus, you are one smart cookie."

"Thanks. Like I said, I had to meddle in policy issues I
normally wouldn't touch with a ten-foot pole. But I didn't
see where my responsibilities—even my oath, when you
got right down to it— gave me any choice." She took a
deep breath, letting it out almost like a long, protracted
sigh. "They would have fiddled and faddled and done their
best to keep a lid on it. Put the brakes, as soon as they
could, on the space program of our country because they
wanted the money for something else—and put them on,
even harder, on any other country's. Now, they can't. With
every American citizen—the whole world—knowing of
the tremendous advances we could get from studying the
Bemmie base on Phobos and here in Melas Chasma . . ."

"And Rich and Jane say there are plenty of indications
there may be other installations on the moons of Jupiter
and Saturn," Helen added.

Madeline nodded, still looking up. "They can't keep a
lid on it, now. If nothing else, even if it turns out we can't
decipher any of the Bemmie secrets, we'll have several
interplanetary ships built that'll last for decades and an
ongoing and self-sustaining presence on Mars. The genie
will be out of the bottle. It'll be a mess, I know. But at
least it'll be a dynamic mess, that gets us out into space
and starts providing us with protection before anything
happens."

She shrugged, the gesture being as difficult as it always
was in the tight-fitting suits. "I'll still keep any military
secrets restricted. But that's never more than a short-term

business, anyway. The main thing is that the human race will now come boiling out into space. Where we won't be sitting ducks, any longer. Hopefully, my country will remain in the lead, but if it stops being so at some point . . . Well, in the end, I figure that the national security of the United States doesn't mean much if it isn't part of the security of the whole human race. So piss on it. These things all tend to even out in the wash, give it long enough."

Finally, she lowered her head. She could never stare at that starblaze, for too long. As glorious as it undoubtedly was, eventually she started seeing LaFayette's face in the constellations of a maniac galaxy.

"I'd like to go to our bubble now, Joe. I love it, in there."

"Sure, sweetheart." He took her by the hand and started leading her away. "Me, I'm just happy to still be here. My notion of 'security' is a lot more tightly-defined than yours, I'm afraid. After all that's happened—two crashes, exploding lab, collapsing tunnel—Joe Buckley is mainly just wondering why he's still alive."

"Oh, look!" exclaimed A.J. "Is that a meteor I see streaking toward us?"

The chorus responded. "SHUT UP, A.J.!"

Rich Skibow emerged from the rover. "Hey, A.J.—can you make up another of those rings? Jane said 'yes'!"

# AFTERWORD

For reasons of cost, the four diagrams below were converted to black-and-white for this edition of *Boundary*: maps showing the journey of Thoat across Mars to finally reach Bemmie's home base and the illustration of NIKE. Color versions of these pictures can be accessed online at my LiveJournal gallery: http://pics.livejournal.com/seawasp/gallery/00004pq8.

I can also be contacted through my LiveJournal itself (http://www.livejournal.com/users/seawasp/), where I will also often talk about my current and future projects and anything else that interests me.

You can also find both myself and Eric Flint on Baen's Bar (http:bar.baen.com); my conference is Paradigms Lost, while his is Mutter of Demons. Come visit; we love to talk with readers. Thanks very much for reading *Boundary!*

Ryk E. Spoor November, 2007

# IMAGES

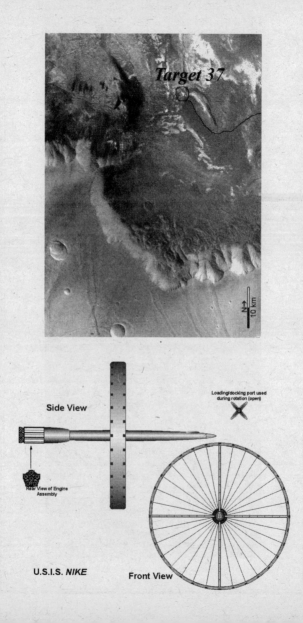

**Target 37**

Z
10 km

**Side View**

Loading/docking port used
during rotation (open)

Rear View of Engine
Assembly

**U.S.I.S. *NIKE***

**Front View**

# IF YOU LIKE...
# YOU SHOULD TRY...

**DAVID DRAKE**
David Weber

**DAVID WEBER**
John Ringo

**JOHN RINGO**
Michael Z. Williamson
Tom Kratman

**ANNE MCCAFFREY**
Mercedes Lackey

**MERCEDES LACKEY**
Wen Spencer, Andre Norton
Andre Norton
James H. Schmitz

**LARRY NIVEN**
James P. Hogan
Travis S. Taylor

**ROBERT A. HEINLEIN**
Jerry Pournelle
Lois McMaster Bujold
Michael Z. Williamson

## HEINLEIN'S "JUVENILES"
*Rats, Bats & Vats* series by Eric Flint & Dave Freer

## HORATIO HORNBLOWER OR
## PATRICK O'BRIAN
David Weber's Honor Harrington series
David Drake's RCN series

## HARRY POTTER
Mercedes Lackey's Urban Fantasy series

## THE LORD OF THE RINGS
Elizabeth Moon's *The Deed of Paksenarrion*

## H.P. LOVECRAFT
*Princess of Wands* by John Ringo

## GEORGETTE HEYER
Lois McMaster Bujold
Catherine Asaro

## GREEK MYTHOLOGY
*Pyramid Scheme* by Eric Flint & Dave Freer
*Forge of the Titans* by Steve White
*Blood of the Heroes* by Steve White

## NORSE MYTHOLOGY
*Northworld Trilogy* by David Drake
*A Mankind Witch* by Dave Freer

## ARTHURIAN LEGEND
Steve White's "Legacy" series
*The Dragon Lord* by David Drake

## SCA/HISTORICAL REENACTMENT
John Ringo's "After the Fall" series
*Harald* by David D. Friedman

## SCIENCE FACT
*Kicking the Sacred Cow* by James P. Hogan

## CATS
Larry Niven's Man-Kzin Wars series

## PUNS
Rick Cook
Spider Robinson
Wm. Mark Simmons

## VAMPIRES
Wm. Mark Simmons